Michelle Paver was born in Malawi; her father was South African and her mother is Belgian. They moved to England when she was small and she was brought up in Wimbledon, where she still lives. After gaining a first in biochemistry at Oxford she became a lawyer and was until recently a partner of a large City law firm, specializing in patent litigation. She has now given up the law to write full-time. *Without Charity* is her first novel.

WITHOUT CHARITY

Michelle Paver

CORGI BOOKS

WITHOUT CHARITY
A CORGI BOOK : 0 552 14752 4

First publication in Great Britain

PRINTING HISTORY
Corgi edition published 2000

1 3 5 7 9 10 8 6 4 2

Set in 10/12pt Sabon by Kestrel Data, Exeter, Devon.

Corgi Books are published by Transworld Publishers,
61–63 Uxbridge Road, London W5 5SA,
a division of The Random House Group Ltd,
in Australia by Random House Australia (Pty) Ltd,
20 Alfred Street, Milsons Point, Sydney, NSW 2061, Australia,
in New Zealand by Random House New Zealand Ltd,
18 Poland Road, Glenfield, Auckland 10, New Zealand
and in South Africa by Random House (Pty) Ltd,
Endulini, 5a Jubilee Road, Parktown 2193, South Africa.

Reproduced, printed and bound in Great Britain by
Mackays of Chatham plc, Chatham, Kent.

WITHOUT
CHARITY

CHAPTER ONE

Early March, the Present

'I'll be back by eleven thirty,' Dominic shouted from the kitchen. 'You'll be here to let me in, won't you?'

Sarah was in the shower shaving her legs. 'Hang on, I've got an early start tomorrow, I'll be in bed before—' She heard the clatter of his keys as he tossed them on the table, and the door slammed shut behind him.

An aversion to carrying keys was one of the few things which irritated her about Dominic. He, on the other hand, never saw the problem. Why *should* he take keys? Driving in London was purgatory, cabs were the only way to get about, and she was usually home first to let him in. On the rare occasions when she was out on a shoot, he could always work late in Chambers till she got back.

By nine thirty that evening she had done a load of washing, chaired two frustratingly inconclusive production meetings, spent three hours on the phone debating two pages of shooting-script with a writer who thought it was perfect and a director who wanted another writer, done the weekend shopping in the annoyingly expensive corner shop, and annotated a one-inch stack of pre-production notes. With ideas for the feature still buzzing in her head, she fixed a plate of cheese and crackers and a whisky and soda, turned on the gas-log fire, and forced herself to curl up with an undemanding thriller her brother had lent her the week before.

From half past eleven she began to listen for Dominic, despite the fact that he always came home at least an hour after he said he would. Every time a car door slammed she lost her place in the paperback, and she read the last chapter twice without grasping the ending.

A video wasn't much better. Listening for steps on the stairs, she pressed the 'pause' button so often she nearly jammed the expensive new VCR. She thought about tackling the next stack of notes but decided against it. If she started on them she'd be up all night, and she was due in Oxford at half past eight the following morning.

By one o'clock she was reduced to tidying the flat. That meant viciously shuffling his papers into stacks and piling his unironed shirts on his side of the bed. He *knew* she had an early start tomorrow. Surely, *surely*, he'd be back by two?

He wasn't.

She had a bath, leaving the door ajar to listen for the phone, then settled down doggedly to watch the rest of the film. She awoke at three o'clock to find Atlanta burning.

The bedroom was a cold uninviting chaos of improvised curtaining and unopened boxes, and clearing the duvet of clothes, paperbacks, and Dominic's mobile phone woke her up thoroughly. She swung between fury at what would now be an exhausted tomorrow, and horrific images of a fatally injured Dominic slumped bleeding in the wreck of a taxi.

At four thirty the buzzer jolted her awake, as it did every other tenant in the building. Sick with fatigue she fumbled for the door. His apology, which she ignored, was perfunctory, and after a whisky-laden kiss he slid under the duvet and fell instantly asleep.

She shut her eyes and the birds started up. In Notting Hill that only meant a handful of pigeons and a magpie thudding down onto the roof, but it was more than enough to keep her awake. Beside her, Dominic whiffled peacefully into the pillow.

She tried everything to soothe herself to sleep. A BAFTA award ceremony, with Dominic – sleek as an otter in his dinner-jacket – sitting in harmony with her mother and brother and applauding as she accepts Best Television Documentary. A Sunday supplement article on the successful married couple surrounded by dogs and books and enormous plants, and possibly children. Pensioners in Sainsbury's shakily thanking her for giving voice to their memories; hardened teenagers moved to tears; her mother proudly cutting out her reviews to show to the neighbours.

None of them worked.

In the end it took a rather tedious story about being the only earth-woman among a lot of handsome, admiring, and interestingly metallic Martian men. She was asleep before she could think of a plot.

Six o'clock in the morning, and still dark outside.

Dominic was no longer in bed when she emerged from the bathroom towelling her hair. He was fully dressed in the kitchen, making coffee.

He brought in a mug for her and put it on the

sitting-room table, then sat on the arm of the sofa, cradling his own mug in both hands.

'You're up early,' she said.

'So are you.'

'I've got to be in Oxford by half past eight.'

'Lord, your *meeting*! I forgot. Sorry about last night.'

She sipped the coffee, lips annoyingly unsteady against the rim of the mug. 'It must've been some party.'

He shrugged. 'It snowballed. Head of Chambers came in just as I was leaving, so I had to stay.'

'You knew I had an early start.'

'You'd already gone to bed.'

'I waited for hours. Next time, take your keys.'

'You should've told me you had a problem with letting me in.'

'I wouldn't have had a problem if you'd been back by eleven thirty like you said.'

'I was wrong. Sorry.' He didn't sound it. He sounded bored. An intelligent man forced to reason with an unreasonable woman.

Reasoning with him never worked. In any case, his barrister's training would come into play and all he could think about was winning, which he always did. He knew precisely when to admit and when to deny, when to confess and when to avoid – and she could never predict which he'd do next. But she couldn't help feeling that somewhere along the way the point of it all had got lost in the rules of the game.

She caught sight of them both in the overmantel mirror. Dominic impeccable in charcoal-grey suit, striped Gieves & Hawkes shirt, and ultra-subtle Lanvin tie. She in an unflattering chrome-yellow bath-towel smudged with mascara, her face sallow and bony from a winter spent indoors, her brown hair clinging damply to her shoulders. In the bleak overhead light she didn't look thirty-five, she looked *forty*-five.

Dominic didn't look like a man of forty-three who had been out for most of the night. He looked as he always did: not exactly handsome, but so at ease with himself and so sharply aware of the physicality of others – especially women – that he was widely regarded as such. The thick, cropped dark hair like the pelt of some sleek predator; the watchful black eyes beneath the emphatic brows; the pugnacious jaw. He was built like a navvy, with broad workmanlike hands she had always found viscerally attractive.

God, she thought, we really are chalk and cheese. No-one would guess in a million years that we're related. Let alone lovers.

'Sarah.' He put down his mug and walked over and placed his hand on her throat. For a moment he caressed the angle of her jaw, looking down at her with an odd mixture of appraisal and regret. Then he released her and returned to the sofa. 'It's like this,' he said, leaning back and crossing his legs. He sounded as if he were embarking on a prepared speech. 'We've been together for nearly two years, and I think we've reached the point when we should either marry or split up. And I've decided I don't want to marry you.'

Above them, another magpie thudded onto the roof.

Sarah blinked. 'You want to split up,' she heard herself say in disbelief.

'Yes.'

She said: 'We've just started living together. We've taken the flat till July.'

He didn't reply.

'You never said there was a problem.'

'I've only recently decided that there is.'

'*Decided?*' She groped for comprehension. 'I thought we were – I thought it was working.'

'How would you know? I've hardly seen you over the last few months.'

'You mean, I've been working too hard.'

He inclined his head in silent assent.

'I don't understand,' she said slowly. 'We both work too hard. We always have. But you're saying that now, for some reason, *my* work has become a problem.'

'Sarah. I really, *really* didn't want to get into all this.'

'I'm sorry,' she said simply, 'but I do. I need to understand.'

He sighed. 'Very *well.*' He sounded weary, as if forced to deal with an unusually obtuse judge. 'Since you insist, I'll try to explain. The problem is this.' He paused. 'When I stop work for the night, however late it is, I can have a couple of drinks, or three or four, and forget about it. However critical the case happens to be, I can just switch off. I don't stay *immersed.*'

'And I do.'

'You know you do.'

'That's how you make a film about someone's life. By staying immersed.'

'My point exactly. You're stuck in the past, Sarah. And it's always someone else's past.'

'So what are you saying? That you're chucking me because I make documentaries?'

He ignored that. 'I just think you need to ask yourself *why.* Why do you keep delving into other people's pasts? What are you trying to find?'

She realized she was still clutching her mug. She thought about putting it on the table and decided against it. She didn't think she'd get there without spilling it. Her hands were cold. She was surprised they weren't visibly shaking. 'I think', she said, 'there must be someone else.'

'Oh, *Sarah*.'

'All this psychobabble about my work. It's a smoke-screen. And even if it's true, it wouldn't suddenly make you want to split up. You wouldn't do that till you'd found someone else first.'

That made him blink.

'Do I know her?'

He ran his thumb along his lower lip. 'She's not what this is about.'

'Satisfy my curiosity. Who is she?' It was important to appear rational, if only to herself. She doubted if he was fooled for a moment.

He sighed. 'Very *well*. As it's so important to you. It's Caroline Harris.'

'*Caroline?*' She almost said, 'how *could* you?', and it flashed across her mind that the old clichés were true, people really did say things like that when their world had just been overturned.

Caroline had worked at Timescape for nearly as long as she had. They had never been close friends, but after struggling together through four years of crises and panics and unexpected successes, it almost felt as if they were.

But Caroline, Sarah reminded herself, was married to an investment analyst at Goldman Sachs and only worked part-time, because she wanted to. Caroline could hardly be accused of getting too immersed in anything. Except, presumably, Dominic.

13

He guessed her thoughts. 'It isn't psychobabble and it isn't a smokescreen. In the end it really *does* come back to your work. You're trying too hard to find whatever it is you've lost, and I think you're looking in the wrong place.'

She met her own gaze in the mirror. Her face was so composed it was frightening. The hazel eyes steady, the wide mouth firm. Not at all like a woman who has just been dropped from a great height.

Her glance shifted to Dominic's reflection. He was studying her coolly, as if mildly intrigued as to what she would do next. Woman in mirror watching man watching woman. A nice shot, concise and powerful. *Hell*, why couldn't she stop thinking in film?

She didn't know if he truly believed what he had just said about her work, or if he was just using it as a convenient excuse. In the end it didn't matter.

Five minutes later, he asked her what she thought she was doing.

Without stopping to dry her hair she had pulled on jeans, hiking boots and an oversize sweater, and was charging about the flat wrapping aspidistras and yucca palms in black plastic bin-liners.

'What the hell are you doing?' he said again.

'If I left these with you, they'd be dead in a week. And if I don't wrap them up when I take them out to the car they'll die. It's freezing out there.'

'Don't be ridiculous, you can't move out *now*!'

'Why not? You want to split up and you've found someone else. The last thing I want to do is to stay here.'

'But you don't have to leave *today* – '

She paused with a plant pot in her hands. 'Oh yes. Yes I do.'

Packing didn't take long. She had been so busy since they moved in that she hadn't had time to unpack most of her books and clothes. Her furniture was still in her own small studio in Battersea, which she had rented out when they took the flat together.

Already it was seven o'clock. She'd have to forget about Oxford. 'I take it', she said, 'you've got time to help me load my car?'

He glanced at his watch and the corners of his mouth turned down. 'I'd *like* to, but I'm due in court at ten. And this judge really doesn't like—'

'Oh, fuck the bloody judge!'

For the first time since she had known him he was lost for words. He picked up a box of books and followed her downstairs.

The radio was full of cheerful snow warnings as she headed north out of London. The sky was a low threatening grey. Everyone kept their lights on as they crept up the M1 through freezing fog.

She hadn't had time to have the heating fixed in her aged Golf, and as it wheezed up the slow lane she wished she'd got round to buying a gadget for plugging into the cigarette lighter to make coffee. All she could find in the glove compartment was a box of horribly expensive mint creams which she'd bought Dominic for Christmas, but decided not to give him when she heard him say how much he loathed them. She tried one but it tasted like frozen soap so she spat it out.

Halfway to Coventry she pulled into a lay-by, and with cold-numbed fingers dialled Timescape on Dominic's mobile. She must remember to post it back to him, along with the sweater she was wearing.

15

Giles sounded suspiciously relaxed about her cancelling Oxford. 'Sweetheart don't be silly, of *course* I don't mind! Listen, why don't you take some time off? You deserve it. You've been flogging yourself into the ground. And don't *worry*, we can manage!'

Oh, Christ. They all knew. They must have known for weeks. She managed to keep her voice level until she cut the connection.

The windows quickly fogged over, and in the frozen shut-in stillness the noise of her crying seemed to come from outside herself. It was alarming. Like being trapped in a box with a wild animal.

Obviously the family with the Ford Explorer in front of her thought so too, because the young mother in the leopard-print skiing jacket took one look at Sarah, packed her two small boys indignantly into the back, and drove off.

After a while Sarah's sobs subsided into hiccups. She blinked at herself in the rear-view mirror. Her nose was red and her hair had dried in matted strings. Her eyes were brown blobs in swollen pink mounds. She looked like a prawn. She stretched her lips into a smile. The effect was ghastly. 'He's not worth it,' she said to the apparition in the mirror. 'He is just not *worth* it.' If only she could make herself believe that. But the truth was, she had believed the exact opposite for nearly two years. She had been so far from seeing this coming that when he had started his speech, she had actually thought he was about to propose. And she would have said yes. She had been so obtuse it was terrifying.

Suddenly she felt exhausted. All she wanted to do was sleep. 'Come on, you,' she said. 'Let's get you to Mum's.'

It was snowing heavily by the time she turned into

the little street of terraced houses in the suburb of south Coventry. Her mother had only moved there six months before, and Sarah wouldn't have recognized the house if it hadn't been for the scarlet Murano glass jug in the lounge window. Her father had teased her mother so much when she bought it, his own taste being almost Japanese in its subtlety, that it had never been seen after they got back from Venice. Not until the day of his funeral, when it had appeared without explanation on the mantelpiece of the old house in Putney. Maybe her mother had taken comfort from it, remembering how gently he had laughed as he tried to coax her out of her sulk. It was better to remember him like that than at the end, when he'd been too weak to get to the loo on his own.

Her eyes filled. She blinked furiously. Not now. Not *now*.

Shirley Dalton opened the front door and gave her daughter a hard, unsurprised stare. She said bluntly, 'I knew this would happen. Get inside before you catch your death.'

Sarah didn't catch her death, she caught pneumonia.

CHAPTER TWO

Mid-May, the Present

Sarah propped herself up on her elbow, moved her legs over the side of the bed, and slowly, slowly sat up. Sweat broke out on her forehead. The blood roared in her ears.

The bed, her home for the past five weeks, was a mess: a dispiriting litter of tangerine peel, crumpled tissues, video cases and paperbacks.

She ought to clear it up. She ought to take a bath and wash her hair and put in her contact lenses. Dab Clearasil on the burgeoning spot on her chin which was signalling the onset of her period like a beacon.

She would do all those things. She would. As soon as the blood stopped roaring in her ears.

She was careful not to catch sight of herself in the mirror on the opposite wall. The doctor had told her not to worry, the weight would come back on eventually and her colour would improve. Yes, but when?

Downstairs a key turned in the front door. Her brother's voice rang through the house. 'Sarah? Sarah!'

She closed her eyes. 'Up here,' she called. 'Is Jenny with you?'

Nick's reply was careful. 'Parking the car. She'll be along in a minute.'

'Right.'

She heard his step on the stairs, then his tanned good-looking face was towering over her.

He blinked when he saw her. Then he dropped a kiss on her cheek and wedged himself into the small pink armchair which their mother had installed for visitors. He raised an eyebrow at *One Hundred and One Dalmatians* on top of the television. 'I thought you'd already seen that.'

'Three times, and still counting. It's therapy. I'm adopting Cruella as my role model.'

He forced a grin. 'Well that's a step in the right direction.'

There was a silence. Then he said abruptly, 'Christ, Sair, the famine's over! There's food in the shops.'

'So I heard.'

'I thought you'd be looking *better*. No wonder Mum's worried.'

They heard steps on the stairs, and Jenny came in with a self-consciously bright 'Hal*lo!*' Her gaze came to rest on Sarah's sludge-brown sweatshirt and elderly black leggings, and she pressed her lips together and smiled.

To fill the silence Sarah asked about Verbier.

'*Exhausting*,' said Jenny, perching on the arm of her husband's chair. 'Taking one's children skiing is the most overrated pleasure in life.'

Nick put his arm round her waist with a casual intimacy which made Sarah look away. Since Dominic, she had avoided all contact with the married, the

19

cohabiting, and those still in love. Which meant just about everyone she knew.

Her sister-in-law wore a sleeveless Liberty print dress in soft shades of green and rose, with flat strappy sandals and pearl earrings. She looked like a teacher in an expensive girl's school: the kind whom mothers like for her sincerity, and fathers for her unthreatening prettiness.

Sarah asked after the children, and Jenny gratefully took up the baton and talked about ballet lessons and the debate over a second Labrador. 'But that's enough about *us*,' she said eventually, 'what about you? How's the— um.' She broke off with an embarrassed smile. 'You really *do* look better, you know.'

To help her out, Sarah smiled back. They both knew that Jenny had been on the point of asking about Sarah's job, because that was what she always did. Jenny asked about Sarah's job, and Sarah asked about Jenny's children: both feigning interest and trying not to patronize; both picking their way round each other's sensibilities.

Only now Jenny would have to think of something else to ask about, because Sarah no longer had a job. Timescape had dressed it up in a lot of talk of cut-backs and rationalizations, but the truth was they hadn't relished the prospect of Sarah, the old love, working alongside Caroline, the new. And as Caroline's father was something important in the City *and* a shareholder, it was Sarah's contract which wasn't renewed. Hints had been dropped that things might be different in about, say, six months' time. But no-one had suggested what she was supposed to do in the meantime.

'I almost forgot,' said Nick, drawing an envelope

from his back pocket. 'Letter for you. Must have arrived after Mum left.'

'Who's it from?' Sarah asked, too casually.

He read the address on the back and frowned.

If it had been from Dominic he would have said so immediately. Nick had never liked Dominic and had been openly relieved when they split up, but he knew his sister.

Suddenly Sarah was alarmingly close to tears. She lay back on the pillows and shut her eyes. 'Whoever it is,' she said savagely, 'they can bloody well wait.'

She felt Nick and Jenny exchange glances. Jenny murmured that she'd love a cup of coffee, and she and Nick disappeared downstairs.

Two months on, and still this bleak, uncomprehending, desolate hurt. This paralysing sense of utter worthlessness. You could blame it on the pneumonia for all you were worth, but it didn't make it any easier to handle. Not when the post arrived every morning with nothing from Dominic.

Her mother had sent back his mobile phone and his sweater the day after they split up, but he had acknowledged neither. Nor had he telephoned, or left a message at Timescape. Nor had he sent Sarah a cheque for his half of the rent, which she had paid in advance when they took the flat in January. She had kept that quiet from her mother, who would have been outraged.

The worst of it was that she still missed him as intensely as when they first split up. Sometimes she would shut her eyes and imagine him lying beside her: his solid warmth, his rich emphatic voice; his smell of cigars and expensive aftershave.

She turned onto her side, and from the bedside table

21

her father smiled down at her. Her 'substitute father', she called the photograph, as it took the place of the memory she no longer had.

'Well, Dad,' she told it, 'that's another man gone.' The photograph smiled back at her, inscrutable. She had given up trying to imagine what he would have said in reply.

Julian Dalton had been much older than his wife. A tolerant, well-read, sharply humorous man, he had made a good living with a popular column in the *Daily Telegraph*. He was fifty when he met Shirley Read at a press convention. She was twenty-nine: an intense, opinionated junior reporter on the *Coventry Informer*.

The marriage had been stable but not particularly happy, for Mrs Dalton could never get over the difference in their backgrounds. She was a third-generation Socialist who lived and breathed the Party; he was very definitely 'a cut above'. Early in the marriage they lapsed into silence on the subject, as if recognizing that it was the only chance for peace.

Then when Sarah was fourteen and Nick nearly sixteen, their father developed backache. When it didn't clear up after a month the doctors had him in for tests, and a fortnight later they diagnosed myeloma. He told his children one Sunday after lunch. 'I'm afraid it's terminal,' he said gently. 'I'm unlikely to live for more than a couple of years. I'm sorry. We'd better just pack in as much as we can over the next few months.'

Nick went into the garden and hiccupped for hours behind the hydrangeas. Sarah didn't cry at all. She tried to imagine her father dead, and found that she couldn't.

A year later, as she was walking home from school,

it occurred to her with a shock that they wouldn't have much to remember him by when he was dead. A handful of photographs, mostly from the Sixties when she and Nick were small, and his cuttings book, which their mother had kept for years out of a kind of exasperated affection: pages and pages of the *Telegraph* column on everything from politics to wildlife to art. But as far as his background was concerned, all Sarah had gleaned from her mother's occasional waspish little asides was that his father had been a well-to-do French wine-grower, and his mother an Englishwoman with distant connections to a Lincolnshire barony. Sarah had no idea if he had been happy as a child, or what his parents had been like. They had both died decades before she was born. She had never even seen a photograph of them.

Until then, she hadn't given it much thought. She'd always assumed that because her father was older than her friends' fathers, that was the way it was. But now the fact that she knew so little struck her as appalling.

As soon as she got home, she went to the small downstairs room which they still called the study. By then her father could no longer manage the stairs, so they had replaced his desk with a bed which they called 'the divan', and to keep up the pretence that the room was still a study, Mrs Dalton had sewn a bed-cover in a dark masculine tartan. But no-one could do anything about the smell: a stale fug of unwanted food, hospital dressings, crumpled bedclothes and sweat. It was never mentioned, and sometimes Sarah wondered if only she noticed it, and felt disloyal.

'Hello, muffin,' said her father. 'Did Miss Horton like the Wolsey essay?'

She pulled a face, and leaned down and kissed his

papery cheek. A yellow crust had collected at the corner of his mouth, and she rummaged in her schoolbag to give him time to wipe it away. Mum had told her it had been a so-so day, with a lot of breakthrough pain.

She ate a handful of Garibaldis from his biscuit tin and they argued about Wolsey. Then she asked him shyly to tell her a bit about his parents.

His dark eyes widened with astonishment. 'This is a bolt from the blue. Why now? Is it something for school?'

Already she wished she hadn't asked. She had never seen him so disconcerted. 'Um, no. I'd just quite like to know, that's all. But only if it's OK with you.' She couldn't tell him that she *needed* to know, so that she could store it up for when he wasn't there any more.

Her attempt to avoid the truth failed. 'Sarah Charity Dalton,' he said with the beginnings of a smile, 'you are absolutely *hopeless* at dissimulation.'

She was relieved. He only called her by her full name when she had made him laugh against his better judgement, like the time when she was eight, and had coloured in all the illustrations in his first-edition *Orley Farm* as a surprise. And this time, when he called her by her full name, it was special, because she knew that her middle name had been his mother's. Charity Elisabeth D'Authon. He had anglicized his surname when he moved to England – to prevent, he said, the inevitable misspellings.

She put her head on one side. 'Please, Dad. I won't tell Mum.'

He shut his eyes. 'The thing is, I'm not feeling all that grand today.'

'Then forget it,' she said quickly. 'It doesn't matter. Honestly.'

For a few minutes he didn't speak, and she thought he had fallen asleep. Then he said, 'Sorry, muffin. But you're right to want to know. I've been a bit remiss about it. And I'd like to tell you about them. Is tomorrow all right?'

'Dad, forget it. It doesn't matter.'

He smiled. 'Of course it matters. Tomorrow. Definitely.'

His face had changed so much over the past year. His skin hung on the bones as if it was two sizes too big. Sarah had heard her mother tell a neighbour that they had to be incredibly careful that he didn't fall over, as his bones were 'like glass'. Now Sarah couldn't look at him without imagining a skull of fine, brittle glass beneath the exhausted skin.

The next day she begged to be allowed to stay home from school so that she could be around when he woke up, but her mother wouldn't let her, and by the time she got back he was already asleep. He had had a bad day, and had been liberal with the morphine to get it over with. Sarah felt obscurely guilty, as if in some way she was to blame. The following morning she had to leave early for a French test, so she didn't see him – and the same afternoon he had an appointment at the hospital, and while he was in the waiting room he had a heart attack and died. The doctors said his heart must have been weaker than they thought, because of all the drugs.

Apart from a small pension from the *Telegraph*, there were only a few thousand pounds in the building society. Despite his background, Julian Dalton hadn't been a wealthy man. His father's vineyard had succumbed to blight just after the war, and over the years a string of unlucky investments had carried off the rest of his inheritance. Besides, he had never been that interested in money.

So Mrs Dalton put the house on the market and started looking for work. It never occurred to her to seek help from her husband's family. For one thing, it would have offended every one of her principles. For another, she couldn't stand them. Julian's only surviving relatives were the Hardys: Harriet Hardy was a distant relation of his mother, and therefore also connected to the barony. To make matters worse, she had married a doctor of independent means, and they had two brilliant and (according to Mrs Dalton) thoroughly 'stuck-up' sons, Dominic and Alex. The final *coup de grâce* was that the Hardys had snubbed the Daltons by not attending their wedding. As a result, Sarah and Nick had gone through their entire childhood without ever meeting the 'Other Side'.

So the house in Putney was sold, Mrs Dalton and her children moved to a semi-detached in Wandsworth, and she wrote domestic features for women's magazines. She never spoke about her husband to her children, but they sensed that although she grieved for him, she also resented his death. It was as if he had withdrawn from a long-standing argument when she was just about to win.

Sarah took longer than the others to get over her father's death, though she never understood why. It wasn't as if she had been his favourite: he hadn't *had* favourites. But for her the loss was absolute in a way that it never was for Nick. Her father had vanished from her life with a completeness which appalled her. Within a week of the funeral she could no longer remember his face, or his voice, or the way he had walked before the cancer deformed his spine. She never even dreamed of him. Julian Dalton simply wasn't there any more in her head. Memory had been all that was left of him, and now she had lost that too.

Sometimes she would toy with the idea of finding out more about his background, as if this might reconstruct the memories she had lost. But she could never bring herself to start, or even to ask her mother for help, because even thinking about it brought back all the old heartache about his death.

The kitchen door slammed and Sarah heard steps on the stairs. Nick elbowed open the door carrying a tray with three mugs and a packet of ginger snaps. Jenny followed, gamely cheerful.

Nick glanced at the photograph and gave his sister a searching look. Shrewd, pragmatic, perceptive Nick. The envelope, she noticed, was back in his pocket.

She reached for a ginger snap she didn't want. 'So who's it from?'

'Actually,' said Nick, 'it's from Alex Hardy.'

That was so absurd that Sarah burst out laughing. 'Oh, now that's perfect! Now I've heard everything!'

Jenny's smile became uncertain. Nick watched his sister narrowly.

She imagined their whispered conversation down in the kitchen. 'Who's Alex Hardy?' 'He's only fucking Dominic's fucking younger *brother*!' 'His *brother*? Oh *no*! Poor Sarah!'

And poor Alex, too. Alex the younger one, always in the shadow of his dazzling brother. Alex the solicitor, the also-ran to the glamorous barrister. Alex with the beautiful unstable wife who had been in and out of therapy for years – the wife who had had affairs with most of his colleagues, a fling with Dominic, and finally left her husband for a tax barrister fifteen years his senior.

Sarah pictured Nick telling Jenny all about it. 'And that was that, as far as Alex was concerned. When Helen left him he just cracked up. Dropped out of law, sold his house, went underground. Absolutely gutted. Goose cooked.'

When she had first heard the story, Sarah had secretly rather liked the notion of two brothers fighting over the same woman. Now her lack of judgement appalled her. If Dominic could cuckold his own *brother* . . .

Nick was still watching her. She returned his stare without a flicker.

She had absolutely no interest in anything Dominic's brother might have to say. Since the Helen affair three years ago, Alex and Dominic hadn't spoken to each other, so it was hardly likely that Alex was writing to tell her that Dominic had repented and wanted her back.

Nick held out the envelope. 'Go on. Read it. We're not leaving till you do.'

'Oh well,' she muttered, 'in *that* case.'

Spidery black handwriting sprawled across a sheet of A4 copy paper. It had clearly been written in haste.

'*Dear Sarah, I understand you've been ill and lost your job. I have a suggestion which would help us both. I have contacts with the Board of Governors of Harlaston College, which as I'm sure you know used to be Harlaston Hall, the seat of the Pearce-Staunton family.*'

'As I'm sure you know . . .'

Sarah set her teeth. All she *knew* was that 'Pearce-

Staunton' was the family name of the barony to which her grandmother – and presumably Alex and Dominic as well – had been related, and that the barony was now extinct. Beyond that it was a blank. She found Alex's casual assumption that she knew all about it intensely annoying. And it shocked her to see the name scrawled on the page with such familiarity, when for her it evoked all the horror and suddenness of her father's death.

'*You'll also be aware*', Alex continued, '*that the Hall was sold just after the First World War, and is now the European wing of the University of Allantown, Wisconsin. Next year is their fiftieth anniversary. They want to commemorate it with a history of the place, and they need someone to write it. Someone with a background in historical research, but with enough flair to make it readable. (From what little I know of the Pearce-Stauntons, that shouldn't be difficult; they were a colourful lot.) I thought you might be interested. The spring semester ends on 31 May and Harlaston will be empty for the next three months. You'd have the run of the house, and of course you'd be paid. Or if you'd prefer, you could live in Hynton, a village about a mile away from the Hall. You might enjoy the work, particularly as I understand you want to find out more about the family. Call me. Regards, Alex. (PS Dominic never comes down here.)*'

Without a word Sarah handed the letter to Nick.

She wondered who had put Alex Hardy up to it. And whether she would be this angry if he hadn't added that postscript. And why had he mentioned her wanting to find out about the family? Had someone told him? Had *Dominic* put him up to this?

Dominic's words on that last morning in Notting

Hill came back to her. Searching for what she'd lost in other people's pasts. But if he *had* put his brother up to this, surely it meant that he still cared about her. Didn't it? She despised herself for the surge of hope the thought produced.

'Interesting,' said Nick, cutting across her thoughts.

'Manna from heaven,' said Jenny briskly, with a glance at her watch.

'It sounds', said Sarah, 'like a put-up job.' She looked at their blank faces. 'Well, since when do things like this fall out of the sky, just when you happen to have split up, lost your job, and got ill, all in the space of a couple of weeks?'

Nick's reply was blunt. 'What does it matter? Someone's trying to help you. Why don't you let them, for once?'

She stared at him. 'You're not seriously suggesting I take this job.'

'Yes I am. Seriously. Where's the downside?'

'The downside is that I can think of a dozen better ways of spending my summer.'

'Oh come on,' said Nick. 'I thought you'd always wanted to find out about Dad's family.'

'I wouldn't be finding out about Dad's family. I'd be dishing the dirt on the aristocracy for the titillation of Middle America.'

'You're beginning to sound like Mum.'

' – and even if I'm wrong, even if every Pearce-Staunton since Adam was so civic-minded they make Abraham Lincoln look like a social delinquent, what on earth makes you think I'd want to spend my summer with the Hardys?'

'You wouldn't be spending your summer with the Hardys! You wouldn't even see Alex, the man's a recluse, and as for Dominic, look what Alex says in the PS!'

'How do you *know* Alex is a recluse?'

Nick opened his mouth and shut it.

'It was you,' said Sarah. 'You put him up to this.'

'All right, it was me. So shoot me. In fact, there wasn't much putting up involved, it was all Alex's idea. He jumped at it. Said it solved a problem for him too.'

'I'm sure it does, but I'm still not going to do it.'

Nick sighed.

They both knew he couldn't push her too far, not when the imbalance between them was so great. All the advantages were on his side: the stable marriage, the steady job, the big house, the children.

She said firmly, 'Nick, it was sweet of you to go to all this trouble and I know you were only trying to help. But for the last time, I do not *want* this job. I mean it.'

He stood up. 'Well, I mean it too. You have *got* to take this job. Christ, it makes sense for about a dozen reasons! You can't stay with Mum or you'll drive each other round the twist. You look like you need a spell in a sanatorium, let alone the country. And frankly, you need the money. Take the bloody job!'

CHAPTER THREE

21 May 1900
Hynton, Lincolnshire

Their belongings had been set down in the road by the garden gate, the carrier's wagon had rumbled off in a haze of dust, and Charity Fosdyke scanned the new village for signs of a schoolhouse.

She didn't know what she'd do if Hynton didn't have one. Getting a position in a school was her last defence against ending up behind the shop-counter at Aspland's.

In Sedgefield where she had grown up there had been a Board school, and Miss Coulbeck the parson's daughter had paid her a shilling a week to wipe the noses of the younger children. Ninepence went to her mother, and threepence into the mustard tin in her trunk. But Sedgefield was eleven miles away now. And Tilburne – which had a National *and* a Higher Grade school – was six miles away. Between here and Tilburne there was nothing but baking cornfields, and an enormous park behind miles of grey stone wall.

Hynton, drowsing in the afternoon heat, didn't look big enough to have a school. A row of eight tiny cottages faced half a dozen larger ones across a green – or rather, across an expanse of baked dust where a green had been. In the middle stood a pump and a thirsty-looking lime tree beneath which a tortoiseshell cat was comprehensively licking its paws. Doors and windows stood open to catch the breeze, but apart from a black wicker baby-carriage and a small pinafored child leaning on a gate, the village seemed deserted. At the far end of the green, past a shop with a sign advertising Aerated Ginger Beer, the road disappeared down an avenue of elms, where a church spire poked above the treetops.

Maybe the school's down that way, thought Charity. Please God, let there be a school.

The 'end house', their new home, stood a little apart from the other cottages, at the point where the road split to go round the green. It was larger than their cottage in Sedgefield, but clearly hadn't been lived in for months. The other gardens were bright with hollyhocks and red-hot pokers, but the end house had nettles, ryegrass, and a strong smell of cat. To make matters worse, a flock of starlings was waging war in the plum tree shading the front door. Charity hoped her mother hadn't noticed them. Her mother *hated* starlings. They reminded her of the fens and Cousin Ruth.

Mrs Fosdyke was standing guard over her horsehair sofa. She was sugared with dust from head to toe, and her arms were tightly crossed to stop herself trembling. She was furiously grinding her teeth. She had strong white teeth which she cleaned every night with a rag dipped in salt, and she ground them whenever she was frightened. Charity had grown up with that grinding sound.

Mrs Fosdyke had bitterly opposed the move. 'What do you *want* with a new job?' she had berated her husband. 'What makes you think this Lord Harlaston will keep his word any more than the old Duke who nearly landed us in the poorhouse? Besides, you're a jobbing stonemason – just one up from a letter-cutter – not an artist-in-residence, an' it's a village church you'll be working on, not Lincoln cathedral! When it's finished they'll lay you off, an' then where'll we be?' On the long bone-jolting ride from Sedgefield she had maintained a rigid silence, unbroken even by the sight of the Hall, a fairy tale castle floating on a hill above the village.

The 'end house' was the last straw. It wasn't much more than a large cottage, but its name had shaken Mrs Fosdyke badly. She had lived in cottages all her life; 'houses' were for those several notches above her on the ladder. 'It's on the wrong side of the green,' she said contrarily, glaring at the end house as if it was an armed foe. 'Same side as the farm-workers' cottages. Where's the sense in that, I ask you? Putting a posh house on the wrong side of the green!'

'It isn't on *any* side,' Charity pointed out. 'It's at the end. That's why it's called the end house.'

'Wrong side of the *road*, then. I can't be doing with that. What'll folk think?'

Charity picked up their basket of provisions, pushed open the gate with her hip, and waded through the long grass to the porch. 'Father's round the back putting Bella in the sty. I said I'd make some sandwiches, but the kitchen's a sight, so I thought we'd have a picnic instead.'

Warily Mrs Fosdyke followed her into the garden. 'That'll give them something to talk about,' she muttered. 'New family eating outside like a pack of Gippoes.'

'*They*' were the shadowy regulators who ruled her life: swift to censure, yet strangely prone to overlook good intentions and believe the worst.

Mrs Fosdyke parted the long grass and peered through the parlour window. Charity joined her, and their two reflections stared back at them. Both were of middle height, with good figures, regular features, straight dark hair, and the strongly marked fenwoman's eyebrows which Mrs Fosdyke detested.

Charity studied herself in the window. This, she thought, is how you will look behind the counter at Aspland's. No. This is how you *would* look, *if* you worked at Aspland's.

Aspland's would be a perfectly good job; it was just that, if she took it, she would still be there in thirty years' time.

Maybe if Hynton didn't have a school she could take in sewing from the Hall. Although if Mr Burridge the carrier was right, the servants at the Hall weren't exactly overworked. The Family rarely visited, for Lord Harlaston was away fighting Dutchmen in South Africa, and Lady Harlaston – said to be the most beautiful woman in England – made no secret of her preference for London. Only the little lad and his governess lived there for most of the year.

Her mother summoned her courage and disappeared round the back to explore, and Charity started making jam sandwiches on the lid of the basket. The heat lay on her skin like a coating of dust. Her stays throbbed, her petticoats clung to her legs, and her black straw hat gave off a sickly-sweet smell of hot varnish. She longed to go inside and have a proper wash, but it was still too soon to attempt an entry to the house.

Her mother returned looking slightly less grim. 'Can't hardly see in, the window's so filthy.'

Charity's hopes rose. 'So it's bad, then. It'll be needing some work.'

Her mother cast her a suspicious glance. With a snap she shook out her pocket handkerchief and gave the doorknob an admonishing rub. 'Take a month of Sundays to make it fit for a Gippo.'

Later, when Mrs Fosdyke had finally taken the bull by the horns and gone inside, Charity's brother erupted through the gate. His jacket and breeches were colourless with dust and his cap had been trampled and crammed back onto his head. 'Mr Burridge let me ride Snowflake to the first milestone an' I ran all the way back an' found five snails for Bella!'

'That'll make her feel at home. Did you find a school?'

Will didn't answer. A clump of dock had caught his eye, and he was brushing his fingers against the flowers to catch the rusty pollen.

'Will. *Will!*'

'Sorry. I axed, but Mr Burridge says the nearest one's three miles away at Moxby, an' he knows for a *fact* the job's taken. Can I have another sandwich?'

So that's that, thought Charity.

Maybe it was a bit of a crazy plan. Saving pennies for a typewriter. Teaching herself stenographic shorthand at night. And after that? After that it all became rather vague. She had visions of typing letters for attorneys, or sermons for a vicar. And of not working at Mr Aspland's.

'Charity.' Will's blue eyes watched her thoughtfully. 'Sorry 'bout the school.'

She took off his cap and slapped the dust out of it. 'Doesn't matter. I'll think of something else. Who trod on this, then?'

'Snowflake. Then me.'

She ruffled his barley-coloured hair.

He studied the pollen-prints on his sandwich and frowned. 'D'you think the lads here are going to like me?'

'Bound to.'

'No, *really*.'

Why, she thought, am I always having to lie? Her brother was brave, quick-witted and hard-working, but he didn't fit in. He didn't have the same sense of what was appropriate as other people did. At Sedgefield he had been at the bottom of the children's pecking order, and only his size and the catapult she had given him had kept him from being regularly beaten up. He didn't like birds'-nesting, tipcat or kites, and he didn't care if he was laughed at for listening to the stories in Sunday School, or quoting the embarrassing bits from the Bible. He only did that because he liked the names, but he never thought of telling anyone.

To make matters worse, when he was eight he had fallen out of a tree and gone deaf in one ear. Charity had a shrewd idea that being half-deaf suited him nicely, for it meant he could cut himself off whenever he liked. It didn't suit his mother. When the school medical officer listed Will as 'defective' she was incandescent. Three years on, the quickest way to rile her was still to say that her son was simple. Sometimes she would urge her husband to stand *up* for his son, but he never did. Mr Fosdyke never stood up for, or to, a soul. Sometimes Charity thought that the chief aim of her father's existence was to go unnoticed by everyone, including his own family.

'It'll be better here,' Will said gravely, cutting across her thoughts. 'This time I'll really try. I'll even play cricket.'

Charity had to laugh. 'Now *that* I'd like to see!'

It was a week before Mrs Fosdyke felt entitled to unlace her boots, change into her grey Indiarubber softs, and sit down at the kitchen table with a cup of black tea and a slice of bread and butterine. Charity could have finished off the rest of the loaf and slept till Sunday.

The table had been scrubbed to whiteness, the walls freshly limed, and the mysterious intricacies of the new Yorkshire range blackleaded twice. *On His Master's Grave* had been tacked above the fireplace in the parlour, *The Glory of Omdurman* occupied the stairwell, and *The Sybarite's Reward* hung beside the kitchen door, where Mrs Fosdyke could see it from the sink. The end house wore an exhausted, vanquished air, like a very bad child who has finally been subdued after a long struggle.

Every article of the family's linen had been boiled, blued, mangled, sprinkled, ironed and aired, to get rid of the travelling dirt. No-one mentioned the fact that they had spent the last week in Sedgefield doing exactly the same thing, to keep it nice for the journey.

'I can't be doing with a weekly wash,' said Mrs Fosdyke. 'It's so poor-looking. Like we've barely enough to cover our backs! What'll they *think*? If only we had enough linen to last a decent six weeks!'

'I heard there's a woman takes in laundry,' said Charity. 'Maybe we could get her to help from time to time. Otherwise your hands will get too stiff to sew.'

Mrs Fosdyke stared at her. 'Since when can we afford a washerwoman?'

'It'd be worth the extra sixpence now and again. We'd lose more than that if you can't sew.' Her own hands, cradling her favourite cup with the violets round the rim, were chapped and swollen, and smelt of Vinolia Soap and Reckitt's Paris Blue. The whole house smelt of Vinolia Soap and Reckitt's Paris Blue.

' "The *extra sixpence*"? And how do we find *that*, my duchess? Stop your father's penny a night for his half-a-pint?'

'I wasn't saying that.'

' 'Course, it'd be different if you were working at Mr A's.'

Charity put down her cup. 'No it wouldn't. I'd have to find bed and board in Tilburne and we wouldn't be any better off.'

'You meet a nice sort of person at Mr A's. Got to think of that at your age. Great girl of nineteen.'

Mr Aspland was the standard by which Mrs Fosdyke judged all others. His shop on Market Square (Ladies' Fashions, Gloves and Haberdashery) had no equal in the county, and his home in Rainbow Villas, where he lived with his plump wife and even plumper daughter, was what everyone should aspire to. It was Mrs Fosdyke's dearest wish to see Charity settled in a villa exactly like it, with a garden path edged in pottery scrollwork, and a parlour with a bay window and a stuffed owl on the mantelpiece.

Charity had nothing against Rainbow Villas. But Mr Aspland did business with a commercial traveller called Mr Hatch, a plump young man with speckled jowls who had taken to gazing at her wistfully. And whatever else might happen, she knew with absolute certainty that she was not going to end up in Rainbow Villas with Mr Hatch.

She tried a change of subject. 'Maybe they need some help with the sewing up at the Hall.'

'Maybe? *Maybe?*' Her mother's voice was shrill. 'An' I s'pose *"maybe's"* going to pay the butcher? Or d'you want me to give up my tuppence a week for the funeral club?'

'Of course I don't. But—'

' – you'll be after the Pig Club money next. An' if Bella's taken poorly, why, we'll just call in the knacker an' have done with her—'

' – Mother, *listen*. I'm not for a moment—'

' – an' why stop there? There's always your father's threepence for his bit of plug—'

'Oh really! As if I'd ever!' Charity got to her feet with a screech of chair-legs and crossed to the open door.

There was a long reverberating silence. When at last she turned round, her mother was blinking down at her cold tea.

Charity said quietly, 'You were the same at my age. You took a job thirty miles away from your village.'

'Not because I *wanted* to. Because I *had* to. Because of Cousin Ruth.'

Charity bit her lip. She had grown up with the shadow of Cousin Ruth. Cousin Ruth, who had gone to the bad. Though what she had actually done was never made clear.

Shakily Mrs Fosdyke polished her spectacles on a corner of her apron and replaced them on her nose.

'With a blot like that on the fam'ly name you've got to be *twice* as respectable as everyone else. That's why I want you at Mr A's. An' if you turn him down now, he'll not ask you again. There's no second chances for folk like us.'

'I know. That's why I'm not going to work for him.'

Mrs Fosdyke took off her spectacles and polished them all over again. She polished them for a long time. Then she put a saucer over her bread to save it for Will, washed and dried the tea things, and set them with admonishing firmness on the dresser. 'Work to be done,' she muttered. 'High time we made a start.'

Charity fetched the work-baskets from the parlour. Mrs Fosdyke laid her sewing cloth over her lap and took a chemise from the pile.

Half an hour passed in strained silence.

When Charity could bear it no longer, she put down the shirt she had been buttonholing and looked across the table at her mother. 'What can I get you, Mother? The Fricassée of Creamed Lobster or the Potted Grouse?'

Mrs Fosdyke licked the end of her thread and squinted at her needle. 'Well, now let's see. I think I could just fancy a bit of that Almond Pudding.'

Charity went to the dresser and took down an old tin of Fry's Concentrated Cocoa ('Strength, Purity and Flavour') from which she extracted an oilcloth package. She unwrapped a dog-eared, grease-spotted shilling volume.

When she was settled in her chair again, she opened the book and read aloud: 'The Young Housewife's Daily Assistant. *Chapter Fifteen, Part Three, Receipt Eleven. A Baked Almond Pudding. Beat eight eggs and*

41

*mix with a pint of good boiled cream and a quarter of
a pound of powdered sugar—'*

'A *pint* of cream!' muttered Mrs Fosdyke, shaking
her head in disbelief.

*'Beat well together and put to them half a pound of
blanched sweet almonds ground fine, and a quarter
pound of warm butter. Add four ounces of jar-
raisins stoned and chopped small, and two gill of
brandy—'*

'I'd leave that out myself,' put in Mrs Fosdyke.
'Brandy's just a wicked spoiling of decent food.'

'I think I might try it once, just to see what it's like.
*Line a pie dish with paste, pour in the mixture and
bake till a good golden colour. If liked, serve with a
Sabayon Pudding Sauce.'*

'If *liked*!' Mrs Fosdyke put her hand to her cheek
and her eyes became distant. 'If liked,' she murmured
again. Then she picked up her sewing. 'Go on, then.
Read us another.'

The next week passed smoothly. Mr Hare's shop was
tried and found wanting, but no more so than the one
in Sedgefield had been. Mr Goldsbrow the blacksmith
patched the bathtub for tuppence ha'penny, and as he
wished Mrs Fosdyke a very civil good morning, he was
pronounced 'a cut above'. At daybreak Mr Fosdyke
would shamble off to St Hybald's with his tools
clinking in his apron, and at five o'clock he would
shamble back covered in stone-dust, and spend the
evening nursing his half-a-pint and talking pigs with
his neighbours, and trying to keep out of his wife's
way. Charity got no closer to finding her extra job, but
she and Will walked along the river-bank to Shotley
Farm, where Mrs Corlett hired Will as a day-lad at

three shillings a week. The village boys kept their distance.

The days slid by. Monday was washing-day and every other Monday was secret washing-day, when the family was confined to the kitchen and the house was festooned with damp linen to hide it from the neighbours. Tuesday and Wednesday meant ironing and sewing, and on Thursdays Charity and her mother walked to Tilburne with the finished piecework and collected a fresh batch from Mr A. Friday meant household mending and shopping, and was Will's second-worst day – worse even than house-cleaning on Saturday – because by Friday Mr Hare's chitterlings were high, and marked down to eightpence a pound. Sunday was *everyone's* worst day, because on Sunday Mrs Fosdyke had nothing to do.

She didn't mix with the village women, but in the third week, when Charity bought a piece of pasteboard in Tilburne and wrote *Dressmaking and Plain Sewing* in her clear looped hand, the village women started coming to them. Hynton had a blacksmith, a grocer-postmaster, two bricklayers, a carpenter-wheelwright, and a shoemaker, but it hadn't had a dressmaker for years.

Even so, at first only the hardiest women would brave Mrs Fosdyke's scrutiny, for she had a way of listing their physical defects out loud with unflinching candour, and her own figure was unnervingly good, though she resented compliments. But she had a flair for concealing her customers' weak points, her prices were fair, and she could reckon yardages in her head to the nearest farthing. No-one liked her, but she soon had work from all the better families in Hynton. The daughters of Shotley Farm had made a preliminary inspection, and Mrs Bowles the parson's wife had expressed an interest in regard to her children's night-clothes.

So when Charity and her mother heard a rap on the kitchen door one Monday afternoon, they took it for another customer.

It wasn't. It was a boy with a note: a piece of expensive cream-coloured writing-paper folded in two.

'From Mrs Jordan,' the boy said, panting from running in the heat. At their blank faces his eyes widened with astonishment. 'Mrs *Jordan*! Under-*house*keeper at the Hall!'

Mrs Fosdyke's face drained of colour. 'What have we done?' she whispered, taking the note between finger and thumb.

The boy laughed as he ran down the path. 'Why, nothing, missis! Least, not that I knows of!'

When he had gone, Charity turned to her mother. Her heart was racing. Maybe this was the extra work she had been hoping for. 'Aren't you going to open it?'

'I knew this would happen,' muttered Mrs Fosdyke. 'I knew we should of never left Sedgefield.'

Gently Charity took the note from her fingers. 'Please. Let me read it.'

It wasn't an offer of work. It was an invitation to tea the following Thursday in Mrs Jordan's rooms in the servants' wing. Mrs Fosdyke, Charity, and even Will, were invited.

Mrs Fosdyke began to grind her teeth. 'We can't go. Not possible.'

'Whyever not?'

'How can we? I've nothing decent to wear for a place like that.'

'What about your dark prune?'

'What? You can't wear your Sunday best to a Thursday tea!'

'Then the everyday grey lawn, with the best collar and cuffs.'

'Look like a proper washerwoman in that, wouldn't I? Me with my knuckles all red and swollen.'

'Mrs Jordan wouldn't mind. She works too.'

'Works? *Works?*' Mrs Fosdyke's eyes glittered. 'She's *under-housekeeper at Harlaston Hall!* Don't you know what that means? Well I do, I was in service! It means she's at the top of the tree! Only the butler an' the housekeeper come above her. She's got the cook an' the second cook at her beck an' call, to say nothing of all those housemaids an' parlour-maids an' laundresses an' footmen, an' I don't know what else besides!'

'Wear the dark prune, Mother. With the everyday collar and cuffs.'

CHAPTER FOUR

18 July 1900
Orange River Colony, South Africa

This is the fifth farm they're going to burn today, and the men are tired. Robert, Lord Harlaston, is as weary as they are. When they have finished, he will call a halt for the night. It will make a change to see cooking-fires burning instead of barns.

On the FID map in his saddle-bag, the smallholding is described as 'Nooitgedacht Farm'. Nooitgedacht. He knows enough Dutch to translate that as 'never thought'. Never thought what, he wonders. That a party of English soldiers would one day ride in off the veldt and burn it to the ground?

The farmhouse is the usual tin-roofed cube: a child's drawing of a farm on the vast brown veldt. There is a garden which in summer will have marigolds, and in the dip beyond the barn there are ducks bobbing on a pond. It could be an English millpond, were it not for the clumps of sisal, and the egret folding its wings.

The men of the farm are of course long gone, and have taken their livestock south into the hills. Undeterred, Private Jessop has found a goat, which he has tethered to a eucalyptus tree. He and Sergeant Atkins stand guard over the animal, stamping their feet in the bitter wind and coughing the dust from their lungs.

Private Webb comes round the side of the farmhouse. Dust coats him in ginger, the same colour as his hair. In exasperation he rubs his temple with a grimy finger. Robert has seen him make the same gesture since they were boys together at Harlaston. 'It's not taking, sir,' says Sam, spitting into the dust. 'We could start it off proper with a drop of that lamp-oil.'

'No lamp-oil,' Robert replies. 'Take hay from the barn.'

Sam squints up at him. 'Lot quicker if we just—'

'The barn, Webb. Look sharp.'

'Yes, sir, Captain Pearce-Staunton sir!'

Sam's tone borders on the impertinent, but Robert lets it pass. He has a reason for wanting the lamp-oil saved. It will be night soon: a moonless night of absolute dark. The Dutch women and the boy will need lamps to light their way, if they're to find help.

Help. Why deceive himself? They won't find help out here. They will be left without shelter in the bitter east wind, with no homesteads left standing for miles around, and the nearest refugee camp a four-day trek across the veldt.

The jingle of a bridle behind him. He turns to see Second Lieutenant Marchand urging his horse forward.

'The men are awfully tired, sir,' the young subaltern says. 'I wondered if it would be possible – that is – well, sir, I mean, I say.' He is fresh off the steamer from Southampton. Still a boy, and not yet bold enough to say what's on his mind. Robert can guess. 'It's bitterly cold, and these are women and children,

47

sir – and what would it matter if we did leave a house or two standing in this God-forsaken country?'

'Mr Marchand,' Robert says, 'the sooner we get on with it, the sooner it will be over. Please carry out my orders.'

They get on with it. Within minutes, heat buckles the farmhouse roof. Thick black smoke curls beneath the eaves. Flames burst with ear-splitting cracks from windows and doors. Marchand's English hunter squeals, but Robert's ugly little bush-pony merely pricks his ears and twitches his scrawny withers. He is used to fires.

The Dutch women and the boy stand in the grass amid their possessions and watch their home burn. The women could be English cottagers' wives, with their sun-bonnets and light-blue eyes, and their print dresses faded from many washings. It has taken Robert a while to get used to that.

At first the grandmother was the most vituperative, but now she leans heavily against an old piano piled with mattresses, and her lips move in silent prayer. These people have such a simple faith in God: so simple, and so very, very strong. Beside her, the younger woman still holds the jug she had fetched when first she saw the dust-cloud of the English soldiers – and, mistaking their intentions, drew water for the officers to drink. Her daughters, sturdy girls of perhaps fifteen and twelve, stand watch over their little brother, as if to prevent him launching a solo attack against the enemy. He cannot be more than eight years old, which must be why he isn't out on commando with his father and brothers.

It is the boy who holds Robert's attention now. Something about the child brings his own son to mind,

48

*although the Dutch boy is well-built and handsome –
unlike Linley, who must wear a lung-protector all year
round, and will always be plain. But the look in the
eyes is the same. Bereft and uncomprehending. Frightened of him.*

*Linley in the conservatory. Hiccupping with horror
over the shattered tray of orchids.*

No. He won't think about that now.

*The fire is intensely beautiful against the dark blue
sky, and it is with some reluctance that Robert turns
his mount to leave. Behind him the veldt is pocked
with fires, as though a medieval warlord has passed
that way.*

*Moving off at the head of 'B' Company, he casts a
final glance over his shoulder.*

*The women have remained with their possessions,
but the boy has followed the soldiers through the
grass. He is powdered from head to foot with cinnamon dust, but his eyes are a startling light-filled blue.
He looks like a statue Robert once saw in Egypt.*

*'You'll never find me now,' the Dutch boy calls after
him in perfect English. 'No matter how hard you look,
you'll never find me now.'*

His clear voice cuts Robert to the heart.

Someone whistled the reveille, and with a shudder-
ing gasp, Robert awoke.

He lay waiting for his heartbeats to return to
normal. He had an obscure sense that his dreams had
been troubled, but he couldn't remember why. He was
cold. His eyelashes were sticky with frost, and he had a
crick in his neck from using his saddle as a pillow.

Sitting up and looking about him, he saw that he
was among the first to awaken. His men slumbered on
the slopes of Brandlaagte Hill, rolled in greatcoats like

the dead on a battlefield. Twenty paces away, fog shut out the world, and beyond the fog hung the silence of midwinter. No birdsong broke the stillness of the veldt. They could have been on the moon.

Some of the men sat up and began to curse.

Robert drew his revolver strap over his shoulder. He felt light and cold with hunger. He wondered if he would need to make another hole in his belt.

Hoarfrost crunched under his boots as he made his way down to the rifle-wall where the kaffirs were stoking a fire under Sam's watchful eye.

Robert's second in command, Lieutenant Jordache, was still asleep in the lee of the wall. Marchand was already sitting by the fire on an old ammunition crate on which Sam had scratched 'Officers' Mess' in charcoal. Marchand was softening a dog-biscuit in his coffee. Like the rest of them, he was bearded and grey with soot, but somehow he still managed to look like a newcomer. The edge of a blue and green striped slipover showed above his tunic collar. Home-knitted, no doubt, by his mother or sister. He couldn't be more than twenty: the same age as Robert when he had obtained his commission and gone to the Sudan – was that really fifteen years ago? But surely, *surely*, he had never been as raw as this?

Marchand saw him coming and gave him a smile of great sweetness, and Robert forbore to point out that he had just wolfed down half his day's rations. Instead, to get rid of him, he sent him off on signal duty. He didn't feel up to another skirmish over the ethics of what they were doing. Over the past few months he had had the same debate with half a dozen Marchands: all of them new to the notion of following orders, and all shocked to discover that Johnny Dutchman looked just like them, and read his Bible rather more frequently.

Robert felt disinclined to explain that he did not enjoy torching farmhouses any more than they. What he *did* enjoy, perversely, was the danger and discomfort of the veldt. The cold, the wind, the hunger. The scramble for cover where there was none. The rattle and whine of bullets among the rocks. It was like inhaling a deep lungful of cold air after years of being shut in by the fire.

Sam handed him a steaming mess-tin of coffee, and he sat on a crate and took a long blistering pull. 'You're up early, Webb.'

Sam's lip curled. 'Got to keep an eye on the bloody darkies, sir.' Sneering seemed to be his way of dealing with the Dark Continent. He sneered at the kaffirs for being black, at the Boers for being Dutch, and at his comrades for not being from Hynton. Only Robert's horse came in for a measure of approval, and even that was qualified because Mahomet wasn't Lincolnshire bred.

Robert dismissed him, and Sam went off to sneer at his rations. Robert sat nursing his coffee while the camp came to life around him. Men huddled over fires, spitting and swearing. Horses threw down their heads to cough.

The fog was lifting, the veldt coming into view below. It was at its worst in July. Cold, parched, blackened by fires. And always the endless wind and the endless dust and the endless silence. Only the odd lonely hawk swinging in the sky, which made it feel even emptier.

They had had no contact with England since leaving Bloemfontein six weeks ago. With Boer commandos

51

raiding the station garrisons every few days, no-one was laying bets on when the next mailbags would get through. They could have been back in the Dark Ages. Robert found this curiously restful, and wondered why.

In the breast pocket of his tunic was his son's last letter. A crayoned picture of the boy's pony and a few laboriously blotted lines. The drawing was simple but accurate. Slipper had indeed grown so fat that he was practically spherical.

It was raining, Linley explained, so he was not allowed to ride Slipper, which was a shame but Pickering had let him choose a pineapple for Great-Aunt Stella's visit. The orchids were fine now. With best wishes your son LINLEY PEARCE-STAUNTON.

Why had Linley written that about the orchids? Surely they had sorted it all out months ago? Why did the boy still feel the need for reassurance?

Those damned orchids. In his reply, penned quickly before leaving Bloemfontein, Robert had been careful not to mention the wretched things. Now he wondered if that had been a mistake. It had happened in January, a week before he left Harlaston for South Africa. He and Violet were having tea in the Blue Drawing-Room when they were startled by a splintering crash from the conservatory. Robert found his son standing in the Orchid House, chalk-faced and beyond tears, amid the wreckage of a tray of *Sophronitis coccinea*. The boy's ears – those awkward ears which so irritated his mother – were glowing beacon-red. He seemed to have stopped breathing altogether.

'What's this?' Robert was curt. The Orchid House was expressly out of bounds, and the plants were rare.

Such depths of horror in the myopic brown eyes. 'I d-didn't mean to, sir, I promise! Now I've *killed* them.'

'Nonsense! Nonsense. Where's Gibbs? Surely it's time for bed? Gibbs!'

But the governess did not appear, so Robert stooped and put his hand on his son's shoulder, and together they made their way out of the Orchid House. Robert was surprised at the smallness and delicacy of the child's bones. It was like handling a young hare.

In the Long Gallery he paused. 'We'll tell Pickering to replant them straight away, shall we?'

The boy looked up at him doubtfully. 'But aren't they already dying, sir?'

Robert was surprised. Perhaps his son was not as dull-witted as Violet thought. 'Nonsense,' he said. 'Orchids are tougher than that.'

Of course the boy was right, and the plants soon died. But within days, Robert's cabled order to Veitch & Sons had arrived and Pickering effected a nocturnal replacement, so the child never found out. It was a sentimental gesture of which Robert felt ashamed, and he ordered Pickering to keep it to himself.

He knew he could count on the head gardener's discretion, for Pickering adored Linley. All the staff did – at least, according to old Bowles. 'I daresay, my lord, it's the little cherub's *cheerfulness*,' the rector had confided to Robert with unfortunate spittle-laden enthusiasm. 'And always so *surprised*, God bless him, and so genuinely *gratified* if the servants can spare him the time for a little jest or a bit of nonsense.'

Ten yards away, a solitary hyrax popped out of its hole like a squirrel and surveyed Robert with twitching nostrils.

He smiled to himself. Choosing a pineapple for

Great-Aunt Stella! Well, Stella owed it to him to savour every bite, and he would tell her so in his next letter. God alone knew when he would taste pineapple again.

Marchand came running down the hill and handed Robert a flimsy yellow page torn from a notebook. 'Helio for you from Bethlehem, sir! Thought I'd bring it myself as it was marked urgent!'

'PRESENCE REQUIRED BETHLEHEM STOP,' Robert read. 'COME ALONE STOP. DECENT CLARET WAITING STOP. HUNTER STOP.'

He handed it back to Marchand, who read it and looked visibly impressed. 'That wouldn't be Lieutenant-General Sir Archibald Hunter, sir? The column commander?'

'It would.'

'Oh, I *say*.' He looked hopeful. 'But he can't have meant that literally, sir, I mean about your going alone. Bethlehem's a day's ride from here. You'll need someone to go with—'

'I'll take Webb.'

'But sir, can't I—'

'No, you can't. Mr Jordache,' he added to the first lieutenant, who was approaching the Mess. 'Take command and wait here for further orders. And find Private Webb a horse.'

'Yes, sir,' said Jordache, without a flicker at Marchand.

And for God's sake, Jordache, Robert added silently, keep the boy out of trouble.

The exterior of Bethlehem General Store was lavishly decorated with pink and white plaster mouldings which reminded Robert of birthday cakes. From the square came the usual barely controlled clamour of the military. The creak and groan of gun-carriages and wagons, the crackle of whips; the shouts of kaffirs and the curses of men. But in the small walled garden at the back of the general store, all was peace and silence.

The garden was no more than a couple of hundred yards square, but, apart from a narrow brick path, every inch was planted with vegetables and the twisted little Colony peach trees which yielded hard yellow fruit at Christmas. In the far corner, a patch had been cleared for a rickety table and two cane chairs, and on the table someone had placed a green tin tray painted with yellow roses, a decanter, and two crystal tumblers.

Lieutenant-General Sir Archibald Hunter poured two generous measures of whisky and lit Robert's cigar. 'That chaos out in the square,' he murmured, shaking his head. 'Quite takes one back to the Sudan, doesn't it, old chap? Same effortless muddle always waiting in the wings.'

Robert smiled.

For a while they smoked in companionable silence. Robert tilted back his chair and gave himself up to the fine, clean taste of the whisky and the sunlight on the cabbages.

'My dear fellow,' Hunter said suddenly. 'I suppose you know you look bloody awful? At first I wasn't even sure if it was you.'

Robert did not reply.

'I know you chaps are down to half-rations,' said Hunter, 'but don't these people keep any *food* on their damned farms?'

'My orders are to burn their damned farms, not harvest their crops.'

Hunter glanced down at his drink. 'I take it you don't object to that?'

'Of course not. They're my orders.'

'Then why do I sense that, if you were in command, this would not be happening?'

Robert laughed. 'My dear Archie, one may always say that!'

'My dear Robert. This is me you're talking to.'

Robert blew a smoke-ring and watched it float away over the peach trees. 'Very well,' he said. 'It isn't working.'

'It'll work in the end.'

Robert shrugged. 'Then from what I've seen, the end will be a damned long time in coming. They're a resolute lot, the Dutch.'

Hunter put down his tumbler. 'That was why I wanted to see you.'

Robert waited.

'We need someone to go and tell the chaps back home.'

'Tell them what?'

'That we still have some way to go before it's over.'

Robert considered that. ' "We" ' need someone to tell them. Who is "we"?'

When Hunter smiled, the corners of his mouth turned down, giving him the look of a tired circus clown. 'I could never fathom why you made such a damned fine officer. You always ask the questions one never should.'

'Very well. I'll ask another. Who else knows about this?'

'My dear fellow, that's the same question! Only I and one or two others. That's as far as I'll go.'

'I'm afraid I'm still being rather obtuse. You have

staff officers for this kind of thing. Come to that, you have politicians and newspaper correspondents. You don't need me.'

'We need someone who knows what he's talking about.'

Robert tilted his head back and blew another smoke-ring.

Hunter's eyebrows rose in astonishment. 'Good Lord. I thought you'd jump at it.'

'If I'd wanted to go into politics, I'd have done so. I'm not a bloody diplomat.'

'It's bloody diplomats who got us into this mess.'

'But surely Whitehall doesn't imagine —'

'That's *exactly* what Whitehall imagines. Worse than that, it's what Whitehall is *saying*. The whole country's giving thanks that the war's nearly over, while here we are in overwhelming numbers, signally *failing* to over-whelm a handful of illiterate cattle-farmers —'

'But I told you, I'm no diplomat —'

'My dear fellow, that is not the point! The point is, you are related to half the Cabinet and you went to Eton and Oxford with the other half. They'll *listen* to you. The more so since you speak from first-hand experience, *and* you're not some damned croaker bleating about women and children. Incidentally,' he lit another cigar, 'it lies within my power to sweeten the pill just a little. I should so like to be able to bring a smile to the face of the glorious Lady Harlaston.'

Which, thought Robert, means a spot of home leave thrown in if I say yes. Suddenly he felt tired. 'Tell me, Archie. Do I have a choice?'

Hunter swirled the whisky in his glass. 'Not really, old chap.'

'Well then.' He stood up. 'It looks as if I'm your man.'

Five days later, on the verandah of Henderson's Hotel in Durban, Robert leaned back in his chair to read his letters, and resisted the temptation to open his aunt's before his wife's.

Violet's first letter had been written in April at St James's Square. The prose was so seamless that he wondered if she had written it out in draft first, as she used to do when they were just married. At the time he had found that rather touching.

'*Dearest, I am in the last stages of exhaustion!*' Which, it transpired, was his Aunt Stella's fault for spoiling her Saturday to Monday with a lot of particularly objectionable people. Why, Violet wondered, did Liberal politicians feel it their duty to entertain '*Jews, Americans, actresses, and cabinet-makers? Où sont les convenances? Aunt Stella of course handled them all quite beautifully, but those Symonds girls! I know they are awfully clever and you rather liked them once, but I feel certain that you would have been scandalized had you witnessed Olivia's tenue on Sunday. Red and grey peau de soie, mon ami, at breakfast!*'

Robert closed his eyes and summoned up a picture of breakfasts at Wynburne. The galleried dining room aglow with spring sunshine; the table a dazzle of damask and Sèvres and great crystal bowls of gardenias and roses.

He skipped to the end, where Violet had penned a few lines about Harlaston. '. . . *which reminds me, I have at last engaged a stonemason for the work you wanted put in hand at St Hybald's. I take no credit. It*

was all Dickon Webb's doing. Apparently, he pur-
loined the man from dear old Georgie!' Robert smiled
at the idea of his estate manager, gentle Dickon Webb,
poaching so much as a rabbit from the Duke of Kyme.
Sam had probably put his older brother up to it. *'. . .*
Webb tells me we're giving the man "the end house",
wherever that is, for it seems that he has a family
(artisans always do, do they not?) I've no idea what he
is to do, but presumably Dickon can instruct him. I
only mention it at all to prove that I have not quite
forgotten your beloved Harlaston, emballée *as I am!'*

His aunt's letter, also written in April, was pure
Stella: a torrent of social and political gossip which
made her sound much younger than her forty-five
years. It reminded him – if he needed reminding – why
Stella and her sisters had been the linchpins of Society
for over twenty years. Stella, Lily and Margot: known
to their friends as 'the Three Graces', to their acquaint-
ances as 'the Harpies'.

Robert read it slowly, to make it last. Stella's gossip
always amused him, although sometimes he wondered
what she said about *him* to her friends. His aunts were
three supremely shrewd, self-confident women. He had
learned the value of silence while still a boy.

As he was turning to his wife's second letter, he
became aware that Sam had returned and was waiting
at the foot of the steps. His own respectable bundle of
correspondence was stuffed into his breast pocket.

'What's the news from Hynton?' Robert asked, as he
opened Violet's letter.

'Oh, this an' that, sir,' Sam said evasively.

Robert suspected that most of Sam's letters were
from the more daring of the local girls, among whom
he was known as a 'regular catch'. But Sam Webb

would not be caught until he wanted to be, and as yet there was no sign of that happening.

'Message for you from the general, sir.'

'Yes?' Robert did not look up from his letter.

'Invitation to dinner tonight, sir.'

'Mm-hm.'

Violet's second letter was dated the 20th of June. Over four weeks ago. Again it was very beautifully written, and definitely the product of several drafts, although unusually for her it did not even cover two sides. Normally she made sure that she filled precisely four.

'The general, sir? Shall I say you'll accept?'

'. . . please be assured that everything conceivable was done. Moreover I am told that he did not suffer greatly. As soon as he showed the slightest fever, Gibbs summoned Dr Young, and throughout the night they administered cold compresses and iced champagne. In the early morning, when Dr Young diagnosed diphtheria, he straight away sent me a wire. I was staying with Aunt Margot at Belgrave Square, and of course we left for Harlaston at once. We arrived in the early evening, but Linley had died that afternoon.'

'Sir? Is anything wrong? Sir?'

CHAPTER FIVE

Wednesday 15 August 1900

The knock at the end house door could not have come at a worse time. They should have left for Mrs Jordan's twenty minutes ago, but Mrs Fosdyke was still in her chemisette. 'Whoever it is,' she hissed to her daughter, 'get *rid* of them!'

'What d'you *think* I'm going to do,' snapped Charity, 'ask them in for tea?'

She couldn't take much more of this. And it was all so horribly familiar, because it had all happened before, eleven weeks ago. Then as now, Mrs Fosdyke had been off her food with worry about Mrs Jordan's tea, and to their mutual horror the dark prune had hung on her like a scarecrow when they tried it on. Then as now, they had been up all night taking it in. The only difference was that eleven weeks before, Mrs Jordan's tea had been summarily cancelled when the little boy at the Hall had died, and the whole parish had been plunged into mourning.

Then suddenly last week *another* invitation had arrived from Mrs Jordan. And this time it didn't look as if Mrs Fosdyke was going to get a last-minute reprieve.

Whoever was at the door knocked again. Charity closed her eyes. If it was Ruby Corlett asking yet again if her gored skirt was ready, she could whistle for it.

She went downstairs and opened the door, and came face to face with a soldier. A compact young man in khaki, with thick ginger hair and hard features, and cool, confident grey eyes.

For a long moment they faced one another on the doorstep. Then the soldier took off his wide-brimmed hat. 'Private Samuel Webb at your service, miss. Keeper Webb that was. And will be again, when the war's over.'

No-one had put himself at her service before. Charity wondered if she should thank him for it. Instead she said, 'We were just going out.'

She flushed. The baldness of it hung in the air between them.

'I know,' he said, to her surprise. 'You're having tea with Mrs Jordan. I was passing, so I thought I'd look in and show you the way.'

It dawned on Charity who he was. 'You're Mr Webb's *brother*. The one that's in the war with Lord Harlaston and came back on leave.'

His features contracted. She realized that he didn't like being referred to as someone's brother. And to be fair, there wasn't much of a family resemblance. Mr Webb the estate manager wore a baggy corduroy suit and old-fashioned side-whiskers which made him look like a walrus. Private Webb's uniform fitted as if it was made for him, his puttees were immaculate, and he sported a severely clipped red-gold moustache. Charity wondered if he might be a little vain – though if he was, it was probably justified.

He hardly glanced at her as they waited on the doorstep for Mrs Fosdyke, but she knew he was taking her in.

She wondered if he liked what he saw. She had given up wishing she was pretty when she was sixteen. But at least her Sunday best fitted her well, and the skirt was long enough to hide the worst of her boots. They were square-toed lace-ups like a farm-girl's, and she hated them.

Will thundered down the stairs and was instantly sent back to collect their mother.

Charity longed to ask Private Webb about the Hall. He must know all about it, for she noticed he hadn't said 'Mrs Jordan at the Big House', or 'Mrs Jordan at the Hall', but simply 'Mrs Jordan', which indicated an impressive familiarity.

The Hall. Her stomach dropped at the thought of it. In half an hour she would be there, along with her mother and Will. Please God, let them behave normally for once.

She cleared her throat. 'It was good of Mrs Jordan to send us another invitation. We didn't know if she meant us to accept it or not.'

'Why wouldn't she?'

'Well, we wondered if it was just for form's sake. I mean, it still seems quite soon after the little boy – we thought the Family mightn't like it.'

'Oh, you needn't fret about that. Far as they're concerned, it's business as usual.'

She must have looked puzzled, for he allowed himself a brief soldierly smile, which made his rather stony face attractive. 'They're not like us, Miss Fosdyke.

Don't you go making that mistake. They don't feel things like we do.'

'I see,' said Charity, not seeing at all.

'Robert? Robert.'

' – my dear?'

'I have poured your tea.'

Robert took the cup from his wife's hand and looked at it. Then he went to stand in the door of the summer-house. Tully and Max, the spaniels, padded after him and slumped panting at his feet.

Violet said, 'You were asking if there will be many to dine with us this evening.'

'Why, so I was.'

'I thought I had better keep it small, to allow you to acclimatize. We shall be twelve.'

'To acclimatize?' Robert gave the expected smile. 'And I thought I was doing so well! Have I been a brute?'

Violet beautifully returned his smile. 'You could never be that. Though I am rather glad that you spared me your beard. I had a letter from May Hunter. Archie said you resembled the Caliph of Baghdad.' She gave a becoming little shudder. 'No, I meant rather that Harlaston must seem such a change for you, coming from the war.'

A *change*. Poor Violet. Her gift for understatement was masterly.

He felt like a stranger in a magic kingdom. Or like a prince who returns from a foreign land to find that spells have encircled his realm and shut him out.

He was dreaming. He had been dreaming since stepping off the train at Tilburne four days before. It was a dream from which he longed to awaken.

From the summer-house, the view across his realm was dazzling. The roses were at their most resplendent: great banks of scarlet, vermilion and gold, throbbing with colour against the cool white marble steps. Peacocks picked their way across the lawns, luminous sapphire on rich emerald. The great house floated like an apparition in the heat: a magnificent confusion of turrets and cupolas and fantastic statuary.

And while Harlaston slumbered, his subjects tended it with dreamy slowness. An under-gardener raked gravel in the Chinese Walk. The old grey gelding drew the mower across the quoits ground. Beyond the park wall the reaper-binders puffed steam over the cornfields, and the yellow wagons rumbled towards the Home Farm. Nothing broke the spell. Everything was part of it. An intricate clockwork mechanism wound up by the prince before he went to war, and now operating perfectly without him.

And at the heart of his realm sat the young princess of inhuman loveliness, in her high-collared mourning of vaporous white. A green-eyed, golden-haired waterspirit of pearly perfection, exquisitely come to rest amid silk cushions and Spode.

'In fact,' he said, 'what strikes me most is the food.'

'The – *food*?' echoed Violet, as though he had said something indelicate. Her gaze strayed to the curate stand which the footman had set at her elbow, with its strata of madeleines and preserved ginger.

He had no idea what she thought he had been doing in South Africa, but plainly it had never entered her head that he had managed fewer than four ample meals a day. Nor had she noticed the really singular thing: that he could not now enjoy what was put before him. Something got in the way. A fullness in the throat which made it difficult to swallow.

She moved a little dish of lemon slices a fraction to the left. 'I also tried to keep the numbers down for the weekend, but I'm afraid I haven't done very well. They were invited weeks ago, d'you see. And I promised Aunt Lily that we'd take Aubrey for the holidays. Shall you mind terribly?'

'I shan't mind in the least. I shall enjoy it.'

She took up a Japanese fan. 'Of course, there will be no question of a shoot. Everyone understands that we shall be very quiet.'

Robert smiled. 'Including the pheasants?'

Violet did not return his smile. 'And you do remember that next week is the Hynton fête? It will be impossible, I know, but we cannot avoid putting in an appearance. Then, the following week—' she fell silent.

'The following week?'

A faint flush visited her cheek. 'The Ball. On the first of September. Three days before you go back. Such a bizarre idea, to give a ball at the beginning of September. But then, everything your grandmama did was bizarre, was it not? I had no *intention* of allowing it to go ahead this year, but Aunt Stella suggested it might be inappropriate if I did not. The war, d'you see? People expect it of one. I fear you'll find it awfully trying.'

Poor Violet. Since his return she had behaved so curiously, as though he were entitled to the lion's share of grief. As though she had not been the boy's mother but merely a trusted secretary, who in his absence had striven to maintain *les convenances*, and was now delicately avoiding any allusion to what lay beneath.

'*I hope I did well?*' she had written, describing the

66

white funeral lilies, and the locks of their son's hair which she had sent to her mother and each of his aunts. With particular horror he had pictured the tiny envelopes addressed in his wife's graceful hand – so much more elegant than their contents, the mouse-coloured hair which had never stayed flat despite the frequent application of wet brushes. The same graceful hand had conscientiously penned a description of each offering of flowers on the back of its accompanying visiting-card: '*Mrs Edmund Sewell, wreath of gardenias and laurel leaves*'; '*Sir Reginald and Lady Wyatt, spray of white roses and palm leaves bound with white ribbon . . .*' With unfailing tact she had placed the cards on a salver and left it on his desk for him to find. He knew without being told that all those who had sent flowers – and there had been many – had been promptly rewarded with a charming note of thanks, referring in gratifying detail to their particular offering.

'The poor darling simply needs *time*,' Aunt Margot had told him when he saw her in London. 'But she is young. There will be other children. And, of course, she will be all the better for seeing *you*.'

His aunt's faith in him was touching, but misplaced, for he knew that Violet found his presence disquieting – and that she would have preferred it if he had stayed in South Africa.

He would have preferred it too.

It was the strangeness of the whole affair which struck him most forcibly. Was this how grief felt? This unfamiliarity with all that was most familiar? But he had known grief before, and it hadn't been like this. When his grandmother had died. Above all, when his brother Spencer was killed. That had been grief. That deep tearing sense that the world was empty. Suddenly he longed to be back on the veldt with his men, who could sob and howl like children at a comrade's death.

Violet was watching him, her lovely face pale. 'Dearest. Are you displeased?'

'*Displeased*?' An odd word to use, when Linley's lonely little ghost was there at her elbow.

'The Ball. I hope I did well not to cancel?'

It wasn't her fault. It wasn't anyone's fault. Leaning down, he touched her forehead with his lips. 'My dear,' he said gently, 'of course you did well. You did perfectly. I have never known you to do anything else.'

Sam would never understand the aristocracy. Not if he lived to be a hundred.

He and Lord Harlaston were going round the stables, with Sam noting things down in his stock-book. Sam's mind was only half engaged, for he had troubles of his own. Ted Wilcox had been doing a worryingly good job of keepering in his absence, and Sam needed to find a way of suggesting the opposite to Lord Harlaston. Also, he had to get away in time to walk Mrs and Miss Fosdyke home from their tea with Mrs Jordan.

But, in the middle of these reflections, it struck him. He had been back at the Hall for four days, and *nothing* had been said about the little lad. Not a word had been overheard by the footmen, the parlour-maids, Lord Harlaston's valet, Lady Harlaston's maid, or indeed any of the upper servants. And now here they were, waiting for Walker to lead Viscount to the mounting-block, and everyone was acting as if nothing had happened.

'My son has died,' Lord Harlaston had said on

the verandah in Durban, without raising his eyes from the letter, and two hours later he was dressing for dinner. *Dressing for dinner!*

Somehow Sam had muddled through his duties. Polishing the boots, laying out the linen and the dress uniform. Somehow, Lord Harlaston had got himself dressed while his batman dropped things.

Only once did matters take a different turn, when Sam accidentally brushed something off the bureau. The thin oilcloth parcel which contained the little lad's picture of Slipper. He knew what it was because Lord Harlaston had shown it to him when it arrived. As Sam bent to retrieve the picture from the floor, Lord Harlaston had snapped, 'Leave that,' and Sam, startled, had looked up and met his eyes. And wondered if Lord Harlaston was really as unfeeling as he had always thought.

They had grown up together. Sam and Dickon, Spencer and Robert. Together they had raided the strawberry beds, and smoked their first cigarettes behind the greenhouses.

Sam had always loved Spencer best. Everyone did. Spencer with his golden hair and open face, and his simple-hearted zest for hunting and having fun. In a way, Spencer had been a lot like Dickon – though it was strange that in his own brother Sam found such traits contemptible.

And it was strange, too, that Spencer and Robert had been so close, when they were so different. Robert, the younger by a year, had taken after his brilliant unsettling grandmother, whom Sam had *hated*. Not that he hated Robert. But he had never felt easy with him. How could you feel easy with a man who enjoyed Greek poetry as much as he enjoyed a pheasant-shoot, and who as a child had once thrown a kitten off the conservatory roof, to teach it to fly?

They said he'd been magnificent in Egypt when he got the news of Spencer's death. Middle of a regimental polo game. Just stood there on the field reading the telegram. Then folded it in his pocket, remounted his pony, and got on with the game.

The family gave out that it had been a quick death from a broken neck, but Sam knew better, for he was there. And when the new Lord Harlaston arrived at the Hall three weeks later, he had sat Sam down in the gun-room and fixed him with his dark foreign-looking eyes, and forced him to tell the truth. How Spencer had hung on for two whole days with his chest crushed in by the pommel of his saddle, and Dr Young had put enough morphine in him to stun an ox, but the maids still had to stop their ears as they ran past the door. Even that Robert had taken without a flicker.

With a start Sam realized that Lord Harlaston was already in the saddle. 'Wake up, Sam! I said, have we covered everything?'

Sam glanced down at his book and his heart sank. Only one item left. 'Sorry, my lord. The fact is, um, what do we do about Slipper?'

Walker, checking Viscount's girth, shot him a pitying look.

Sam glanced up and met Lord Harlaston's eyes. And knew that they were both thinking of the same thing. A child's crayoned attempt at a fat black pony.

Lord Harlaston managed better than he. The Poynters needed a mount for their little girl, he said. Slipper would be just the thing. Sam must see to it directly.

'Very *good*, my lord,' said Sam.

A sharp glance warned him to keep his distance.

Or had Sam only imagined that? *Had* he?

Because he couldn't understand how a man could lose his only son, and still behave to all the world – yes, even to his own wife – as if it had never happened.

Maybe that was the secret of the aristocracy. Maybe they knew how to cover things up better than everyone else.

'You did perfectly. I have never known you to do anything else.'

As Violet went to her rooms after tea she was borne upwards on a warm wave of approbation.

She had been right, right, *right!* She had been *right* to have languished in this dreadful place – just as she was *right* to begin seeing people again. At last, after weeks of ennui, she could re-enter her element. And she would be magnificent.

She took pleasure in the sight of her maid, in faultless black frock and organdie apron, holding open the door of her room. 'Mary. We have a *very* great deal to do. We must begin to go out again in Society.'

'Yes, my lady.'

'And I know that you will help me as only you can, because you are a treasure.'

Mary's pretty face flushed with pride.

'Now, then.' Violet looked about her with satisfaction. Her rooms had been her first attempt to introduce good taste to Harlaston, and they had been a complete success. They had once been Robert's grandmother's: a terrible old harridan whom Violet had loathed. Grandmama Adela had stood for everything she detested: intellect, enthusiasm, and an utter disregard for form. When at last the old witch had died, Violet was triumphant. She astonished her husband by claiming the rooms for her own, and then with joy in her heart she ripped out every vestige of purple velvet and jet fringing, and replaced it with lemon-coloured silk and *Louis Seize*. She eliminated Grandmama Adela as thoroughly as an exorcist. Then she worked her way through the rest of the house, banishing the worst horrors to the attics. The giant Venetian griffins, the disgustingly lifelike Nubian slaves, whose sly enamelled eyes used to follow her every move.

She knew that she hurt Robert when she did these things, for in his way he had loved his grandmother, but she was unrepentant. Stamping out Grandmama Adela was her one indulgence.

'You will need pencil and notepaper,' she told her maid. 'I shall need a list of every gown, every bodice, every day-dress – in short, every *item* – of white. And I do not need to tell you that I mean *white*. Not oyster or ivory or cream. And I shall need another list of the greys.'

'And – the mauves, my lady?' ventured Mary, whose principal asset was a thorough knowledge of form.

Violet considered that. 'No. Not mauve. I agree that in theory it counts as mourning, but I cannot believe that in this case it would be correct. He was no longer an infant, he was nearly eight.'

She moved to the window.

She had been wearing lavender on the day the boy died. Lavender *faille* with a bolero of cream *passementerie*. And the pearls which Robert had given her for Christmas.

The boy had always been irritatingly plain, but the

72

illness had made him perfectly hideous. And that awful, awful smell. Dr Young had said it was peculiar to the disease, as if that was supposed to provide some sort of excuse. It did not. It was simply revolting.

Her gaze drifted to the stable-block, where Robert was setting out for a ride across the park. Her heart swelled with pride. He was so handsome. So beautifully reserved. And so effortlessly *comme il faut*. He had chosen to stay in uniform while on leave, and she knew that he had not given a thought to whether it was the correct thing to do. Doing what was correct came naturally to him. And it *suited* him so.

Before they were married, Grandmama Adela had taken her aside and slyly warned her: 'To date, my grandson's tastes have happened to coincide perfectly with what Society demands of him, but do not let that deceive you, my dear. It does not mean that he is deficient in free will. I look forward to observing how he conducts himself, should a divergence ever occur.' Violet hadn't understood what the old woman meant, except that she was trying to frighten her. She did not succeed.

'Mary,' she said without turning her head. 'We shall need something very simple for the dinner on Saturday. There is a Worth evening bodice. Pearl-grey chiffon over charmeuse. It will be perfect. See to it.'

The wind was strong on Hynton Edge, rushing up through the uncut wheat with a hot dry rustle. Charity hung back on the fringes of the wood. Her mother and Will had already passed beneath the trees, and Private Webb was waiting to hand her over the stile.

The great house floated below her: a self-contained city from a storybook. To her surprise and dismay, she didn't like it. There was too much of it; its presence overwhelmed.

What's *wrong* with you? she thought.

Mrs Jordan's tea had gone without a hitch, her mother and Will had behaved beautifully, and they'd even been given a sewing commission. She should have been overjoyed.

But she knew what was troubling her. It was the hectic look on her mother's face. The look which said that when the fall came it would be a hard one.

'Miss Fosdyke?' Private Webb extended his hand.

You're daft, she told herself. Stop worrying. Sufficient unto the day is the evil thereof.

As she climbed over the stile and entered the trees, the sound of the wind dropped to nothing. A distant rook cawed. A vole rustled through last year's leaves. You could hear a twig fall. Private Webb had said that as Hynton Wood was a pheasant covert, they wouldn't have been allowed in if he hadn't happened by when they were leaving Mrs Jordan's.

'Enjoy your tea, did you?' Politely he included Mrs Fosdyke in the question, but she was picking sloes behind them and didn't hear. Surprisingly, she had taken to Sam Webb from the outset, no doubt because of the extreme propriety of his demeanour. Besides, after the success of the tea, nothing could faze her. Even Will had been permitted to run off on his own, as a reward for his total silence at Mrs Jordan's. Charity suspected that that had been due to the statues at the Hall rather than any sustained effort at good behaviour. Before today, the only statues he had seen had been effigies in church; he had been profoundly shocked to learn that stone animals could stand upright, crouch, snarl, and attack each other.

'The tea', said Charity with feeling, 'was a miracle.'

And yet when they had started out from the end house, things had not promised well. Mrs Fosdyke had *hated* the big house. 'I don't *care* if they're only marble! I wouldn't put up with 'em if I was Lady Harlaston. All they nasty untidy wild animals sitting about on my roof!' She had only regained her composure when they turned into the service road and the Hall was lost from view behind the kitchen gardens. She knew where she was with asparagus beds.

But she had fallen in love with Mrs Jordan's rooms in the upper servants' quarters, and what had helped about Mrs Jordan herself was the fact that her bodice pulled at the collar, and its patriotic khaki did nothing for her complexion.

At first the under-housekeeper had been fearfully reserved, but she had relaxed when she perceived that her guests could be trusted to maintain the proper distance. Charity had guessed correctly, and the purpose of the tea was indeed to assess their suitability for taking in sewing from the servants' hall. Once they had all established their respective positions, things had proceeded smoothly. There had been no talk of the fens, Cousin Ruth, or the Prince of Wales – all of whom came in for a thrashing when Mrs Fosdyke was frightened.

Private Webb held back a bramble branch, and Charity thanked him with a smile.

Five minutes passed in awkward silence. To their left, a path branched off to a clearing, and Charity glimpsed pale green water and a dragonfly's rainbow dart. She would have liked to have taken a closer look, but Private Webb gave no sign of turning aside, and she didn't feel inclined to ask him to. He might take it as encouragement, and she wasn't sure that she wanted to encourage him.

At last he said, 'I hear you're taking a position in Tilburne.'

'Who told you that?'

'Your mother.'

'Well she's wrong,' she said curtly. 'I have no intention of working at Aspland's, if that's what she said.'

'What's wrong with Aspland's?'

'Nothing. But I can do better if I stop right here.'

'How?'

'You must've seen the sign in the window. We take in sewing.'

'But that's not what you meant.'

She felt her face growing hot. She didn't want to talk about it, and she didn't like the way he was firing questions at her. 'I'm saving,' she said.

'For what?'

' – For a typewriter.'

'A typewriter? What d'you want with one of them?'

'To make a living, same as everyone else!' That had come out more sharply than she'd intended. She added: 'You can do fifteen sheets a day if you practise. The going rate's tuppence a sheet.'

'That's good, that is. That's fifteen shillings a week.'

'Yes I know. I did the sums too.'

She caught a gleam in his eye, and wondered if he had been needling her for fun.

They reached the edge of the wood and he helped her over the stile. They were on the Moxby road, about a quarter of a mile west of the village. Charity fiddled with her umbrella. She felt snappish and unwomanly. Perhaps it was simply lack of sleep.

Private Webb ran a forefinger over the band of his khaki hat. 'Mrs Fosdyke says you like books,' he said at last. He made them sound like some kind of outlandish animal.

'I do when I can get them. I'd join the lending library in Tilburne if I could afford it, but it's two shillings just for the deposit.'

He nodded slowly. 'Maybe I can help. Mrs Bowles – the parson's wife – she likes books too, but she's been poorly for years. I've heard she's in want of a reader. I could put in a word, if you like.'

In the lemon silk rooms the peace had splintered like a scent-bottle smashed against the wall.

'All you ever do in *life*', said Violet between her teeth, 'is care for my things! You lay out what I tell you to – the correct hat and veil and shoes, the gloves and the wrist-bag and the parasol. That is what you *do*.'

'Yes, my lady.'

'And when I return, you put everything away. After, *after*, you have made sure that if it needs brushing, it is brushed, if it needs cleaning, it is cleaned, and if it needs mending, it is mended. Is that so very complicated?'

The girl swayed. If she hadn't been a maid she would have fainted.

'So do me the courtesy of explaining why the *one* item in my wardrobe which will be appropriate for the first dinner of any consequence in months – explain why it was put away with a rent in it? No, I do not want to hear excuses. I merely want it repaired. Of *course* there's no time to send it to London, you stupid creature! You will simply have to see that it's mended here.'

'M – my lady?'

'My lady?' she mimicked. 'I won't be *your* lady for

77

much longer if it's not mended by Saturday. Now get out and take the wretched thing with you!'

The stillness after the girl had gone was profound. The only sound was the discreet ticking of the clock on the mantelpiece.

Violet stood in the middle of the room feeling wretched. She put her hands to her temples. No, no, *no*! She would not *let* this spoil everything. Not when it was going so well.

She went to the secretaire and poured three drops of laudanum into a sherry-glass of water.

Rest. She needed rest. Her little lacquered couch looked so inviting. *Why* hadn't the wretched girl stayed to help her into a tea-gown?

She lay down and waited for the first drowsy swell of the opiate to bear her away. The glow of sunlight on her eyelids darkened to amber and she drifted down. Down into the amber glow.

She is nine years old. Playing with her dolls in the schoolroom at Chisholm Grange on a dark Sunday afternoon a week before Christmas.

She *hates* Christmas.

The horror of it begins weeks before, with the long tearful sessions with Frau Schickemeier. Struggling to learn some awful German poem by heart. She has nightmares; she lives in terror of the moment when she must stand alone in the drawing-room before Papa and Mama and their guests, and recite.

She is thinking of that now as she plays with her dolls, when suddenly, like a lightning flash, she *understands*.

She realizes that of all her dolls it is only the prettiest, with the freshest waxen skin and the most elegant gown, that she ever takes to the park. She never takes the ones that are grubby and *demodé*; those she throws in a corner and forgets. And now at last it dawns on her: *other people feel exactly the same as her*.

None of the grown-ups wants poetry at Christmas. Schiller is boring. All they want is something pretty to look at which won't interrupt their conversation.

Christmas Day comes. She hears the guests entering the drawing room. She holds her breath. Then the screen is taken away, and there is a gasp of delight as the Little Mermaid is revealed in all her fragile beauty. She reclines on a couch which has been draped in azure velvet to resemble waves. Her hair is an undulating mantle of palest gold. Her thin child's shoulders are roped with borrowed pearls. Her tail is a scaly miracle of sea-green silk. She *adores* her tail. She has made Frau Schickemeier's life miserable for days, hunting down the exact shade of satin she had in mind. She has been unstoppable. Indefatigable. She has never worked so hard on anything. The costume hurts savagely, crushing her legs and constricting her ribs so that it is hard to breathe. But it is *worth* it. For the first time ever she is a complete success. Papa and Mama and all the beautiful ladies and elegant gentlemen are smiling and applauding. Their admiration laps at her in waves. She was right, right, *right*.

She closes her eyes and lets the waves carry her away.

After Sam Webb had left them at the gate, Mrs Fosdyke let herself be persuaded upstairs for a nap. Mr Fosdyke seized his chance and departed quietly for the Dolphin, Will disappeared, and Charity went out for a walk on her own.

She had a lot to think about. Private Webb. Mrs

Jordan. The Hall. But most of all, the position with the parson's wife, which lit up the future like a firecracker.

She walked past the Green and out onto the Tilburne road. It was the same route they had taken earlier when they were going to Mrs Jordan's, but so much had happened since then that it felt like days ago.

On her left, fields of tawny stubble stretched down to the river. On her right rose the tall stone wall of Harlaston park. Ahead lay the crossroads, where Cragg's Lane swung towards Shotley Farm, and the drive turned into the gates and swept up to the Hall.

The shadows were lengthening and the wind had dropped. The fields were deserted. Her skirts whispered like satin over the straw carpeting the road.

There had been so many changes since they'd come to Hynton. Sedgefield, her world for nineteen years, had already faded in her memory – as if someone had covered it with a vast outlandish shawl of peacock colours.

Maybe Mrs Bowles would lend her some books. Maybe the rector owned a typewriter. Maybe he wanted his sermons typed. Maybe she would become a private secretary and go to London. The possibilities multiplied. She felt elated and afraid.

The horseman was at the crossroads when she saw him. He had halted at the park gates and was looking the other way, while his splendid chestnut gelding tossed its head at the flies.

He was in uniform, with a wide-brimmed hat turned up on one side like Sam Webb's. But because he was an officer and not a private, he wore knee-high calfskin boots instead of puttees.

Charity noticed the black band on the sleeve of his tunic and her stomach turned over. Lord Harlaston. It had to be. It was his little boy whose memorial tablet had just arrived from London, and which her father was preparing to instal in the chancel.

To her horror, he turned his mount and started riding slowly towards her. She had no choice but to walk on to meet him, or appear ridiculous.

He sat his horse beautifully, with the reins in one hand and the other resting lightly on his thigh. But he did not look about him, or seem to notice when a pheasant erupted from a clump of poppies and ran across the road in front of his horse. To Charity's intense relief, he was too preoccupied to be aware of her existence.

She was wrong. As they drew level, and still without looking at her, he touched his crop to his hat. It was a graceful, impersonal courtesy, and it made her feel like a duchess. She acknowledged it with a nod.

He was unnervingly grand and handsome, with very dark hair, a fine sunburned face, and brilliant black eyes. He reminded her of the colonel in *The Glory of Omdurman* – except that his jaw wasn't fashionably round, and his moustache was neither waxed nor curled. Her mother would have admired the cut of his uniform, but she would have said that he was far too lean.

Watching him ride away, it occurred to her that her nod had probably been presumptuous, or even impertinent, and she ought to have dropped him a curtsey instead. If she got the position at the rectory she must ask Mrs Bowles.

If she got the position.

The sun was low in the sky. Lord Harlaston had gone.

Please God, let her get the position.

CHAPTER SIX

Early June, the Present

April is not the cruellest month. June is, when all it brings are cold north winds and relentless rain, and when the very notion of summer becomes incongruous. In Lincolnshire, June can feel like the middle of winter.

'Nearly there,' said the taxi-driver bitterly.

Sarah dug her fingers into the fake-fur seat-cover as they lurched round another bend. The orange acrylic felt warm and greasy and smelt of cigarettes.

She turned her head and stared out of the window. Five minutes earlier, the driver had swung off the main road and was now meandering through barren farming country in a blatant attempt to inflate the fare. She was too exhausted to protest. Huge fields of sodden corn and sugar beet flashed past. No hedgerows, no dry stone walls, no lacy drifts of cow parsley or hawthorn. A charmless landscape of bleak grey skies and the odd spinney of windswept trees.

Her train had been late and had arrived in Grantham at the same time as the five thirty from King's Cross. She had been swamped by a tidal wave of London commuters, barking into mobile phones and spitting fury at anyone with more than a briefcase. In the end she gave up and stopped with her luggage in the middle of the concourse, and the tide flowed around her and passed on.

She found a trolley behind a hamburger stand and started for the taxi rank. Her legs felt wobbly. Black spots floated before her eyes. A tramp lurched out from behind a Railtrack notice-board and shouted in her face: 'A *bullet* in yer eye! I *know* you!' His eyes were hot and liquid in a face as rough as tree bark. Welcome to Lincolnshire.

Rejecting a lift from her brother began to look like a mistake. On the other hand, rejecting a lift from her mother had been a necessity. Mrs Dalton hadn't stopped trying to prevent her from taking the job since she got Alex's letter.

Rain spotted the windows. The driver put his foot down to attack another bend. 'You'll need a car,' he said for the fifth time.

'I had to leave mine in Coventry for repairs. My brother's bringing it in a few weeks.'

'You can't get by without a car out here. This is lonely country.' He sounded affronted, as if she had recklessly underestimated what he had to put up with.

She wondered what unfaithful wife or lost job or other corrosive failure had caused such bitterness, and whether she was going to escape being told. She often got them: the angry, resentful ones. They seemed to sniff her out in cafs and queues. A listener who wasn't going to protest or walk away.

'Summer's nothing,' he said with contempt. 'Winter's the worst. People go mad. It's the loneliness. One time, boy I was at school with, lived on a farm.

83

Bashed his dad to death then killed himself. Cut his own head open with a saw.'

That must have taken some doing, she thought tiredly.

Dominic would be angry if he could see her now. 'You don't need this,' he'd say. 'You've been ill. Tell him to shut the fuck up! Why can't you just *tell* him?'

Dominic. He would approve of what she was doing. Wouldn't he? Focusing on her own family rather than someone else's.

She hoped he never found out. He would think it was all his doing.

She looked down at her hands. They were yellow and bony, like those of an old woman. The pneumonia had taken away most of her looks and all of her self-confidence. How in all seriousness had she ever thought she could keep a man like Dominic?

They were approaching a village. A sign flashed past. Hynton. Where Alex Hardy lived. It was hardly more than a hamlet, with a war memorial on a green surrounded by cottages of cherry-red Victorian brick. Weekenders' cottages: their windows dark, their paint-work self-consciously pristine. No shops, but three pubs – or rather, two pubs and the Old Forge, a 'Wine bar with Restaurant'. Down side-roads she glimpsed cheaper-looking bungalows. A child's bike discarded on a pavement; a sports ground; a village hall.

Then they were out in the fields again, with a high grey wall of lichen-crusted stone on the right-hand side.

A break in the wall, and the cab lurched into a drive. They passed between two towering lodges of window-less granite. Craning her neck, Sarah saw white marble lions sleeping on top. The gates themselves were lost in dripping banks of rhododendrons twenty feet tall which hedged a driveway of stately-home proportions. They crossed a Palladian bridge spanning an artificial lake, and began to climb.

Minutes later, a house came into view on a ridge above them. It towered against a backdrop of dark grey sky and cedars of Lebanon and it was appalling. Far worse than anything Sarah had imagined, and about a hundred times bigger. A nightmare wedding-cake of baroque and neo-Gothic stonework, bristling with turrets, cupolas, crenellations, gargoyles and lions.

She had been expecting an English manor-house of no more than moderate dimensions. Perhaps something on the scale of Sissinghurst, or maybe smaller: a Lincolnshire version of Howard's End, with mellow golden brickwork and a pleasantly overgrown terrace, and an ancient wisteria framing the windows. This was a hundred Albert Memorials rolled into one.

Could it really be true that Charity Elisabeth D'Authon, her own grandmother, had been related to *this*?

Jesus, thought Sarah. No wonder Mum's got a thing about Dad's family. A hundred Albert Memorials must be a bit hard to take if you've voted Labour all your life.

They swung through a pair of yawning gates the height of a London bus and crunched to a halt in a vast round carriage drive, in the middle of which a naked Perseus rescued a struggling Andromeda from a pond. An enormous forked stairway of white marble led up to a pair of huge doors, in the manner of the stairs at the Villa d'Este. To the right, more steps led up towards terraced expanses of garden, with more lions, and what looked like cast-iron wolves attacking cherubs. To the left, an arch surmounted by a clock-tower led through to still another courtyard.

'The service wing,' spat the driver with a jerk of the head. 'Bigger than the main house, only you can't see it on account of it's on a slope. Out of sight, out of mind. That's what they thought of servants in those days. Bastards.'

Sarah stopped listening. In a few minutes, when she felt stronger, she would tell him that she had changed her mind and please would he drive her back to the station. Her mother needn't have worried. This over-blown monstrosity had nothing to do with her, or her father, or her grandmother. She was going home.

As she was forming this intention, the front door swung open and a man came down the steps to the car.

'They've made up the master bedroom for you,' said Alex. 'The bathroom works, and the view's good. I've left the heating on, as it's so cold.'

After one look at her, he had shouldered her bags and taken her straight upstairs without attempting to show her round. They had passed swiftly through a vaulted entrance-hall thronged with marble knights, and up a staircase whose more nightmarish aspects were mercifully sunk in shadows.

The bedroom had all the intimacy of a minor parish church. Three tall sash windows rattled in the wind, and grey silk curtains heaved dismally in and out. A four-poster bed shrouded in ice-blue brocade was flanked by two monstrous gilt chairs, and a porphyry escritoire the colour of raw steak. Against the opposite wall stood a mahogany wardrobe as big as a garden shed. The mantelpiece was black and white marble, and had unmistakably once been part of someone's tomb. The name of the original occupant, on a plaque above the fireplace, had been carefully erased.

All Sarah could muster was a watery smile, and the lift of the eyebrows that people give when they can't think of anything positive to say. With every passing minute the extent of her mistake was becoming clearer. This horrible place didn't want her, and she didn't want it. She wanted to sit down on the bed and howl.

Alex gave no sign of having noticed that anything was wrong. He left her standing in the bedroom and went down to fetch the rest of her bags. Then he suggested that he show her the kitchens.

'I got some groceries for you,' he said as they started back down the miles of corridor. 'Hynton doesn't have a shop, but you can borrow my car whenever you want. There's a Sainsbury's just outside Tilburne.'

'Tilburne.'

'The nearest town with shops. You went through it coming from Grantham.'

She didn't feel like explaining that, no, she hadn't gone through Tilburne, because she'd let the taxi-driver rob her blind on the scenic route.

It was a small comfort to find that at least in the kitchens, the Gothic revival had been banished by gleaming expanses of strip-lit steel. A bottle of whisky on the table beside a box of groceries was like an old friend beckoning in an unfamiliar pub. Sarah hadn't had a drink in ten weeks. Her mother wouldn't tolerate pneumonia and alcohol in the same house, and she hadn't had the energy to make a stand about it. She was embarrassed by the surge of gratitude the bottle evoked.

'Give me a call when you've settled in,' Alex said when they were back in the entrance-hall. 'If you want to make a start, there's a box-file in the Library with some papers I've pulled together. What's left of the family portraits are in the Long Gallery. Most of them went years ago. It's just the two Singer Sargents left. The last baron and his wife.'

Right, she thought firmly, that's the Long Gallery out for the time being. She didn't feel strong enough to tackle anyone even remotely related to Dominic. It was bad enough having to deal with his brother.

'There are no ghosts,' Alex said briskly. 'The cleaners come once a week on Tuesdays, and the gardeners are pretty unobtrusive. You may come across the head gardener from time to time. Name's Larry Hinde. He lives in Moxby, about three miles away. He doesn't like to talk.' He glanced at her. 'Apart from that you'll be left alone. If you want anything, I'm down in Hynton. The Old Rectory, near the church. Number's on the fridge.'

'Right.'

'You can see the church spire from your bedroom. It's only a mile or so down the drive. Or if you prefer, there's a path through the woods.' He paused in the doorway, as if he expected her to speak.

For something to say, she asked how long he had lived at the Old Rectory. Three years, he said, and abruptly changed the subject by showing her how to lock the front door.

Three years was pretty much straight after Helen had left him, which would account for the change of subject. His defensiveness annoyed her. What do you *think*, she felt like saying, that I *want* to talk about your problems?

'I should also tell you,' he said, 'that Stephen will be staying with me for the summer holidays.'

'Stephen?' she echoed blankly.

'Stephen my nephew. Dominic's son.'

Oh, *Christ*.

'In fact, he's here now. Clare brought him down for half-term. She's going abroad on business at rather short notice. I didn't know he'd be coming, or I'd have called you to let you know.'

She nodded, pressing her lips together. 'No, no, that's fine.'

'It isn't fine, and I'm sorry. But I couldn't say no. She had nowhere else to leave him. He's only ten.' He went down the steps and stood on the gravel, his face in darkness. 'Clare's already gone back to London. As you know, Dominic never comes to Harlaston.'

It angered her that he thought it needed saying, and she swung the great door shut with more force than necessary.

By the time she had found her way back upstairs, her head was pounding and her palms were damp. She lowered herself into one of the gilt monsters and surveyed the bedroom. Her laptop lay like a sacrifice on the raw-steak escritoire, surrounded by her cowed-looking luggage.

She glanced at her watch. It was eight o'clock.

She had a bath in seven feet of claw-footed, scroll-topped cast iron beneath a chandelier of pink Bohemian crystal. Then a bowl of cornflakes, eaten standing at the door of the fridge, followed by two large whiskies and a couple of aspirin.

After the second drink she began to feel better, not least because Dominic would have been horrified at the thought of drowning good single malt in Sainsbury's ginger ale. Then she took an extra duvet from a neighbouring bedroom, crawled into the four-poster, and fell instantly asleep.

She didn't dream. When she drifted back to consciousness her first thought was that, for the country, the birds were keeping extraordinarily quiet. Then a glance at her watch told her it was half past three in the afternoon.

Rain rattled the windows. She opened the curtains on an overwhelming view of rainswept parkland dotted with trees. Beyond it, rain pocked the ornamental lake, and beyond that, the valley of the Lyde was a misty green blur. Hidden among the trees to her extreme left, she could just make out the spire of what must be Hynton church.

The sky was heavy with more rain. Exploring could wait. She padded back to bed and dozed for another hour, sensuously aware of the solitude and the patter of rain on the windows. Drifting in and out of consciousness, it occurred to her that for the first time in her adult life there was nothing she had to do that day. Or the next, or the next after that. No-one was coming to see her, no-one was waiting for her to call, no-one was counting on her to meet them. She could stay in bed for a week doing nothing, or have breakfast at midnight.

A couple of hours later, she pulled on jeans and a sweater and padded downstairs to the kitchen. In her mother's house in Coventry when you switched on the lights, the shadows scuttled for cover like mice. At Harlaston they were huge extravagant monsters: sharp-toed dinosaurs crouching slyly behind cupboards. She liked the thought of them: large shadowy pets that didn't need feeding. Perhaps she would stay after all. At least, for a while.

The night before, she had shoved Alex's box of groceries unexamined into the cavernous fridge. Now she sorted through it, vaguely aware that she was taking three times longer than she should have done. Standing for minutes at a time frowning at a pot of yoghurt, wondering where to put it.

The groceries were those of someone who lived alone, didn't like shopping, and didn't care what he ate. A large jar of instant coffee and several cartons of long-life milk; cornflakes, rice, ham, tinned tomatoes, eggs; apples, potatoes, cabbages and sprouts; sliced bread for the freezer, butter, crackers, a block of Cheddar cheese, two large bars of fruit and nut, and a wine box of Chilean Sauvignon Blanc.

Some of last night's irritation seeped away. He might be Dominic's younger brother, but at least he was an effective shopper. With this lot she didn't have to go out for days. If she wanted to, she could stay inside for a week without seeing a soul.

And Alex would leave her alone, she was sure of that. She didn't need Nick to tell her the man was a recluse. She could tell that just by looking at him.

It had been a relief to find him so different from his brother. But if he was different from Dominic, he was also a world away from the relaxed, approachable young man he had once been.

When they were growing up, she and Nick had only met the Other Side once, six months after their father died. The Other Side had invited them to Sunday lunch. 'The Sunday Lunch Disaster', as it became known in the Dalton household.

The tension between Shirley Dalton and Harriet

Hardy had been palpable from the start: a simmering amalgam of social rivalry, a new widow's bitterness towards a wife, and plain old-fashioned antipathy. And Cawthorpe Lodge, a large double-fronted Victorian house set amid fields just north of Bourne, was not designed to put Mrs Dalton at ease.

The age difference between the 'young people' had reduced conversation to monosyllables. At fifteen, Sarah was by far the youngest. Alex, nearly twenty-one, was a fresher at Oxford. He had just started going out with Helen, who, to Sarah's intense relief, was holidaying with friends in the south of France. Dominic, in his final year at Cambridge, was twenty-three, and impossibly remote.

All Sarah wanted was to be ignored. But then Dominic and Alex decided to skip the pudding and take the dogs across the fields to the Cawthorpe Arms, Nick traitorously decided to go too, and the adults ganged up and said Sarah should go with them for the exercise. Sarah refused. Alex tried to help by pointing out that even if the landlord allowed Nick in the pub, he'd draw the line at Sarah, so she'd have to wait outside with the dogs, which wouldn't be much fun. That had the effect of prolonging the debate and making Sarah wish she could sink into the floor.

It was a scorchingly hot and windy August day. The fields were full of crunchy brown stubble, wilting sugar beet, and glistening bales of straw like huge Swiss rolls. Vermilion poppies drooped beside the path, reminding Sarah of the border on her mum's toaster. The dogs – two overwrought English setters called Scylla and Charybdis – went racing off across the fields, then realized it was too hot, and lagged behind with their tongues hanging out.

Dominic did most of the talking. He ignored Sarah, and Nick took his lead and ignored her too. She trailed unhappily behind with the dogs. Alex walked in front of her with his hands in his pockets, humming under his breath and looking about him with the barely contained happiness of the newly in love. He didn't say much, and Sarah could see that Nick wasn't as impressed by him as he was by Dominic, so she wasn't either. But she also noticed that Dominic talked mostly about his brother's girlfriend. He called her 'Troy', because he said her face could launch a thousand ships. Sarah thought that was incredibly dashing, but Alex only laughed and told Dominic not to exaggerate.

Until then, Sarah had been proud of the 'outfit' she had cobbled together in the teeth of her mother's objections. Flared white jeans, a long-sleeved mauve T-shirt which she secretly thought of as Arthurian, and a silver chain-belt which reminded her of her favourite painting of Guinevere. But now, hearing Dominic talk about Helen in Antibes, she knew she was nothing but an overdressed schoolgirl. The belt in particular struck her as ludicrous. She agonized over whether to keep it on and suffer, or take it off and risk the horror of being noticed.

They came to a drainage dyke fifteen feet deep, and walked along the edge. The sides were rank with nettles and frighteningly steep, and at the bottom lay an oily scum of waterweed. The track was treacherous with leftover straw; it was like walking on satin. Sarah was terrified she would lose her footing and fall in. If that happened, the humiliation would kill her.

She felt horribly fat, her long hair was a tangled mess, and her nose was greasy from the sun. They crossed a pasture of young bullocks with neat Egyptian heads and insolent stares. It was like walking past a gang of workmen on a building site.

After a while Alex glanced back at her. It was far too hot, wasn't it? he said. Couldn't country walks be dismal? He was taking the dogs back to the house, did she want to come too, as she didn't seem to be enjoying it much either?

She was furious with him for noticing and brusquely refused. He paused, as if to say something further, then shrugged, and took himself off with a good-natured smile.

Outside the Cawthorpe Arms she waited under a tree with a warm orange juice, feeling as if everyone was staring at her. When at last Dominic and Nick emerged and they had trailed back to Cawthorpe Lodge, Alex was in the kitchen feeding the dogs, and the atmosphere in the dining room had curdled beyond redemption. Mrs Hardy had said something unforgivable about Coventry (Nick and Sarah never learned what) and Mrs Dalton had chosen not to ignore it, and said something equally unforgivable back.

The Daltons and the Other Side did not meet again until Mrs Hardy's funeral seventeen years later. By that time, Dominic was an established barrister who people were predicting would take silk, Alex was a soon-to-be ex-husband and ex-solicitor, and Sarah's own star in television was in the ascendant.

And now it's 'all change' once again, she thought numbly, as she put a slice of bread in the toaster.

She had arrived on a Wednesday. By Friday afternoon, after more sleep than she thought herself capable of, she began to explore. After all, she needed to find a place in which to work.

Exploring should have been easy. Her first job in

television had been researching the Gothic revivalists for a feature on George Gilbert Scott which never got made, and the Hall was a classic E-plan, with two wings flanking a massive central section surmounted by a cupola which would not have disgraced a small cathedral. But Harlaston's guiding principle seemed to be that nothing was as it appeared. Or, less charitably, that a lot of it was fake. Mock tapestries had been stencilled straight onto walls. Swags of pink damask were in fact tinted plaster. Alcoves of polished walnut turned out to be nothing but flat *trompe-l'oeil*. Wall-panels swung open on hidden stairways, while imposing double doors revealed nothing more interesting than a cupboard full of cleaning equipment. Sarah found that she had to climb the main staircase to reach the conservatory on the *ground* floor, as well as the front reception rooms on the *first* floor. Often she would start off east and end up west, with no idea how she had arrived there, nor how to get back.

She wondered what her father had made of it all. He had only mentioned Harlaston once, when she was twelve. She had been devouring everything she could find on English stately homes, having read *Rebecca* and fallen in love with Max de Winter, and one day she had come across a few lines on the Hall in a library book. 'Pity there's no picture,' her father had said. 'I went there once. It's quite a sight.' When she asked him what it was like, he thought for a moment, and smiled. 'Abandon taste, all ye who enter here.' At the time she hadn't known what he meant. She did now.

The University of Allantown had wisely confined serious teaching to the servants' wing, which had become the Humanities Complex and the students' lodgings. The State Rooms in the central section had been lavishly restored and kept for the reception of guests. Sarah wondered what the citizens of Wisconsin made of it all.

'*The visitor's expectations are lulled*', said the dog-eared booklet she had found in the downstairs washrooms, '*by the austerity of the Doric entrance-hall. Only the somewhat alarming display of gigantic marble weaponry*', it added without apparent irony, '*gives a hint of what lies ahead.*'

What lay ahead was an aesthetic maelstrom. A reckless jumble of neo-Gothic, neo-classical, rococo and Jacobean, shoe-horned into a succession of vast rooms which had been decorated with '*very variable discrimination*'.

The Library at the head of the main stairs was an ersatz medieval Great Hall, with flabby bronze centurions and lurid faux-malachite bookshelves. Its windows were brilliant with Pre-Raphaelite stained glass, but so high-set that Sarah had to climb on a chair for a sight of the lawns. She was rewarded with a ruby-tinted view of two enormous lions guarding an imposing set of steps which led to the cedars on the ridge. One lion dozed like a spaniel, his chin resting on huge, crossed front paws. The other was crazily awake, with staring eyes and a lunatic snarl. It would be important to find a place to work where she was out of his line of sight.

The Gold Drawing-Room, which also opened off the main staircase, was not going to be that room. It had mouldings relentlessly picked out in indigo and maroon, and across the ceiling three fat seraphs trailed vines of unbotanical roses. The walls were decorated with what the booklet called '*slightly frightening Flemish gilt strapwork*'. Next door, the Ivory Room had a green mosaic floor which made Sarah dizzy, and a view across the South Lawns directly into the jaws of the mad lion. At first glance, the State Dining-Room was promising, with sweeping views across the valley of the Lyde. But it had two oddly pagan sideboards of oxblood marble, and twelve basalt pineapples worryingly suspended from the ceiling.

On the fourth day, Sarah began to like the Hall.

She was sitting with a mug of coffee on the Sandalwood Staircase. Naked plaster putti swung from the shoulders of blatantly overmuscled slaves. More putti ('*a whole gyration of the little fellows*') clambered up porphyry columns towards three painted upper storeys that didn't exist. In a *trompe-l'oeil* gallery above her head, a plaster Father Time brandished a sickle in one hand and a floor-plan of Harlaston in the other.

Someone had *built* all this. Someone – someone distantly related to her own grandmother – had conceived this outrageous design, and had poured all their wealth and energy into making it rise from an English hillside. They had chosen the *boiseries* and the ormolu griffins, and had racketed around Europe buying up graves and resurrecting them in bedrooms. Not, presumably, because they believed that anything would harmonize with anything else, but simply because they enjoyed each thing for itself, and to hell with the consequences.

And the sickle was *real:* suspended high above her head like a ghost at a feast. For the first time since breaking up with Dominic her curiosity returned. Why would anyone put a sickle at the apex of their *pièce de résistance*? Was it the architect's not-so-subtle revenge on an over-exacting client? Or a Victorian version of the slave's whisper: *Caesar, thou art mortal*?

She wondered how her grandmother had fitted into all this. Had she motored down from London for weekends in the country? '*Darling* old Harlaston, *such* a lark!' Or had she been more of a poor relation? A genteel governess figure whose only function was to make up the numbers at dinner?

Downstairs, someone knocked at the front door.

Three loud raps of the great brass knocker, filling the stairwell with echoes.

Sarah froze like a burglar. At eight thirty on a Sunday evening it would hardly be tourists, or the cleaners, or someone from the village. It was probably Alex, she thought in irritation. Ambling up after four days' silence to check that she was still alive.

She started down the stairs. Angry with herself for that first ridiculous surge of hope that it might be Dominic – come to say sorry, *sorry*, he'd been an *utter* fool, and *please* would she forgive him and take him back.

It wasn't Alex or Dominic. It was Clare, Dominic's ex-wife.

CHAPTER SEVEN

'Sarah.'

'Clare.'

'I've brought a bottle and a corkscrew. Can I come in?'

She wore an oatmeal cashmere polo-neck under a nubuck jacket, taupe jeans, and calfskin paddock boots. No jewellery except a Patek Philippe wristwatch and plain gold earrings half-hidden by smooth blond hair. Her face was arranged in a tight, friendly smile, and her green eyes met Sarah's with studied ease.

The smile didn't waver as Sarah rummaged for an excuse and came up with nothing.

They had met only once, at Mrs Hardy's funeral four years before. At that time Clare had been at the hub of the Hardy clan: the wife of the richer and more prominent son, mother of the only grandchild, and driving force behind the faultless funeral arrangements. It was less than a year later that divorce had sent her spinning out into the wilderness. But not for long. Within six months she had joined a health club, lost twelve pounds, and regained the PR job she had given up when Dominic's career became a full-time occupation. 'She's a *doer*, is Clare,' he had told Sarah in their first heady months together, when they used to lie in bed and talk for hours. 'Thick as a brick and she knows it – but God, can that woman *manage*! She's so single-minded it's terrifying.'

Sarah knew she was being managed now, though she couldn't imagine why. It could hardly be Clare's idea of fun to spend Sunday evening drinking with her ex-husband's latest cast-off. Any more than it was hers.

'Look, I know I'm the *last* person you want to see right now,' said Clare, settling into an armchair and getting to work on the bottle. 'But I had to postpone the Algarve till Tuesday so I thought I'd just pop down for a last peek at my little monster, and it suddenly seemed ridiculous to pretend you're not here. What an *amazing* room.'

They were in the Jade Ante-Room, which Sarah had finally chosen as a study because it was less exhausting than the others. The walls were stencilled in jade green on gold with a courtly tapestry of panthers, lilies and peacocks. Above a serene white fireplace a gilt mirror reflected a dusty infinity from its sisters on the opposite walls. A bay window gave onto the South Lawn, with a side view of the sleeping lion. The only concessions to Gothicism were a three-foot bronze dwarf clutching a bell-pull, and twelve marble cherubs joyously chasing each other about the doors and mirrors, as if they had just escaped from someone's tomb.

'Incredible,' Clare murmured. 'I *must* get Hugo down here, he's always on the lookout for new locations.' She gave a fond chuckle. 'The man's incorrigible! Never lets up. But you know what media people are like. Did you think it was Alex at the door?'

Sarah was startled. 'What? No. Why?'

'You looked so crestfallen when you saw it was only me.'

'Thick,' Dominic had said, 'but not without perception.'

Sarah sipped her wine. It was New Zealand Blanc de Noir, dry and excellent. 'I wasn't expecting anyone. I was on my way to bed.'

The corners of Clare's mouth turned down. '*Poor* old you! Alex told me you've had pneumonia – though I must say you don't *look* too sick. In fact you quite put me to shame, with my white city face. Must be all those country walks and early nights. And never having to get dressed up – what *heaven*! What a glorious view of the grounds. Stephen adores them. He's doing some kind of project for school. Could you bear it if he wandered around from time to time?'

Is that what this is about? Sarah wondered in exasperation. Making sure that the wicked ex-prospective-stepmother – or whatever I am – doesn't feed her son poisoned Kit Kats if he comes too close? She doubted that Stephen needed much protection. At the funeral he had been a solid six-year-old version of his father, with the same fearless gaze and determined chin. 'Of course I don't mind,' she lied. 'He can come whenever he likes.'

'That's sweet of you because now my job's taken off he'll be spending his holidays with Alex.' She played with the clasp of her watch. 'Poor little thing was absolutely shattered when Dominic left. Completely turned against him. Calls him his 'ex-father'. But he does so desperately want another one. Sometimes I even suspect him of plotting to get me and Alex – ' she laughed. 'Poor little tyke! We'd be hopeless together.'

Sarah said carefully, 'It must do Stephen good to get out of London.'

Clare nodded as if she had said something profound. 'And Alex is a *much* better role model than Dominic. Not that I don't still admire Dominic in many ways, but he's a horrendous example for a child. Always putting people down. That's why he and Alex don't see eye to eye.'

'I thought it was because Dominic had an affair with Alex's wife.'

Clare regarded her serenely. 'Hardly an affair, Sarah. Helen was never more than a one-night stand.' In the silence that followed, she refilled their glasses. 'God, he's a bastard. But I just keep telling myself that he didn't get Stephen. I did. And that's what counts. In any relationship, it's the children that count.'

Sarah, a childless thirty-five with no immediate prospect of becoming otherwise, and unsure how she felt about that, wondered what it would have been like to have had a baby with Dominic.

Perhaps he *was* a bastard. But that was hardly the point. The point was, she still wanted him back. She missed his wit and his phenomenal capacity for hard work, and the wiry black hairs on his wrists, and the over-emphatic way he talked – Sarah darling, you're *absolutely* right.

Her head was swimming. She had drunk too much, too quickly. She stood up. 'I'm afraid it's bed for me, Clare,' she said firmly.

Clare had been gone for an hour, but her relentless point-scoring had left an aftertaste.

It was too early for bed and too late to wander

down to a pub, where in any event she might bump into Clare again. So she threw on a jacket and let herself out of the conservatory and onto the West Terrace.

After four overcast days the sky had cleared. The wind had dropped and the night air was fresh with the scent of rain-washed leaves. The grounds of Harlaston glistened in the light of a nearly full moon.

She wandered through the French knot-garden and out onto the West Lawn. Ahead of her, the ground climbed steeply towards the tree-covered darkness of Hynton Edge. A nude St Sebastian, bristling with arrows, stoically contemplated a boarded-up summer-house.

She thought back to the last time everyone had been gathered together, at Mrs Hardy's funeral at Cawthorpe. A raw November afternoon on the edge of the fens.

Alex and Helen had still been a couple then, although probably only just. Helen had been in one of her upbeat phases and had dazzled them all. Sarah couldn't remember Alex at all; already he seemed to have withdrawn into the background. Clare, Dominic and Stephen were still a family – or thought they were – and Sarah's own career had just taken a quantum leap after *Memsahib*. On the strength of its success, Mrs Dalton had swallowed her pride and come to condole grimly with the Other Side, bringing Nick, Jenny and the children for additional support. Dominic was the only one who wasn't there. For the last three weeks, as Clare told everyone, he had been in Hong Kong on a case for South China Power. The other side's expert witness had just taken the stand and he couldn't possibly be spared.

It was a few months after the funeral that things began to unravel. Helen had the affair with Dominic, or one-night stand or whatever it was, and then left Alex for good. Alex astonished everyone by resigning from his City firm – where he was managing partner of the litigation department – and buying the Old Rectory in a matter of weeks. Then Dominic left Clare.

Sarah met him a year later, at a Sunday brunch in Belsize Park. She didn't particularly like Sunday gatherings. Sunday was her only non-working day, and she preferred to spend it in the companionable solitude of her flat. But this was a special case, a good friend's first shaky attempt at socializing after the end of a long relationship.

London was in the grip of an Indian summer, and the guests spilled out of Emma's living room onto the tiny patio, where they stood around dodging the wasps between the clematis and the Russian vine. They were mostly media people in urban combat gear, with a sprinkling of slightly self-conscious academics, and Dominic. Big, forty-something, mordantly witty, and unashamedly well-dressed, in dark grey Italian wool shirt and trousers, charcoal vicuna jacket, and expensive loafers. He looked like a highly educated *Mafioso*.

He was the first man she had met in three years who wasn't threatened or antagonized by her success in television, and from the start he let her know that he was attracted. They both knew they were distantly related, though neither had any idea exactly how. All they knew was that they both had some connection with 'a rather grand old barony', as Dominic put it. And both remembered the Sunday Lunch Disaster.

Dominic had laughed as he studied her with his

direct obsidian eyes. 'Isn't this *marvellous*, a long-lost relative! D'you think it's going to count as incest? I do hope so, I've always longed to try it. Come on, let's get out of here and grab a proper lunch.'

At the time, Sarah had thought such directness wonderfully original. Now it struck her as embarrassingly trite.

A breeze from the park scattered raindrops from the beech trees at the edge of Hynton Wood.

Why is it so much easier to exchange confidences in the dark, even with oneself?

The time had come to be honest about Dominic. That same intent dark gaze had had its effect on Clare Walker and Helen Hardy and Caroline Harris, and a host of others both before and after Sarah Dalton. And it would continue to do so long into the future. The result would always be the same. A pool of damage spreading outwards like a stain, with Dominic stepping aside to keep his shoes clean.

He had sloughed off his first family in a matter of months, and now he had done the same to her. He wouldn't be back. To pretend otherwise was merely self-delusion. He didn't feel about her – probably never *had* felt about her – any differently than he had about the others. And now he no longer felt about her at all.

Much later, she dreamed she was walking in the fields at Cawthorpe. It was the day of the Sunday Lunch Disaster. She was fifteen, and desperate to impress Dominic and Alex as they crunched over the stubble. But suddenly she realized that although she was an adolescent, they were both adult men in their forties, and they looked straight through her as if she didn't exist.

Half-awake, she pressed her wet face into the pillow. Poor Alex. Poor Helen. Poor Clare. Poor Stephen. Bloody, bloody Dominic.

'*Animum lucrum sequitur*,' said the green glass motto in the Library window. '*The motto*', the booklet explained, '*was chosen by the First Baron Harlaston in 1347. Strictly as a matter of heraldry, the words are of course redundant. It is the shield, the supporters, the mantling and helm, which together comprise the Pearce-Staunton achievement. What the untutored*', it added severely, '*would call a coat of arms.*'

Sarah, one of the untutored, made a note to look up the Latin. But she knew enough to guess that *lucrum* meant money. The First Baron didn't sound as if he had favoured his spiritual side.

What the Americans are after, Alex had said when she telephoned him in May, is a lively account of Harlaston's history. The site's been inhabited for eleven thousand years; they want its story. But I'm not an archaeologist, she had protested, I did medieval history. I know, he'd replied. I'll do the early stuff. Just start with Crécy and work your way up. Oh, fine, Alex, that's nearly seven hundred years! So? He'd sounded puzzled. You've got the whole summer. That had made her laugh.

But sitting at a table in the Library with the rain pouring down outside, she was curiously reluctant to begin. After a broken night she felt tired and heavy-eyed. The aftertaste of her dreams still lingered: a pervading sense of humiliation and failure.

What if, deep down, she didn't really *want* to learn about her father's background? What if she still harboured some half-admitted childish fear of a family curse, or an inherited taint – or perhaps simply a fear of uncovering mediocrity?

Or was the answer more prosaic than that?

After all, what had really changed since yesterday, when she had been looking forward to making a start? '*Clare*', she wrote on her notepad, and surrounded the name in a halo of little spikes.

The fact was, when Clare had 'dropped in' the night before, she had brought Dominic with her. She had let him in and shown him round and now here he was in the Library, pacing up and down and chuckling at the centurions and telling Sarah that she wasn't up to this.

Sarah put him firmly out of her mind, and opened Alex's box-file.

It contained a jumble of yellowing papers in no discernible order. A privately published book of plates featuring the Pearce-Staunton mausoleum and the village church; a motley collection of household accounts which left her hands red with dust; a brittle roll of newspaper cuttings from 1917; an auctioneer's catalogue and some further cuttings from the following year, and a slim typewritten history dated September 1948.

And that was it.

For an estate over six hundred years old, it was pitiful. Alex couldn't have tried very hard. 'CRO – Lincoln', she wrote. '*Colindale Newspapr Reg; Church recds? Regimental Histories?*' The family history had been written by someone who described himself rather pompously as '*Aubrey Hamilton Vincett-Searle, the only son of the Honourable Lilian Vincett-Searle and the last surviving grandson of Augustus, the Seventeenth Baron*'. Whoever he was, he plodded with pitiless thoroughness through the centuries, from the ennoblement of the First Baron after a skirmish in the Hundred Years War to the sale of the Hall to Jesuits in 1918, and its subsequent acquisition by the university. Sarah flicked through the pages and wondered how she was going to spend three months on this.

Reading between the lines of Aubrey's manfully whitewashed account, the Pearce-Staunton males had favoured under-age heiresses, gambling, bankruptcy, and whores – at least, when they weren't engaging in what Aubrey Vincett-Searle called the family's *'distinguished tradition of military service'*, and what Mrs Dalton and the good people of Wisconsin would probably call the suppression of ethnic minorities.

The Pearce-Staunton women had had a horrible time. Most had died appallingly young after bearing large clutches of sickly children. The rest had succumbed to typhoid, tuberculosis, and what sounded like clinical depression. The only one who seemed to have had any fun at all was the Seventeenth Baroness, Adela – and she had quite possibly been delusional. At any rate, Aubrey, her grandson, had clearly been petrified of her, as had her husband – who in 1852 had let himself be coerced into commissioning plans for a magnificent new Hall to replace the old Jacobean manor-house, in a blatant attempt to outstrip the Duke of Kyme's enormous country seat at Dunsford. A quarter of a million pounds, fourteen architects, and twenty-four years later, Harlaston Hall was finally finished, and the Pearce-Stauntons moved in. Sixteen years after that, 'Grandmama Adela' was dead, leaving her collection of 'Italian grave furniture' scattered about the Hall, and her ashes displayed in the Library in a Biedermeier compotier of emerald glass. According to Aubrey, the ashes were misplaced *'through a servant's negligence'* in 1917.

'But how marvellous!' Sarah could hear Clare say. *'I must show this to Hugo, he's always looking for fresh material!'*

Dominic would probably also find the story entertaining. And no doubt he would embrace the Pearce-Staunton males as soulmates.

Reluctantly, Sarah skimmed the rest of Aubrey's account. With the accession of Robert, the Nineteenth Baron, the account took on the more vivid colours of personal recollection. Aubrey dealt at some length with the Nineteenth Baron's unexpected succession after his brother broke his neck in a hunting accident; with his early marriage to an immensely rich heiress (*'the very lovely Violet Redfearn'*, with whom Aubrey had obviously been in love); with his heroic conduct in the Boer War, and finally with his ten years serving with his regiment in India until the outbreak of the First World War. 'The very lovely Violet' turned out to have been pretty long-lived, for she was eventually laid to rest beside her husband in the family mausoleum on the 15 December 1947, *'prompting this writer to take up his pen in her honour.'*

Sarah sat back in her chair.

There was no mention of anyone who might have been her grandmother, but then, she hadn't really expected that there would be. In fact, Aubrey's account was pretty much as she had anticipated. A moderately depressing little rewrite of family history which strove to portray womanizing, gambling, and conspicuous consumption as the work of philanthropists and model family men.

And maybe thirty years from now, she thought,

some biographer will portray Dominic as a disinterested and humanitarian judge.

Dominic. Bloody Dominic. Everything kept coming back to him.

She didn't want to read any more. Nor did she feel inclined to seek out the portraits in the Long Gallery and put faces to Robert and Violet, the last Baron and Baroness. That would only make the whole thing real. And she was fast discovering that she didn't want to make *any* of it real. The notion of spending a whole summer with the Pearce-Stauntons was preposterous. Ploughing through their depressing little story and failing to come up with anything about her grandparents, while she struggled to keep Dominic out of her head, and his ex-wife and ex-son swooped down on her whenever they liked.

She went down to the kitchen, made a mug of coffee, and drank it standing at the sink. The window looked out onto what had once been the servants' yard. It was as spare as a German monastery, with looming rust-streaked walls and a few tiny wide-apart windows. True to form, the Pearce-Stauntons had kept all their ostentation for the front.

What had it been like, she wondered, growing up in this over-decorated mausoleum at the dawn of the new century, when your family owned most of the surrounding countryside and your Empire owned half the world? It must have taken a regiment of servants to run the place – and to all of them you would have been 'Lord Harlaston', or 'the Honourable this or that', whatever your age or theirs. You would have grown up believing you could do whatever you liked.

Although, of course, some people didn't need to be

taught that. Dominic had managed perfectly well on his own.

The final item in the box-file was a newspaper cutting which Sarah had missed on her first flick through, and which had nothing to do with Harlaston. Alex must have scooped it up by mistake.

Charles Alastair Hardy MD, father of Dominic and Alexander, had died peacefully on 21 May 1995 at the age of seventy-one, and had merited a couple of paragraphs in the *Cawthorpe Clarion*.

'*He led a full life which he enjoyed to the hilt . . . brought up his sons to care about others and tell the truth . . . immensely proud of their achievements . . . very greatly missed.*'

To care about others and tell the truth.

Sarah thought about Alex in his self-imposed exile, who seemed to care for no-one, including himself. And Dominic, who cared *only* for himself, and ignored the truth except when it suited him.

Her gaze shifted to the window with its brilliantly coloured coat of arms. The Pearce-Staunton achievement. A motto about money and a string of selfish and unhappy lives. And meanwhile, thirty miles down the road, a country doctor who had failed to bequeath his humanity to his sons.

She dragged her chair to the window and climbed onto it, and stood watching the gardens sink into twilight.

A small boy emerged from the cedars of Lebanon and came slowly down the Lion Steps. He was solid and dark, with a fearless gaze and a determined chin. Scowling, he placed a finger on the nose of the lunatic lion, and his lips moved in intense and secret communication. He was Dominic, thirty years younger.

111

Sarah had indulged in the usual fantasies about having Dominic's child. Trite little stories in which the child – always mysteriously beautiful and talented – brought out the caring side in the outwardly hard-as-nails father. It was humiliating to recall them now.

She climbed off the chair, sat down cross-legged on the parquet floor, and pressed her fists to her eyes.

You bloody *fool*. *Whatever* made you think you'd be up to this?

Summer in the country, away from it all. Straight into a tangled mess of wrecked marriages and sibling rivalries, and single-parent children who just happened to be the only offspring of a horribly recent ex-lover. Her first instinct had been right. She should never have let her brother talk her into this. Coming to Harlaston was the worst possible way she could imagine of getting over Dominic.

Alex answered the phone on the eleventh ring. He sounded preoccupied, as if he had been immersed in something and was still coming to the surface. 'Hallo? – Sarah? Is that you?'

' – Alex.'

'Is anything wrong?'

'Yes. This is. I'm sorry but I can't do it. You'll have to find someone else to write this thing.'

CHAPTER EIGHT

The Old Rectory turned out to be a large run-down house of ochre brick set back from the road in a tangle of overgrown garden. It had ivy growing all over it, and spiky fretwork eaves which made Sarah think of cake-frills.

Alex was waiting for her on the porch. Yellow light streamed from behind him onto the broken flags of the garden path. He wore the same sagging tweed jacket and brown cords with whitened knees he had worn on the day she arrived, and the same tan checked shirt, faded from many washings. 'Come inside and have a drink,' he said.

The sitting room was spacious and high-ceilinged and might once have been elegant, but it looked as if Alex had stopped unpacking halfway through and never bothered to finish. Three sofas, upholstered in coffee-stained red and white striped ticking, sagged beneath cardboard boxes of books and piles of ageing newspapers. On a rug in front of the French windows stood a line of translucent, expiring spider plants. Around the walls, eight extraordinarily beautiful botanical prints in expensive lacquered frames had been hung with blatant unconcern on whatever hooks were already in place.

Alex threaded his way to the far end where a very large partner's desk defined a rectangle of pure order. A green glass reading-lamp cast golden light on burgundy leather, and three mahogany in-trays held sheaves of yellow copy-paper. An Apple-Mackintosh on a side-table gave out a steady alien purr.

Nick had told her that Alex was working on a book. 'Some kind of local history, I think, but *really* historical, all the way back to fossils. Trouble is, it's non-commissioned, so it'll never get published. Pretty sad when you think about it. All that potential. Oxford First, top ten law firm, partnership at thirty. And now look at him.'

Alex bore no resemblance whatever to his brother. He was tall and spare and sandy-haired, with light analytical eyes in a sharp-boned face. Sarah thought he looked like the kind of man who might design a new fiscal strategy or a nuclear bomb.

On one corner of his desk stood a row of crystal tumblers and a half-empty bottle of Bruichladdich. Without bothering about ice or asking Sarah if she wanted soda, he poured them both a stiff drink. 'Clear a space anywhere and sit down,' he said over his shoulder.

Beside her on the sofa lay a copy of Seinfeldt's *Encyclopedia of Medicine*, open at a glistening colour plate of a ripe bubo. *The Decameron* had been placed across it, with the place marked by a Power Rangers pencil. Sarah tried and failed to come up with a link between Alex's book on fossils, and Italy in the grip of the Black Death.

'Those are Stephen's,' said Alex, handing her a tumbler. 'Put them on the floor if they're in the way.

He won't bother us. He's in the garden. Now. What's this about?'

She twisted the tumbler in her hands. 'I'm really sorry. I shouldn't have taken this job.'

'Can you tell me why?'

'I was a coward. I should've stayed in London and faced up to things instead of running away.'

He gave her a lopsided smile, and she realized that what she had said applied equally to him.

The silence between them lengthened. He made no attempt to break it.

She tried again. 'Last week when you told me Stephen was here, I said I didn't mind. I was wrong.'

He waited for her to go on.

'I can't spend a whole summer being reminded of Dominic. I just can't.'

'I thought you came to Harlaston to find out about your grandmother.'

She looked at him. 'What difference does that make?'

'If you leave now, aren't you letting Dominic dictate what you do?'

'That's a nice try. But it won't work.'

He went to the desk for the bottle and topped up their drinks. 'You haven't answered the question.'

'Please don't try to talk me out of this.'

'I'm not. I've no interest in persuading you to stay if you don't want to. I simply think—'

'I'm not letting Dominic dictate what I do. It's more complicated than that.'

'All right.'

'It isn't only *about* Dominic.'

'Fine.'

'Stop agreeing with me. You're behaving like a therapist or a bloody lawyer.'

'I am a bloody lawyer,' he replied mildly.

She placed her drink on the coffee table. 'I don't understand myself why I took this job. But you're right, I did want to find out about my grandmother. I suppose I thought that as she was related to the Pearce-Stauntons, somehow I might learn something which would tell me a bit about Dad. But I've realized that until I deal with this thing with Dominic, I can't—'

'She wasn't related to the Pearce-Stauntons.'

Sarah blinked.

'Your grandmother wasn't *related* to the Pearce-Stauntons.'

'How do you know?'

He looked puzzled. 'Well of course I know. William Fosdyke was my grandfather.'

'Who was William Fosdyke?'

'Who was—? He was your grandmother's brother. But you knew that, surely.'

'Wait a minute. Your grandfather and my grandmother were brother and sister?'

'Well, yes.'

'So you – you and Dominic – you're my second cousins?'

He looked nonplussed. 'What did you think we were?'

'I – didn't really know. Just some sort of relations.'

He looked down at his hands. 'I'm sorry, I thought you knew a bit more than that.'

'Um, no, actually. Mum and Dad didn't – they didn't see eye to eye about family history.'

He waited.

'Mum hates anything to do with the upper classes. So you can imagine, Dad's family bugs the hell out of her.'

He thought about that, then slowly nodded. 'Yes. I can see how that would be.'

'I know it sounds weird, but they never talked about it. At least, not in front of Nick and me.'

'But surely when you started seeing Dominic – didn't he tell you?'

'He said he didn't know either.' Suddenly it sounded like something from a French farce or a Restoration comedy. Here she was, sitting opposite a 'distant relation' who had suddenly revealed himself to be her second cousin, and for the past two years she had been sleeping with *another* second cousin who had known all along, but hadn't bothered to tell her.

Judging from Alex's expression, similar thoughts were going through his mind. 'Dominic', he began carefully, 'likes to keep the Fosdyke side of things under wraps.'

'Why? What's so awful about the Fosdykes?'

'Nothing. They were just a bit too humble for him, that's all. You know what he's like.'

'Too *humble*? Now I'm really confused. Mum disapproves of Dad's family because they're too *posh*. And anyway, why the hell would she bother to disapprove of the Pearce-Stauntons at all – and I know she does, she was horrified when I took this job – if they've got nothing to do with us?'

'Well, I suppose that part's understandable. I mean, a woman of her generation—'

'What do you mean, it's understandable? What's her generation got to do with it?'

Alex gave her a strange look. 'You really don't know anything, do you?'

She swallowed. 'Obviously not.'

'Didn't your father – didn't he tell you *anything*?'

'He was going to. But I kind of – I left it too late to ask. And then he – ' she drew a deep breath, 'he died.'

Alex contemplated his drink. Then he put it on the floor and leaned forward with his elbows on his knees. 'Look. Sarah. I think this is something you need to talk about with your mother, not me.'

'Why? What's wrong?'

'Nothing's wrong.'

She felt herself getting angry. 'Don't patronize me. Just tell me what the hell you're talking about.'

'No.'

'*Why?*'

'Because you've been ill, and this is important, and I don't think I'm the right—'

'I may have *been* ill, but I'm better now.'

'You don't look it.'

'Thanks.'

'Listen. It's nothing sinister. Nothing bad about your father. Or your grandmother. I just think you need to talk to your mother.'

'Mum?'

' – Sarah? *Sarah?* What's wrong? It's nearly midnight! Where are you? What's happened?'

'I'm fine, Mum. I'm at Harlaston. I'm fine.'

'You don't sound fine.'

'I'm kind of – confused.'

'Right, that's it. Pack your bags. I'll be there in three hours and we'll be home for breakfast.'

'Mum I'm *fine*. I just need to talk to you.'

'What about? What's this about?'

'It's about Dad.'

'Oh, *Sarah*. What's Alex been telling you now?'

'Nothing. That's sort of the point. He said I should ask you.'

'I *knew* no good would come of this. Didn't I tell you? What earthly *good* d'you think you're doing, rummaging about like this?'

'Please, Mum. Just tell me about Dad's parents.'

'Sarah love I really, *really* don't want to go into this now.'

'Mum. Please. I really, *really* do.'

The headstones in the churchyard tilted like skiffs at low tide. It was half past four in the morning, but already it was getting light. A few yards from the south porch, an enormous domed shape loomed like a bomb-shelter. The Pearce-Staunton mausoleum. Sarah gave it a wide berth, but she still managed to bark her shins on the railings hidden in the grass. The Victorian obsession with ownership: they even put their dead behind bars.

The church door gave at the first push, and she inhaled a dusty school-assembly smell of chrysan-themums, wax polish, and vinyl-covered seats. She couldn't find the light switch, but beneath an orange plastic night-light shaped like a flaming torch she found a box of candles and lit one. Smiling Third World faces sprang to life on a cluttered notice-board. A rakish cardboard camel announced the dates of Scripture classes for the under-tens.

Stepping out into the darkness of the nave, she left the clutter of the present behind, and the strong sinewy lines of the fourteenth century fountained overhead. Images in brass appeared on the flagstones beneath her feet. Good steady Lincolnshire names: Annis Stamfast,

Alaster Mordaunt, Margaret Cavel, William Kempe. The lady, the merchant, the widow, the priest.

She found the Pearce-Stauntons where one would expect them to be: prominently displayed in the chancel, near the altar. A collection of elaborate wall-tablets adorned with marble drapery, rifles and laurel wreaths. These must be the family highlights, the exemplars of the 'distinguished tradition of military service'. According to Aubrey, only those who had died in battle were honoured with a tablet inside the church.

Her heart began to pound as she moved closer to read the names. Eustace Sidney, 1843–85: Abu Klea. Charles Merivale, 1854–79: Isipezi Hill. Julius Addison, 1825–41: Gujarat. Jocelyn Seymour, 1821–54: Inkerman. Osborne Mawdley, 1826–85: Allahabad.

Robert Percival.

They had put his memorial in pride of place, six feet up on the south wall, between the sacristy and the altar rail. A perfect alabaster tablet, no expense spared. No rifles, no drapery, no wreaths, no fulsome quotations. Just a severely classical border and crisp, elegant Roman lettering. The stone had been allowed to speak its own translucent beauty.

Robert Percival D'Authon Pearce-Staunton.

Sarah's grandfather.

'My *grandfather*? Mum, what do you *mean*?'

There had been a pause on the other end of the line. Then her mother said, 'Dad always meant to tell you. He just never got round to it. And I suppose I didn't help much.'

'Wait a minute. You really mean this. Robert the Nineteenth Baron Harlaston was my grandad.'

'Yes, love.'

'And someone called Charity Fosdyke, who was no relation to the Pearce-Stauntons, was my grandma.'

'Yes. But I don't know where you got the idea—'

'So who the hell *was* Charity Fosdyke?'

Her mother sighed. 'I don't know much about her. It was so long ago. She was – a village girl. A dressmaker.'

'A dressmaker. I thought she was related to the barons. I thought my grandad was French.'

'Oh Sarah, love, don't get upset. I can't imagine where you got those ideas. We never said anything like that.'

'You never *said* anything, that's the whole bloody point! We had to piece it together from whatever we could pick up. No wonder we got it wrong.'

Another pause.

'Well? What else can you tell me?'

'I can't.'

'Come on, Mum, this is no time to play hard to get.'

'Sarah. I can't. I don't know any more.'

'What *is* it with this family? You were only married to the man for seventeen years!'

'We didn't talk about it. He knew how I felt so he avoided the subject. I suppose it was more my fault than his.'

Outside in the churchyard, the dawn chorus was gathering strength. Sarah went and sat in a pew and leaned back and shut her eyes.

Robert Percival D'Authon Pearce-Staunton. A model of Edwardian rectitude, or a ruthless womanizer – depending on whether you believed Aubrey Vincett-Searle or Shirley Dalton.

But whatever he may have been, the facts were beyond doubt. In 1908 he had got a village girl pregnant, and packed her off to the Continent to avoid a scandal, and Julian D'Authon had been the result. Charity Fosdyke hadn't had a chance. Not against the massed ranks of the Pearce-Stauntons.

Authon was the name of a village in the *département* of Seine-et-Loire; Sarah had looked it up in an atlas. Perhaps it had been the site of the First Baron's heroics in the Hundred Years' War. That would explain its adoption as the middle name of the Pearce-Staunton males. But what explained Charity Fosdyke's choice of surname for her son? Had she done it to blend into her unfamiliar surroundings in south-western France? Or had she still been in love with her seducer, and taken his name as a pathetic reminder of her one catastrophic brush with greatness?

'I've no idea, love,' her mother had said. 'I really don't know any more than what I've told you. I know it sounds strange, but, like I said, your dad and I never talked about it. I didn't want to know.'

'Then how can you be so sure that it *was* Lord Harlaston?'

'Well, your dad told me that much! And I saw his birth certificate when we got married. There's no doubt about it, it's his name, large as life. Robert high-and-mighty bloody Pearce-Staunton. Doesn't seem possible in the twentieth century, does it? I'm sorry, love. I really am.'

Her poor mother. No wonder she had struggled so hard to keep it quiet, and had resented the Other Side for knowing the secret. A deeply conservative woman despite her socialist principles, she had felt her husband's illegitimacy as an outrage and a disgrace.

And Julian Dalton? What had he felt about the circumstances of his birth?

Sarah couldn't imagine him caring very much one way or the other. He had judged people by what they were, not by what they were called.

But somehow, that wasn't the point. For once, Sarah found herself siding with her mother. Her father had been a gentle, loving, tolerant man. He hadn't deserved to be handed a marked deck of cards at the outset.

Nor had he deserved to be scratched from the family tree with a sweep of the pen. And that was exactly what Aubrey Vincett-Searle had done. By baldly stating that the last Baron had left no surviving issue, he had coldly, deliberately written Julian Dalton out of the family.

Or maybe – and this would be still worse – maybe he had simply never known of Julian Dalton's existence.

Shafts of early morning sunlight were beginning to strike the altar. Sarah snuffed out the candle and rubbed her face.

Dear God, she thought. From Restoration comedy to *Upstairs, Downstairs* in a single night. What the hell do I do now?

She had spent most of the night roaming the State Rooms, trying to summon the courage to enter the Long Gallery and confront her grandfather's portrait. She had failed. She wasn't ready to face the man who had ruined her grandmother's life, but to whom she owed her own.

'What are you feeling?' her mother had asked timidly on the phone.

What *was* she feeling?

Anger and contempt for the Pearce-Stauntons. Sympathy and exasperation for her mother. Pity and admiration for her grandmother, who had somehow managed to raise her son in the teeth of it all, and had done a pretty good job, all things considered. And above all, love for her father – who hadn't allowed the past to sour his life or that of his wife and children.

If she backed out now, it would all be forgotten. Someone else would tell the story of Harlaston Hall, and would no doubt portray Robert, Lord Harlaston through Aubrey-coloured spectacles.

The sun's warmth began to steal into the church. Shafts of gold lit an effigy on a table-tomb. A Tudor Pearce-Staunton, with bland stylized face and hands piously joined.

> *Adam of Hearlastun somtym was I*
> *Now ended this worlds pylgramage*
> *In blyst heuen everlasting lyf*
> *Iesu send me and Agnes my wyf*
> *Such as ye be such were we*
> *Such as we be such shall ye be*
> *Therfor pray you hertily for cheritee*

Sorrow and anger lodged in her throat.

Yes, pray you heartily for Charity, and for Julian her son, who should be up there in the chancel along with the others – along with Eustace and Osborne, and Robert Percival bloody D'Authon Pearce-Staunton – but who instead has been wiped from the slate as if he never existed.

Pray heartily for Charity and for Julian. Pray for them both. For no-one else ever will.

Blindly she got to her feet and left.

CHAPTER NINE

Thursday 16 August 1900

On the morning after Mrs Jordan's tea, Charity had a 'preliminary interview' with the parson to discuss the post of reader to his wife. To her slight annoyance, Sam Webb walked her to the rectory gate. He seemed to think that, as he had put her forward for the position, the outcome would in some way reflect upon himself.

The rectory was an imposing double-fronted mansion surrounded by an acre of well-clipped garden. It had a glossy black door with a brass knocker, and beautiful white fretwork eaves.

She was so nervous that she received only jumbled impressions of Dr Bowles's study. Brilliantly coloured rugs and walls of books with softly gleaming spines; the syrupy smell of the parson's maple and rum tobacco; his grin, as broad and yellow as a split melon. It took a few minutes to realize that the grin had nothing to do with smiling. Dr Bowles was one of those people who bare their teeth out of shyness.

'You'll excuse me, Miss Fosdyke, if I seem a little perturbed! I popped over to the vestry a short while ago, and *just* missed Lord Harlaston who had called to see me most *unfortunately* while I was out! So *very* provoking of me not to be in! Now, what were we saying?'

It was not the best way to put Charity at her ease. In the space of a five-minute walk she had gone from the anonymity of the end house to a place where lords dropped in without warning. She felt as if she was in the branches of some huge tree, staring down at the ground.

The parson asked her about her schooling and she answered in monosyllables. Luckily he seemed to interpret that as humility, and was so pleased that he arranged for her to see his wife on Saturday afternoon, the day after tomorrow. It was all over so quickly that Charity could hardly take it in, and she remained silent as she was shown out of the study. Sam Webb, who was waiting by the kitchen door, seemed to take her silence for ingratitude, and left her smartly at the rectory gate.

She found her mother in turmoil when she got back. A boy had brought another note from the Hall, and Mrs Fosdyke had been summoning the courage to read it. She was standing in the middle of the kitchen, holding it gingerly between finger and thumb. 'He said it's *urgent*!' she whispered, as if the note could hear. Charity took it from her and opened it. As she read, her hand moved slowly to her throat. 'Something's up,' she murmured. 'You're to go to Mrs Jordan at once.'

Mrs Fosdyke's eyes were black with terror. '*What? Why?*'

'She doesn't say. Just that a situation has arisen. That's what she says, a situation – and it's most urgent and please to come at once, Edith Jordan.'

Mrs Fosdyke grabbed her hat, then stared at it blankly. 'It's Will. He did something terrible at the tea. I knew he was being too good.'

Charity folded the note and put it on the table. Her mother was right. With Will, anything could happen. Like the time when he had freed all Mr Pechey's rabbits to save the old man from sin, because Leviticus says eating rabbits is wrong.

Mrs Fosdyke insisted on going up to the Hall alone, so Charity spent a distracted two hours finishing a pile of corset covers ready for the weekly trip to Tilburne. It occurred to her that if Will had done something terrible, she might be wasting her time. There might not *be* any more trips to Tilburne, or any interview with Mrs Bowles at the rectory on Saturday afternoon.

It was nearly noon when she went into the parlour and found her mother sitting in silence on the horse-hair sofa.

Mrs Fosdyke still wore her hat and gloves, and she had placed her hands on either side of her as if she had meant to push herself to her feet, but had then forgotten to do so. Her face was composed, with just a faint redness around the eyes and nostrils.

'What did he do this time?' Charity asked quietly.

'What's that, child?'

'What did Will *do*?'

'Why, nothing. Least, not that I know of.'

'Then what did Mrs Jordan want?'

A faint smile touched Mrs Fosdyke's lips. 'You'll never guess. Not in a month of Sundays.' Slowly she rose to her feet and took Charity's hand in hers. Her gloved fingers were feverishly hot.

Something was laid out on the parlour table. It was thin and flat, about the size of a tea towel, and wrapped in a length of clean nainsook. Tenderly Mrs Fosdyke peeled back the wrapping, and filled the room with enchantment.

It had the subtlety of mother-of-pearl, the delicacy of breath on a frosty morning. It was a fragment from a waking dream which had drifted in through the end house window.

Mrs Fosdyke's voice shook. 'It's from the House of Worth. Embroidered applickay'd chiffon over silk.' She drew off her glove and passed a cracked red hand over the bodice. Not touching. Merely tracing the patterns in the air. 'See how *fine* that openwork is? All they little butterflies an' curly leaves? That's weeks of eye strain, that is. An' that collar! You can't *see* the boning, it's so fine! An' three inches high if it's anything. They say her ladyship has a throat like a swan.'

'Lady *Harlaston*?' Charity looked from the bodice to her mother. 'This is hers?'

'Whose else would you think, lovely thing like that?'

Baroness Harlaston. The consort of the slender sunburned officer who had acknowledged her with such graceful courtesy on the Tilburne road.

It seemed incredible that something as intimate as an evening bodice should have found its way down from the Hall to the end house. In one swoop it brought the dwellers on the hill shockingly close. Too close for comfort.

Charity tried to picture the woman who might wear such a thing. She imagined her gliding about a ballroom in the arms of her handsome husband. They circled endlessly beneath crystal chandeliers: silent, slender, impossibly beautiful. 'Look at that waist,' she said quietly. 'You wouldn't think anyone could have a waist as narrow as that.'

'See where it's torn?' her mother whispered. She pointed to a ragged inch-long tear in the chiffon on the left-hand side. 'Her ladyship must've snagged it on her jewels. Miss Mitchell – that's her lady's maid – she put it away an' never noticed. Oh, she was in a proper state when I got there. Came down herself an' begged me to help. *Begging* me.' Her eyes glittered. 'It's the only thing that's right for the grand dinner on Saturday night. They don't know what they'll do if I can't mend it.'

'*Can* you mend it?' said Charity doubtfully. The tear looked as cruel and final as a rent in a mayfly's wing.

Her mother's lips tightened in her peculiar mirthless smile. 'Well, now. Maybe I can.' She began to pace, and her gaze turned inward. 'First we'll need needles and silk,' she muttered. 'We'll start for Tilburne at once. If Mr A's doesn't have 'em fine enough, we'll go on to Grantham. Maybe even Lincoln. London if we have to. Can't let her ladyship down when she's counting on me.' She hurried off to fetch her funeral fund from the top shelf of the dresser.

As Charity was putting on her hat in front of the mirror, she caught sight of the bodice behind her on the table. Suddenly it seemed a mocking presence, silently belittling all her efforts. Her hopes of the rectory position, the typewriter, her mother's feverish excitement at what after all was just a piece of mending. She pushed in the last hatpin and left the parlour without a backward glance.

In the end it proved unnecessary to go further afield for needles and thread, as Mr A did not let them down. They returned in the furnace heat of the afternoon with everything Mrs Fosdyke required, and she spent the evening planning in the parlour while Charity made pepper-and-lard sandwiches in the kitchen.

At two o'clock on Friday morning the family was awakened by the scraping of furniture downstairs. Charity found her mother on her knees in the parlour, dusting the skirting-board. 'Stone-dust,' she muttered. 'That man just tracks it in in shovelfuls, all over everything. No, my girl, I'll not go upstairs till I'm good an' ready – an' *that* won't be till I've got this place fit to work in!' Three hours later she had donned her dark prune with a fresh collar and cuffs, and wrapped a starched pillow-slip about her head. Then she disappeared into the parlour with orders not to be disturbed on any account.

Charity got the shopping done but there was no chance of doing the baking: cooking had been outlawed because of the smells. Instead, she made a start on the week's sewing, bracing herself for a howl of despair from the parlour, and rehearsing what she would say in the interview with the parson's wife the following afternoon.

The interview.

Every time she thought of it her stomach dropped, and she felt again the same dizzying apprehension she had experienced as she sat in the parson's study.

That evening, she made a sandwich tea which she and her father and Will had in the front garden, as Mrs Fosdyke had detected smells coming from the kitchen. In response to an enquiry over the wall from Martha Bacon, Charity crisply declared that they had found a wasp's nest and were sulphuring the place out. She knew without being told that her mother would regard any breath of the truth as the blackest betrayal of Lady Harlaston.

Everyone except Mrs Fosdyke went to bed early, and no-one slept much.

On Saturday morning at half-past four, Charity awoke with a pounding heart from a nightmare in which the parson's wife had died suddenly in the night. 'There'll *be* no interview!' cackled Lady Harlaston's grey chiffon bodice as it fluttered out of the window and up to the Hall. 'There'll *be* no position! So much for your foolish, ridiculous little plans!'

Lying on her back and gazing up at the rafters, it occurred to Charity that in her dream she had felt no pity for the parson's wife: only desolation at the loss of the position. She was surprised at her own ruthlessness.

Her next thought was that it was suspiciously quiet downstairs. To judge from the light, it was nearly five. Usually by this time her mother was already busy in the kitchen. She threw a shawl over her nightgown and went down to the parlour.

She found her mother sitting on the sofa, her face rosy in the early morning light. The Worth bodice lay before her on the table in a cardboard shirt-box she had begged from Mr A.

It was impossible to tell that the bodice had ever been torn. Instead, where the rent had been, a new butterfly had settled on the pearl-grey chiffon. Its delicate openwork wings exactly matched its sisters around it – but, as space had been limited, Mrs Fosdyke had depicted it in the act of alighting on its chosen petal, teetering with precarious insect grace and half-closed wings.

'Where'd you learn to sew like that, Mother?' murmured Charity. 'I never saw anything so fine.'

Mrs Fosdyke's face was dreamy and at peace.

131

'Parson's wife taught me when I was just a snippet. Used to have me stay behind to do her smalls.' She passed her hand over the new butterfly, like a blessing. 'I couldn't take anything home, I'd have dirtied it, so she let me work in her house up village. Oh, I *loved* it there. All so neat, everything in rows. Proper paraffin lamp in winter, mug of tea with milk.' She paused. ''Course, that was before Cousin Ruth went an' spoilt it all.'

'Don't start on that. You'll only upset yourself.'

Her mother wasn't listening. She closed her eyes and rubbed the back of her neck. 'When Cousin Ruth happened it all went bad. They had to let me go without a reference. Said it wasn't right for the children if I stayed. I thought I'd die of the disgrace.'

'Why don't you go on upstairs and rest?'

Mrs Fosdyke studied her daughter with a dispassionate eye. 'You've got a chance to be free of all that, my girl. Play your cards right, don't breathe a word about Cousin Ruth, an' your Sam'll marry you.'

'He's not my Sam.'

'Soon will be, though. You keep yourself respectable, don't let him have what he wants. An' you'll see.'

Charity went through to the kitchen and started taking down cups for breakfast.

The rector's study was no preparation whatsoever for Mrs Bowles's drawing room. To Charity, entering it alone and with extreme trepidation, it was one long astonishment. Flowers were everywhere: on the papered walls and the chintz curtains, and on the Indian shawls festooning the piano. Knick-knacks cluttered every surface. Peacock feathers in vases made

132

of paste and sea-shells; Japanese fans on side-tables; a stuffed blue and yellow parrot in a clump of ferns.

Clearly Mrs Bowles was a great reader. A Bible and a peerage, both shiny and new-looking, took pride of place on a japanned table behind the sofa, while well-thumbed novels and journals lay scattered about on the rugs. *The Illustrated London News*, Mrs Corelli, Seton Merriman. When Mrs Bowles indicated an armchair, Charity had to remove *At the Point of a Bayonet, Sheer Pluck*, and a tabby kitten before she could sit down.

It was all wildly intriguing and unexpected. More luxurious than she could have imagined, but also astonishingly haphazard and untidy.

The same went for Mrs Bowles herself, a kindly heron stretched to an alarming length on a cretonne-covered sofa. Her tea-gown of painted muslin badly needed a pressing, and although the beading on her cap must have cost a fortune, her fuzzy brown hair-piece looked as if it hadn't been combed in days. She was clearly not at all strong. Although only in her early forties, she had the papery complexion of long illness, and deep caramel-coloured shadows around her eyes. After taking tea she lay back on the cushions, and the housemaid whisked away her two baleful, muddy-skinned children. But she was keenly interested in Charity, and displayed an invalid's passion for excessive detail.

The interview passed in a blur of nerves, with Mrs Bowles doing most of the talking. She had lived in Hynton for most of her life, 'knew everyone', and loved to gossip – which she called 'keeping up with developments'.

'So,' said Sam Webb afterwards as they walked

home beneath the elms. 'The parson's wife was pleased with you, was she?'

'I suppose so,' said Charity.

'She must of been, she kept you long enough. What did she say?'

'She wants me twice a week on Tuesdays and Thursdays, from three till five.'

'How much?'

'Sixpence an hour.'

'There you are then! You'll have that typing machine in no time. All you needed was a chance to start you off.'

It was her cue to thank him again, which she did, although she couldn't help thinking that he was rather too keen on hearing her say it. It was Charity Fosdyke who had secured the position, not Sam Webb.

She wished he would leave off talking for a while, so she could think in peace. She needed time to take it all in. To get over this fluttering sense of apprehension and excitement.

And she was doubtful if there would be much time for reflection when she got home. She had no idea how the Worth bodice had been received up at the Hall, and it was beginning to worry her. Her mother had set out to deliver her precious burden well before noon, but she had still not returned by the time Charity and Sam had set off for the rectory at a quarter past four.

When they reached the end of St Hybald's Lane they saw Will swinging on the end house gate, watching out for their return. He spotted them and came racing across the Green. 'Come an' *see*, come an' *see*! She got a reward for the mending!'

Sam gave Will a cool look and said to Charity, 'I'll be on my way, then.'

'You could step in for tea if you want,' Charity said.

'Best be going. Things to do up at the Hall.'

'Right, then. Well. Thank you for walking me home.'

He gave her a curt nod, flicked another cool glance at Will, and left. Watching his stiff back as he walked away, she wondered if she had offended him by not thanking him enough.

Will tugged at her hand. 'Come *on*, Charity! Ma's waiting to tell you all about it!'

'I'd just left Mrs Jordan's,' Mrs Fosdyke told her when they were settled round the kitchen table, 'and was starting on my way back, when what should happen but down runs that young lad that brought the note on Thursday.'

Will, who had heard it several times already, watched his sister intently for her reaction.

' "I'm to give you this for your trouble," says the lad, an' holds out a parcel tied up in newspaper an' string. "With her ladyship's thanks," he says. "Oh," says I, "I'm sure I never expected nothing more," meaning Miss Mitchell's silver shilling an' Mrs Jordan's cup of tea. An' do you know, my girl, when I undid that string an' saw what it was, I went all fainty. I was so done up I had to sit down there and then on the grass to recover myself.'

'Show her, Ma,' prompted Will.

Mrs Fosdyke went into the parlour and returned moments later with a thick, shiny magazine about the size of a tea tray.

'It's called *The Queen*,' said Will unnecessarily.

With her forefinger Mrs Fosdyke traced the gilt lettering. Her lower lip trembled. 'It's the last word in the Paris designs. With her ladyship's *thanks*.'

*   *   *

The following day was Sunday, and the best day the Fosdykes had had since moving to Hynton. Rain in the night had at last brought some freshness to the air, and Mrs Fosdyke was too taken up with her magazine to force strict observance of the Sabbath on the rest of them.

As a result, Will was allowed to run off on his own, and Mr Fosdyke enjoyed a pipe after church at his friend Mr Goldsbrow's and a quiet afternoon on a chair on the front step with *Pearson's Weekly*. Mrs Fosdyke sat in the parlour all day studying the plates in *The Queen*, and after tea she and Charity chose gowns for each other.

'There now.' Mrs Fosdyke turned up a lithograph of a Doucet visiting-dress with a tiny bolero and leg-of-mutton sleeves. 'That one'd suit for your reading at the rectory. "*Dark blue velvet with pouched bodice and waterfall skirt.*" Made for you, that is. With your colouring you couldn't go for anything subtle, but you'd look smart as a new pin in that.'

It didn't rain again, and by the evening the freshness had given way to stifling heat. The following day dawned hotter than ever, and when Charity came downstairs she knew instantly that the harmony was over.

Mrs Fosdyke sat at the kitchen table with *The Queen* spread out before her. She was still in her Sunday best and clearly hadn't been to bed at all, for she was surrounded by little squares of brown wrapping-paper which she was feverishly covering with sketches of gowns, hair-styles, and jackets.

'What are you *doing*?' Charity knelt to pick up some squares which had fluttered to the floor.

'Nearly finished,' muttered Mrs Fosdyke. The sound of her grinding jaws was like the ticking of a clock. ''Nother couple of hours an' I'll have copied the lot. It'll be back in Miss Mitchell's hands before the clock strikes noon.'

'*What?* But Mother, Lady Harlaston doesn't want it back! It's a magazine. She must have dozens of them!'

'Not our place to say, is it?' snapped Mrs Fosdyke. 'For all we know she's *counting* on having it back. She'll need it for ideas for her next party, won't she? An' here I am, keeping what's not mine. It's not right, an' I can't be doing with it!'

Charity shut her eyes. Her instinct had been right: they had been flying too high, and if she didn't take care, her poor mother would come crashing down. She certainly would if she went up to the Hall in this state.

'What if you're wrong,' she said carefully. 'What if Lady Harlaston *did* mean you to keep it? She'd be offended if you—' she stopped when she saw the panic in her mother's eyes. 'I tell you what. I'll take it to the parson's tomorrow afternoon.'

'The parson? What would he know about—'

'Not him. *Mrs* Bowles. She'll know what to do. She told me she's known Lord Harlaston since they were children. She's bound to know what his wife would want. Don't fret. Mrs Bowles will know what to do.'

CHAPTER TEN

Letter to Mrs Myles Gifford
Ridgewell Terrace, Chelsea
Friday the seventeenth of August, 1900
Hynton Rectory, six o'clock in the evening

Dearest Loelia,

Do not be alarmed that this comes to you in another's hand. It is only because this morning I took my first steps on the lawn (yes, my first in three years!) – and now dearest Ederic insists that I should not exert myself, but must instead give dictation. Well I shall not spare him, for I have a New Cause – or rather, a new protégée! *But I must come to that later, for Ederic disapproves of my jumping into the middle of things.*

So, dearest sister, are you and yours quite well? Here at Hynton we are all going on excellently, though the heat has made poor Ederic feel fearfully seedy. (As for Theo and Flora, we struggle constantly to keep them out of the sun!) I too go on very well indeed, which brings me to the best news of all: Dr Young says the beastly spinal carriage is no longer needed! It is wicked to call it so when Ederic bought it at such terrible expense, but it is such bliss to lie on a proper sofa and know that I may absolutely get up for five minutes and walk about!

Saturday the eighteenth of August, 1900
half past six in the evening

Yesterday I was more fatigued than I realized, and had (metaphorically) to lay down my pen. Thankfully I am now recovered, and may write this myself. Moreover, Ederic is upstairs dressing, for there is to be a very grand dinner at the Hall, and Lord Harlaston insisted that his 'old friend' should make up the party! I am so happy. Dearest Ederic has no society here, and rejoices in the talk of educated men.

There, I am such a muff! You must be wondering why Lord Harlaston is in England at all. Everyone is thrilled, for he has three weeks' home leave in rec-ompense for some important secret duty discharged in Town. It is all very exciting, for we have the Fête in a week's time, and of course the Harlaston Ball. You may wonder at so many engagements in this time of mourning for our leading family, but Ederic says it is courageous of them to put a brave face on their grief while doing their duty to maintain morale in wartime. He is right, of course, and I feel for them with all my heart. I cannot but recall the desperate time after our little Perry was taken.

But there, I must not become maudlin. I shall move on apace to jollier things. I have not yet told you about our excitement of yesterday afternoon, when who should be announced but Lord Harlaston himself! As calm and frank as you please, and quite mahogany from the African sun. He accepted a cup of tea but ate nothing, not even a morsel of Rose's ginger sponge which he used to plead for as a boy, but he stayed with us for fully twenty minutes, and then absolutely smoked a cigar with Ederic in the garden.

What a delightful treat it was! Afterwards, however, I could not help but remark to Ederic that our noble guest looked fearfully drawn, and that I detected a perceptible strain in his manner. I fear that he found the sight of our darling Theo – an embarrassingly grubby little seraph in his new sailor suit – something of a trial, although he did his best to conceal it. I have known the same distress, however, so am able to sense it in others.

Now on to the dinner this evening, on which I have something to impart which I fear may cause you no little distress. Loelia, I am convinced *that Ederic's invitation was purely Lord Harlaston's doing, and that* Lady Harlaston had *very much rather it had never been extended. 'But how can this be?' you will ask in perplexity. It is decidedly hard to explain, for one could not imagine a more courteous and well-bred hostess – and yet I* do *feel it, in innumerable little acts and omissions which perhaps only a wife's eye can detect. I am just thankful that the Lord has spared my own darling from perceiving it himself, for I could not bear the distress it would cause him, knowing as I do his boundless admiration for his patroness. I confess that at times I have had to struggle to master my* anger. *(Yes, anger, Loelia! There, what sedition! You perceive what a tigress I am become in defence of my loved ones!)*

The same day, nine o'clock in the evening

I had to rest after my outburst, and am now contrite. Furthermore, Ederic came down looking immensely distinguished, and the children became overexcited. Now that peace is restored, I will return to the New Cause to which I alluded at the outset.

Do you remember, Loelia, the old fen tigers of our youth at Willow End? Those secretive souls who lived in hovels and slept on reeds, and supped on water-rats and eels? Well, such a fen tiger we now have in our midst! Or rather I should say, a fen tigress. The good woman has disguised herself as a respectable village seamstress, but when one was born in the fen country, one is not easily duped.

Yes, we have a new family in Hynton, and though they only are of the artisan class I am prodigiously intrigued. From the French windows I have observed them en route to their devotions, and Ederic has furnished me with several diverting accounts. Thus I now put before you a little sketch of the famille *Fosdyke, of my own devising.*

The father, who rejoices in the name of Jack, is a fine-looking fellow of the heavy Dutch type frequently encountered among our Lincolnshire labourers, which Ederic tells me dates from the Restoration, when we brought over men from the Netherlands to assist in draining the fens. Fosdyke père *has frank china-blue eyes, fair hair, and a stolidly handsome countenance which flushes carmine the instant he is addressed by his superiors – foremost among whom he clearly numbers his wife.*

The son, William, is a well-built and handsome lad of eleven with a remarkably sweet disposition for one of his station in life. He is much given to reading the Bible, with which he is admirably familiar, although sadly he is what our locals call 'half-sharp'.

So now to Fosdyke mère, one Alice Fosdyke, who is dark of countenance and small of stature: too small for beauty, but well-proportioned. From what I have glimpsed beneath the inevitable Watteau hat the features are not without distinction, but the expression is unusually fierce. Ederic calls the good woman a true daughter of the Jutes, who peopled this region in ancient times. I would characterize her quite simply as a fen tigress — for she has a certain clenched quality: a sense of resentful energy rigidly held in check, as if she feels constantly threatened with opprobrium. I do believe that I perceive a whiff of a Family Secret — and you know how I adore secrets!

So now what of the Daughter, whom I intend to make my Project for the summer? Here are the particulars.

It is important to understand at the outset that to the casual observer there is nothing remotely remarkable about this girl. In stature and colouring she takes after her mother, and hence is not tall enough to be called handsome, although she is agreeably well-proportioned. Quantities of (alas) straight dark hair are dressed in a becomingly simple pompadour, with, mercifully, no attempt at one of those unsightly 'Alexandra fringes'. The complexion is sound and neither pale nor rubicund, and the features have definition but are not distinguished: ordinary brown eyes with rather pronounced dark brows, a neat nose, and lips of the matte raspberry hue which is sometimes seen in brunettes. In short, she can lay no claim to being a beauty, but neither is she absolutely plain. It is not an arresting face, but I fancy it belongs to that type which improves steadily upon acquaintance.

I have done it again, haven't I? I have leapt into the middle without explaining how I encountered her in the first place. This omission will be rectified forthwith.

You will be aware that recently I have developed a selfish desire for entertainment, and have therefore been in search of a Reader. Last week, my prayers were answered – for young Samuel Webb suggested to Ederic that Fosdyke fille *(whose name is Charity) might try for the post, as she is not entirely destitute of education, having been a 'scholard' (sic!) at the Higher Grade School at Tilburne before her education ended at the age of fifteen. Thereafter, and unusually for a rustic, she returned to assist her mother at home, rather than going into service. (Mrs Fosdyke seems not to share the countrywoman's aversion to seeing her offspring distinguish themselves: further indication, if it be needed, that she is indeed a remarkable woman.)*

Eventually Ederic overcame his misgivings and the girl was sent to me in the drawing-room. Loelia, I took to her at once. She had donned her 'best' for the occasion, which had been got up with not a little taste. A simple costume of dark green gabardine trimmed with black Nottingham braid, a blouse of white lawn with quite tolerable pin-tucking, black woollen gloves (poor creature!) and a black straw hat trimmed with a new green riband. The hands (when at my request she drew off her gloves) are neatly turned, although naturally coarsened by work. I could not make out the ankles as they were encased in a pair of rather unsightly boots of which I suspect she is painfully

143

conscious, for she coloured and tucked them beneath her skirts when she felt my glance.

Fearing that I had wounded her by my thoughtlessness, I swiftly rang for tea. In retrospect that may have been a mistake, for the sight of the spirit-lamp seemed to persuade her that tea in educated homes is an entirely different ritual from that to which she is accustomed, and she would accept only a plain biscuit and a cup of tea with neither milk nor lemon (and both tea and biscuit remained untouched throughout the interview). She was too nervous to look about her – a point in her favour, for I do dislike rustics who gawp – but she watched shyly as I poured the tea, and I sensed a natural curiosity and desire to improve which I found charming.

To proceed. The girl listened to me with a pleasant, restrained eagerness, and answered my enquiries with a frank and ready intelligence. It straight away became clear that she adores reading, but that due to insufficient funds she can admit to an acquaintance with only a handful of volumes from her schooldays. Lives of the English Princesses, Pyecroft's English Reader, The Traveller's Library, and Laneton Parsonage comprise her literary universe to date.

We then proceeded to an 'audition', and here I fear you may deplore my choice of text. Partly to determine if the girl can handle unfamiliar prose, and partly to test her moral reflexes, I had her read a passage from Jane Eyre. Be assured that it was one of the more innocuous passages: the scene in which the heroine observes the guests at Thornfield playing charades (I had to explain the term, and she seemed enchanted to have learnt a French word!) The result was highly gratifying, for she reads fluently and with expression, *and her voice is pleasingly low-pitched, with the Lincolnshire burr not so pronounced as to be disagreeable (in fact, it is rather engaging). Patently she enjoyed the text and wished to learn more of the story – but when I told her the respective positions of Mr Rochester and Jane (I didn't reveal that he is already married, I have some scruples!) she was very properly severe in her judgement of them both.*

I should perhaps correct any impression that the daughter shares that desperate sense of a hidden grievance which is so marked a feature of her mother. In the daughter there is only an unforced natural dignity which is the quality I find most attractive about her, and which marks her out as not being from the common mould. In short, I believe her to be capable of considerable improvement – hence at last my Project.

I have it in mind to effect that improvement myself. Slowly, of course, and not to any degree which would be inconsistent with her station in life. A subtle correction of certain little faults of diction and vocabulary; an inculcation of gentler manners and demeanour; a judicious course of reading. If I am successful, who can say but that she may not make a very creditable assistant in some dressmaker's establishment – and thence a worthy match with some sort of junior clerk?

Later, eleven p.m.

It is very late and I am fatigued. Please please do not be disquietened. It is nothing that a few days' rest will not correct. Still, I had better close now, and

*leave the development of my plans to a future letter.
Do write soon, darling Loelia, for I long to hear your
news.*

> *Your devoted sister
> Gwendolen*

CHAPTER ELEVEN

Dr Bowles was baffled.

He did not understand why he was here, halfway down the enormous dinner table, in front of the curiously unsettling centrepiece.

He reminded himself that as a quondam Fellow of Caius, he might hold his head high in whatever company he chanced to be. But that was an empty boast in the State Dining Room at Harlaston Hall, in the middle of a Society dinner for thirty-eight. In such a milieu, intellect was immaterial, for he was not *clever*. Nor had he grace of face or form.

So why had he been invited? He could only surmise that his distinguished patron wished to speak with him, as he had tried to do the other day in the garden. The thought made him hopeful and afraid, for Lord Harlaston had not sought spiritual counsel since he was a boy.

In the meantime, he told himself stoutly, there was a great deal to be enjoyed, oh yes *indeed*. Before him lay a veritable forest of Baccarat crystal and an armoury of Georgian silver, and his lap was festooned with a napkin the size of a small bath-sheet. And *how* the children would adore the great silver *compotiers* ranged down the middle of the table, and filled with figs and pomegranates and grapes!

But he would have enjoyed it so much more had not the centrepiece loomed so disturbingly near. He had always found orchids *indecorous*, with their fleshy petals and gaping mouths. There was something voluptuous about them which made him feel subtly mocked.

'Ederic dearest, you are an old silly,' he could hear Gwen say. 'Fancy regarding *flowers* as unnatural!' Thinking of his wife made him feel suddenly better.

And *how* she would enjoy hearing of the dinner on the morrow! Oysters *à la demi diable*, turtle soup, turbot *à la Russe*, boned snipe with quail forcemeat, saddle of lamb, *salade Nantaise* – and a truly superlative *Bavaroise Impériale,* which he was still attacking with vigour. He knew he would dream about the wines for months to come.

A footman, resplendent in the Baroness's colours of aquamarine and fawn, bore down on his empty glass, and he blushed for his vulgarity of mind. He took another gulp of champagne and immediately realized that he ought not to have done. His head was swimming. He must *not* become tipsy. Not when Lord Harlaston might wish to talk after dinner.

'Bowles, I should like to speak to you,' he had said as they'd walked across the rectory lawn. Flattered and flustered, Dr Bowles had maintained what he hoped was a respectful yet encouraging silence. He waited for his patron to mention his poor little boy, but, to his surprise, what followed seemed instead to relate to the war. Hazarding a guess that his patron was concerned for the men he had left behind, Dr Bowles ventured that God would protect His soldiers in such a just cause. 'But I wasn't thinking of soldiers,' said Lord Harlaston, narrowing his eyes against his cigar smoke like an Eastern potentate. 'I was thinking of civilians. For them, at times, the Lord seems to care very little.' There was an edge to his voice, and Dr Bowles was quite taken aback. But just then little Theo had bounded up with his new puppy, and no more was said.

And now, although his patron was as courteous and attentive as always, Dr Bowles was not deceived. He saw how frequently the sombre glance would stray to the great silver centrepiece and lose itself among the orchids.

But if it was not the loss of his son, then what could be afflicting so fortunate a man? Surely Lord Harlaston had everything which mortal clay could desire? And how *could* he remain troubled for long, when he was married to the most beautiful woman in the Empire? That thought brought tears to Dr Bowles's eyes, and another gulp of champagne was needed to restore his composure.

The object of his admiration could just be glimpsed at the far end of the table through a jungle of ruby-shaded candelabra. That is, she could be glimpsed if he leaned discreetly forward and twisted his head quite sharply to the right. Her gown was of some filmy pearl-grey stuff which clung miraculously to her magnificent figure. Her complexion was as radiant as that of a Raphael madonna.

But a withdrawn and distant madonna, it had to be owned. His murmured condolences on entering the drawing-room had been met by one of her cooler glances. He understood *entirely*. Who was he to aspire to her confidence?

'The Golden Couple', the Press had called them in the summer when they wed. Dr Bowles had been assiduous in collecting the clippings, and had preserved them in a little book, the existence of which not even Gwendolen was aware.

For a moment he allowed himself to picture the wedding night at Langham's Hotel. The velvet curtains shutting out the gas-lit London street; the high mahogany bedstead; the crimson counterpane and the snowy mountain of pillows. And those two Olympian beings, their bright limbs intertwined for the very first time. The Golden Couple.

Giddily he bent his nose to the bubbles in his glass.

'The last time I saw you play as badly as this', the Earl of Minto remarked to Robert after dinner, 'was at Abu Shendi, when you blamed it on the state of our table.'

'Which, as I recall, was the door of the commissionaire's office,' Robert replied. 'Rather harsh, don't you think, Algy? I was coming down with yellow fever at the time.'

'Precisely. And since you ain't got the same excuse tonight, I shall show you no mercy.'

'Then be warned, my dear fellow, I shall extend the same courtesy to you.'

Algy laughed.

Dusting his cue, Robert reflected on how easy it was to conceal one's thoughts from others. He watched his friends drift between the supper table and the ash-stands, secure in the knowledge that they were far enough from the ladies to be able to talk without constraint. His friends adored the Long Gallery to the same degree that the ladies, Violet in particular, detested it. By day it had more than a hint of the mausoleum about it, but by gaslight it achieved a gratifying Miltonic splendour. Gasoliers fashioned like small malevolent gargoyles cast an infernal light on his grandmother's fearsome oil-paintings, while the anguished gaze of St Agatha on her rack lent piquancy to écarté and bridge.

He stifled a yawn. Tomorrow there would be morning service, followed by breakfast. Then riding for the energetic, then luncheon, a sketching party for the ladies, boating on the lake, tea, croquet and quoits, dinner, and finally the inevitable smoking and billiards. And on, and on, and on, in this petty pace . . .

To his dismay, he wanted none of it.

And yet, on the long ride from Bloemfontein to Bethlehem, he had thought with longing of these languorous summers at home. He loved them precisely *because* of their stately predictability. So why could he take no pleasure in any of it now? Instead he found himself sleepwalking through the days, and jolting awake at night from nightmares he could never quite remember. It was puzzling, it was perverse, and it made him angry with himself.

He watched Algy increase his score with an evil flourish.

Robert old fellow, he told himself, you really ought to stop taking everything so seriously. Perhaps you simply dislike losing at billiards.

But he knew there was more to it than that. Something was cutting him off from everything he knew. He found himself observing the rituals of his life as though through some high clear wall which deprived everything of savour. Wasn't there a line in the Bible about apples turning to dust in the mouth – or was it ashes?

He had tried to dismiss it all as selfish fantasy, reminding himself that others were in mourning besides himself. It had not worked. He knew – he *knew* – that no-one else was experiencing what he was going through. They *could* not have acquired this urgent habit of searching the face of any boy he encountered – gentleman's son, village urchin, or London street Arab, it didn't matter who – for some trace of the well-known countenance. It was impossible that they *should* have acquired such a habit, for the simple reason that he sought not the face of his own son Linley, but the blunt, handsome features of the Dutch boy at Nooitgedacht Farm.

He hadn't the Devil's own idea why that should be, and there was no-one whom he could ask. The London doctor he had consulted with some awkwardness the day before leaving Town had put it down unconvincingly to an overworked nervous constitution. His few close friends were either in South Africa or India, but if they had been in London he would not have sought them out. And talking to anyone in the family was out of the question. The last recourse was, he supposed, the Church.

The Church was nodding off on the corner of a divan, with a tumbler of brandy and seltzer water about to slide off his knee.

Poor old Bowles. Violet had been cold to him before dinner. Why did she dislike the poor fellow so much? She herself attributed it to his unfortunate appearance, but Robert suspected there was more to it than that. Violet was not intelligent, but at times she could be extraordinarily shrewd. Had she sensed the change which had overtaken the old fellow when his wife became ill? The increased avidity for the crueller passages of his beloved classics – the bloodier and more anatomical the better, particularly if coerced young virgins were involved.

Well, what of it? thought Robert wearily.

A taste for literary depravity was a harmless enough vice in a man who shrank from speaking a harsh word to a maidservant. And presumably it was better than picking up streetwalkers or cornering housemaids. Robert had friends who did both without compunction.

'You're musing again,' said Algy. 'If there's one thing I can't stomach, it's a man who *muses* when he should be playin' billiards. You must pay the penalty and tell me your thoughts.'

'I was musing', Robert said lightly, 'on the differences between men and women.'

'Ah,' said Algy, with a significant lift of his eyebrows. 'Muse on, m'dear fellow! I've been an admirer of the weaker sex all my life, but I'm dashed if I'm any wiser than when I was a boy.'

It was common knowledge that for the past twelve years, Algy had kept a stout red-faced mistress in Holywell Street. His wife Sophia had known about it since the beginning. Indeed, there were those who maintained that she had assisted in the woman's selection.

Robert smiled to himself. It was a far cry from the comfortable vagueness of boyhood, when he had whiled away rainy afternoons by browsing through his grandmother's botany books – from which he had gleaned the notion that ladies and gentlemen procreated by brushing against each other, like flowering plants. Algy's right, he thought. I must stop musing, or I shall end up like poor old Bowles, with a well-thumbed volume of Ovid locked away in my desk drawer.

The thought amused him so much that to Algy's consternation he began playing better than he had done all evening.

Before going to her apartments, Violet liked to tour the state rooms with Paige, talking over the arrangements for the following day. Since Paige was a paragon among butlers and the arrangements were invariably perfect, she found this a soothing prelude to retiring.

Tonight, however, she dismissed Paige and walked the rooms alone, finally coming to a halt before the windows in the Jade Ante-Room. She would have liked to have opened one to gain some relief from the airless heat, but the thought of ringing for a footman made her weary. Instead she stood gazing out at the Lion Steps.

It was a view she particularly loathed. But then, she loathed everything at the Hall. How could she do otherwise, when she was leered at from every corner by blowsy seraphs and bulging serpents? She was counting the days till she could decently return to St James's Square.

But tonight something more profound was keeping her from her rest. In the course of the day, she had been overtaken by an awareness that she was *at fault* – and to be at fault was a thing she detested above all else. It was the strongest feeling she knew.

But in what *way* was she at fault? She could recall no duty she had overlooked, no disagreement or unpleasantness. The house party was proceeding perfectly, as she had known it would. And yet the sense of wrong-doing was so strong that she caught her breath. She set down her lamp on a side-table and gazed at her reflection in the window.

Suddenly she was back at her grandmama's house, sixteen years earlier.

'You're to play out here, and don't go snooping,' Millie had said, leaving her outside the footmen's cottage. Lately, Millie had found lots of errands to take her to the stables. Violet didn't mind. She liked being with Millie on Frau Schickemeier's free afternoons, for between the loose-boxes and the tack room there was a little alleyway in which she could play hopscotch. But this afternoon, the sky clouded over and the alleyway turned cold. She became indignant. It would be warm in the footmen's cottage – and yet here she was, made to wait outside like a lackey!

Afterwards, she remembered how dirty the window pane had been, and how a spider had crouched in a corner of the sill. A small grey spider with a tight shiny body that would pop like a grape beneath one's boot.

Inside the footmen's cottage she could see Bates and Millie standing close together. Bates had his hands about Millie's waist, and his fingers were taut and shiny, like the bunches of sausages which hawkers sold on streetcorners. Millie was moaning as Bates chewed at her face – but to Violet's lasting horror she was neither struggling nor pulling away.

Violet turned sharply away from the Lion Steps, her heart pounding. *Why* should she remember that now?

Once again she is in the stable-yard on that long-ago afternoon. This time she is practising carriage-drill. Straw skitters across the cobbles. She smells horse-dung and hears the scrape of hooves. Grandmama Atherton is watching her as she steps up into the brougham. 'No no *no!*' the old lady barks from the couch which the footmen have carried out for her. '*Right* foot first onto the step!'

Bates stands waiting for Violet at the carriage door. The steps are steep, but somehow she manages to get inside the brougham with only her gloved fingertips brushing his arm. She turns to descend. One, two, thr— one of the horses shifts its weight and the carriage tilts ominously. As she leans on Bates she meets his eyes. He *knows* she was watching through the window. He knows that she knows, and he takes pleasure in the knowledge. She will never forget the complicity in his eyes, or the moist swollen fullness of his lips.

For years afterwards she tells herself that *spooning*, as Millie calls it with an ungainly blush, is confined to the labouring classes. Nothing like that occurs between people of her sort. Then she met Robert, and the world changed.

She was seventeen years old and in her first Season, and she knew instantly that they must marry. Gentlemen *ought* to be tall and dark and cultivated and discreetly admiring; ladies *ought* to be beautiful and fair and delicate. One of them must be very wealthy. That it should be she was the crowning perfection.

They had known each other for four weeks when he proposed. Her parents were delighted, and his formidable aunts took her to their bosom. Only Grandmama Adela narrowed her eyes and smiled a smile of great cynicism, which Violet ignored.

From then on, the affianced couple saw little of each other, for Violet must concentrate on her trousseau, and there was a great deal to do. Paris for gowns, Vienna for furs, Rome for gloves and shoes, London for hats. It took over a year, but it was worth it.

On her wedding day she achieved her destiny. She was discussed and admired in every newspaper in the country.

The wedding night was horrific.

When they returned from the honeymoon she went straight to her mother at Chisholm Grange. But she had no words to describe it, nor was she even sure she should try. Perhaps it was some unspeakable aberration peculiar to her new husband – and if it were, wouldn't it be a betrayal to reveal it, even to Mama?

But somehow Mama had guessed, and to her daughter's lasting astonishment had explained with appalling calm that what had so distressed her was something to which *all* women must submit (*all*? Even Mama? *Mama and Papa*?). Though never more than submit. Mama was very clear about that. 'Your distaste is *entirely proper*, my darling, and does you great credit. You must find a way to retain your dignity without allowing this to diminish your regard for Robert. He is a good man, and from what I gather has shown exceptional patience and restraint. He will make you a fine husband.'

A *fine husband*? What did that mean, when such a horror swam beneath the surface?

At first, being with child was a glorious relief. Then her waist began to thicken, and relief gave way to loathing. Mercifully, the event itself was a blur – as were the months of nervous prostration which followed. Laudanum for her nerves, brandy to stop her fainting. All she remembered was the wonderful peace of her cool, clean, solitary bed. In many ways, it was the happiest time of her life.

And Mama had been right. Robert *had* proved a

fine husband. Gentle, considerate, admiring, and restrained. But Violet never overcame her bewilderment. How is it possible, she would ask herself, that an act which is the blackest sin a woman can commit *before* marriage should suddenly become her bounden duty the moment *after* the vows have been exchanged?

Behind her, the clock struck two. If she did not retire soon she would be *affreuse* in the morning.

'Violet?' Robert spoke from the doorway. 'It's rather late. Are you unwell?' He came towards her, his face saturnine in the glow of the lamp he carried.

For an instant they regarded one another in silence. 'Thank you, *mon cher*,' she said at last, 'I am quite well. I was just about to go to my room.'

'I too. Let me carry your lamp.' He took hers from the side-table, and together they moved towards the door. 'Are you sure you are well?' he asked. 'This evening I thought you seemed – distracted.'

'Distracted? Why do you say that? I hope I did not in any way neglect—'

'That is not what I meant.'

'And yet you meant something.'

He paused. 'To be frank, I thought it most pronounced towards poor old Bowles.'

'Oh, really! Is that all?'

'My dear, I know he is not what you would choose in a guest, but—'

'Frankly, I think I treated him with a great deal more indulgence than he deserved. Approaching me in the drawing-room in that fawning manner! Why, I thought he meant to press my hand! *Il n'est pas de notre monde, mon cher, et vraiment, ce n'est pas de ma faute!*'

'*Mais oui, ma chère, il* est *de notre monde. Parce que je veux qu'il le soit.*'

His voice was low and troubled, and she wondered if her conduct had caused him pain.

Was this why she felt at fault? But that was absurd. What she sensed went deeper than coolness to an obnoxious guest. 'Perhaps', she admitted gracefully, 'I *was* a little too distant.' She put a hand to her temple. 'I am sorry. This has all been something of a strain.' She knew as soon as she lifted her eyes to his that she had won.

'What a cad you married,' he said softly. 'The first engagement after – after Linley – and all I can do is carp.'

Graciously she met his apology with her own. 'And I too am sorry. We will visit the Rectory together, the minute the last guest has left.'

He stood looking down at her. 'Violet,' he said in a low voice. 'I wondered—'

'You know, Robert,' she put in quickly, 'you were right, I do not feel quite myself. I believe I will have Mary prepare one of Dr Young's powders.'

A moment's pause, then he inclined his head with that courtly reserve which was what she admired most in him.

Later, after she had sent Mary away, she stood in her peignoir gazing out of the window. The avenue of limes was a dark snake winding down to the stables.

It had come to her. She knew why she felt at fault.

In the course of the day, as she moved among her guests, she had caught in certain glances an elusive questioning. The son and heir is dead, they seemed to say. When will the beautiful Lady Harlaston provide another?

She pressed both hands to her temples.

It was the *boy's* fault. Silently she railed against her son. For being awkward, for being plain. For being dead. For putting her through *that* again.

Body and mind revolted at the thought. *It could not be*. Not when she had promised herself on her wedding night that she would never, ever submit to *that* again.

CHAPTER TWELVE

Will hated his new job.

He hated the early morning walk past Gunnerby Wood, with his boots hissing through the long grass and the mist sneaking between the trees like an army of ghosts. He hated the shouts from the surrounding fields where the gangs stoked the steam-reaper and bound the corn: men and boys working together, fitting in.

He had only lasted a week as a kitchen-boy at Shotley Farm. Then he'd asked Mrs Corlett's Ruby if she was named after the woman in Revelations arrayed in purple and scarlet, and they'd demoted him to rook scaring on the spot.

Things like that were always happening to him. At first people liked him, but then he would say something they didn't understand, or wander off in the middle of a cricket match, and they'd feel let down. But he was used to that. It no longer bothered him very much. In fact, if it hadn't been for Ned Webb, he'd be doing all right.

Ned Webb. His stomach clenched.

Ned was three years older than him, with a ferret's red-rimmed eyes, and a scraping of pimples across his chin. He had a knack for sniffing out weaknesses, and would latch onto them with his terrier's teeth and not let go till his victim screamed for mercy. Last spring, he and Jim Bacon had caught a mole in a bucket and stuck skewers in its eyes and ears for a laugh. 'Where's the harm in it?' Jim had said with a jittery giggle. 'Blind an' deaf to start with, wannit? Can't hurt what's not there. Though yur should'er heard it flammering about in that old bucket! Good half-hour it took, never would'er thought it last that long!'

Jim wasn't so bad. He didn't hate Will the way Ned did. None of the boys did.

The trouble had started when Ned's uncle got sweet on Charity. At first Ned's rage had puzzled Will. Then he had worked it out. Keeper Webb the bachelor was the most feared man in Hynton: his thrashings were legendary. Keeper Webb the lover was not. And Keeper Webb was the source of all Ned's power.

Will didn't want to think about Keeper Webb. He didn't like him, and he knew Keeper Webb didn't like him back. And he couldn't bear the thought of losing Charity. She was the only one who could cope with their mother, the only one who didn't think he was simple. If she married Keeper Webb, Will would die.

'Eh there! *Mole!*'

Will froze.

Ned Webb and Luke Morris and Jim Bacon were standing at the edge of the wood. They had come up on his deaf side, like they always did.

'You bin talkin' to yourself again, Mole,' said Ned.

'Bugger off,' said Will.

'We *heard* yur, Moley.'

'Bugger *off* or I'll do you!' With what? he wondered,

his palms prickling with sweat. His catapult was useless. He'd spent his last pebble an hour ago.

'I'll *do* you!' mimicked Ned. The others sniggered. 'Daft as muck but he thinks he can *do* Ned Webb! Moley. Mowdy-warp.' The glint in his eye made it more than just a taunt at Will's deafness. It made Will think of that mole, flammering about in a bucket with skewers in its head. He began to feel sick.

'I got a job fur you, Moley,' Ned said softly.

A low murmur of voices reached the rectory kitchen, and across the table, Charity and Rose exchanged awkward smiles.

Poor Rose. She didn't know how to treat Charity, who was neither proper visitor nor proper staff. In the end she had opted for a friendly, impenetrable silence. She must be longing for the bell so that she could see out Lady Harlaston, settle Charity back in the drawing room, and have the kitchen to herself again.

That would suit Charity perfectly, provided she didn't have to meet Lady Harlaston in person. *The Queen* was a dead weight in her lap. She had been curling the corners of each page into little rolls.

Mrs Bowles had misunderstood her spectacularly from the start. She had been delighted with what she mistook for Charity's 'delicious little scheme' of wanting to return the magazine to Lady Harlaston. And when Rose put her head round the door and announced that Lady Harlaston's dog-cart had been spotted in the lane, Mrs Bowles decided, horrifyingly, that this would be the perfect opportunity for Charity to carry out 'her little scheme' in person.

The last thing Charity wanted was to carry out the 'scheme' in person. It wasn't *her* scheme, it was Mrs

Bowles's, and it was far from being delicious. She considered mumbling an excuse and escaping out the back door, then pretending to her mother that Mrs Bowles had confirmed it, and *The Queen* was indeed hers for keeps.

The parson's wife would have been horrified to have learnt that Charity was contemplating a falsehood. 'Dare to be true!' she had quoted with flashing eyes that very afternoon, '*nothing* can need a lie!' Dear, innocent Mrs Bowles. These days in the end house, everything needed a lie.

The drawing-room bell rang and Rose pushed herself to her feet and rustled out of the kitchen. Voices grew louder, then fainter, as doors opened and closed. Charity shut her eyes. Relief washed over her.

Rose put her head round the kitchen door. 'You're wanted, Miss! Mrs Bee says to go round the side an' meet her at the gate to catch 'em before they go. I'm to take out a chair so she can see 'em off without tiring herself.'

This is ridiculous, Charity told herself, looking down at her trembling hands. It's only a magazine. And she's probably very nice.

'Ah, Charity, there you are!' Mrs Bowles's chair wobbled alarmingly on the gravel as she leaned back.

Out in the lane stood a graceful high-sided dogcart in which sat a lady in vaporous white. Between the dogcart and the rectory gate, Lord Harlaston sat astride his big glossy chestnut horse.

Charity's face flamed. Rose hadn't said anything about *Lord* Harlaston being there as well.

'Lady Harlaston, Lord Harlaston,' Mrs Bowles said graciously, 'may I present my little reader, Charity

Fosdyke, who has undertaken the somewhat daunting task of enlivening my afternoons.'

Charity curtseyed.

Lord Harlaston gave her the same distant salutation he had bestowed on the Tilburne road. His face betrayed no flicker of recognition.

Lady Harlaston's acknowledgement was less perceptible than her husband's. In the brief glance which Charity allowed herself, she saw a profile of alabaster perfection beneath a great veiled hat trimmed with white organdie roses. A white silk dust-coat broke softly over skirts of snowy *mousseline de soie* to reveal a long narrow foot resting on a footboard; a thoroughbred ankle sheathed in a stocking of gossamer lisle, and an unbelievably delicate shoe of dove-grey suede: pointed of toe and narrow of heel, and fastened across the instep by four impossibly slender straps and four tiny smoked-pearl buttons.

The reins lay loosely in Lady Harlaston's immaculate gloved hands. The reins were a mere formality. It was inconceivable that the beautiful grey carriage-horse would do anything other than wait in perfect stillness for her command.

Charity averted her gaze, and found herself contemplating Lord Harlaston's hand resting on his khaki-clad thigh. He had not yet drawn on his gloves, and his hand was brown from the sun, with long narrow fingers and a vigorous tracery of veins across the back.

'. . . so it occurred to me,' Mrs Bowles was saying, 'that as my lady was so *kind* as to call on the very afternoon when I and my little reader seek diversion, we might afford Charity the privilege of soliciting my lady's views in person.'

All heads turned towards Charity. Even Lord

Harlaston's horse gazed at her curiously through its lashes.

Charity forgot her cobbled-together speech and said baldly, 'We thought your ladyship might want her magazine back.'

Behind the veil two peerless green eyes flickered over Charity and blinked once, and fine golden brows delicately rose. Lady Harlaston raised her lovely head to her husband with a tiny incredulous frown.

'It came from Miss Mitchell with your ladyship's thanks,' said Charity. 'But we didn't know if it was given or lent.' Spoken out loud, it sounded even more preposterous, and she caught an amused glance from Lord Harlaston. She coloured deeply. Of *course* the wretched thing was a present! Wherever did her mother *get* her ideas? And how could she have *let* Mrs Bowles persuade her into looking such an utter fool?

'*Lent?*' echoed Lady Harlaston, sounding faintly affronted. 'How is it conceivable that I should *lend*—?'

' – or that you should want it back, my dear,' put in Lord Harlaston smoothly, 'when I fancy the editors of those magazines pay a good deal more attention to you than you do to them.'

'Oh Robert, how you do exaggerate.' Lady Harlaston smiled up at him, and it seemed to Charity that she didn't believe he exaggerated at all. 'But I remain at a loss. Who is Miss Mitchell? Do I *know* a Miss Mitchell?'

'It must be a mistake,' said Charity. 'I won't trouble you further, I'll just—'

'Yes, why don't you go back inside,' said Mrs Bowles hastily, seeing her little scheme running aground.

But Lady Harlaston was implacable. 'Ah, I fancy I

begin to see. The girl means *Mary*! My *maid* has used my name for her own ends. Now that is too provoking.'

Charity and Mrs Bowles exchanged alarmed glances.

Lord Harlaston appeared to have stopped listening. He and his horse were gazing thoughtfully up the lane.

'I really do not believe that I ought to let that pass,' Lady Harlaston said softly. 'Mrs Bowles, I understand your committee is collecting trifles for some kind of a – a prize draw, is it?'

Mrs Bowles looked startled. 'Indeed yes, my lady. For the fête. Although we like to refer to it as a *tombola*.'

'Just so.' The beautiful lips curved in the ghost of a smile. 'Well you must send your girl here up to the Hall. I shall see to it that "Miss Mitchell" provides one or two trifles of her own.'

Again Charity felt herself reddening. 'Your girl' made her sound like the rectory washerwoman.

She saw now how improbable the whole episode of the magazine had been. How impossible that a woman like Lady Harlaston should have seen fit to thank a village dressmaker with *any* sort of gift – or indeed that she should have cared a straw for such a 'trifle' as a torn bodice. Somewhere between Miss Mitchell and the end house, things had got royally garbled.

Charity recalled the strained curve of her mother's neck as she copied yet another fashion plate onto a scrap of paper. She resolved that the end house would never learn the truth about *The Queen*. As far as her mother was concerned, it would remain a present from Lady Harlaston 'with her thanks' – and if that poet of Mrs Bowles's really thought that nothing ever needed a lie, then he didn't know Alice Fosdyke.

She glanced up to find Lord Harlaston watching her. She had the uncomfortable impression that he sensed her antipathy towards his wife, and was amused by it.

Nor had Lady Harlaston's casual demotion of Charity to a rectory servant been lost on Mrs Bowles. 'What a generous notion that is, my lady,' she said crisply. 'But I regret that Charity already has more than her share of duties for the fête' – serenely she ignored Charity's startled glance – 'though if it suits, I shall send a boy for whatever your maid can spare.'

Lady Harlaston flicked the reins on the grey's gleaming rump. 'As you wish,' she murmured as the dogcart began to move off.

'Remember me to your sister,' said Lord Harlaston to Mrs Bowles, touching his crop to his hat. He sounded as though he meant it, and Mrs Bowles's heron face flushed with pleasure.

When they had gone, Mrs Bowles put her hand on Charity's arm. 'I've been meaning to ask you about the fête,' she said unconvincingly.

'I've been meaning to ask if I could help,' Charity put in quickly.

'Perhaps you might assist in packing up the leftovers after the tea. Yes, that will do very well. There are always those who are too infirm to attend the meal, but who nevertheless merit a share of the comestibles. And it is complicated, as they all receive different things. I have a list.' She patted Charity's hand. 'And that way, you can enjoy yourself first, and make yourself useful afterwards. Will that suit?'

'Mrs Bowles,' said Charity gravely, 'that will suit very well indeed.'

Walking home, she decided that it would be important to be properly dressed for the fête, particularly if she was to have official duties. The typewriter could wait for a few more weeks. On her next visit to Tilburne she would devote some of her savings to a pair of buttoned boots.

'There,' said Violet as they emerged from the elms and turned towards the park. 'Have I redeemed myself from charges of callousness *vis-à-vis la famille Bowles?*'

'In full, my dear,' replied Robert, 'had charges ever been brought, which they were not.'

He wondered why women invariably disliked his wife. It had been amusing to watch Gwendolen Bowles closing ranks with the village girl. Amusing and all too familiar. With the girl it was understandable: the natural antipathy of a handsome young woman for a beautiful one. But Gwen? It could hardly be that. The last time he could recall her uttering a word about her own looks had been when they were ten, and she had declined to play Polyphemus to his Odysseus, on the grounds that she had two perfectly good eyes, not one.

Dear Gwen. She had been so bubbling with enthusiasm for her protégée that she quite failed to notice how tedious Violet found her conversation. 'Delicious, quite *delicious!*' Gwen had exclaimed as she regaled them with the eccentricities of her protégée's family. A downtrodden father, an unbalanced mother (nicknamed 'the fen tigress' by Gwen), and an idiot brother. The poor little thing. Perhaps that was why she took walks by herself on the Tilburne road.

He thought she had appeared to more advantage on the road than she had just now. On the road she had been walking fast, with a swinging step and a queenly carriage, like a girl in a Millais painting. Outside the

169

rectory she had been prickly and gauche, and the natural warmth of her colouring had appeared irritatingly unsubtle beside the exquisite Violet.

'I should like you to tell me', said Violet, gazing straight ahead of her, 'why you have been so fearfully quiet.'

He was startled out of his reverie. 'Have I been quiet?'

'You know you have.'

'I do apologize.'

'I did not mean just now. I meant since you arrived from London. You have been – distracted.'

'I suppose I have.'

'Would you care to tell me why?'

He hesitated. 'It will sound absurd. But I'm having difficulty sleeping.'

She stared at him.

'I keep having nightmares. Though I can never remember what they're about. I told you it would sound absurd.'

She gave an irritated little laugh. 'I confess it does! Perhaps you ought to see Dr Young and ask him to give you a powder.'

' – Perhaps I ought.'

She rearranged a fold of her dust-coat. 'Is it – has it to do with Linley, do you think?'

A wagon had pulled up on the verge to let them pass, and the usual salutations were exchanged. As they entered the park, Robert wondered how he should answer. Violet was oddly defensive about their son, as if his death had put her in the wrong. 'I don't know,' he said carefully. 'I think perhaps it might. But also, in some way I don't yet understand, with the war.'

'The *war*?' she echoed in astonishment. Then understanding dawned, and she allowed herself the smallest moue of irritation. 'Oh Robert, *tell* me this has nothing to do with those wretched reports of yours in Whitehall!'

He cast her a curious glance. 'You know about those?'

'One can hardly avoid knowing, *mon cher*. Not when one is accosted by disgruntled statesmen at one's own house party.'

'Really? And what was one told?'

She gave the reins an impatient flick. 'I was given to understand that you spoke out rather too frankly against this – policy – or whatever it is – of clearing the veldt.'

'You mean, of burning farms, and rendering women and children homeless.'

'There is no need to couch it in such emotive terms.'

They rode on for a while in silence. Then Violet said: 'I am sorry, *mon cher,* but I regard your concerns as entirely misplaced. There is a war on, you are a captain in Her Majesty's Army, and you have orders to carry out—'

' – ah yes, and hundreds of others besides myself receive the same orders and carry them out without complaint, so why shouldn't I?'

A faint flush bloomed on her cheek. 'Is what I say unreasonable?'

'It's not unreasonable. It's merely beside the point.'

'Then what is the point?'

He met her eyes. He couldn't tell whether she genuinely wished to understand him, or whether she simply wanted to hear his argument so that she might knock it down. 'The point is,' he said slowly, 'I have become tired of waging war on women and children.'

'Oh well really! If you are going to descend to melodrama!'

'It's hardly melodrama. It's what I do.'

'But not you alone.'

'Why should that matter? I'm not responsible for other men's consciences, thank God. Only for my own.'

'But good heavens, Robert! These "women and children", as you call them – they are adequately cared for—'

'Oh yes, and some of them may even have a fighting chance of survival!'

Violet had reined in her horse and was staring at him. 'Is that any reason for you to speak to me in such a tone? I had not thought I deserved this from you!'

There was silence between them. For once, Robert was not inclined to apologize.

What the devil is the matter with me? he wondered, as they proceeded up the drive. He had had the same discussion with old Bowles, whom he'd finally collared in the churchyard that morning. The rector had trotted out precisely the same arguments as Violet, and Robert hadn't believed a word of it, but at least he hadn't fallen out with the old chap. A pity he had not been as fortunate with his own wife.

The Hall was drawing near before either of them spoke again. Then Violet said smoothly, 'Perhaps you are right, *mon cher. Au moins, en partie.* Perhaps you are simply a little fatigued.'

'I was just about to say the opposite – that I haven't enough to do. Perhaps I shall take old Bowles's advice, and fling myself into the harvest festivities like a good landlord.'

Violet shuddered. 'Oh Lord, the fête. Just as long as

you don't expect the landlord's wife to *fling* herself into them too.'

Robert looked down at her exquisite Madonna face. 'Of course not, my dear,' he said quietly. 'I never expect that.'

CHAPTER THIRTEEN

July, the Present

'I did you some notes on diphtheria,' said Stephen Hardy, dropping out of the pear tree and handing Sarah a sheet of A4. 'Yuk. *Grim.*'

'Thanks,' said Sarah. 'Is Alex in?'

He shook his head. 'But he said he'd be back for lunch.'

'Hell. This is getting ridiculous!'

He fished in his jeans pocket. 'He left the keys in case you wanted the car. And he said if you're going to the Savacentre can you get him a bottle of Laphroaig, a pound of Cheddar, and a packet of water biscuits.'

Bloody Alex. He hadn't been exactly forthcoming over the past five weeks. He was always too immersed in his own research to pay much attention to hers. Not that she needed help with the book, that was coming along fine. It was her own private research that had ground to a halt. 'When you see him,' she told Stephen, taking the keys, 'tell him I've *got* to talk to him, and there's no point putting me off because I won't give up.' She sighed. 'On second thoughts, don't bother. I'll catch him later. D'you want to come to the shops?'

Stephen frowned. 'I would, but I've got two days of observations to write up for the bat sanctuary.'

'OK. I'll see you later. Thanks for the notes.'

How like Stephen, she thought as she pushed the trolley around Sainsbury's, to have the keys to Alex's Saab and not even be tempted to sit in the driver's seat. And how like Alex to have left a ten-year-old in charge of his car, his house and his computer. 'This is the deal,' Stephen had explained to her on one of their walks. 'If anything goes wrong while I'm using the Mac, I've got to buy a new one. And on my current allowance I reckon that'd take me about thirty-nine years. So actually I'm pretty careful.'

She glanced at his immaculately typed précis of Gregson & McDonald. She hadn't asked for it but he'd done it anyway, as diphtheria was what had killed Linley Pearce-Staunton. '. . . *a gelatinous off-white pseudomembrane in the nasopharyngeal and/or laryngeal areas . . . exposes a raw bleeding surface over which the membrane rapidly re-forms . . . characteristic odour . . . fatality.*'

Poor little Linley. Grim indeed.

Everything to do with the ill-fated Linley fascinated Stephen. Here was a child only three years younger than himself who had died – actually *died* – for no other reason than that the doctors hadn't been able to save him. In Stephen's world of TV dramas, doctors pulled off miracles every day. Death happened to criminals, sidekicks, and the very old. Linley's bleak fate outraged his sense of justice. It was as if, he said indignantly, Linley had been thrown out of school, shut out from everyone's birthday, and forbidden everything for ever, without having done anything wrong. Which wasn't, Sarah thought, such a bad way of putting it.

Liking Stephen had come as a surprise.

They had met for the first time in the churchyard, the day after she decided to stay at Harlaston.

She had found it impossible to settle down and make a start on the book, so instead she had taken a battered architectural handbook from the Library and wandered down to St Hybald's.

'*Strikingly sumptuous nave and chancel*,' said the handbook, '. . . *with some good C15 stained glass of Christ Rising from the Tomb attended by angels (not all of them genuine), and a C14 wall-painting in the North Arcade of a crouching figure from a Weighing of Souls*'.

A weighing of souls.

She had sat in the front pew contemplating her grandfather's beautiful alabaster tablet. 'You thought you'd got away with it, didn't you?' she murmured. 'You thought you'd covered your tracks. Well you can't hide from me. I'll find out the truth. And then I'll put you in my book for everyone to read.'

The blank immaculate stone gave nothing away.

Outside, the churchyard was vivid with wych-lime and elder, the emerald grass studded with yellow hawkweed. Swifts wheeled and darted about the Pearce-Staunton mausoleum. According to the handbook, it had been built by the Seventeenth Baroness, Aubrey's extraordinary 'Grandmama Adela', who had also masterminded the building of the Hall. '*A violently idiosyncratic High Victorian* tour de force *built of pink Aberdeen granite in the manner of a Doric temple . . . it houses two amazingly overblown*

176

effigies of the Seventeenth Baron and Baroness . . . truly, this was one woman's bid for immortality.' The baron was in full dress uniform, bizarrely adopting the pose of the Dying Gladiator, while Adela reclined, like a Saint expiring in Ecstasy, beneath a congregation of weeping seraphs.

It was all very picturesque, and would make a terrific cover for the book. The trouble was, Adela was no longer just an entertainingly crazy peeress with delusions of grandeur. She was Sarah's ancestor. She was the woman who had raised Sarah's grandfather from the age of five, and had quite possibly passed on to him her own peculiar brand of egotism, thereby setting in train the events which had led to the seduction of Charity Fosdyke and the birth of Sarah's father.

The mausoleum was not just another colourful location shot. Her *grandfather* lay in the underground chamber beneath it. Her genes, crumbling to dust inside these walls.

She clambered down the ivy-choked steps which led to the chamber. At the bottom, rusty iron doors bristled with Victorian symbolism. Broken lilies drooping over scythes; snatches of poetry on tattered pennants. She was picking at a moss-covered panel with her ball-point when an indignant voice behind her asked what she thought she was doing. She turned, and came face to face with the boy she had seen talking to the stone lions at Harlaston. He was so like his father it was heartbreaking. The same heavy brows, the same belligerent thrust of the lower lip. 'What are you *doing*?' he said again.

'Reading,' she said shortly.

'No you weren't. You were scraping bits *off*. I saw you.'

'It's only moss. There's an inscription underneath that I want to read.'

'Why?'

'Because', she said with elaborate patience, 'this is where my grandfather's buried, and I want to see what it says. Now please go away and let me get on with it.'

He didn't. He sat behind her on the steps reading the inscription over her shoulder. She could hear him breathing unselfconsciously through his mouth. He smelled of chocolate biscuits and Wright's coal-tar soap, both of which she later discovered he loved. After a while he said, '*My* great-grandfather's under an ash tree next to the south porch.'

'I know. He's next to my grandmother. They were brother and sister.' She put down her notebook and turned to face him. 'You're Stephen Hardy, aren't you? I'm Sarah Dalton. We're cousins a few times removed.' She would have liked to have left it at that, but she didn't trust his mother to have told him the unvarnished truth. 'I'm also your ex-father's ex-girlfriend. And in case you're wondering, I became his girlfriend *after* he divorced your mother.'

He met that with an unblinking stonewall which would have made Dominic proud. Then he said, 'It's just that you were scraping bits off. They take ages to grow.'

'What do?'

'Lichens. That's not moss. It's lichen. I'm doing a project on it. There's this running battle between the genealogists and ecologists. I support the ecologists.' To prove his point he held up a Bart Simpson exercise book.

'Lichens are important.'

178

Important to whom, she was tempted to ask. But she had read somewhere that one shouldn't use sarcasm on children. Besides, that was the sort of thing Dominic would have said.

In a rare moment of openness Alex had summed up his nephew. 'He's into ecology, history and disease. In fact, anything which explains why plants and animals and especially people do what they do. The divorce hit him pretty hard. He doesn't understand why things like that happen. I suppose he's trying to make sense of it all.'

Stephen was peering down the steps. 'Have you been inside?'

'Not yet. But I can see through the cracks.'

'What's it like?'

'Dark. Mouldy. Piles of coffins and urns.'

'Yuk.' He looked at her hopefully.

'Some day, but not right now. I'm hungry and I've got a crick in my neck.'

As they were walking back through the churchyard, he asked what she was doing at Harlaston, and she told him what she knew about their ancestors. She could see him mentally bracketing her grandfather with the only other adulterer he knew, and making up his mind to back Lady Harlaston to the hilt. 'My lot are luckier than *them*,' he said with a scornful toss of the head in the direction of the Hall.

'Why?'

'Because *they're* all down in that horrible stinky old crypt. Jeez. Grim. Nicer up here where you can see what's going on.'

That had been over a month ago. Since then, she had found to her surprise that she liked Stephen more and more as she got to know him. She also felt sorry for him. Alex seemed to be the only person who spent any time with him.

But, at times, a warning note would sound at the back of her mind. Be careful, it said. This is Dominic's son.

Sainsbury's was quiet at this time of day. The girl at the checkout gave Sarah's card a contemptuous swipe and fixed her eyes on the middle distance while the receipt was printing out. She had inch-long fingernails painted lemon yellow, and she had served Sarah half a dozen times without ever saying a word. It had become a game to try to get her to open her mouth.

'Pretty colour,' Sarah said, packing Alex's provisions in a separate bag. She was rewarded with a suspicious stare.

Her mother would have said that propitiating shop assistants was proof that Sarah had been on her own too long. She didn't know the half of it. She would have been horrified to learn that the only people her daughter had talked to since coming to Harlaston – apart from herself, Stephen and (occasionally) Alex – had been the cleaners, half a dozen clerks at various county records offices, and Nick, once, when he had called to say that her car still wasn't ready.

'You've got this appetite for being alone,' Mrs Dalton had said in one of her phone calls, which had become longer and more frequent since she told Sarah about her grandfather. 'I don't know where you get it from. God knows your father wasn't like that and thank heavens your brother isn't either.'

What she didn't know was that it was no longer an appetite, it was a necessity, for Sarah had lost her nerve. She didn't want to go anywhere or see anyone, and she had an overriding sense that she wouldn't be able to cope if she did. She knew it was irrational – probably just a combination of pneumonia and Dominic – but that did nothing to increase her confidence. It seemed unbelievable that she had once held down a job in television, or that she ever would again.

Sometimes she wondered if Alex guessed what had happened to her. The day after she met Stephen in the churchyard, he had ambled up to the Hall and suggested they might convert the Jade Ante-Room into a proper study. He helped her set up her laptop and printer on a student's desk in the bay window, then wandered off to the Science Complex and came back with a small green filing cabinet which he put beside the desk. He found a spare kettle in the refectory, and then added a row of Snoopy mugs and three willow-patterned tins containing tea, coffee and powdered milk. Finally he brought in a television and a VCR from the refectory, and two sagging blue armchairs from the bursar's office. 'There,' he said, dusting off his hands. 'A bolt-hole to be proud of.' His tone was neutral, so she let it pass.

'And what have you got to show for all your weeks in purdah?' Shirley Dalton had said in her last phone call. 'Are you doing anything at all on that book they're paying you to write?'

'Yes, actually, Mum, six hours a day. I've already got as far as the Civil War, so you don't need to worry about it. Any research on the grandparents is strictly in my own time.'

'Six hours a day? You're working too hard! If you're not careful you'll have a relapse.'

But what *did* Sarah have to show for her spare-time efforts? Not a great deal. In fact, five weeks on, her grandparents were as elusive as ever.

To begin with she had been optimistic. She had Aubrey's family history as a starting-point, and Aubrey was her great hope, for she had worked out that he had probably known the Nineteenth Baron at first hand. If he'd been middle-aged in 1948 when he wrote his account – born, say, some time in the 1880s – he would have been about fifteen years younger than the Pearce-Staunton boys. Maybe he had visited them. After all, Robert and Spencer had been his cousins.

But when it came to Robert, Aubrey's account provided only the bare bones of a carefully expurgated life. '*A progressive landowner, Fellow of the Royal Society, decorated officer . . . awarded the Distinguished Service Order at Suakin in 1888 . . . resigned his commission on the death of his brother and returned to England . . . despite crippling death duties and widespread agricultural recession, kept the ailing estate intact . . . Served in South Africa from 1900–1903 with the 2nd Battalion of the Lincolnshire Regiment . . . mentioned in despatches after an incident in the Orange River Colony in December 1900 . . . expeditions to Peru and Ecuador between 1903 and 1905 . . . served in India from 1905 till 1915 . . . After Cambrai, awarded the Military Cross . . . left no surviving issue . . .*'

Diligently, Sarah had followed up the leads buried in Aubrey's account. From the regimental histories she had learned that whatever her grandfather's other failings, he had not lacked physical courage – although, tantalizingly, the records for the years 1903–1914 had been lost in the Blitz, and all her enquiries to the various private archives had so far gone unanswered. From the Royal Society she had learned that he had dabbled in science: the expeditions to South America had produced three new varieties of orchid. And from the memorials he had commissioned in St Hybald's, she guessed that he had not been afraid to break the family tradition which decreed that only those killed in battle rated a tablet inside the church. He had commemorated his son Linley with a medallion by Sir Edward Brock, bearing a child's head in exquisite bas-relief, and his brother's tablet also bore a bas-relief, this time of a saddle, bridle and hunting-horn, with a stark inscription: '. . . *killed in a hunting accident, aged twenty-six; Cat.101 l.9.*' It took Sarah a while to trace the reference. '. . . *Atque in perpetuum, frater, ave atque vale.*' Catullus's grief-drenched farewell to his dead brother.

So her grandfather had known his classics, hadn't been afraid to flout tradition, had quite possibly loved his brother and his son, and hadn't believed in an afterlife: '. . . *and in eternity, brother, hail and farewell*' didn't sound like a man who expected to be reunited with his loved ones in the next world.

But that was as far as she had got three weeks ago, and since then she had come up with no new leads. Astonishingly, she could find no photographs or papers relating to the Nineteenth Baron or his wife. All the family memorabilia had apparently disappeared in an auction in 1918. The two Singer Sargents had been sold along with the rest, but according to the guidebook, after Lady Harlaston's death in 1947, Aubrey had tracked them down, bought them, and finally bequeathed them to the college.

Sarah's own father's papers had literally gone up in smoke. Her mother had told her, with a shade of defiance, that when he died she had only kept his cuttings books and their marriage certificate. A

183

marriage certificate, her tone implied, was more than *his* father could have managed. For several nights Sarah had lain awake picturing bundles of letters consigned to the flames, until her mother told her not to be ridiculous, there hadn't been anything like that or she'd have kept it, she wasn't daft.

There were no relatives left alive. Robert's wife Violet had been an only child, and Aubrey had died a bachelor in a rest home in Hurstpierpoint in 1972. War, illness and celibacy had claimed the rest of the family. As far as Sarah could tell, she and Nick were the only surviving descendants.

The quest for her grandmother was even worse. There was simply nothing. No photographs, no letters, no traceable relatives (apart from Alex and Dominic). No mention of her in the parish records. The brick wall erected by the Pearce-Stauntons to keep out the scandal remained intact. Poor people didn't leave traces when rich people didn't want them to.

Alex was her last remaining hope.

For heaven's sake, she thought, as she drove back to Hynton, his grandfather was Charity's *brother*. He must know something. Beside, she could hardly ask Dominic.

As she pulled up in front of the Old Rectory she was mentally composing a strongly worded note to leave on the door, when Alex came out onto the porch. He wore hiking boots and had a rucksack on one shoulder.

'Alex,' she said without preamble, 'we will make a date *now* for that talk about the family. It won't take long and I absolutely will not take no for an answer.'

'How about now?'

She blinked.

184

He eyed the groceries in the back of the Saab. 'That stuff will keep, won't it? If Stephen remembered to ask about the cheese, we can have lunch.'

She sometimes forgot that he had been a lawyer. Like his brother he knew the value of a well-timed concession.

CHAPTER FOURTEEN

'I don't think I'll be much help,' said Alex, clearing a space for her on the least cluttered sofa. Stephen was in the kitchen, noisily washing celery to go with the cheese. 'What do you want to know?'

'Everything you know about your grandfather and his family. And obviously mine too. Where they lived, whom they knew, what they were like.'

He sat opposite her with his legs crossed at the ankle and one arm along the back of the sofa, as unselfconscious as Stephen. Dominic, she thought, would have presented a more polished front: head tilted back, eyes narrowed in thought. But then, Dominic had always been intensely self-aware. It was one of the things which had attracted her in the beginning.

Stop it, she told herself. Stop making comparisons.

'I really don't know very much,' Alex said, watching Stephen place a mug of celery on the table, where it dripped all over the crackers. 'My grandfather died before I was born. There's a wedding photo somewhere. I'll get it in a minute.'

'But you must know *something*. I mean, didn't your mother ever talk about her father?'

He thought about that. 'She used to say he was *odd*.

And that *his* mother was *mad.*' He gave a twisted smile. 'My mother didn't have much time for mental illness. She and Dad were pretty much of the "pull yourself together" school of psychiatry.'

Odd. Mad. No time for mental illness.

A memory surfaced from the Sunday Lunch Disaster. Alex's mother describing his girlfriend's 'mood swings' while he was out of earshot. 'So *sad*,' she had said, 'so *sad* that Helen hasn't got her feet more firmly on the ground.' Harriet Hardy had been a practical woman, proud of her ability to call a spade a spade. It had occurred to Sarah at the time that she used the one-syllable word like a lid, slamming it shut on the tangle of human woes.

Perhaps Alex thought so too. He was gazing ahead in abstracted silence.

Mad. Sad.

Even in her early twenties, Helen had been in and out of therapy, and over the years she had got steadily worse. According to Nick, the divorce had been 'bloody', and Alex had blamed himself. He looked as though he was still doing so.

'And was he?' Sarah said. 'Odd, I mean.'

Alex surfaced, and nodded. 'Oh yes, I think so. At least, in a conventional sense. But he wasn't mentally ill. He was deaf in one ear, that's all, and in those days that sort of thing isolated you. Especially if you were poor.' He spread his hands. 'He probably just withdrew into himself. That's what your father thought.'

'*My* father?' Sarah stared at him.

He nodded and took a stick of celery from the mug. Stephen, quietly butchering the Cheddar, cast Sarah a curious glance.

'When did you talk about this with my father?'

'He gave me lunch a few times when I was about fourteen. I was going through a bit of a rough patch. Didn't he tell you?'

'No. He – no.' She coloured. He wouldn't have, would he? One didn't mention the Other Side in front of Shirley Dalton.

Alex didn't seem to notice. 'I'm afraid I wasn't very good company. I was hating every minute of Winterbourne, and didn't spare him a single detail.'

'Wasn't that the same school Dominic went to?' Stephen asked.

Alex nodded.

'Why did you hate it?'

'No privacy, too much noise, too many drugs.' To Sarah he added, 'I was getting up the courage to change to a grammar school. Your father helped a lot.'

'How?' said Sarah and Stephen together.

'Mainly by listening.' He smiled. 'Thankless task. I talked for hours. One thing I remember, though. He said, for Christ's sake just do it, and if it doesn't work, at least you'll have tried.'

'And did you?' asked Stephen. 'Change schools?'

'Yes. But don't get any ideas. You *like* St Cyprian's.'

Stephen squirmed, and tried to hide a grin.

'It was then that he mentioned my grandfather,' Alex went on. 'He said something about William Fosdyke going his own quiet way and learning not to care what other people thought.'

Suddenly Sarah didn't want to hear any more. It felt all wrong, having to ask Alex what her own father had said. In a strange way it made her jealous. She had the same prickly, hot-and-cold sensation she'd felt when Dominic told her about Caroline Harris.

From the way he was looking at her, Alex had guessed what she was feeling.

She said, 'Do you remember anything else?'

'I wish I did. But I'm afraid I was too self-centred to concentrate on anyone but myself.'

'Didn't my father say anything about my grandmother?'

'I'm sorry, no.' He paused. Then he said gently, 'And he really never talked about her to your mother?'

She shook her head. 'I told you. She hated the whole idea. A bit extreme, but that's Mum. I suppose I can hardly blame her. I used to think it was the class thing. But *illegitimacy*! She must have found that pretty hard to take.'

'What's illegitimacy?' said Stephen.

'Look it up,' said Alex automatically.

Sarah twisted her watch-strap, and frowned. 'Dad would have told me if he'd lived long enough. He wanted to. In fact, that was one of the last things he said to me.' She drew a breath which turned into a gulp.

Stephen blinked.

Alex contemplated his cheese and cracker. 'I'll go and find that photograph.'

She had recovered by the time he came back. The photograph he handed her showed a solemn young couple on their wedding day. It bore an illegible photographer's signature across the lower right-hand corner, and had been faded around the edges to make a tasteful oval. Judging from the bride's cloche hat and uneven hemline, it had been taken some time in the 1920s.

Sarah studied the young man's face. 'My God,' she

murmured, 'I had no idea. He was gorgeous. Like a young Gary Cooper.'

The young man was in his early thirties, and clearly ill at ease in his best suit. He had thick, wavy fair hair, large light-filled eyes, and an extraordinarily beautiful mouth. It was not the face of a half-deaf village stonemason, but that of a young World War One flying ace, or the first officer over the top at the Somme. No wonder his bride looked so smug.

Alex said: 'I've just remembered something else. I have a great-aunt – well, more of a great-grand-aunt, and she's only related by marriage. But she might remember something.' He handed her a Post-it sticker bearing a scribbled address.

Sarah looked at it in disbelief. Why the hell hadn't he mentioned this before? What *else* might he remember, given time?

'Sarah – ' he looked thoughtful. 'What you said about your mother. Class-consciousness and illegitimacy. I'm not sure that's the whole story.'

'What do you mean?'

'Because *my* mother was just the same. She hated anyone referring to your grandparents. And she wasn't someone who cared about class.'

Oh, no? thought Sarah, in a waspish echo of her own mother. Like Mrs Dalton, Alex's mother had moved up in the world when she married, but she had left her own family firmly behind her. Shirley Dalton, on the other hand, had had a house-painter father and a mother who had cooked at the local comprehensive, and it had never occurred to her to forget about either.

Alex went on, 'In some ways, your mother and mine are – were – quite alike. Both intensely practical people, and pretty brisk when it comes to what my mother used to call "high-flown emotion".'

'What are you getting at?'

He looked uncomfortable. 'This is difficult. Of course, I don't know what your parents' marriage was like. But as for mine, well, they were affectionate to each other, but more like friends than lovers.'

She stared at him.

Stephen's mouth fell open.

'You see,' Alex said abruptly, 'I think what your grandparents had together made people like your mother and mine feel inadequate. No, inadequate's the wrong word. Deprived.'

'But – he – Lord Harlaston – he seduced her.'

'God, no. Who told you that?'

'My mother. But that's what happened, isn't it? He seduced her and packed her off to France to have the child.'

He was shaking his head. 'That's not what I gathered from your father at all. Look, I don't know how it turned out in the end, but I got the impression that for a time at least, there was real feeling between them.'

'What do you mean?'

He looked at her. 'They were in love.'

' – *What*?'

'That's what I gathered from your father.'

There was silence in the sitting room.

'I think *that's* what your mother couldn't take,' said Alex. 'Not the illegitimacy. The love.'

CHAPTER FIFTEEN

Saturday 25 August 1900

When Charity saw Lord Harlaston again it was at the Hynton fête.

It was the first time she had been in Harlaston park. When she entered the drive and the great green expanse suddenly opened out around her, she felt an absurd desire to run back to Hynton. Ahead of her lay a shimmering lake bordered by tall poplars and spanned by a broad stone bridge. At one end, an octagonal ice house hid in a grove of walnut trees; at the other stood a white marble boathouse like a miniature castle. On the grass by the lakeside, green canvas stalls clustered about an enormous blue and white striped pavilion. Red, white and blue pennants fluttered in the breeze. And, far in the distance, the Hall floated in majesty: beautiful, unattainable and remote.

'Very properly done,' Mrs Fosdyke said bravely, clutching her husband's arm. 'I doubt if Moxby or Stainton Hamer could put on anything as fine.'

Lord and Lady Harlaston arrived just before tea-time. Before then, the Fosdykes watched the foot-races and the high-jump, the magic-lantern show, the Chinese conjuror from Grantham, and the cricket match between Hynton and the Hall. Mrs Fosdyke was at her best, bolstered by the thought of Lady Harlaston's magazine, her daughter's position at the rectory, and her new collar of Nottingham lace. To everyone's relief, Will was unusually subdued.

Sam Webb was barely in evidence. Apart from a hurried nod on his way to oversee the paddle-boat rides, he left Charity alone, although there seemed to be an understanding among the other single men that they should keep their distance. His behaviour vexed Mrs Fosdyke more than it did her daughter. Charity was still undecided about Samuel Webb, and secretly relieved when he left her in peace.

At four o'clock a line of carriages was seen coming down the drive, and shortly afterwards the crowd drew apart to let Lord and Lady Harlaston and their guests through.

Lady Harlaston was dressed entirely in white, as she had been when Charity had first seen her outside the rectory. This time she wore a pouched Russian blouse with a tiny grosgrain bolero, a bell-shaped skirt and a huge windmill hat with bird of paradise feathers and a white spotted veil. She kept her eyes on some remote prospect known only to herself, and her gloved finger-tips barely touched her husband's arm.

Her lack of expression enchanted Mrs Fosdyke. But then, everything about the gentry enchanted Mrs Fosdyke – from the gentlemen's panama hats and white linen suits to the Dowager Lady Lydford's magnificently rigid black silk dress. She pronounced Lady Harlaston's figure 'Quite, quite perfect. *Look* at that bosom!' But although she admired the cut of Lord

Harlaston's uniform and judged him a 'very fine-looking gentleman', she thought he was 'far too lean, and ought to wax his moustaches'. Fortunately, her remarks went unheard by all except her family.

Charity watched the couple's slow procession towards the tea pavilion, and was both relieved and disappointed when they passed her by without recognition. It was obscurely upsetting to be so close to them. They seemed like some separate species of humanity: taller, slenderer, and more beautiful than everyone else.

The Moxby Friendly Society band struck up, and folk followed the gentry to the tea pavilion, and its six long rows of trestle-tables. The lower cottagers from Hynton, Moxby and Stainton Hamer took the first row, the unmarried labourers the second, and the third was occupied by farmers and smallholders. The Fosdykes shared the domain of the better villagers, while in the fifth row, Dr Young and his wife headed a mixture of curates, nursemaids, and the children of high-table guests. Among these Charity spotted Theo and Flora Bowles, silently working their way through a strange meal of cold sausages and peppermint rock. The final row was reserved for the Hall staff, with Dickon Webb at its head. Sam Webb's place remained empty throughout the meal.

According to Mrs Goldsbrow, this year's spread was particularly lavish. There were hams, cold chickens, veal pies, roast sirloin, stuffed chine and jellied tongue, with plum duff and Dundee cake to follow. Drink flowed freely: lemonade for the children, sweet milky tea for the women, and great foaming cans of beer for the men. 'Now Alice, let me *be*,' Jack Fosdyke told his wife in a rare show of spirit, as he recklessly poured himself another half-tumblerful. 'Harvest-home feast comes but once a year.'

To her annoyance, Charity was unable to take pleasure in the meal. She wasn't hungry. She simply wanted to get through it and go home. Her mother put down her lack of appetite to a growing fondness for Sam Webb, and was delighted.

'Charity,' said Will suddenly, towards the end of the meal. 'Where are all the peahens?'

'What?' she said abstractedly.

'The peahens. You know. We saw one by the melon-beds on our way to Mrs Jordan's.'

'Oh. You mean the peacocks.'

'*No*. The pea*hens*!'

His voice was so strained that she looked up in surprise. Above his tight ha'penny collar his face was flushed.

She leaned across the table and wiped his forehead with her handkerchief. 'You've eaten too much. You'll get a bellyache if you're not careful.'

'But where are the *nests*?'

'How should I know? I don't think they've got any, this time of year.'

Will's lips went white. He stared down at the pink and brown humbugs on his plate. 'They *got* to have nests,' he said loudly, just as the band stopped playing with a flourish.

'*Hush!*' hissed Mrs Fosdyke across the table. 'Can't you see the parson's just stood up?'

The parson's speech was composed entirely of thank-you's: to Lord and Lady Harlaston, the Fête Committee, the band, God, and Lord Lydford for judging the vegetables. Lord Lydford's speech came next and sent many people to sleep. Mostly they woke up when Lord Harlaston got to his feet to present the prizes, and toast the harvest and Her Majesty. He didn't speak for long and everyone laughed at his jokes: the women because he was handsome and the men because he had been generous with the beer. Charity thought he looked tired, and did an excellent job of pretending to enjoy himself.

Lady Harlaston sat through the speeches without smiling, and clapped her gloved hands twice at the end of each one. Charity wondered why she had bothered to pin up her veil, when she ate nothing and merely sipped a cup of tea.

'Afternoon, Miss Fosdyke,' said a familiar voice behind her. It was Sam Webb, cool and well-brushed as always. His face was innocent of apology. Plainly he saw nothing wrong in ignoring her all afternoon. Perhaps he assumed she was thankful for any time he could spare her.

He turned to her mother. 'Mrs Fosdyke, I wonder if I might take Miss Fosdyke for a stroll after tea.'

Mrs Fosdyke opened her mouth to reply, but her daughter folded her napkin and stood up without looking at him. 'It'll have to be later,' she said crisply. 'I've got duties to attend to.'

After a pause, Sam stood back to let her pass. The curl of his lip told her that he accepted his punishment with reasonable grace.

It had become oppressively hot in the pavilion, and she was glad to get out in the breeze. Her duties could wait. First she would take a stroll along the lake. Perhaps some time on her own would dispel this prickling sense of discontent.

She had the waterside to herself. Most people were still at their tea, and only a handful strolled between the stalls, or emerged discreetly from the 'refreshment' tents tucked behind the trees. The air was thick with the smell of beer and roast beef and trampled grass. Beneath a clump of willows, a group of grooms smoked and sucked their teeth, and argued about how fast Lord Lydford's motor could go. Horses dozed in clouds of flies, their manes and tails braided with wilting ribbons.

She started down the avenue of poplars. It was deliciously cool. Wood pigeons cooed in the branches, and now and then she heard the plash of a mallard landing on the lake. Through a tunnel of green shade she could see the white glimmer of the boathouse. She began to feel better.

She had almost reached the boathouse when she saw the man and woman standing in the deep shade under the eaves.

The man had his back to her. He wore a tweed cap, a short drill jacket with a farm-worker's red neckerchief, breeches, and heavy workboots. All she could see of the woman was a pink sprigged frock, a straw hat of the cheapest sort, and two rough countrywoman's hands clasped about the man's neck.

The man held the woman tightly in his arms. Her fingers were deep in his sandy hair, kneading the back of his neck. Mouth strained against mouth, hip against hip, thigh against thigh. Then he bent to lift her, and Charity saw the powerful flex of his shoulders, his buttocks straining his breeches. The strength in his gaitered calves. The woman hooked one leg about his thigh and her petticoats fell back to reveal a broad expanse of pink flesh above a coarse black stocking.

Charity knew neither of them. They were simply a man and woman of the lower sort taking their pleasure in a secluded patch of shade. She turned on her heel and left them to their business. After she had gone fifty yards, she stopped for breath. She pressed her back against a poplar and stared up into the shivering emerald leaves. Her cheeks burned. Her heart was racing. She kept seeing the tautness of the man's shoulders beneath his jacket. The woman's fingers deep in his hair.

She knew what went on between men and women when the candle was snuffed, but she hadn't had much in the way of sweethearts herself. You didn't, when you had a mother like hers. There had been Mr Plaistow at school when she was thirteen, whom she had loved from afar for his short-sighted blue eyes and his beautiful, beautiful hair. She used to watch it flop down over his forehead as he sat at his desk, its soft brown waves so clean and shining that she wanted to stroke it as she would have stroked a newborn kitten. Then, when she was sixteen, a letter-cutter who worked with her father took a fancy to her. He never spoke, but one Sunday he presented himself at their cottage in his best suit with a chrysanthemum in his buttonhole. Mrs Fosdyke sent him packing and he didn't come again.

After that there was only Tom Logan, when she was eighteen.

Tom Logan lived in Sedgefield with his parents and worked as a hedge-layer. He was big and shy and never acknowledged Charity's existence, but one July evening when she was walking back from Tilburne, he plucked up his courage and jumped on her from behind a haystack. He was almost as terrified as she, and his fumbling attempt to claim her came to an abrupt end when she sank her hatpin into his buttock.

But Tom Logan had been utterly unlike what she had witnessed behind the boathouse. Tom Logan had knocked the breath out of her, and jabbed his elbow painfully into her breast. He had smelled of sweat, onions and stale cheese, and had bellowed like a bull when she stuck him with the hatpin.

The couple behind the boathouse had been struggling too, but struggling *together* – in an intense wordless world which contained them alone.

She put the back of her hand against the tree-trunk and felt its roughness against her skin. She wondered what it would be like to be held as that labourer had held his sweetheart. To sink her fingers into a man's hair and feel his mouth on hers.

'*The Better Poor*', said the heading on the lengthy handwritten list which Mrs Bowles had given Charity. It was split into four columns: '*Infirm*', '*Indispos'd*', '*To be encourg'd*', and 'Not *deserving, but in gt need*'. Some names had notes scribbled beside them: '*avoid cheese*'; '*no hardbake (teeth)*'; and, surprisingly, 'no beer!' beside the name of Sam Webb's elderly father, Tom. Against each name was a precise description of what they should receive and in what quantity.

Mrs Bowles was right: plating up the leftovers was a formidable task, despite plenty of help. Even Will had offered to take a box to old Mr Pickering behind the stables. But by half past six all but the most fly-blown bits and pieces had been sent on their way.

Journeymen had begun to dismantle the pavilion, and the roads to Hynton and Moxby were dotted with tired little groups straggling homewards. The lakeside had the exhausted air of departed festivities. Scraps of bunting rolled in the breeze, and a lady's hat-feather fluttered in the reeds.

The gentry had been the first to leave. Charity, working in what Mrs Bowles called 'the field kitchen', had stopped to watch Lord and Lady Harlaston's brougham start up the drive. As it moved off, Lord Harlaston had turned to his wife and made some remark, and Lady Harlaston had nodded once, without looking at him.

Charity thought: she doesn't even need to look at him, she knows him so well. That's what it's like for people who love one another. They understand each other's every gesture, their every feeling.

The thought made her feel inexpressibly lonely. She put down the paper bag she had been filling with ginger biscuits and went to the women's refreshment tent to wash her face.

By the time she got back, Sam Webb was waiting for her. He was lighting a Woodbine, holding it casually between thumb and forefinger in a manner much copied by the Hynton boys. He didn't ask if she minded him smoking, and she guessed he meant to pay her back for keeping him waiting.

He offered her his arm and she took it without a word. 'Your mum and dad went home,' he said. 'I told them I'd have you back by half past seven.'

They walked in silence towards the bridge. It occurred to Charity that her mother would be delighted if she could see them now: they were behaving with such propriety that they might as well be brother and sister.

She thought of the couple behind the boathouse and tried to imagine herself doing such things with Sam Webb. She couldn't. The fact that he was good-looking didn't help at all. Maybe if he was taller and thinner, and darker.

Stop it, she told herself. You're being ridiculous, even thinking of it. You're like a schoolgirl with a crush on the teacher. Just because he's rich and handsome, like a prince in a fairy tale. You should know better, you're nineteen years old. Besides, it's not fair on Sam.

To break the silence she said, 'You missed a splendid tea.'

He shrugged. 'I'm not a great one for fancy food. 'Sides, I was called out. Some lads got into the Screed and baited old Corlett's shorthorn.'

'Were they hurt?'

His lip curled. 'Not by the bull they weren't. But they won't forget the feel of my belt in a hurry.'

'Will used to go bull-baiting in Sedgefield. I don't think it ever did the bull any harm.'

He snorted to signify his doubts about her brother's ability to cause harm to anything.

She was nettled. 'He was good at it. He's a fast runner.'

'Really.'

Again they walked in silence. Then Charity said, 'Come to think of it, where *is* Will?'

Sam looked irritated. 'How should I know?'

She thought for a moment. 'He was very quiet all day. At tea he looked downright ill.'

'Must of gone home with your mum and dad.'

'But you said he didn't.'

'I never.'

'Yes you did, you said, "your mum and dad went home". You didn't mention Will.'

'Well what if I didn't? Who cares? Can't the lad find his own way home?'

'It's what he gets up to before he does that worries me.'

He stubbed out his cigarette and lit another. 'That's his lookout.'

Suddenly Charity said, 'Where do they keep the peahens?'

'*What?*'

'The peahens. Peafowl.'

Sam stared at her.

'I just remembered. He was asking about them. Where do they keep them?'

'Nowhere, this time of year. They just wander about. Why? What are you on about now?'

She caught her lip between her teeth. 'Is there anything in the Bible about peahens?'

After Will left Mr Pickering's cottage he started back down the service road. But instead of going down to the junction with the Tilburne road, when he reached the stables he skirted the reserve garden and came out into a patch of waste ground behind the greenhouses. The shadows were lengthening. The clock in the clock-yard had just struck seven.

Mr Pickering had said that when the peahens were laying, they had to be put in the sheds behind the greenhouses. He said it was the devil of a job fetching them in because you had to seek out each nest wherever the wretched birds had made them, in hedges or old barrels or whatnot, then steal up behind them and cover them with a black cloth. Then you had to carry them, nest and all, into the sheds.

Will had listened politely, although his only concern was the whereabouts of the sheds.

Above the rot-heaps the hot air shimmered. The

pungent smell of compost caught at his throat. Shading his eyes with his hand, he scanned the greenhouses for signs of movement. Nothing. A stroke of luck. The greenhouses were out of bounds. He'd be for it if he was caught.

But it wasn't the thought of a thrashing that made his heart jerk unevenly in his chest. It was the thought of what Ned, Luke and Jim would do to him if he turned up next Friday without a peahen's egg on a string.

Tribute, Ned had called it, with that glint in his eye. Got to prove you got the balls to be one of us.

But there won't *be* any eggs, Will had protested. Not this time of year.

'Course there will, said Ned. Peahens are special. Not like other birds. Peahens lay all year round.

And Will had believed him, because he knew in his heart that peahens were indeed magic birds, who could do things that other birds could not.

Tribute, Ned had said. You bring it on Friday, or else, Moley. Mowdy-warp.

Jim and Luke had clutched their sides laughing.

CHAPTER SIXTEEN

Robert wandered out onto the south terrace and lit a cigar. Perhaps tobacco would dull the throbbing in his temples. It was his own fault. At the fête he been bored, and had overdone the champagne. But he almost welcomed the headache. He knew what had caused it and he knew how to get rid of it. These days, that made a refreshing change.

Shadows stretched across the lawns. The Lion Steps glowed in the evening sun. Apart from Tully and Max panting at his feet, he had the grounds to himself. Violet had gone to her room to rest, and most of the staff were at their evening meal.

He wandered past the sleeping lion and into the Rose Walk. Tully clattered happily after him, but wise old Max thumped his tail and stayed where he was.

The Rose Walk. A tunnel of scarlet, coral and peach, glowing like sunspots against closed eyelids. Sweet, drenching perfume catching at his throat. How odd, he thought, that Violet, who deplored excess, should prefer this walk above all others in the grounds. Although perhaps it wasn't so odd after all. An admiration for roses, even in excess, was *appropriate*.

And to be appropriate was the chief aim of his wife's existence.

He reached the arbour at the end of the walk. From here he could go no further, unless he chose to scramble up the banks on an unconventional route to the arboretum. Or unless, he remembered suddenly, the old path was still there behind the arbour. Winding through a thicket of elder and blackthorn before emerging onto the service road opposite the stables. He hadn't thought about it in years. Hadn't been down it since he was a boy, when he and Spencer had used it as a short cut to the stables if they had forgotten to order their horses the night before.

The path was still there. Tully crashed joyfully ahead, unable to believe his good fortune.

He found the stable-yard deserted. Horses dozed with their heads over the doors of their loose-boxes. His old grey cob, Xerxes, whinnied a welcome.

'Hello, old boy,' Robert said softly. 'Too hot for you, mm? I know. Poor old chap.'

The cob's amber eyes were liquid and resigned. His nose was warm grey velvet in Robert's palm.

Walker the head groom came hurrying across the yard, wiping his moustache with his handkerchief and looking cross. 'Were you wanting anything, my lord?'

'No, Walker. I didn't mean to take you from your meal. I just came to – to see how Xerxes is getting on.'

'On the mend, my lord. Fetlock's still hot, but my bread poultice is doing the trick.'

'Ah, good. Good.'

Walker waited in pointed silence. At this hour, and without having ordered horse or carriage, Robert's presence in the yard was tantamount to trespass.

'Well,' said Robert, 'go back to your meal. I don't need anything else.'

'Very good, my lord.'

The groom watched until Robert was clear of his domain.

Outside the stables Robert hesitated. He didn't want to return to the house, but if he continued down the service road he would pass the gardeners' cottages, and doubtless encounter the same polite resentment he had received from his groom. He could scarcely blame them. He never came this way. They must be wondering what was wrong. He could not have told them, for he didn't know himself. Except that nothing and nowhere seemed right any more.

I am out of sorts, he thought, whatever that means. Old Bowles would tell me to count my blessings, and Dr Young would give me a sleeping-powder. And Violet? What would Violet do, save agree with them both, and suggest that I take more rest?

Whistling for Tully, he rejoined the path as it wandered off into the cool of the elder wood.

The wood smelled of nettles and leaf-mould and dust. A closed world, timeless and secretive. Spencer felt extraordinarily close. A twelve-year-old Spencer, scouting with an eleven-year-old Robert. 'Not *that* way, you muff,' Spencer said. '*Never* the same path there as back! We've got to confuse the enemy.' 'Muff yourself to the nth power,' retorted his brother. 'We haven't even decided who the enemy is, so how do we know what's going to confuse him?'

Amazingly, the old railway carriage was still there in the clearing, although the tide of rubbish had risen against its sides. Broken barrels and gutta-percha tubing, and Pickering's old galvanized spraying engine which Robert had ridden when he was six. On the carriage's dark green door the familiar legend was still legible if one knew where to look: *'Ruston and Hornsby Ltd, Lincoln'*.

Whatever had possessed his grandmother to build a railway at Harlaston? She had intended it to be the last word in the domestic transport of coal. The wagon would have trundled down a specially constructed viaduct to the top floor of the servants' wing, whence the coal would be lowered to collecting-points inside the house. The only problem was that it had taken more coal to power the engine than could conveniently be transported – or so the under-footmen had steadily maintained until the scheme was dropped.

Meanwhile, the abandoned carriage had made a wonderful clubhouse for boys; the starting-point for countless expeditions to steal ice or eavesdrop on the dimly understood smut of the journeymen's bothy. It was inside the carriage that a ten-year-old Robert had smoked his first cigarette, of some nameless and searing tobacco donated by Tom Webb.

Robert waded through the nettles and peered through the window. A bird's nest crumbling to dust on the rotting velvet. A small deadly coil of nightshade insinuating itself through a hole in the roof.

He stood with his back against the door and blew smoke-rings, and thought of Spencer and Linley and all his other ghosts. Somewhere a blackbird trilled its pure sweet song. The throbbing in his temples lessened, eased by the rough indifferent life around him.

A splintering crash of glass not far off. A boy's indignant cry, then a man's voice, raised in anger. Then the boy's voice again: cultivated, outraged and shrill. 'Dickon! Dickon! *Where's Dickon?*'

207

Robert closed his eyes. Surely someone would hear the uproar and tell them to be quiet?

No-one did.

Instead the noises grew louder and more piercing, and suddenly Aubrey burst through the trees shouting for Dickon. He had lost his hat, and his white linen suit was smudged with grass-stains. His long bony face was purple with fury. He was dragging a village boy by the ear: a stocky lad, a good deal younger than himself, who hung his flaxen head and followed his captor with the hopeless step-anywhere plod of the condemned. The boy was bleeding freely from a long gash across his forehead, but seemed too wretched to care. Behind them came an irate Sam Webb, and a girl in a dark green dress and black straw hat whom Robert recognized instantly as Gwendolen Bowles's protégée – although he always thought of her as the girl on the Tilburne Road.

They had not yet seen him.

He stepped away from the railway carriage and said, 'What the devil's going on?'

They all saw him at once, and their round-mouthed astonishment would have been comical if his headache hadn't viciously renewed its attack behind his eyes. Tully began to bark relentlessly, unsure whether to welcome Aubrey or menace the intruders. Robert told him firmly to be quiet.

Aubrey was panting. Sweat beaded the coppery down on his upper lip. '*Sir!* I found this – this *sneak* – prowling about behind the greenhouses! And when I challenged him, *he ran away*! I gave chase and we – fell into some frames. And he *must* be the same prowler I saw near the conservatory last night because—'

'No he's *not*, my lord!' thundered Sam. 'Meaning no

disrespect to Master Aubrey, but that just can't be! The lad was coming back from taking Mr Pickering his box of eatables, that's all!'

'Well if he *was*,' cried Aubrey shrilly, 'why was he *lurking* behind the greenhouses?' Robert noticed he didn't explain what he had been doing there himself, but it wasn't hard to guess. The fruit-room was adjacent to the greenhouses. Presumably both boys had been after apples. 'He's a *sneak*!' Aubrey repeated. 'Dickon should take him before a magistrate!'

Robert rubbed his temple. 'He *is* before a magistrate. Thank you for bringing this to my attention, Aubrey, but I'm sure Sam and I can handle this without getting Dickon involved as well.'

'With respect, sir, it's not Sam's responsibility, it's Dickon's.'

An ill-judged remark, which darkened Sam's brow still further.

Robert said, 'Aubrey, would you be very kind and go to the house and ring for some iced tea for your cousin Violet? She asked me to have some sent up a while ago and I rather selfishly forgot all about it. There's a good fellow.'

'Oh, sir, of *course*. At *once*.'

Robert watched him go with a mixture of exasperation and amusement. The poor boy never passed up a chance to be of service to Violet, with whom he had fallen painfully and rather publicly in love the previous summer.

'Now then,' Robert turned back to the little group in the clearing.

Throughout the fracas, the cause of it all had stood in trembling silence with his head bowed. The girl was bending over him, binding his forehead with a large lawn handkerchief which Robert suspected must be Aubrey's. To judge from the way she handled the boy, she was as angry as he was frightened, and in no mood to administer more than rough comfort.

'Come here, boy,' said Robert in his best magistrate's voice.

To his surprise, the boy gave no indication of having heard. He did not move until the girl put her hand on his shoulder and propelled him forward. Then he raised his head and met Robert's eyes.

Robert's cigar froze on its way to his lips. He felt the blood leave his face. Beneath the thatch of flaxen hair the boy's face was shockingly, unmistakably familiar. He had the broad cheekbones, the short straight nose, and the appalled, unblinking blue eyes of the Dutch boy at Nooitgedacht Farm.

Robert forgot to breathe. For an endless agonized moment he and the Dutch boy stared into each other's eyes.

At last Robert said hoarsely, 'What – what's your name?'

The boy made no answer. He went on staring at Robert with his great, round, dread-filled eyes.

Robert fought the urge to shake him into speech. Anything to break this terrifying silence. 'What's your *name*?' he repeated.

Sam was looking at him curiously. 'His name's Will, my lord. William Fosdyke.'

'Why doesn't he speak for himself? Is he mute?'

Sam opened his mouth, but it was the girl who replied. 'He can speak perfectly well, my lord, but he's deaf in one ear, so sometimes he misses things.'

He cleared his throat. 'I see. I see. So this is Jack Fosdyke's boy.'

'Yes, my lord,' the girl said.

Normality was filtering back. The scattered fragments slotting into their familiar pattern.

Now that he knew, the boy's resemblance to the big stonemason was unmistakable. He should have noticed it at once. He felt dizzy and slightly sick.

Sam, the girl, and William Fosdyke were waiting for him to speak. He glanced from the blond boy to the dark-haired girl. 'He – he is your brother?'

'Yes, my lord.'

Slowly he nodded. 'And you read for Mrs Bowles. Is that not so? We met the other day.'

She inclined her head in an odd little gesture which was midway between a nod and a bow. It was the same gesture he had seen her make on the Tilburne road. For a village girl she had a prickly dignity. He wondered where a stonemason's daughter – he wished he could remember her name – fitted into the Hynton hierarchy. 'And which ear is it?' he asked.

'My lord?'

'You said he's deaf in one ear. In which one?'

She touched her forefinger to her earlobe. 'The left one.' She was unable to hide her perplexity, and clearly wondered what had caused his extraordinary reaction to her brother.

He put his hand on the boy's shoulder and turned him so that the good ear was towards him. Then he stooped down to his level. 'Well, boy. Were you near the conservatory last night? That's the glass house on the other side of the Hall. Tell me the truth, now.'

The blue eyes widened. 'I *never,* sir! Not after dark!'

The unexpected qualification made Robert smile. 'You're not supposed to go there at all. But why especially not after dark?'

'For fear of the lions, sir.'

'The lions. Ah, yes, of course.'

The boy had been watching his lips, but now he raised his eyes to Robert's to see if he was being mocked. He looked as though he might be used to that.

The girl came to her brother's defence. 'He's only a little deaf, my lord. There's nothing wrong with his wits.'

He glanced at her. 'You misunderstand. He makes perfect sense. I was wary of those lions myself, when I was his age.'

She bit her lip. Her expression – half-puzzled, half-vexed – was the same she had worn outside the rectory, when Violet was sharpening her claws.

With some reluctance he turned back to the boy. 'Now, William. What were you doing behind the greenhouses? You oughtn't to have been there, you know.'

'Yes sir, I know. I'm very sorry.'

'So why were you?'

He swallowed. 'I need a peahen's egg by next Friday.'

Behind him, Robert heard the girl's exasperated 'Oh, *Will*!' and Sam Webb gave a disgusted snort. Robert frowned. 'A peahen's egg in August? I'm afraid you'll have to wait until spring.'

The boy swayed. His lips turned grey. 'I can't.'

'Why not?'

But from the look on his face, Robert realized he would not receive an answer. William Fosdyke no longer heard nor saw what was around him. He was staring into his own secret world of unimaginable dread.

Robert straightened up, aware that Sam was watching him. 'I'm not inclined to take this further. Get him home before he faints.'

'Yes, my lord. Thank you very much, my lord.'

'And Sam – don't be too hard on him. He seems honest enough.'

Sam gave a grim nod.

The girl did not add her thanks to Sam's, nor did she apologize for her brother, and Robert liked her for that. But as the odd little trio was starting off along the path, she turned and looked back at him, as if about to speak. Then she seemed to think better of it, and left.

Robert stood and watched them go.

It had been a surprise to see her with Sam Webb, for at the fête he had been sure she was alone.

But on reflection, what was so remarkable about Sam Webb courting her? She was a handsome, intelligent young woman. Sam had good taste.

Suddenly he felt a stab of pure jealousy. Sam would marry that girl with her clear brown eyes and her honey-coloured skin, and they would raise a brood of healthy clear-eyed children.

His cigar had gone out. He dropped it on the path and ground it beneath his heel.

'So when did you meet Lord Harlaston?' said Sam as they made their way past the kitchen gardens.

They had stopped at the stable pump to wash Will's face, and were now pressing on towards Hynton.

What a fool you were, Charity told herself savagely. To think you might actually get through a whole day without something going wrong. And of *all* the people to bump into, it would have to be him. What must he think? That you spend your time covering for your family, that's what. And he'd be right.

Beside her, Will walked as stiffly as a tin soldier, his eyes remote and unseeing. For once she had no urge to comfort him. He was lucky to have escaped without a thrashing.

And now Sam had fallen into this queer, bitter mood, and she must find a way to get rid of him before they reached the end house, so that she could give her mother an edited version of events which would exclude all mention of Lord Harlaston. Her mother wouldn't be able to cope with that.

Suddenly a great weariness came over her. Her life stretched before her in an endless succession of edited versions and half-truths and coverings up.

'He said you'd met,' Sam said again.

'They called at the rectory last Tuesday afternoon when I was reading for Mrs Bowles.'

'Ah. So you met Lady Harlaston too.'

'Only to look at.'

He stripped a switch of hazel and slashed at a clump of poppies by the side of the road. 'I remember the first time I ever set eyes on her. Eight, nine years ago. Never seen such a beautiful woman in all my life. Not before nor since.' He seemed to take no pleasure in the thought.

'She's very lovely. But she was quite unpleasant to me.'

Sam snorted. 'You just say that because she's so beautiful.'

They walked on in silence. Then Charity said, 'Why do you say a thing like that? I said it because it's true.'

But Sam wasn't listening. He was glowering at the

ground, hands jammed in his breeches pockets. 'Why is it some men got everything and others nothing? If the parson could tell us that in his sermons he wouldn't want for listeners.'

She knew without being told that he meant Lord Harlaston. 'And how does it help to get bitter about it? Who knows what you'll make of yourself in a few years?'

Again he snorted.

'What about all those plans you were talking about? Learning to mend motors and starting your own garage—'

'Oh, yes,' he sneered, 'fine plans they are! How am I s'posed to learn about motors, when Lord high-and-mighty bloody Harlaston won't be buying a motor till the war's over! An' of course, that's *his* decision, 'cos *he's* the one with the money.'

'He didn't seem high and mighty to me. It was kind of him to let Will off the hook.'

He turned on her. 'It wasn't *kind*! Folk like him aren't *kind*! They please themselves! He just couldn't be *bothered* to prosecute, that's what! Not on his home leave, not with all his parties an' his fancy friends an' his lovely wife!'

She made no reply, and they walked on in silence.

But Sam was wrong. She was sure of it. A prosecution had been the last thing on Lord Harlaston's mind during his odd little conversation with Will – although what *had* been on his mind was anyone's guess. Clearly, something about her brother had shaken him badly. He had studied Will's face with such intensity, narrowing his dark eyes like someone blinded by the light. But later, when he had regained his balance, he *had* been kind. Saying what he did about the lions, to put Will at his ease. As they were leaving, she had been tempted to explain to him that her brother thought peacocks were magic birds which *could* lay eggs in August. He would have understood, and it would have explained Will's bizarre behaviour, and proved he wasn't simple. But at the last moment she had decided against it. He was a lord. He wasn't interested in what her brother thought about peacocks.

'What do you think he was doing,' she wondered aloud, 'all alone in there?'

'Who?' said Sam.

'Lord Harlaston. Smoking his cigar in that funny old wood. And what was that shed thing he was leaning against?'

He spat. 'Railway car. One of the old witch's harebrained schemes. We used to play in it as lads.'

'You and Dickon?'

'An' Lord Harlaston an' his brother. The one that was killed.'

'You used to play with *them*?'

'Why not? We were much of an age.' He paused, remembering. 'You'd think I'd of been the underdog, being the youngest. But it was always Dickon.' There was contempt in his voice, and resentment – as if his brother's docility had been a kind of betrayal.

Maybe, she thought, that was the reason Lord Harlaston had sought solitude in that old wood. To remember the brother who was gone. 'You never told me you used to play with them.'

He beheaded another clump of poppies. 'Why should I? Only fools tell folk things they can't use. My dad told me that when I was a lad. Only worthwhile thing I ever got out of the old bugger.'

She studied his pale, severe features. At times he

wasn't an easy man to like. 'I don't understand you, Sam Webb,' she said quietly. 'Not at all I don't.'

His lip curled, and for the first time that day he looked pleased. 'That's good then, isn't it? 'Cos you don't need to.'

To everyone's surprise, Mrs Fosdyke took Charity's version of events without a murmur. 'Boys get into scrapes,' she said, with the nearest she ever got to a shrug. 'It's not as if he did anything terrible, is it? As long as he learns by his mistakes, I say there's no harm done.' When Sam dropped in for tea he backed up Charity's account, and spent most of his time talking to her mother.

It was strange, Charity thought the following Tuesday as she left the rectory and crossed to St Hybald's on an errand for Mrs Bowles, but she got on best with Sam when they were with other people. With her parents or any of the villagers they were far more of a couple than they ever were on their own.

Thinking about that, she entered the south porch and elbowed open the door. Her arms were full of the tomatoes, artichokes and marrows which made up the rectory's contribution to the harvest festival. It was because of the artichokes that she didn't see Lord Harlaston until she was halfway up the nave.

He was sitting with his back to her in the front pew, just below the pulpit. He hadn't heard her come in. His head was bowed, and he was leaning forward with both forearms resting on the rail. As Charity watched, horrified at having blundered upon a solitude he must deliberately have sought, his head sank fractionally lower, and his shoulder-blades sharpened beneath his tunic. It was a slight movement, but so fraught with feeling that her one thought was to leave silently while she still could.

She wasn't aware of making a sound, but to her horror he turned and fixed his eyes on her. 'What do you want?' His voice was rough.

'N-nothing,' she stammered. 'I'm sorry. I'll come back later.'

'You came in here for a purpose, surely.'

She glanced down at the burden in her arms. 'To put the vegetables round the pulpit.' She was immediately conscious of how absurd that sounded.

'Very well. Put them round the pulpit.'

Having blurted out the truth, she could think of no way to escape. Colouring deeply, she walked up the nave and knelt to lay down her ridiculous burden. Vegetables escaped across the flags. She was horribly aware of being watched from a distance of less than six feet.

After a painfully long pause he said: 'I've forgotten your name.'

On her knees and with an artichoke in one hand, she turned to look up at him. The sun streamed through the windows and made her blink. 'Charity, my lord. Charity Fosdyke.'

His gaze wandered to the altar and lost itself.

Silently she began recapturing the vegetables.

'So, Miss Fosdyke.'

She jumped.

'What do you think of the lesson?'

'The lesson, my lord?'

He nodded towards the tablet above her head. 'Deuteronomy nineteen, twenty-one. If I remember correctly it's the one which begins: "*And thine eye shall not pity; but life shall go for life, eye for eye, tooth for tooth.*" I forget the rest. D'you think that applies to children?'

' – My lord?'

'You heard me. Do you think it applies to children?'

She looked down at the vegetables in her lap. 'Well. Yes. It applies to everyone.'

'You misunderstand. If it's an eye for an eye and a tooth for a tooth, is it also a child for a child? In other words, if one harms a child, is one's *own* child harmed in return? Is that how it works?'

She guessed that he was coming down with a fever. His eyes were too bright and he spoke too fast, with the irritable impatience of a sick man. His dark hair was wet with perspiration. Perhaps he was suffering from what her mother still called the yellow shakes. Hadn't Sam said you could catch that in Africa as well as in the fens?

'Come, Miss Fosdyke, you've a tongue in your head, answer me. If one harms a child, is one's own child harmed in return?'

She swallowed. 'I don't think so. That wouldn't be fair.'

'How so, not fair?'

'Because you mightn't *have* any children.'

He gave a brief bark of laughter. 'I hadn't thought of that! Though God knows it's obvious enough.'

'You're not well, my lord. I'll go and fetch help.'

'I'm perfectly well. Why does everyone find excuses for me?' He looked down at his hands and frowned. 'I am perfectly well.' When he spoke again it was in a low voice, as if talking to himself. 'But what if one *did* have a child? What then? What if – what if there was a war. Here, in Lincolnshire. And what if an enemy captain came and surrounded Shotley Farm. Ordered

219

everyone out, then set fire to the place.' Slowly he shook his head, and Charity saw how the sweat had curled the hair above his collar. How his lashes trembled as he closed his eyes. 'It's winter, it's fearfully cold. Old Corlett's away fighting for his country, and his wife and daughters must stand in the cold and watch their house burn. The enemy captain watches with them. Then he rides off at the head of his men, and leaves the women and children to fend for themselves. But this isn't Lincolnshire. They can't just walk across the fields and put up at the Dolphin. They've been abandoned on that great, empty, bitterly cold plain. No food, no shelter. The smaller children probably won't survive.' He spread his hands, as if to let something fall to the floor. 'What would one think of such a man? A man who could commit such an act not once, but many times over? Dozens of farms. Dozens of dogged little groups dragging their wagons across the veldt. Would one absolve him of guilt merely because he was following orders?' Once again his gaze sought the altar. 'What would it matter in the scheme of war if he'd ridden away and left those pitiful little houses standing? But I didn't. Not a single one. I was so damnably thorough.'

Charity no longer thought he was ill. Heartsick perhaps, but not ill. He seemed to be trying to work something out. Something which mattered so terribly that the usual rules of behaviour didn't apply. That was why he was here. Why he had sought solitude in this village church rather than in the grand painted chapel at the Hall.

She knew she should find some way to give him back his solitude. Perhaps she should slip out through the vestry, or simply get to her feet and hurry down the nave as quietly as she could. He wouldn't see her go. He had forgotten she was there. But she couldn't bring herself to leave him.

'At one of those farms,' he went on, 'there was a boy about my son's age. We left him on the veldt, just like all the others. I enquired about him afterwards but of course he couldn't be traced. He had gone. Swallowed up in the camps, if he ever got that far.' His right hand made a fist about the left, and he stared at it as though it belonged to someone else. 'Linley and the Dutch boy at Nooitgedacht Farm. I dream of them every night. And they're always together. I can't keep them separate. I can't – untangle them in my mind. I didn't understand why, but now I do. I know – I *know* – that my son died for his father's sins on the veldt.'

'Oh, no,' Charity said. 'That can't be.'

He looked at her. 'I accept that. What I've just said is impossible. The timing's wrong. My son died three weeks *before* Nooitgedacht. I know all that. But I don't believe it. I just cannot see', he broke out savagely, 'how such acts – such crimes – can be so utterly without consequence. What I did was *wrong*.'

It was very quiet in the old church.

Charity glanced down at her lap. When she raised her eyes, he was looking at her. 'It was wrong, was it not? Tell me the truth.' His eyes were black and frighteningly intense. 'Tell me. Tell me the truth.'

His hands were still clasped. They were good hands. They reminded her of those of the effigy she liked to look at during the parson's sermons. But because he was a man and not an effigy, there were black hairs on the wrists, and the base of the left thumb bore a small triangular scar, and there were scratches across the backs where he had pulled aside the branches as he walked through the wood.

The truth.

The flagstone was cold beneath her hand. Dust floated in shafts of sunlight.

She could hardly do other than tell him the truth. Not in church, right in front of the altar. Not after witnessing his own painful search for meaning.

He no longer belonged to a race apart. He was simply a man who needed to hear the truth. 'I think,' she said softly, 'I think – yes. It was a terrible thing to do.'

He stood up. The scrape of his boots echoed through the church. She had forgotten how tall he was.

'Get out,' he said brusquely. 'Finish that later. Just – get out.'

CHAPTER SEVENTEEN

Late July, the Present

The man in the painting didn't look the type to have fallen in love with a dressmaker.

According to *A Short Guide to Harlaston Hall*, the portrait of the Nineteenth Baron had been painted in 1892, a year after his marriage. He had been twenty-seven. Sixteen years later, at the age of forty-three, he had fathered Julian D'Authon: either as the result of a backstairs seduction – or, if Alex was to be believed, in the grip of something altogether more improbable.

Singer Sargent had depicted him in full evening dress, in a graceful pose reminiscent of one of Saki's elegant young cynics. He stood with one elbow resting on a bookcase, the other hand half withdrawn from a trouser pocket. His clothes had been sketched with confident impressionistic brushwork, his surroundings sweepingly evoked: a sliver of light on a gun-barrel; a profusion of orchids in a great *japonais* bowl; the satiny ear of a spaniel curled beneath the desk.

By contrast, the face had been painted with photographic precision. Sarah thought him handsome, in an officer-and-a-gentleman kind of way. Confident fine-boned features and an intelligent height of brow. An unusually decided curve to the lower lip. The hair and moustache were very dark, the eyes remarkably so: black, almond-shaped, and curiously Latin in the directness with which they engaged the viewer.

It was impossible to tell from his face what sort of man he had been. One could imagine him conducting a love affair or a *coup d'état* with equal aplomb, with no-one the wiser as to his motives.

Who and what had he been to Charity Fosdyke? A hedonist out for casual gratification? Or a man who had found love where he least expected it?

Sarah searched for traces of herself or her father in those thoughtful, worldly features. Perhaps there was some similarity in the shape of the eyes and the modelling of the mouth. Or perhaps she was trying too hard. But one thing was certain. Between father and son there was one striking difference. Julian Dalton's vivid sense of humour had never left him, even at the end. The lines of his face had arranged themselves for laughter. About Robert Pearce-Staunton there wasn't the trace of a smile. Perhaps he had found posing for Singer Sargent a tedious affair.

His wife, on the other hand, looked as though she had loved every minute of it.

Violet, Baroness Harlaston, had been just twenty years old when she sat for Singer Sargent – a full two years after her husband's portrait was painted. Perhaps she had waited to regain her looks after the birth of her son.

And what looks they were. No wonder Aubrey had run out of superlatives. She was the ideal of Edwardian beauty made flesh: a paragon of brittle Meissen delicacy and narrow-lipped refinement. And that figure! It must have been very perfection in an age which proclaimed sensuality incompatible with femininity, but demanded a pouter-pigeon bosom, a breathtaking waist, and discreetly lascivious hips.

Unlike her husband, her expression revealed everything about her. She knew she was beautiful, and she revelled in it. '*I have made my appearance my life's work,*' her wonderful eyes seemed to say, '*and behold: I have succeeded beyond anyone's wildest dreams.*'

The painter had understood very well what was most important to his sitter. He had lavished as much care on the subtle sheen of her aquamarine gown, on her opals and pearls and vaporous eau de nil wrap, as he had on the chilly perfection of her face. And he had surrounded her with the coded trappings of wealth. Singer Sargent pretending to be Gainsborough: he must have enjoyed that. The rose garden in which she sat evoked the aristocracy's links with the land. Formal walks and classical statuary, and a park fading to blue in the distance. At her feet he had placed a nondescript plant with muted grey leaves and heathery flowers. '*The indigo plant*', the booklet explained, '*is a reference to the Baroness's father, Sir Gregory Redfearn, who made a fortune in the dyestuff after the Behar Mutiny of 1859.*'

Insignificant pink florets which produced a dye of midnight blue. An exquisite beauty christened with leaden symbolism for the fortune she would inherit. Singer Sargent, that most worldly of painters, must have relished the ironies.

Sarah contemplated the perfect Edwardian couple and thought of her grandmother, the faceless dressmaker from Hynton.

'Alex must have got it wrong,' she said aloud, and

her voice raised a faint echo in the Long Gallery. 'He can't have been in love with Charity Fosdyke. It doesn't make sense.'

Lord and Lady Harlaston stared coolly back at her, giving nothing away.

Two days later, she was sitting at her desk watching a pair of magpies strutting about the lawn when Stephen walked in.

He pulled a grey clothbound book from his knapsack. 'It's about the fens,' he mumbled, without looking at her. 'Alex remembered that Charity's parents came from there, so he thought it might help.'

She thanked him for the book and passed the biscuit tin across. He ate four chocolate digestives, still without looking at her. She wondered what was wrong.

At last he said, 'You're going to see that old lady tomorrow, aren't you?'

'Alex's great-grand-aunt? Yes I am. How did you know?'

He shrugged. 'She called him to check up on you.'

She was half-hoping he would ask to come with her. Ridiculous to admit it, but the thought of going to London on her own was making her nervous.

When the silence had gone on long enough, she asked what was wrong.

His forehead creased. Then it came out in a rush. 'I told my mother you're going to London and she said could you meet her for lunch 'cos she really wants to see you, and I said yes and Alex was *cross*, he said I shouldn't arrange things for other people. You're not cross, are you?'

'Of course not,' Sarah lied, hoping the truth didn't

226

show in her face. So much for total honesty with children.

'*Please* have lunch with her. Hugo's being mean again. He's almost as bad as Dad— Dominic. And she thinks you don't like her 'cos she's not clever enough. But you do like her, don't you? It'd *really* cheer her up if you had lunch with her.'

'Of course I will,' Sarah said.

Surprisingly, she was glad the following day to have something to do. She had two hours to kill before her appointment with Mrs Favell, and London was even more of an assault course than she remembered. Pneumatic drills roared at every corner, and she had forgotten how hard you had to concentrate to dodge the *Big Issue* sellers and the backpackers standing in the middle of the pavement consulting their maps. Had there ever been a time when she had felt part of all this?

There were reminders of Dominic everywhere. On the cab journey from King's Cross she passed the wine bar where they used to meet after work, and the shop where she had bought his birthday present, and the travel agent's where she had researched their next holiday. She had left the brochures in the flat in Notting Hill. Perhaps he had taken Caroline Harris instead.

Gratefully she sank into a chair in the packed Covent Garden restaurant where Clare had booked a table. Maybe Mum's right, she thought. Maybe you're becoming a recluse, like Alex.

The restaurant was full of smart, supremely confident young people. She realized it had been a mistake to underdress. Her T-shirt and jeans, blazer and loafers were ridiculously out of date, and her hair was pulled back into a ponytail with a tortoiseshell clip her

227

mother had given her for her fifteenth birthday. Maybe after seeing Mrs Favell she would get herself a haircut. Something short and up-to-the-minute, in one of those places that stays open half the night.

'*Sorry* I'm late!' Clare dropped into the chair opposite her. She wore a cream Lycra shirt, black zip-up waistcoat, russet pants, and high-heeled strappy sandals. Bangles and hooped earrings completed the effect, although Sarah noticed that the Patek Philippe watch had managed to survive. Not even Clare had the heart to ditch *that* for retro-chic.

She was full of brittle smiles and seamless chat as she ordered a *salade de rouget* and Perrier. Sarah chose pasta and a large glass of Pinot Grigio. She had a feeling she was going to need it.

I wish, she thought, listening to Clare bemoaning the demands of her job, I wish I was honest enough to say: Clare, why don't you just tell me what you want? That way you could avoid having lunch with someone you dislike and I wouldn't have to fork out twenty-five pounds, which I can ill afford, on a bowl of over-cooked noodles and half a tin of tomatoes. Why the hell did I let Stephen talk me into this?

'So how's my little brat?' asked Clare. So far she hadn't met Sarah's eyes once.

'He's marvellous.'

Clare gave a hollow laugh.

'I mean it. He's smashing. You're lucky to have him.'

'I know. I miss him like crazy. I used to be forever on the phone to the rectory. Must've driven Alex wild. But these days I never seem to catch him. Alex, I mean.' Her tone seemed to link Sarah and Alex in some covert disappearing act.

Sarah applied herself to her pasta.

'You know', Clare went on, watching her, 'people think Alex quit his job because Helen left him.'

Sarah looked up, startled by the change of tack.

'He didn't. It was the other way around. *First* he quit the City, *then* she left him.'

In spite of herself, Sarah was intrigued. 'So why did he quit the City?'

Clare gave an exaggerated shrug. 'He'd had enough of the law and wanted out, so he gave Helen a choice: come to the country or get a divorce. Silly cow chose the divorce.'

It had the ring of truth about it. Sarah had never been able to picture Alex having a nervous breakdown. He was far too self-sufficient. But she could imagine him giving his wife an ultimatum, with his peculiar brand of kind but slightly shocking honesty.

'Stephen *hates* it when people get it the wrong way round,' Clare went on. 'And, of course, Helen's the *last* person to set the story straight. It suits the silly bitch far too well as it is. Much more glamorous to have the deserted husband falling spectacularly apart while she rides off into the sunset with spouse number two.' She pushed an olive round her plate. 'Don't tell me this is all new to you.'

'It is.'

'But surely Alex told you something.'

Sarah felt herself sliding into dangerous waters. 'We never talk about it.'

'Really? How odd.'

Sarah ignored that. 'I never knew Helen,' she said carefully.

'Lucky you.'

Once, before Sarah had learned about Dominic's

affair with his sister-in-law, she had asked him what he thought of her. 'In fact,' he had said, 'she's not really classically beautiful, when you look at her. But my God, that *colouring*!' The colouring was something Sarah remembered from the Cawthorpe funeral. Clouds of jet-black hair, smoky blue eyes, naturally red lips, and a creamy skin which didn't need a scrap of make-up.

According to Dominic, after Alex and Helen were married she was 'always on some course or other – when she wasn't in therapy. Tried any number of jobs. Publishing, advertising, interior design. But something always made them impossible. And it was never, *ever,* her fault. Nothing was ever her fault. Then poor old Alex's career took off and she began to blame *him*. He was stifling her, sapping her confidence. She blamed him for the affairs, too. Said he neglected her, so she had no choice. Silly little thing didn't even have the sense to enjoy them. A great one for *Sturm und Drang,* is our Helen. But because it's Helen, you make allowances. You want to be the one to get through to her. The usual story.'

It had taken Sarah a while to realize that Dominic had spoken from personal experience.

'Do you know,' Clare was saying indignantly, 'for the last four years of that marriage she didn't work *at all*? She had a woman in every day, a therapist four times a week, no children – she didn't want them, though he did, I'm sure of it – and she still didn't have time to cook him a decent meal. I once found him in the kitchen eating olives from a jar because it was the only thing left in the fridge!'

Sarah couldn't help laughing. 'From what I know of Alex he wouldn't mind a bit, as long as he had a tumbler of Glenfiddich to wash it down!'

Clare gave her a suspicious stare. In the harsh city light she looked her age. Her skin was orange and papery from too many sun-lamps.

The coffee came with the bill.

'How's – er – Hugo?' Sarah asked, to break the silence.

Clare gave an impatient toss of the head. 'It's not going anywhere.'

'I'm sorry.'

She shrugged. 'It's better than being on my own. Is Alex seeing anyone, do you know?'

'I've no idea. I don't run into him very often.'

'Really? I thought you borrowed his car all the time. Yours is still being repaired, isn't it?'

Poor Clare. She wasn't very good at hiding her feelings. In fact, she was bloody awful. Her transparency should have been appealing, but it wasn't. Not when the feelings in question were bitterness, resentment, and misplaced jealousy.

Sarah took a fiver and two ten-pound notes from her wallet and put them under the mints on the saucer. 'Please don't *worry,* Clare,' she said briskly. 'Alex isn't avoiding you because of me. And I'm not about to do a rebound onto any brother of Dominic's.'

'I can't help feeling', said Alex's great-grand-aunt, 'that it is a mercy their mother didn't live to see *both* her boys divorced. First Dominic, then Alex. She would have been appalled. I'm not sure *I* wasn't appalled.'

With admirable steadiness for a lady in her late seventies she handed Sarah a cup of tea. Then she settled straight-backed into her chair, clasped her liver-spotted hands firmly in her lap, and crossed her ankles in the approved manner of fifty years ago. They were good ankles, and she was clearly proud of them.

She had the air of many of the elderly people Sarah came across in her work: apprehensive about being interviewed, but ultimately detached. She was old. Nothing this young person said could matter very much.

Sarah decided that her hand-held cassette recorder would remain in her bag unless she could get Mrs Favell to relax. 'In my day one *stuck* at one's marriage,' the old lady said. Her accent was pre-war BBC with a barely detectable Midlands twang. 'That young woman. Helen. *Why* she felt she had to leave Alex I *don't* know. A perfectly *good* young man like that.'

Sarah bit back a smile at hearing Alex referred to in the same decided tones that her mother would have used for an old raincoat: 'You're not giving that to Oxfam, it's still perfectly *good*!'

Mrs Favell glanced at Sarah's ringless hands and her lips tightened for a moment.

She was a short, slight woman with an incongruously heavy bust and a neat face that might once have been pretty. She had dressed with care in clothes which were good but not expensive. A pink floral print dress with a pussy-cat bow at the throat; flesh-coloured nylons and beige high-heeled pumps; a marcasite brooch (looking a little lost on the imposing bosom), matching earrings, a medium-sized diamond solitaire, and a plain gold wedding ring. Her hair was freshly set in crisp silver waves through which her scalp showed a clean, pale pink.

The high heels must be in Sarah's honour, for the receptionist at the 'sheltered community' had explained that Mrs Favell had brittle bones, and must be careful not to fall.

Sarah asked what Mrs Favell had done before her marriage. The old lady gave her a measuring look, and seemed to make up her mind that she meant well. 'I ran a travel agent's in Salisbury. Salisbury, *Rhodesia*, that is. Though I suppose I ought to call it *Zimbabwe* now. Of course, *I* didn't run it, not officially. There was a man in charge.'

'Did you enjoy your work?'

'Oh, I *loved* it! Though naturally, I gave it up when I married.' She placed her palms on her lap, a gesture of finality.

The small sitting room contained a dozen or so framed photographs of children down the decades, but none of a husband. Mrs Favell followed the direction of Sarah's eyes. 'Things were more straightforward in those days,' she said calmly. 'One stepped out together, one got engaged, one married, and one stuck *at* it. One didn't go in for a lot of agonizing.' She gave a slight smile. 'Still. I enjoy my children. And my grand-children. I take it that you don't – that is, *do* you have children?' She looked rather pleased with herself for recognizing the phenomenon of single motherhood.

Sarah shook her head. 'Too much work, I suppose. And maybe a bit too much agonizing.'

They exchanged tentative smiles.

Sarah liked Mrs Favell. There was something un-flinching and honest about her. She decided that at some stage she must come clean and mention her relationship with Dominic. On the telephone she had only explained briefly who she was.

The tiny bungalow looked out onto one of the neat clipped quadrangles of the estate. The sitting room was comfortably furnished with a green three-piece suite, reproduction bookcases, and a large colour television and VCR. A door gave onto an immaculate galley kitchen tiled in yellow, and another onto a sunny peach-coloured bedroom. It seemed unlikely that Mrs Favell had needed to do any special tidying for her visit. Everything had the air of being long settled in its appointed place.

Sarah indicated the oil-painting above the fireplace: a bewhiskered Victorian hunter posing inside the rib-cage of a recently slaughtered bull elephant. 'Dominic's little boy would love that.'

Mrs Favell's face softened. 'Alex tells me that Stephen has a *great* interest in biology.'

For a while they talked about Stephen, and Mrs Favell continued to thaw. Then Sarah said carefully, 'You know, Mrs Favell, I went out with Dominic for nearly two years.'

'Did you *really*?' Mrs Favell gave her a frank re-appraisal. 'I wonder you stood it for so long! I never took to that young man. Though I can see that he's probably frightfully attractive.'

To her surprise, Sarah found herself telling the old lady all about it. About splitting up and catching pneumonia and losing her nerve, and how hard it was to forget him.

'You're well rid of him,' the old lady remarked, 'though you may not think so for some time to come. But just remember. You might have married him.'

There was a silence while they both thought about that.

Then Sarah asked Mrs Favell how she was related to William Fosdyke.

Mrs Favell moved the sugar-bowl a little to one side,

234

in tacit recognition that they had reached the purpose of the interview. 'I wasn't,' she said. 'I was related to his wife, and only by marriage. I was her stepsister.'

'And did you see them much when you were growing up? William and his wife?'

'Not at all, until I was fourteen. Grace – William's wife – was much older than me. She had already left home when I was born. But in 1935 my mother fell ill, and she asked Grace to take me for the summer holidays.'

Sarah asked if she might start her recorder, and there was a brief pause during which the machine was examined and admired. Sarah realized she had underestimated Mrs Favell. The recorder seemed to increase rather than diminish the old lady's confidence. 'They lived in a little house in Stainton Hamer,' she went on, speaking slowly and distinctly for the benefit of the machine. 'William was the caretaker at the local school, though he was a stonemason by trade. From time to time he still helped out in the churches in the parish.'

'Did he ever help out at Hynton?'

The old face softened. 'Oh, yes! That was his favourite. There was a sweet old couple there, the retired rector and his wife. Bowles, I believe they were called. William had known them since he was a boy. They had a most *disagreeable* daughter, as I recall. Flora. She was something high up in the Salvation Army, and she used to come down from London and *boss* them about. It was the only time I ever saw William annoyed.' She smiled, remembering. 'Sometimes he would do odd jobs in St Hybald's, and I would wander off and pick wild flowers. I always knew when he was coming, for he kept three glass marbles in his pocket which he was forever rolling in his fingers. I'd hear them clicking as he came through the churchyard.'

Sarah let Mrs Favell pursue her memories for a while. Then she said gently, 'What was William like?'

The pale old eyes looked through Sarah into the past. The clasped hands opened and closed. 'William – William was wonderful.'

Sarah waited for her to go on.

'Of course, he was *very* handsome, but it wasn't only that. It was his *charm*. I mean that in the true sense. When he listened to you, and of course he had to concentrate because of his hearing, he really *listened*. And you could tell him anything. He couldn't be shocked.'

'His daughter – Alex and Dominic's mother – she used to say he was odd.'

'That sounds like Harriet. And she was right in a way, though it doesn't at all convey what he was like. How should one describe William? Of course, he was extremely well-read, and he knew his Bible, though he wasn't religious. He merely enjoyed the language. I think – I think he tended to *unsettle* people who didn't know him. He told me once that he had to go very *carefully* in this world, because what was straightforward for other people was mysterious to him, and the other way round. He laughed as he said that.' She paused. 'The wonderful thing about Will was that he could admit all that quite naturally to a girl of fourteen.'

'Did he ever mention his sister?'

Mrs Favell's gaze returned to Sarah. She looked troubled. 'Your grandmother. I'm sorry, but he rarely did. You see, Grace became *very* indignant whenever

236

she was mentioned, so he lost the habit. Grace had a great capacity for indignation.'

'Why indignant?'

'Your grandmother wasn't what Grace regarded as respectable. But then, you know about that.'

'I was wondering what *you* knew.'

The pencilled brows drew together. 'Very little, I'm afraid. All Grace would tell me was that your grandmother had been *taken advantage of* by the lord of the manor, and that he'd sent her off to the Continent to have the child. I'm afraid that's what the ruling families did in those days.' She sounded apologetic, as if, by being old, she shared the guilt for the harsh attitudes of the past.

'Did you ever meet my grandmother?'

'Oh, Heavens, *no*! I never even saw a picture of her! You see, she never came back to England. She couldn't, because of what she had done. Of course, it was really what *he* had done – Lord Harlaston – but I'm afraid in those days, it was always the woman's fault.'

Sarah swallowed her disappointment. 'And after that first summer in 1935, did you visit Stainton Hamer again?'

'Only for two more summers.'

'Why only two?'

'Because in 1938 William died.' She said it calmly, but her hands curled together in her lap.

Sarah said gently, 'How did he die?'

Mrs Favell watched the tape going round in the recorder. 'One day he developed a stomach-ache, and the next he was dead. It was peritonitis, you see, and in those days there wasn't much they could do. He was only forty-nine.' She paused. 'I don't think Grace was right for him. She was not a *kind* woman. And kindness is so important. Still. I believe he was happy in his way. He had a talent for making his own contentment.'

Sarah felt her eyes beginning to fill.

The old lady gave her a considering look. Perhaps at her age she found tears a curiosity. 'I'm afraid that's all I can tell you. It isn't very much, is it?'

'On the contrary, I've learned a great deal I didn't know before.'

Mrs Favell did not appear to have heard her. 'There is one other thing which perhaps I should mention,' she said. 'Your grandmother used to send Will picture postcards from France.'

Sarah became very still.

'She sent at least one every fortnight, and she kept it up for, oh, twenty or thirty years. And he would send postcards back, though Grace didn't at all approve. But you see, he had always been very close to his sister. I think he missed her terribly. And she must have missed him too, to judge from the postcards.'

'Did he – did he keep any of her postcards?'

'Oh *yes,* he kept them all. In large pasteboard albums, with each card secured by those little corners, so that he could take them out and read the backs.'

'Did he ever show them to you?'

Her chin went up a fraction. 'Oh *yes*. It used to drive Grace wild! Such *beautiful* cards. All sorts of paintings and photographs. Birds, châteaux, landscapes, cathedrals. Will admired the cathedrals most. He had read a great deal about architecture.'

With enormous care Sarah placed her cup and saucer on the table. 'Do you know what became of the postcards?'

'Grace burnt them all shortly after Will died.'

There was a moment of appalled silence.

'Are you *sure*?'

'Oh, yes, my dear. I made a point of enquiring about them. You see, he had particularly said that he wanted me to have them after he died. I thought at the time it was an odd thing to say, because of course we all thought he'd live for years. Then at the funeral I asked Grace about them, and she told me quite calmly that she had burnt them in the incinerator in the garden. She said she didn't know they were meant to come to me. I'm very much afraid I didn't believe her, and I told her so. We had quite a set-to.' She gave one of her slight smiles. 'That was the last time I saw her. How dramatic that sounds, but in fact it was rather banal. The war came, and afterwards I went to Rhodesia to see my sister, who had married a tea-planter, and then I got married. But I must confess I never made any *effort* to see Grace. I suppose it was foolish, but I always held that business of the postcards against her. You see, I never had a photograph of Will. Those postcards would have been a comfort.'

There was silence in the little sitting room. Muted visitors' voices drifted in from the quadrangle.

Mrs Favell said suddenly: 'Would you like a glass of sherry, Sarah? I believe we are respectably close to six o'clock.'

Sarah replied that she would love a glass of sherry. She watched the old lady fetch glasses on a tray, then return to the cabinet for the decanter. A sensible woman beneath the genteel prettiness, and one who knew her limitations. A pity she had never had the chance to go beyond them.

239

The sherry was spectacularly good: fine and many-layered, and neither too sweet nor too dry. Sarah said so.

Mrs Favell gave a rich snort of appreciation. 'One thing I do know about is sherry! My husband sometimes allowed me to choose a bottle, as it is a *ladies'* drink!'

For a while they gave the sherry the attention it deserved, and Sarah watched the colour return to the old lady's powdery cheeks.

At length Mrs Favell said quietly, 'Would you fetch that box for me, my dear? The little sandalwood one on the window sill.'

Sarah set the box on the table and watched Mrs Favell sort through its contents and extract a brittle yellow envelope. 'This is the only postcard which survived. The picture is of a stained-glass window at Pointe Chapelle. Have you ever been there? I hear it's remarkable. It's a picture of Ruth, from the Bible, which for some reason I liked particularly. Will gave it to me on my last visit. There's nothing of great consequence in the message on the back, but as it *is* from your grandmother, I thought you might care to see it.'

CHAPTER EIGHTEEN

Ruth wore a long blue robe tightly belted over an uncompromising stomach, and clutched a sheaf of corn with ears the size of daffodils. For seven hundred years she had stared down from a window in Pointe Chapelle. Shifty eyes. Potato nose. Mouth turned down in a burlesque medieval grimace.

'*She's either the village idiot*', Charity had written to her brother, '*or a thief pretending to be an idiot. On balance I'd say a thief: if that's gleaning, I'm a Chinaman. Am longing for the holidays – tho' annoyingly, St Benoît breaks up late again this year. Have at last taken yr advice & scrapped landscapes in favour of portraits. Far more interesting, tho' pupils here at Ste Agathe (as everywhere!) won't sit still for 2 minutes. Did you get to York Minster? If so, p/cd please! Proper letter follows next week with sample portraits for comments. Do reconsider & come. Summers at Mazères are ridiculously beautiful. Surely this time G can be squared? Yr loving Charity.*'

The date had been written in the Continental style, with a barred seven and a hook on the one. The seventeenth of June, 1923. By then, Charity had been living in France for fifteen years. She had been

241

forty-two. In 1908, when she had given birth to her son, she had been twenty-seven.

Sarah had copied the text of the postcard into her notebook before she left Mrs Favell, who had politely declined to let her borrow the original. 'Too silly, I know, but I'm sure you understand. I promise to have Reception make you a photocopy first thing tomorrow. You shall have it by first-class post.'

Leaning back in her seat as the train sped through the countryside, Sarah recalled the look of her grandmother's handwriting. An assertive copperplate. The hand of a confident, balanced woman.

It was a chatty postcard, and obviously part of a running dialogue. And there was that tantalizing promise of a proper letter. When Sarah had queried that, Mrs Favell had told her that there had been letters too, but Grace had burnt them along with the postcards.

And that mention of 'pupils' was a puzzle. Mrs Favell thought she remembered Will mentioning that Charity had worked as a schoolteacher in France. But surely if she had taught anywhere, it would have been in south-western France, where Sarah's father had grown up? And yet the address on the postcard was '*Dinan, C.-d'Armor., Bretagne*'. What had she been doing in Brittany? And if she was only visiting, why would she mention pupils?

Waiting for the Grantham train, Sarah had phoned her mother from a call box. Prompting Mrs Dalton with the names on the postcard had taken some doing, but eventually she agreed that the name of the vineyard where her husband had grown up might have been something like Mazères, that it was somewhere near Pau, and that he had attended a nearby school with a name which might have been St Benoît.

242

And if all that was true, it meant that Charity had been longing for the holidays so that she could see her son. At least, Sarah hoped it was what she meant.

She felt a surge of optimism. At last, some leads. Maybe she could trace someone who had been at St-Benoît with her father. And maybe if Charity *had* taught at a school in Brittany in 1923, or had visited it for whatever reason, she might find someone who had been there at the same time. They would be pretty ancient by now, and the chances were it was too late. But one never knew.

What sort of woman emerged from those brief lines on the postcard? A confident woman, amusing and lively, who had looked forward to her son's school holidays, presumably for another 'ridiculously beautiful' summer at Mazères, and had tried her best to persuade her brother to join them.

It was eight o'clock, but the sky was still a luminous blue. The flat Cambridgeshire countryside sped past, superimposed by a ghostly image of Sarah's face. After the new haircut, she looked sharply unfamiliar. Mrs Favell had insisted she make time for it before returning to Grantham, and she was glad she had. It was short and layered, and made her feel younger and more in control.

She wiggled her eyebrows at her reflection, and earned an aggrieved glance from the dough-faced young man sitting opposite.

All in all, she thought, not a bad day's work, considering the way it had started out.

'Alex? It's Sarah. I wondered – could I borrow the car tomorrow?'

'Ah. I was going out. Is it urgent?'

'Well, no, not really. It's just something I want to get on with. I need to go to the Lincoln Archives. But it's OK, I'll call them instead. They can probably—'

'No, that's all right, Lincoln's on my way. I'll give you a lift.'

Coming down the steps the following day, she was surprised to find him alone in the car. Stephen, he explained, was spending the day at the bat sanctuary. He made no comment on her haircut except to give her a slightly more penetrating look than usual – which she thought was taking discretion a bit far, given that in one step she had gone from a ponytail to k.d. lang. He didn't ask about Mrs Favell either, or about her lunch with Clare, or what made it so important to visit the Archives. But as she was in a good mood, she told him anyway, although she left out the lunch with Clare.

'Unfortunately,' she said as they drove through fields of red-gold wheat, 'Dad's school, St-Benoît, stopped being a school in the Seventies. I called them this morning. It's now a training centre for Chinese medicine. About twenty-five miles south of Pau. Do you know Pau?'

He shook his head.

'I drove through it once. It's a funny place. Sort of half French and half English. Something to do with the English presence there after Napoleon.'

'Borderline.'

'Exactly. Maybe she felt comfortable there. Neither widow, wife, nor maid.'

'Mm. And this place in Brittany. Has that stopped being a school too?'

'Ste Agathe? *Mais non!* That's where I got lucky. I called Dinan Town Hall and they put me through to some terrible old woman in *Enquêtes* who took it as a

244

personal slight that I'm not fluent in French. '*Excusez-moi, madame, est-ce qu'il y a un école dans votre ville qui s'appelle Ste Agathe?*' '*Une école, mademoiselle!*' And so on. Blood out of a stone. But I finally established that, *oui, il y a* une *école qui s'appelle Ste Agathe,* but there's *absolument* no point in my contacting it, because they had a reorganization five years ago and threw out all their pre-war records. But eventually she gave me the address of an old lady who used to teach there before the war. So I need to get to a post office, because Mme Lebesque, the old lady, doesn't have a phone and I'm writing to her instead. I suppose it's what you might call a long shot.'

Alex swerved to avoid a family cycling two abreast. 'So why the Archives?'

Sarah cast him a curious glance. After a silent start, he had asked several casual but penetrating questions about how the book for the college was going, and had then moved on to her private research. During the last half-hour he had shown more interest in both aspects of her work than he had in the past six weeks. She wondered what he was up to. Was this his way of checking that she wasn't quietly unravelling at Harlaston all by herself? It occurred to her that after Helen's various breakdowns, he would be pretty sensitive about things like that. And she had noticed that despite his self-imposed seclusion, he had a habit of shouldering responsibility for those around him.

'The Archives', she told him, 'are because of my *second* lead from Mrs Favell. In the Thirties, your grandfather did odd jobs for an old couple in Hynton, the ex-rector and his wife. In fact now I come to think of it, they probably lived in your house. Apparently they had an obnoxious daughter in the Salvation

Army, and as they knew William when he was a boy, I thought if I could trace the obnoxious daughter or her children, they might remember something about Charity too. Of course, it's another long shot.'

He nodded.

'What about you?' she asked. 'Where are you going, if Lincoln's on your way?'

'Springthorpe.'

She had never heard of it. 'Why Springthorpe?'

'Bones.'

She waited for him to elaborate, but he didn't. She suppressed a smile.

They drove in silence for a while. Fields flashed past, checkerboarded with cubes of dark gold straw. The verges glowed with hawkweed, poppies and rosebay willow-herb.

Finally, Sarah said, 'I was wondering when you're going to tell me not to get my hopes up.'

'About what?' He sounded surprised.

'About my long shots. Mme Lebesque in Brittany, and Flora Bowles the obnoxious daughter.'

'I wasn't going to.'

'Really? Dominic used to tell me I'd never make a proper historian because I read too much into things, and because I'm always hoping for a miracle.' She glanced sideways to catch his reaction.

There wasn't one.

'In fact,' she went on recklessly, 'Dominic used to say that I—'

'Sarah.'

'What?'

'Stop it.'

She grinned. 'You know, I had lunch with Clare yesterday. She talked about nothing but you.'

'Oh, Christ.'

'It wasn't *my* fault. Stephen asked me to have lunch with her.'

There was a silence. Then Alex said, 'I suppose this is the stuff of your television dramas, isn't it?'

'What is?'

'Divorced mother with son. Divorced brother-in-law. Rural setting. Cello on the soundtrack.'

'I wouldn't know. I do documentaries.'

'But with your training you can probably think up any number of plots.'

'So could anyone with a little imagination. Now let's see.' She narrowed her eyes. 'Clare helped you over Helen, and you were drawn together. *You* helped Clare over Dominic, and you were drawn together. You helped each *other* over Helen *and* Dominic, and you were drawn together. You took Stephen for the summer in order to get closer to Clare. Clare asked *you* to take Stephen in order to get closer to you. In fact, Stephen's not really Dominic's, he's yours—'

That made him laugh. 'OK, let's talk about something else!'

'All right. Suppose you tell me why for the past six weeks you've been practically impossible to contact, and now suddenly you're giving me lifts and asking all these questions.'

He thought about that. 'When you first arrived, you looked ready for a breakdown. I thought you needed time on your own.'

'I did,' she agreed. 'But then I started getting better. I got stuck into the book, and I started looking into my grandparents' story. Then I ran out of leads and I needed to talk to you. And you were *still* avoiding me.'

'You still weren't better.'

'According to whom?'

He did not reply at once. After a while he said, 'All right, I take the point. It was for you to decide when you felt better, not me.'

'Thank you.'

Perhaps she couldn't entirely blame him. Maybe Helen had preferred him to make the decisions.

But what had it been like for Helen, being married to all that quiet self-sufficiency? Maybe it had sapped her confidence. And if it had, Alex would have been perceptive enough to notice, and blame himself.

Or maybe the truth was simpler. Maybe he was still in love with his ex-wife. From what Dominic had said, Helen wasn't a woman men forgot in a hurry.

Or maybe, she thought, turning to stare out of the window, I should have done television drama after all.

They were nearing Lincoln. Half-finished housing estates alternated with fields of muddy pigs and small shabby rows of shops. They crawled towards a roundabout behind a long tailback following a tractor. Alex changed gear and said, 'Dominic called.'

Sarah turned to look at him. ' – What?'

'Dominic called.'

'When?'

'Last night.'

'Why?'

'I don't know.'

'What did he want?'

'He wants you to call him.'

'*Why?*'

'He didn't say. Just that he'd heard you were at Harlaston and he wants you to call him back.'

Blankly she stared ahead. How did Dominic know where she was? She had had no contact with him since the beginning of March. She was pretty sure neither her mother nor Nick had told him where she was, even assuming he'd contacted them, which she doubted. And Alex wouldn't have told him.

Clare. After yesterday's lunch. Bloody *Clare*. 'What did you tell him?' She tried to sound casual but failed utterly. She felt him looking at her.

'Nothing,' he said.

'You must've said something.'

'I told him you're working. That's all.'

'If he wants to talk why didn't he call *me*?'

'I don't know, Sarah. It wasn't much of a conversation.'

They had reached the roundabout. Alex turned off towards Lincoln.

'Why did you leave it till now to tell me?' Sarah asked. She had trouble keeping her voice steady. 'Did you feel you had to check that I'm strong enough to take it?'

He made no reply.

'I thought I'd got through to you, Alex. I don't need looking after.'

'I'm sorry.'

She drew a deep breath. 'What the bloody *hell* does he think he's playing at? He was the one who ended it. And much as it would do wonders for my self-esteem to be able to slam the door in his face, I find it hard to believe that he's suddenly changed his mind and wants me back.'

'I know. I'm sorry.'

'Don't keep saying that. It's not your fault.'

I suppose, she thought as they pulled up outside the Archives, it isn't only for me that I want to keep

Dominic out. It's for Charity and Will, and, who knows, maybe for Robert as well. I don't want Dominic getting his claws into any of them.

She turned to Alex. 'If he calls again, please don't tell him what I'm doing. Particularly about my grandparents. I know that sounds odd. But he twists things.'

'Of course.'

She got out and was about to close the door when he leaned over.

'Sarah – '

'Yes?'

'You know, you don't have to call him back if you don't want to.'

Surprised, she met his eyes. 'I know.'

'Right. See you at three.' He drove off.

The Lincoln Archives were in one of the less genteel parts of the city, next to an abandoned Wesleyan School for Infants and Girls. Black plastic rubbish bags cluttered the pavement, and across the road was a row of scruffy Victorian cottages and an NCP car park.

The optimism of the past twenty-four hours drained smartly away. In all probability she was on a fool's errand. She could just imagine what Dominic would say. 'Oh, *Sarah*! You're doing exactly what I said you shouldn't, you're getting *immersed*!'

All it took was one phone call and he was back inside her head. Lurking, like the bad fairy at the christening.

The Archive information clerk was a painfully thin, prematurely balding young man who could not have been more than twenty. He had a shy smile and a Mohican-like strip of vestigial fuzz down the middle of his scalp. '*Crockford's Clerical Directory?* No problem *at all*! Pre-war? Hmm. *Interesting.* We'll have to go into the back editions to track this one down.' He must be new to the job, thought Sarah, to be as enthusiastic as this.

Crockford's told her that Ederic Maitland Bowles, MA, D. Phil. (Cantab.), born 1855, had been ordained in 1876, served as curate of St Anselm's, Norwich, from 1876–83, and been rector of St Hybald's in the parish of Hynton and Moxby from 1883 until 1920. So when Mrs Favell had known him in 1935, he had been in his eighties. As well as a daughter, Flora Marguerite, the rector had a son, Theophilus Nestor, who merited his own entry, as he had been a missionary in Nyasaland, where he had perished in the 'civil unrest' of 1922.

Dr Bowles's address was given as The Rectory, Hynton, South Kesteven, Lincolnshire. So Sarah had guessed correctly, and William Fosdyke had been in and out of what was now the home of his grandson, Alex Hardy. She must remember to tell Stephen about that.

Disappointingly, though, there was nothing on Flora Bowles in any of the charity directories, and despite the Mohican's best efforts, Sarah drew a blank. But he allowed her to use the phone in his office to call the Salvation Army, who tracked Flora down with the sort of speed which is rare in research.

'We've just finished putting our records on-line,' said the voice on the phone, which sounded like a twelve-year-old boy scout. Obviously it was Sarah's day for helpful schoolboys. 'Now let me just get into this one.' Click click, click-click. 'Which territory?'

'Oh. England, I suppose. I don't really know.'

Click. Click-click-click. 'Which division?'

'I don't know that either, I'm afraid. All I've got is her name. Could you do a sort of general search?'

A doubtful sigh. 'I *suppose*.' Click, click. Click.

Sarah stared at the Mohican's *X Files* mug full of newly sharpened pencils, and willed the boy scout to use his brain.

'Flora Marguerite Bowles?'

'That's the one!'

'Ah – ha!' Click! 'As from 1938 she was *Mrs Arthur Fielding*. *That's* why nothing was coming up under Bowles. Hm. Important lady. Got her own file. Started out as a cadet in 1911 at Spalding Girls' Home. 1911–21 – Women's Rescue Work. There's pages of this stuff. She ended up a full Colonel.'

'Does it give any family details?'

'Um – no. Deceased 6th October 1988 aged ninety-nine – pity, she just missed her telegram. No, wait. Papers donated Feb. 1989 to Army archives by Mr Leonard Fielding, son. I can give you an address as at 1989.'

'Yes please.'

'The Orchards, Hilltop Rise, South Haverford, East Sussex. You never know, maybe he's still there.'

He wasn't. But the new owners, whom she telephoned slightly guiltily while the Mohican was dealing with another enquiry, had only been in the house for three months and were still forwarding his mail, as they told her with some asperity. Far View Cottage, Little Pluckett's Way, Witherhurst, East Sussex. And no, they didn't have a phone number for him, but would she *please* ask him to get onto the Post Office? They sounded accusatory, as if they suspected her of conspiring with Mr Fielding to waste their time.

She got his number from Directory Enquiries but

decided to wait till she got home to call him. There must be a limit to the Mohican's good nature.

She still had an hour before meeting Alex. She found a post office and sent the letter to Mme Lebesque in Brittany by recorded delivery. Then she bought an apple and a Coke and walked up the hill to the cathedral close. The city centre was humming with tourists, but their impact lessened as she approached the cathedral. She found a place on a low wall in front of the bishop's palace, under a plane tree.

Choir practice had just ended, and a crocodile of choirboys was issuing from the cathedral's Judgement Door. One of them reminded her of Stephen. He had the same stocky build and intense, scowling concentration.

Just like Dominic.

Dominic.

It didn't take long to decide not to call him back.

It wasn't worth it merely to satisfy her curiosity. If she called he would be gratified, which would be unbearable. Nor would it take him long to establish that she still missed him. And, knowing Dominic, by the end of the conversation she would be none the wiser about why he had called.

If he wanted to contact her he would have to try again. And since the only available line to the college was connected to the bursar's answering machine, that meant either leaving a message, calling Alex again, or coming to see her in person. He wouldn't risk the machine and she didn't think he'd get past Alex, which left coming to Harlaston in person. That was the least likely of all. Dominic was the last man to risk having a real door slammed in his face, let alone a metaphorical one.

But the fact remained that she had no idea what he wanted. And why had he called Alex first?

Dominic had always been curiously wary of his younger brother, though they had never openly vied for the limelight. From the start, Dominic had had it all. He was the head boy, the rowing blue, the high-flying barrister with the steady turnover in glamorous girlfriends. But he had always kept a watchful eye on Alex.

Poor old Alex, he used to say. Not bad going for a solicitor. Doing rather *well* till the divorce. Couldn't *win*, though, could he, with a wife like that.

And Dominic hadn't, she recalled, done anything to dispel the notion that Alex had cracked up because Helen left him – although, according to Clare, that was plainly false.

Dominic had always cared so terribly about being first. Alex, on the other hand, didn't seem to care at all. Maybe somewhere along the line he had slipped into the habit of *letting* Dominic win, because he knew it mattered so much to him. Sarah could imagine Alex doing a thing like that. She wondered if Dominic had ever guessed. If he had, it would explain a lot. Maybe that was why he needed to keep tabs on Alex. Because he needed reassurance that his younger brother was one step behind, not one step ahead.

Was that why he was trying to get in touch with her now? Because he didn't like the idea of his ex-girlfriend being in the same village as his brother?

What a mess, she thought tiredly. Maybe Alex has a point, burying himself in a distant past that doesn't include humans. Least of all his own relations.

He was waiting for her when she got back to the car park, leaning against the bonnet of the Saab with his arms crossed, gazing into space. He didn't ask her about the Archives and she didn't ask him about Springthorpe, and neither of them mentioned Dominic. Driving back, they talked desultorily about the cathedral, and what the fens must have been like before they were drained. Outside Tilburne they stopped at a farm Alex knew and bought strawberries. Then they drove the rest of the way home in silence.

She thought she had done a pretty good job of banishing Dominic on the drive home. And she was fairly successful in keeping him banished while she made a cheese sandwich and poured a glass of Orvieto, then climbed the stairs to the conservatory. She curled up in an old cane armchair that smelled of weed-killer and watched a rabbit nibble its way up the slope towards the Japanese Garden. Silence closed over her like a fine settling of dust. Suddenly she had to shut her eyes to stop the tears from coming.

She *wasn't* still in love with Dominic. She knew that. So why this churning sense of bleakness? He was vain, mendacious, and a towering egotist, but he had a peculiar talent for making others desire his approval, and for making them feel a failure if they didn't get it.

Perhaps that was what was upsetting her. Simply the sense of having failed.

She hadn't had much in the way of *éducation sentimentale*. A couple of brief experimental couplings at Oxford with clever, insecure young men who had mistaken her reserve for passivity and her tolerance for lack of perception. A friendship with a co-trainee at the BBC, with some more or less desultory sex thrown in. Both the sex and the friendship had ended when she had landed her first documentary feature, and he had got a children's educational short on lifeboats.

Then Dominic.

With glass in hand, she wandered across the landing and into the Jade Ante-Room, where the bronze dwarf gave her a sly welcoming look. She picked up her father's photograph from the mantelpiece.

It had been taken at some school open day, where he had been the guest speaker. He was often asked to speak at schools, and rarely declined. He said it was good for him, as the children usually knew more about journalism than he did.

She couldn't imagine Dominic talking to a lot of schoolchildren for free.

'You wouldn't have liked him, Dad,' she told the photograph. 'You'd have said he needed taking down a peg or two.'

She wondered if Alex also became maudlin when he was drunk. The thought of Alex becoming maudlin was so incongruous that she started to laugh. She laughed all the way back to the kitchen, where she refilled her glass, took a Kit Kat from the fridge, and went back upstairs.

She drank a silent toast to her grandfather in the Long Gallery, then wandered into the Gold Drawing-Room, where the Technicolor cornicing looked almost mellow in the twilight. Fat white putti struggled to escape wooden garlands wound strategically between their legs.

It was Harlaston at its most exhausting – but comforting in its flamboyance, if one was used to it.

No. She wouldn't *let* Dominic get his teeth into this.

She went back to the study and loaded the VCR with one of her all-time comfort videos and curled up in an armchair. Rachmaninov's Second Piano Concerto boomed out on the soundtrack, and the train steamed into Milford Junction.

She had worked her way through a clutch of paper tissues when the telephone rang.

Alex hardly ever called, so it wouldn't be him. And it wasn't the right time of day for her mother. Moving quietly as if the phone might hear her, she crossed the landing to the bursar's office.

The answerphone clicked, and the bursar asked the caller to leave a message, speaking slowly and clearly after the tone.

'Pick up the phone, Sarah,' said Dominic.

CHAPTER NINETEEN

Friday 31 August 1900

'I'll be gone all day,' said Mrs Fosdyke, skewering her hat with a six-inch pin. 'Don't wait tea. You'll not need more than sixpenn'orth of brisket, an' *don't* use it all. What with the excitement tomorrow we won't want much.'

'I know,' Charity said. 'We went over that last night. Twice.'

Her mother ignored her. The clicking of her jaws was the only sound in the silent kitchen.

It was still only half past five, but already the day had got off to a shaky start. Mrs Fosdyke had been thrown badly off kilter by yesterday's invitation from Mrs Jordan to watch the Ball from the upper servants' quarters. There wasn't enough time to work out what to wear, how late to stay, and whether Will could be trusted to accompany them. Added to which, the trimming on her best black straw was a disgrace, so there was nothing for it but to make a special visit to Tilburne. Charity would just have to do the shopping and baking by herself. It'd do her good, high time she learnt to run a household, she'd have one of her own soon enough, not naming any names, though at her age no-one could say it wasn't before time.

Mrs Fosdyke wasn't the only one out of sorts. Mr Fosdyke had gone to work fretting over a swelling he had found behind the sow's ear, and, since the incident of the peahens, Will had withdrawn deeper and deeper into his silent world.

Charity hadn't slept properly since the conversation in St Hybald's. For the past three nights she had lain awake, going over and over what she had said to Lord Harlaston. Whichever way she looked at it, she had behaved with the most appalling insolence. It was only a matter of time before he turned the whole family out of the end house.

She glanced across the table to where Will sat blinking owlishly at his kettle broth. 'Either eat that,' she told him, 'or go to work. But don't just sit there like a pudding. You're getting on my nerves.'

'Hark at the *duchess* and her nerves!' cried Mrs Fosdyke, giving her hat a final stab.

Will ignored them both. His eyes were fixed on some distant, terrible prospect known only to himself.

'What's up with you?' Charity asked. When he didn't reply she gave a weary shrug. 'Oh, suit yourself. You're not the only one with troubles.'

Mrs Fosdyke snorted. 'An' what troubles have *you* got, I'd like to know? Which bit of ribbon to work into your blouse for tomorrow night, I shouldn't wonder!'

'Isn't it time you went, Mother?' said Charity.

'Can't wait to get me out of the house, can she, the little madam! Far as I'm concerned, the sooner that young man says his piece an' it's all official, the better.

Then maybe we'll get a civil word out of her once in a while.'

'Not everything I say and do goes back to Sam Webb.'

Two spots of red appeared on Mrs Fosdyke's cheeks. 'I'll be off,' she announced, as if she was starting for the North Pole. 'Maybe you'll have learnt some manners by the time I get home.'

The front door slammed.

Charity sat on at the table.

Every time she thought of the conversation in the church she went hot and cold.

How could you *do* it? Why didn't you leave the *minute* you saw who he was? He wouldn't have stopped you, he didn't want you there in the first place. He wanted to be on his own. That's why he was there. To be on his own.

But you had to stay, didn't you? You had to fool yourself into believing he wanted to know what you thought. You! Who d'you think you are, the Duchess of Devonshire? Passing judgement like that.

Oh, yes, my lord, it was a terrible thing to do.

What an insolent, unforgivable, *suicidal* thing to say to the man who owns Hynton and Moxby and Stainton Hamer and everything in between.

The family was ruined, and it was *her fault*. She pictured the despair on her father's placid red features. And what would it do to her mother, with her hard-won confidence and her cherished acquaintance with the upper servants? To have all that publicly snatched away, just when she was beginning to let down her guard. It would kill her.

But it's *done* now, she told herself wearily, in a vain attempt to put it behind her. What will come will come. There's nothing you can do about it now.

To begin with, though, she had thought there might be something to be salvaged from the ruins. She could try to see him. Apologize, explain, say something, anything, to stave off disaster. But when would she get the chance? Never. Not unless he happened to call on Mrs Bowles on the exact afternoon when she happened to be there reading to her. And even if he did, she recoiled at the idea of stammering out apologies in front of Mrs Bowles. The parson's wife was the kindest person she knew, but she had no idea about the conversation in the church. No-one did. And if Charity told her now, days later, Mrs Bowles would be hurt that she had withheld something so important. She might well sack her for dishonesty.

Though of course, if her father got the sack, they would have to leave Hynton anyway, so Mrs Bowles could hardly make matters any worse.

Oh *God*.

She put her head in her hands.

She had even tried praying. She had steeled herself and returned to St Hybald's and stood before the altar and asked Him for help. It was a last resort which she didn't expect to work. No prayer of hers had ever been answered before, and there was no reason to suppose it would be different now.

But the worst of it was that she couldn't stop reliving the conversation in her head. Summoning up the way he had looked. The feverish brightness in his eyes. The sharpening of his shoulder-blades as he leaned forward. His hands.

When she thought about that, she wanted to see him again so badly it was a physical ache. And that made her angry with herself all over again.

A hand touched her shoulder. She raised her head.

Will was standing beside her, about to go to work. For reasons she didn't understand he looked as ghastly as she felt.

'I got to go,' he murmured, hardly moving his lips.

'Well then, you'd better go. You're late as it is.'

He moved to the door. Suddenly he ran back and flung his arms around her shoulders. 'G'bye dearest sister,' he mumbled into her neck.

'What are you doing? What's got into you?'

He tore himself away and ran from the house.

He had left behind his jam sandwich and tea-bottle. Oh well. Maybe missing his dinner would bring him to his senses. It was time he grew up. Time he left behind his dream world of magic lions and peahen's eggs, and learned what grown people had to contend with.

Over the past few days, Robert's study had become a refuge for himself and Tully. It was the only room in the house which had not been rendered uninhabitable by the preparations for the Ball. The din of hammering, the rumble of wagons and the shouts of footmen floated in through the open windows.

Usually, his afternoons were given over to correspondence and estate affairs with his secretary and Dickon, but today he was too restless to deal with either. He sat at his desk abstractedly cutting the pages of a book he had no intention of reading.

Every time he thought of the stonemason's daughter he felt a twist of guilt.

Because of her, he felt lighter in spirit than at any time since Linley's death. Not free of grief nor cleansed of guilt, but better able to live with both, now that he had finally acknowledged them to himself. He owed that to her, for she was the only person who had told him the truth.

And how had he repaid her?

He kept seeing the way she had looked at him when he told her to get out of the church. The blood leaving her face. The clear eyes darkening with shock.

Why had he been so curt with her? What must she think of him?

Perhaps he could engineer a meeting so that he might apologize.

Another twist of guilt. He wasn't being honest with himself. The apology was a sham. A trumpery piece of self-deception. He wanted to see her again. The rest was lies.

A knock at the door brought him smartly back to the present.

It was Sam. Normally he entered with the assurance of a valued servant and stated his business without preamble. But today, to Robert's irritation, he shut the door softly behind him and waited on the rug until he had Robert's full attention.

'If it's not inconvenient, my lord, I wondered if I might have a word on a personal matter.'

With a sense of weariness Robert put down the book and prepared to listen to a renewed attack on the vexed question of the motor. As this was Sam rather than Dickon, he knew that the attack would be carefully reasoned, outwardly respectful, and simmering with barely concealed resentment.

The attack didn't come. Instead he was treated to an impenetrable hypothetical question about what Sam's expectations might be in the event that, for reasons Robert didn't understand, Dickon might 'move on to other things'. The thought of the conservative Dickon moving anywhere was ludicrous. 'What's this, Sam? You're not planning a *coup* to take over the throne?'

Sam flushed. 'A coup, my lord? I'm afraid I don't know what that means.'

'Then you'll have to be a little more direct,' Robert said tartly. 'What is it that you want?'

Sam's chin went up. 'I wouldn't of troubled your lordship the day before the Ball, only I didn't think it proper to wait till we're on our way back to South Africa, so I thought it best to speak out.'

Robert felt his face stiffen. He hoped he was misreading the signals. 'Why, Sam. Can it be that at last you're to be married?'

Sam glowered at him. 'I don't know about *at last*, my lord. But it's true I've decided to choose a wife.'

Robert cleared his throat. 'Indeed. And – who is your – *fiancée*?' As if he didn't already know.

'Jack Fosdyke's girl,' Sam replied coolly.

The omission of her name made Robert repress a flicker of anger. 'Indeed. Surely you can't have known each other for very long?'

'Long enough, my lord.' And mind your own bloody business, said the cold grey eyes.

Robert picked up the book and weighed it in his hand.

His first thought was how to prevent a match which even to a disinterested observer would clearly be a disaster. His second was that, if he did, it would be purely for his own ends. He glanced up at Sam and arranged his features in a smile. 'You have my best wishes, of course. And clearly we can't keep you languishing in that bachelor's room of yours on the off chance that Dickon develops brain fever and hands in his notice. We shall have to find something more suitable for a married man. We'll look into it after the war.'

He thought he sounded abominably hearty and insincere, like a squire in a music-hall comedy. Sam did not appear to have noticed. Perhaps, having secured what he was after, he didn't care.

Best wishes, he thought, when Sam had gone. What an empty phrase that is.

And yet Sam deserved his best wishes if anyone did. He was bright, hard-working, and knew more about the care of pheasants, dogs and horses than any man in South Kesteven. If he ever decided to do the unthinkable and 'move on to other things', half a dozen landowners in the district would leap to offer him a position.

But Robert had never liked him. As boys they had fought constantly. Then when Robert was twelve years old he had blundered into the keeper's back yard and come upon old Tom Webb steadily thrashing his younger son's naked back to the consistency of ground dog's meat. Old Tom never knew that Master Robert had seen him at his work, but Sam, with his breeches round his knees and a stick jammed between his teeth to stop him screaming, had glared at Robert with a rage so incandescent that twenty-three years later the memory was still vivid.

They had never spoken of it, but Robert knew Sam well enough to know that he had not been forgiven for what he had seen.

He went to the window and looked down into the clock-yard.

Whatever had led the girl to accept a man like that? But perhaps she had not accepted him – at least, not

265

yet. Sam had not said that he had proposed to her: merely that he had chosen her for his wife. And in four days' time, Sam, like Robert himself, would begin the journey back to South Africa. Four days. What could be accomplished in four days? Surely nothing irrevocable.

He shut his eyes, overcome by a wave of self-loathing. My God, man, *listen* to yourself! You're no better than old Bowles with his Ovid – or Algy Hepworth with his Holywell Street arrangement. Is that what this is about? Is it? Well then, for Christ's *sake* have the sense to take a mistress from your own kind, and don't behave like a blackguard on your own estate.

Suddenly the study was unbearably hot. He threw the book aside and left the room.

The Ponds in Hynton Wood are a curiosity. They lie in a saucer-shaped depression halfway up the Edge, where Slea Beck begins its descent into the valley of the Lyde.

Between two and three thousand years ago, the people of the region worked the ironstone around the source of the Beck, and when they left, the workings filled and became the Ponds: three small tear-shaped lakes, each no more than thirty feet at its widest, but deep and cold, with water of a peculiar opaque pale green. Anyone leaning over will see mysterious skeletons of drowned weeds through which small red-finned perch glide and flick their tails. Bulrushes rustle in the breeze. Dragonflies dart like blue sparks. Water lilies spread their glossy leaves, their thick white petals enclosing hearts as yellow as wax.

The beeches and sycamores of Hynton Wood do not

encroach upon Pond Hollow, which is enclosed by a belt of tall Scots pines.

It should be a place of peace and beauty.

Will hated it.

To him the water lilies were coffin flowers. The pines were a band of wicked old men hissing curses. On the eastern edge of the Hollow, where a pine had fallen the previous autumn, its tortured root-mass reared above the torn black earth like a vision of hell.

Though it was still early in the morning, the sun was hot on the back of his neck, but his limbs were clammy and cold.

He would have prayed to God if the name had meant anything to him. But God was merely a distant authority, somewhat less dreadful than the School Inspector. God had never helped him before and was unlikely to help him now. When Will prayed, he prayed to Moss Lion, whose eyes were shut in perpetual slumber. For especially weighty matters, such as a spell to stop Charity marrying Keeper Webb, he summoned his courage and prayed to Moon Lion, whose lunatic stare blazed with unbridled power. For the past week, since Segg's Field and the incident of the peahens, he had prayed to them both.

'Mole,' said a soft voice on the slope above him.

Will turned his head.

Ned Webb, Luke Morris and Jim Bacon were standing on the rise at the edge of the pines.

'Well, Mole,' said Ned again. 'I bin' waiting all week. Mowdy-warp.'

'I an't got it,' said Will, his voice rough with anger. 'You knew I wouldn't of. Might as well tell me to fly to the moon an' bring back a bit o' cheese as get a peahen's egg in summer.'

'Now that's an idea, that is,' said Ned. 'I'm partial to a bit o' cheese.'

Behind him Jim Bacon sniggered.

'Liar!' Will cried. 'Peahens only lays in spring.'

Ned ignored him. 'Come on, lads,' he snapped. 'Time we stopped buggerin' about an' got on with it. An't got all day.'

With a sense of detachment and almost relief, Will saw the glint of metal in Ned's hand, and the pile of rusty iron in the nettles at his feet.

By four o'clock the preparations for the Ball had reached the relentless stage, when the staff were beginning to wonder if the remaining twenty-four hours would be sufficient even if they worked all night.

The marquees on the south lawn lay in a deflated tangle of hawsers, like vast marine creatures stranded at low tide. Journeymen sweated to string thousands of tiny candle-holders of coloured glass along the drive and the pleasure-ground walks. On the croquet lawn the dance floor was still only half-built. Engineers bickered over the construction of the bandstand.

For days, wagons had trundled up the service road from the poultry yard, the Home Farm, the kitchen gardens and the forcing-houses. Kitchen boys carted ice from the ice house, and Mrs Shaw and Mrs Walsh had their yearly debate about whether they had brought it up too soon. This year they had more cause for anxiety than usual, for no-one could recall it being this hot in September.

Inside the Hall, an army of housemaids had taken over, and teams of under-gardeners moved like ants between the greenhouses and the state rooms, which were gradually succumbing to a lush tide of greenery.

Great banks of camellias, oleanders and citrus; forests of giant palms; curtains of passiflora and ipomoea; pyramids of orchids.

With his hands in his pockets, Robert walked across the American Ground, followed by a disconsolate Tully who was soon to be locked in the kennels until the Ball was over.

Robert caught sight of Violet's pearl-grey figure gliding across the west terrace. Despite the heat, she and Paige had been patrolling the grounds since the early afternoon, like a minor Inquisition. Violet was in her element. Paige – tall, inscrutable, with a hatchet face like a Bellini Pope – followed two paces behind, looking scarcely less regal.

It occurred to Robert that Violet and Paige made the perfect couple. Both were zealots pledged to an all-consuming cause: the pursuit of Form. Both were united by a common zeal to fulfil their narrow destinies.

He debated what to do next. There were still a couple of hours until he must go inside to bathe and dress for dinner. In the meantime, what? He had forgotten to order Viscount, and to descend un-announced on the stables would create more trouble than it was worth. Perhaps he should take pity on Tully and see that he enjoyed his last hours of freedom with a walk.

He lit a cigar and started northwards, making a detour through the Japanese Garden to avoid the Inquisition on the terrace. Recognizing the start of a favourite walk, the spaniel gave a joyous yelp and bounded up the Lion Steps to the quoits ground, where he ran back and forth barking at Robert to join him. He was four years old and a hopeless gun dog, with a poor sense of smell and a haphazard attitude to commands. Robert liked him for his silliness and extravagant devotion.

He scooped up the spaniel in his arms and climbed over the stile into the wood. Tully licked his chin and wriggled out of his grip, hitting the ground at a gallop and disappearing into the brambles. Robert let him go. He could do no harm. Hynton Wood was no longer maintained as a covert.

After the glare on the lawns it was wonderfully cool beneath the trees. The din of hammers fell away. A leaf spiralled with silent grace to the forest floor. Robert gave himself up to the sharp green scent of summer and the rustle of his boots through last year's leaves. As always on the Edge, he had a sense of centuries of human woodsmanship stretching back into the distant past. It gave him a deep feeling of peace to view his own life as a vanishingly small link in an endless chain.

After ten minutes he reached Pond Hollow in the middle of the wood. The sounds from the pleasure gardens had fallen to nothing. All he could hear was birdsong and crickets and the buzzing of bees. The infinitesimal *plick* as a swallow dipped on the wing to drink.

At the far end of the Hollow stood a pile of logs: the neatly sectioned carcase of a fallen pine which had been left to season. He wandered over to it. The air was sweet with resin, the sun bright on the hot waxen leaves of the water lilies. Leaning against the log-pile, he smoked his cigar and followed the course of a damsel-fly across the pale green water.

The stonemason's daughter and Samuel Webb.

The cold, grimly secretive gamekeeper, simmering with resentment and distrust – and that warm-hearted, perceptive, painfully honest young woman. It was all wrong.

He threw away his cigar and whistled for Tully.

The spaniel came crashing through the brambles and down into the Hollow, where he paused to gulp noisily at the nearest pond before trotting straight past Robert to investigate the log-pile.

Robert found the path which led out of the Hollow and down towards the Moxby road. 'Come along, Tully, we're going. Tully! *Come!*'

Tully ignored him. Something by the log-pile had claimed his attention: a log which had fallen from the stack and rolled down into the crater left by the roots of the toppled pine. The spaniel was snuffling and whining excitedly, his head thrust into a clump of nettles. All Robert could see were quivering hind-quarters and a tensely waving tail.

With a sigh, Robert walked back up the Hollow and scrambled down into the crater. He waded through the nettles and reached down to take hold of the dog's collar.

Then he saw that it was not a log that had caught Tully's attention, but a boy.

CHAPTER TWENTY

He lay face downwards with his arms tied behind his back. His left leg was caught in a spring-trap: one of the old galvanized kind which the under-gardeners still set for rabbits around the kitchen gardens. But no-one had set traps in Hynton Wood for a decade or more.

Kneeling among the nettles, Robert saw eight more traps, staked out around the boy in a double ring about three yards wide. It was only by chance that neither he nor the dog had inadvertently sprung one as they approached.

He told Tully to sit, in a voice which set the spaniel's ears back and dropped him where he stood. Then he sprang the remaining traps with scraps of bark, and turned the boy onto his back.

He had recognized the flaxen hair on sight, and it was with pity and apprehension but no surprise that he found himself looking down at the unconscious face of the stonemason's son.

The boy had been gagged and blindfolded with sacking, and his good ear stopped with beeswax. About his neck hung a placard crudely fashioned from a scrap of old fencing, on which a near-illiterate hand had scratched the letters 'MOL' in charcoal.

Someone had placed him inside this double ring of traps, and cleverly positioned them so that sooner or later he must step in one. The boy would have known that, and no doubt the dread of it had been part of the design of whoever had put him there.

Robert reflected for a moment on the nature of a being which could pinion a child, render him deaf, dumb and blind, and then leave him in the blazing sun inside a ring of bone-cracking traps.

Of course it had to be another child, or more probably a gang of them. This had all the marks of the gleeful brutality of village lads.

Fortunately, when the boy had made his bid for freedom, he'd had the sense to attempt the more difficult but safer route *up* the side of the Hollow, rather than down towards the ponds. If he had taken the latter direction, he would have pitched in and drowned.

'Who did this to you, William?' Robert asked some time later. He was not surprised when the boy answered with a shake of the head. The code was the same, whether it was Hynton or Eton. One did not betray one's peers.

He had revived sooner than Robert expected, after a hatful of pond water poured on the head and a long agonizing drink which he had promptly vomited into the grass. The sturdiness of his limbs and their healthy covering of flesh appeared to have saved his shin from a fracture, but the rusty iron had bitten deep into the calf, which was badly bruised and swollen and crusted with dried blood. The right side of his face was lobster-red from the sun. The left, on which he had lain, was chalk-white and blistered with nettle-stings.

He looked like some woeful, bizarrely particoloured jester.

He sat with his back against the log-pile with Robert's tunic about his shoulders and his injured leg stretched before him. He was shaking like a puppy, as he had been since Robert prised the jaws apart. It must have hurt like the devil, but he had only whimpered and clutched Robert's shoulder, and somehow managed not to scream.

So far he hadn't uttered a word. When Robert removed the wax plug from his ear and asked if he could hear, he merely stared at him with enormous, shocked blue eyes.

'Will,' Robert said again. 'You're not a sneak, and that's good. But you must tell me who did this, so that I can stop them doing it again. You could have been killed.'

The only answer he got was an unblinking gaze which mutely acknowledged the limits of a landlord's authority.

Robert sighed. 'Very well. We'll leave it for now. Let's get this leg of yours cleaned up.'

The boy set his teeth and made an admirable stab at not crying as Robert cleaned off the crusted blood with his wet handkerchief and then used it to bind the wound. But an attempt at levity – pointing out the collection of pocket handkerchiefs he was acquiring – fell dismally flat.

'I n-never, sir!' he stammered, at last breaking his silence. 'M-ma took Master Aubrey's kerchief back *next day*, washed an' ironed, an' gave it to Mrs Jordan in a bit o' paper. She'll do the same with yours, sir, *promise*. Mrs Jordan'll have it tomorrow.'

'No doubt, no doubt,' said Robert, who had no idea who Mrs Jordan was.

But the boy was not to be comforted. The thought of his mother was a fresh cause of woe. 'What'll I *do*! She'll *never* get over this! The disgrace'll kill her!'

'But good heavens, child, there's no disgrace!'

'She'll *take* it as disgrace! 'Tis the *notice* she won't bear. Everyone knowin' an' talkin'. She won't stand the *notice*!'

Which showed, thought Robert, a not unsubtle grasp of feminine psychology. What had Gwendolen Bowles said about the stonemason's wife? A 'fen tigress', pathologically sensitive to slights. She must be sensitive indeed, if her son's first thought was for her.

'Your mother doesn't need to know the details,' he told the boy. 'No-one need know.' He took the placard and tied it to a stone with the scrap of sacking which had served as a gag. Then he lobbed it into the nearest pond. 'There. As far as I'm concerned, you simply trod in a snare which someone left lying about. Are we agreed?'

Will thought about it, then gave a nod.

With a child's ready acceptance of the extraordinary, he had shown no surprise at being rescued by a member of the aristocracy, and Robert liked him for that. In fact, now that he was accustomed to the unsettling Dutchness of the boy's appearance, he found himself liking Will Fosdyke increasingly.

He drew out his watch. It was nearly five o'clock. He considered the options for getting the boy back to Hynton.

The most obvious was to retrace his steps and summon a journeyman to carry him down to the village. But that would mean leaving Will alone in the Hollow – and, despite his rapid recovery, he clearly wasn't in any state for that. On the other hand, he, Robert, was perfectly capable of taking the boy to the village himself. This surely didn't fall within that vast category of tasks which he could perform quite well for himself, but did not, in order to avoid upsetting the staff.

If nothing else, he thought, the sight of the landlord in shirtsleeves with an injured village lad in his arms should give the tattle-tales of Hynton something to tattle about for weeks to come.

But at the back of his mind, he knew that this debate was a sham. The outcome was never in doubt. In the first moment when he had pulled Tully aside and recognized the boy, he had experienced not only pity and outrage but also a shot of pure joy. This was what he had been hoping for. An excuse to see her again.

In the next moment he told himself that the whole point of seeing her again was to prove once and for all that he had been wrong about her. That she was not what he had made of her in his mind, but merely an ordinary village girl. Perhaps a little more perceptive, a little more *aware* than most. But a village girl nonetheless.

'Come on Will,' he said briskly, 'I'll take you home.'

By the time the bells of St Hybald's had rung a quarter past five, Charity had done the shopping and the entire week's baking. The mixing-bowls had been washed and put away, the loaves and ginger buns stood cooling on the table, and the suet pudding was jiggling the kettle-lid on the range.

She hadn't stopped for dinner. A quick cup of tea

and a slice of bread and dripping had kept her going, and now she had her reward. Her father and Will wouldn't be home till six, and her mother wouldn't arrive till some time after that. Which meant that she had three-quarters of an hour – *three-quarters of an hour* – in which to make a start on Chapter Two of *Wanderings of an Oxonian, or Little Sketches of Life and Nature in Italy and France.*

The kitchen was hot and the table cluttered with baking, but it didn't occur to her to take Mrs Bowles's book into the parlour. She disliked the parlour, which reminded her of Sundays. In any event, she couldn't leave the ginger buns at the mercy of Mrs Goldsbrow's marmalade tom, which was loitering outside the open door, ready to pounce.

She settled into her favourite chair and pushed the conversation in the church firmly to the back of her mind. She had thought of little else all day, and was tired of it. Now it was a question of will-power. It would be a waste of a good book if she allowed fruitless worrying to spoil her free time.

'In this region of the Auvergne,' she read, *'the peasants live in a state of the lowest savagery. On one occasion we ventured inside a picturesque way-side hovel, and I confess that I never saw anything like that pestilential interior, festooned with rude vestments and cooking implementia of the most doubtful cleanliness! Fearing the attentions of the* pulex irritans, *we swiftly took our leave.'*

Charity marked the page with a slip of newspaper as a reminder to read it to her mother, who would be enjoyably horrified.

Ten minutes later, when she was deep in an account of the walnut harvest at Salers, she heard the gate creak and Will's voice saying quietly, 'Best to go round the back. We don't use the front door much.'

She shut her eyes in disbelief. Oh, *Will*! To come home *early*. How could he do this to her? And to bring someone with him.

A man's voice said, 'In the kitchen, Will?'

She shut the book and raised her head, just in time to see a liver-and-white spaniel put his nose round the door. Then Lord Harlaston, hatless and in Army blue shirtsleeves rolled up like a journeyman, ducked beneath the lintel and carried her brother into the kitchen.

Wordlessly she took in Will's bandaged shin and extraordinary particoloured face, and the way he rode with one arm crooked about Lord Harlaston's neck like a young maharajah, looking pale and ill, but also shyly and intensely proud.

Lord Harlaston raised his head and saw her, and blinked once. 'It's not', he said, 'quite as bad as it looks.'

No, thought Robert, she is not, after all, what one would call *handsome*. It is simply the colouring and the definition of feature which make one think her so. And the way she holds herself, like a little empress. Even when she's utterly taken aback.

'Mother's in Tilburne,' she said inexplicably, 'though it's not our day for it.' Then the honey-coloured skin darkened as she realized he had no idea what she was talking about. 'What *happened*?'

'He caught his leg in a trap. Please do not distress yourself. I don't believe it's serious. I mean, I don't think anything's broken.'

'A *trap*? Where?'

'Pond Hollow. That's in—'

'He was trespassing? *Again*? Oh, Will!' Then to Robert: 'I'm so sorry, sir – I mean, my lord. He's usually quite good, despite what you must think!'

'It doesn't matter. I'd guess it was some kind of dare which went awry.' He reached into his pocket and brought out a half-crown which he tucked into Will's breast pocket. 'That's for not crying when the trap came off.'

Wordlessly Will touched his finger to his pocket as if it contained the Koh-i-noor diamond.

'After what he's done,' the girl said tartly, 'he doesn't deserve a farthing.' Then she blushed anew, realizing she sounded ungrateful.

She had the most expressive face. In the course of two minutes Robert had watched her register consternation at his arrival in her kitchen, horror for her brother, exasperation at the boy's transgression, and finally a transparent internal debate as to where she ought to put a visiting lord. He solved that for her by depositing Will on one of the rickety chairs around the table, propping up the injured leg on a second, and placing himself on the third. 'Dr Young ought to take a look at that cut,' he said.

She made no reply, save for a brief inclination of the head which could have meant anything. He cursed himself for his obtuseness. Which artisan family could afford the attentions of Dr Young for so slight an ill? She was simply too honest to lie, too polite to contradict, and too proud to admit to her family's lack of funds.

'Perhaps,' he said, trying to smooth things over, 'perhaps you had better take a look at it yourself. I couldn't do more than a rough job at the Hollow.'

She bit her lip, clearly torn between concern for her brother and her duty to her guest. 'But I can't just – that is, would you like some tea, my lord?'

'Thank you, no. The boy. See to the boy.'

Robert watched her move about the tiny kitchen collecting clean rags and some kind of clove-smelling liniment in a blue glass jar. Then she knelt on the floor beside her brother's chair and started to dress his leg. Her expression was self-conscious, but her movements had a surety which he found admirable.

She wore a sprigged cotton blouse tucked into a dark blue skirt and a wide leather belt. Her sleeves were rolled back to the elbow, presumably from the afternoon's baking. Her hands were sturdy but well-formed, with prominent wrist-bones like a boy's. For a moment he was back in St Hybald's, watching those hands arranging artichokes around the pulpit. Jewelled sunlight streamed through the stained-glass windows, splashing her skin with amethyst and topaz.

The conversation in St Hybald's was a mutual awkwardness between them, and he knew it would be for him to bring it up. Here in her own kitchen she would be more circumspect than he had allowed her to be in St Hybald's.

She startled him by asking if he thought someone had done this to her brother deliberately.

He glanced at Will. The boy was watching him, but without anxiety. He didn't seem perturbed by the idea of his sister knowing the truth.

And it would be unconscionable to mislead her after she had been so honest with him in St Hybald's. So he told her about the circle of snares, and the wax, and the gag, and finally about the placard.

Her clear eyes widened as she took it in. 'Who would *do* such a thing?'

'Your brother wouldn't tell me. Perhaps you'll have better luck than I.'

Slowly she shook her head. 'I doubt it. When he takes it into his head not to tell . . . Well. I suppose whoever they are, they won't try again after this.'

'Why not?'

Her cheeks darkened. 'I mean, considering who it was that brought him home.'

'Oh. That had not occurred to me. I hope you're right.'

Tully padded over to Will and placed his muzzle on the boy's thigh.

'He found me,' Will murmured sleepily.

'It's the first time that animal's found anything,' Robert remarked. 'Tully, sit.'

Still with his muzzle on Will's thigh, Tully sat. His tail swept the floor as Will stroked his ears.

The silence deepened. Outside, the sow rooted in her sty. A blackbird alighted on the wall and sang. Will's head sank to his chest. Finally, he slept.

It occurred to Robert that he ought to leave, but he could not bring himself to do so.

As a boy, he had been in and out of countless cottages such as this: gulping down scalding black tea and soaking up the village gossip. And always there was the same earthy tang of potatoes and coal-dust and supper bubbling over the fire, with birdsong and the snufflings of the pig coming in through the open door.

The girl was still on her knees beside her brother, thoughtfully looking down at the blue glass jar in her lap. As her contemplation deepened, her dark brows drew slightly together, like two sharp, delicate wings. Robert thought them extraordinarily beautiful.

He asked if he might reconsider the offer of tea.

She raised her head. ' – I'm sorry. Yes. Of course.'

He watched her fetch cups and saucers from the dresser and set the kettle to boil. A strand of her hair had come loose from her chignon, and he thought how easy it would be to reach over and smooth it back from her cheek.

She turned from the range and gave him a quick, shy glance, which made him instantly contrite. Thank heavens she couldn't read his thoughts. He gave her a brief smile, then glanced away and pretended interest in his surroundings.

The end house was a good deal cleaner than many cottages he had been in. In fact, it was spotless. The tiles had been sanded clean of every speck of dirt, and the table beneath its burden of baking was white from scrubbing. A large sack of potatoes and a smaller one of flour stood in a corner, their tops neatly folded and weighted with stones. On the range a meal was simmering. It smelled of suet and not much else, but the odour was barely detectable beneath the glorious fragrance of freshly baked bread.

The dresser contained the inevitable willow-pattern plates, a pair of milk-jugs commemorating the Golden and Diamond Jubilees, a row of jam jars labelled in a neat copperplate hand, and an artless arrangement of poppies and sweet william in a yellow pottery jug.

It was all no different from countless other cottages he had been in, save for two items which stood out as peculiar to the inhabitants.

The first was the book the girl was reading when he came in, and which, disconcerted as she had been, she

282

had carefully set aside on the dresser. From the title, it was a volume of travel notes of the more or less interminable kind, but she seemed to be enjoying it, for she had placed it on a square of clean linen like a holy relic.

The second was an outstandingly bad lithograph of the kind to be found at the centre fold of the cheaper illustrated newspapers. It had been tacked beside the door, presumably so that the family might benefit from its thumpingly obvious message as they sat around the table. It depicted a plump young woman who had plainly strayed from the path of virtue, and who – through carelessness or some additional misfortune – had been flung from her paramour's brougham on a wintry night. Seemingly impervious to frostbite, she lay weeping in the snow, with the tokens of her shameful luxury strewn about her, while the paramour's carriage rattled off into the distance. 'The Sybarite's Reward' was printed in unnecessarily bold Gothic script beneath.

It was a spectacularly ugly picture, but one with an intriguing ambivalence as to tone – its stern moral message being considerably undermined by the sensuality with which it had been executed. The artist had clearly revelled in the scattered items of luxury: the jewels, the tasselled robes, the tiny Turkish slippers, which he had depicted with flamboyance and something very close to glee. The Sybarite, Robert reflected, looked as though she had thoroughly enjoyed her fall from grace.

The girl set before him a china cup painted with violets. Following the direction of his gaze, she gave the Sybarite a doubtful look. 'I'm sorry, sir – my lord – we don't have any milk.'

'I never take it,' he lied, remembering that villagers never had fresh milk in the summer. 'And thank you, nothing to eat. This will do perfectly.'

She gave the curious little inclination of the head which seemed habitual to her, though he had the impression that she guessed his unwillingness to deplete their stores of baking.

'In South Africa,' he found himself explaining, 'we go for weeks without milk. Tea itself is something of a luxury.'

He was rewarded with a curious glance. She almost smiled. 'What do you drink if you can't get tea?'

'Coffee. Weak, black, and very bitter. Rather like acorn coffee. But it keeps one warm.'

'But – it can't be *cold*, in South Africa?'

'Oh, frequently.'

'I thought it was hot.'

'In summer it is. But since it's at the other end of the world, the seasons are the opposite way around.'

'Oh, of course. So it would be spring there now?'

'Yes. It would be spring.'

They exchanged tentative smiles.

Colouring, she fetched a water-jug and filled an earthenware bowl and put it on the floor for Tully. The spaniel trotted over, his claws clicking on the tiles, and drank noisily. Then he padded back and curled up beside Will's chair.

The girl stood against the dresser with her arms crossed about her waist. 'I wondered—'

'Yes?'

'The Dutchmen. The Boers? That is what you call them?'

He nodded.

'Do they – do they look like us?'

284

He was startled. It was the last thing he had expected her to say. ' – No,' he faltered. 'At least, not – not like you or me. They tend to be fair. In fact, your brother resembles them rather strikingly. That's what I find so disconcerting.'

She nodded, frowning a little, and he wondered how much she had guessed.

Another silence.

The time had come to broach the subject of St Hybald's. He was wondering how to begin, when she said in a rush, 'I hope, my lord, you won't think me impertinent if I refer to what was said last Tuesday afternoon.'

Again she had astonished him. 'Why – of course not. I was about to do the same.'

'I only wanted to say', she began with concentrated intensity, 'that if what I said caused offence, the offence was mine and mine *alone*. If I did cause offence,' she added, 'of course I'm very sorry and I hope you'll forgive me. But the point is that my father had nothing to do with it.'

'Your *father* – ?' Robert was baffled. Then it dawned on him. The notion was so absurd that it made him brusque. 'But good heavens,' he cried, 'this is not the Middle Ages! You can't imagine I'd be such an ogre as to hold what you said against you?'

But of course that was precisely what she did think.

And, on reflection, was it so very far-fetched? The Duke of Kyme frequently dismissed senior members of his staff for disagreeing with him on minor matters. Charity Fosdyke was only a stonemason's daughter, and last Tuesday she had roundly condemned her landlord for his lack of humanity.

He was mortified. This was not at all what he had

anticipated. 'You must understand', he said, 'your father's position – your family's tenancy of this house – are quite, quite secure. I am infinitely dismayed that you should have thought it might be otherwise.'

Not very well put, and apparently hardly reassuring. Her face became rigid with apprehension. She looked as if she was about to cry. He tried again. 'That afternoon,' he said gently, 'I was trying to work something out. You happened to be there, so I asked you a question. A question which was, I admit, of some importance to me. But it was grossly unfair of me to put it to you at all. Do you see? The fault lies with *me*, and me alone. It is *I* who should apologize to you.'

He wished she would look at him. If only she would look at him he would be able to make her understand. But her gaze remained stubbornly fixed on the floor.

'And you see,' he went on, searching for words, 'that is not the worst of it. For when you answered my question in all honesty – for which I'm more grateful than you know – I behaved like a boor. I don't know why. I think it was the shock of hearing the truth after so long. All I can say is that I have been regretting my behaviour ever since.'

Still she would not raise her eyes to his. 'Please try to understand,' he said. 'It is very straightforward. I asked you a question, and you answered it. The matter ends there. Miss Fosdyke, it really is as simple as that.'

Her arms tightened about her waist. At last she raised her head, and their eyes met and held. He realized that he had been disingenuous. They did not live in a world where the exchange of truth between a man and a woman of such vastly separate classes could ever be 'as simple as that'.

The church bell struck a quarter to six. They both jumped.

Tully heaved himself up and went to sniff at the water-bowl. Will murmured in his sleep.

Robert drew out his watch and stared at it. Finally he said, 'I believe I should go.'

Awkwardly she handed him his tunic and handkerchief. Awkwardly he took his leave, and emerged blinking in the sun.

He walked slowly along the Tilburne road and turned into the drive, and Tully trailed after him. Journeymen, stringing up coloured lights between the elms, cast him curious glances. He ignored them.

The drive was tiger-striped with dappled shade. He watched the shadows shift and dance beneath his feet. A silent, unreal world of waving branches and puppet-men, like shadows cast by firelight on the wall of a cave.

Seeing her again had failed to achieve the resolution he had hoped for – and he saw now that he had been wrong to suppose that it would. Instead, he was left with an overpowering sense that he was simply re-entering his own familiar shadow-world, after a brief spell in the light.

CHAPTER TWENTY-ONE

You are allowed this one night for yourself, thought Charity as she finished buttoning her blouse, and after that you must put this nonsense behind you for good.

She took up her hat from the washstand. In honour of the Ball, she had picked a twist of violets for the brim. Her fingers shook as she pinned them on.

She didn't want to think about the future. Or Sam. Or what she would do when Monday came, and Sam and Lord Harlaston left for South Africa. For this one night she would forget about everything except watching the Ball.

She would be safe up in Miss Mitchell's rooms with her mother and Mrs Jordan. She would be safe.

Why then did she have the same exhilarating sense of danger which had swept over her when he was with her in the kitchen? He had looked so much younger and less lordly as he sat there in his blue shirtsleeves, caressing the spaniel's ears, and trying to tuck his long legs under the table. And when she had asked him about South Africa his face had been open and unguarded, and slightly surprised, as if he wasn't used to talking about himself.

Right now he would be up at the Hall getting ready

to greet his guests. He would be wearing his dress uniform: scarlet, with heavy gold braid. He would look beautiful in that.

But it wasn't his looks which gave her this painful twist of longing, but the gentleness he had shown her brother, and the pains he had taken to reassure her over their conversation in church.

She studied her reflection in the looking-glass. Her face had a higher colour than usual, her eyes were darker, her mouth was a fuller, deeper red.

Steps on the stairs. Her mother appeared beside her in the looking-glass.

Mrs Fosdyke looked almost handsome in her dark prune dress, having recently put on a little weight. Her hat was encircled with black taffeta peonies which Mr Aspland had let her have at cost. Their severity had sent her confidence soaring.

She studied her daughter with a critical eye. 'Well I must say, that forest green fits you like a glove. You could have been poured into it. Yes, you're in your looks tonight.'

Charity felt herself flush. To conceal her nerves she executed a deep mock curtsey. 'Must be the prospect of watching all those lords and ladies.'

Her mother raised an eyebrow. 'An' I thought it had something to do with a certain young soldier I could mention.'

Charity did not reply.

'Sam *is* walking us to the Hall, isn't he?' her mother said.

''Course he is.'

'What time's he coming?'

'I don't know. Soon.'

'Charity—'

'Mm?'

'Is something wrong?'

'Why don't you try some of my lavender water?' Charity held out the threepenny bottle Mrs Bowles had given her for tidying her escritoire.

Mrs Fosdyke's eyes widened in astonishment. 'Me? I've never worn scent in my life!'

'You've never watched the Harlaston Ball, either. Go on. Mrs Bowles says a lady's not properly dressed without scent.'

'Well – I s'pose if *she* says it's all right. No, you do it for me. I wouldn't know how.' She put her hands behind her back and leaned forward, and a mottled flush stole up her neck.

'There,' said Charity. 'Now I'll just go and say goodbye to Will, and we can be off.'

'Charity – wait. You look a mite feverish. I wondered—'

'I'm fine. It's just the heat.'

'Are you sure? You've been fidgetty all day.'

'I'm excited. I'm going to a Ball.'

Mrs Fosdyke bit her lip. 'Far as I can see, it's not a good sort of excitement. One minute you look like you'll burst out laughing, an' the next, I wouldn't be surprised if you broke down in tears. You've not fallen out with Sam?'

'Sam?' She picked up her reticule and fiddled with the snap.

'He's not been—' her mother hesitated. 'He's not been pressing you, has he? To do things.'

'No, Mother, of course he hasn't. Sam's not like that.'

'All men are like that with a pretty girl. Specially when they're going off to war.'

Charity placed both hands on her mother's shoulders. 'Don't worry. I'd never do anything I shouldn't. You know that, don't you?'

Mrs Fosdyke's lips worked. She smoothed her daughter's collar. 'I know, my poppet.'

'Well, then. Stop worrying.'

'It's just – you're so *different* from me! You've always had more nerve than me, even when you were a little girl. I wonder where you get it from. An' sometimes I wonder where it'll take you.'

She gave her mother a gentle shake. 'I get it from you.'

'Don't say that.'

Charity tried to lighten the mood. 'Where else would I get the nerve to entertain a lord to tea?'

Mrs Fosdyke gave her peculiar pulled-down grimace. 'Now you're making fun of me. As if I'd ever! I'd drop down dead if he so much as gave me the time of day!'

'No you wouldn't.'

'I still can't believe it. Him in my very own kitchen. You did say it was presentable?'

'Spotless.'

'And he sat right there, at our actual table, and had a cup of tea?'

'Well I couldn't very well put him in the parlour, could I? Not with two dozen corset-covers on the sofa waiting to be finished.'

Mrs Fosdyke permitted herself a snort behind her hand. 'Oh *my*! Oh my *Lord*! Whatever next!'

'What time's Mrs Jordan expecting you?' Sam asked as they walked up the service road, while Mrs Fosdyke followed at a diplomatic distance behind.

'Nine o'clock,' Charity replied. 'We'll have tea in the

Stewards' Hall, then up to Miss Mitchell's room to watch the guests arrive. Of course she'll be too busy to be there herself, but Mrs Jordan says her room's got the best view. You can see right across to the pleasure gardens.' She stopped, aware that she was talking too much. 'It's a shame you can't come,' she added.

'Someone's got to keep an eye on the stables.'

A great amber moon hung above Hynton Edge in a sky of luminous sapphire. Ahead of them the Hall was a looming blackness honeycombed with light.

Looking at it, Charity felt guilty. I must be kinder to Sam, she thought. It's not his fault. To break the silence she said, 'Poor old Will. He hates having to stay behind and miss all this.'

'Brought it on hisself, didn't he?' muttered Sam. 'Didn't ought to of been trespassing in the first place, let alone got a reward when he was caught. If I'd found him I'd of tanned his hide, not given him half a crown.'

'No you wouldn't. Not if you'd seen the state he was in.'

'I bet your mother was proper put out.'

Charity shrugged. In fact, her mother's consternation at Will's injury had been swiftly eclipsed by the unbelievable, exhilarating, terrifying notion of Lord Harlaston taking tea in her kitchen.

''Sides,' Sam said, clearing his throat, 'I don't want to talk about your brother. I've more important things to say.'

Her heart gave a lurch. He wouldn't – not now. Not tonight. Oh please, not tonight.

'I've been wanting to talk to you,' Sam said solemnly.

She looked straight ahead, feeling sick.

He removed her hand from his arm and sank both fists in his breeches pockets and glowered at his boots. 'I want us to get wed.'

She made no reply.

'Well?' he said without turning his head. 'Yes or no?'

' – Sam. Let's not – let's not rush into this.'

'Who said anything about rushing? I've given it thought. It's easy for you. All you've got to do is say yes or no.' Then he added, 'I thought you'd say yes.'

'I – I will. Probably. I just need a bit of time.'

He turned to face her. 'Why?'

They had reached the bend in the service road where the gardeners' cottages sent columns of smoke into the still air. The night had a hot, breathless feel to it, as if a storm was on its way.

Everyone approves of this, she told herself, looking at his sternly handsome face. Your parents. Dr and Mrs Bowles. Mrs Jordan. He's the most eligible man in the parish. He's good-looking, hard-working, and well thought-of. And he wants to marry you.

But all she could feel was how separate he was: how unknown and utterly different from herself. Perhaps all men were as alien if you got this close. She didn't know. She only knew that it gave her an immense feeling of loneliness to be asked to join her life with someone she couldn't begin to understand.

She said: 'It's very soon, Sam. We've barely known each other three weeks.'

'What's that got to do with anything?'

'Well, I don't – I don't even know if you care for me.'

He gave vent to his exasperation. 'Why d'you think I'm asking you to marry me?'

'What I mean is—'

'*I* know what you mean! You mean I don't make pretty speeches an' buy you presents!'

'Of course that's not what I mean—'

'Of course it *is*. I thought you were above all that.'

'Will you *listen* to me? What I'm trying to say is that I don't know you very well. And you don't know me.'

'Yes I do. I know enough.' He hacked at the dust with his heel. 'We could make a go of it, Charity.'

She put her hand on his arm. 'I'm not saying no. Just that I need more time.'

'We'd have a cottage of our own, if that's what's worrying you.'

'I wasn't worrying.'

'Lord Harlaston told me. He promised me a cottage.'

A wave of hot and cold washed over her. 'Lord Harlaston?'

'He gave us his blessing. *He* didn't think it was too soon.'

'When did you tell him?'

'What does that matter? Am I going to get an answer or not?'

'I'm sorry, Sam. I need more time.'

'Maybe you've forgotten', he said with bitter emphasis, 'that I'm leaving the day after tomorrow.'

'I hadn't forgotten.'

He bowed his head. 'All right, then. But promise you'll tell me before I go. I must know before I leave Hynton.'

'Of course.'

'Promise you'll give me an answer by teatime tomorrow.'

294

She was touched by his childish reliance on promises. 'Teatime tomorrow. I promise.'

The telegram arrived as Violet was pouring tea in the Blue Drawing-Room.

Robert watched her take the yellow envelope from the salver tendered by Paige.

Her eyebrows rose a fraction as she skimmed the contents. 'How trying,' she murmured.

'Bad news?' Robert asked.

'It's from Sophia Hepworth, sending their regrets.'

'Oh, really?' He was disappointed. Algy Hepworth had his limitations, but he was kindly and unpretentious, and Robert had been counting on him to help him through the evening. 'I thought they'd accepted weeks ago.'

'They did. That is what is so trying. Though I confess it hardly comes as a surprise.'

'It does to me.'

'Ah but surely, *mon cher,* you have heard? Algy has come the most fearful cropper with his – ' she searched delicately for words, ' – with his *établissement* in Holywell Street.'

'Really? He didn't mention it last weekend.'

'It only came to a head a few days ago. I had a line from Isabel Brabazon on Wednesday. Apparently it was the most appalling *fracas public*.'

He waited, knowing she meant to tell him.

'Apparently it concerned delays in settling his – his *notes d'affaires. Enfin,* it seems Madame Holywell absolutely tracked him down.'

'Tracked him down?'

'To the play at Her Majesty's. She accosted him in the foyer.'

Robert smiled. 'Poor old Algy! I hope he appreciated the irony.'

Violet favoured him with an enquiring look.

He said, 'The play at Her Majesty's is *Resurrection*. A fallen woman seeking redemption.'

'I see,' said Violet, who didn't in the least, as she never read novels. 'Well, I doubt whether poor Algy enjoyed anything about the evening, ironic or otherwise. Apparently the creature made the most dreadful scene.' She shuddered, and he saw how she relished it.

It was one of the quirks of his wife's nature that, although the most refined of women, she displayed intense, almost vulgar gratification when her friends' liaisons ended in disaster. He suspected that she found such scandals reassuring, confirming her belief that relations between men and women are invariably sordid.

'Oh well,' he said, taking the cup from her hand, 'I shall just have to form a cabal with dear old Bowles, and rely on him to get me through.'

Violet studied a plate of madeleines on the curate stand. 'I very much fear', she said at last, 'that you'll have to find someone else with whom to form your cabal.' She turned her head a fraction and addressed the footman behind her chair. 'Thank you, Green, you may go.'

'Why is that? What could prevent old Bowles from coming this evening? These affairs are the high point of his year.'

Violet centred the plate of madeleines on the stand. 'Has it occurred to you that *I* might not care to number him among my guests?'

He looked at her. 'Are you saying you didn't invite him?'

'Why do you look surprised? I see nothing extraordinary in that.'

'But – Violet. How could you do such a thing?'

'Remarkably easily. I took a propelling pencil and crossed the name out of my book.'

'But – don't you realize how mortally hurt the poor old chap must be? He sets *such* store by these occasions!'

' – and I "set store", as you put it, by his not attending them.'

'But why? He never stays more than an hour or so. Just long enough to have a plate of pudding and a little too much champagne, and worship you from afar—'

' – a fact which I try very hard to forget.'

'You'd do better to try to understand, and pity him.'

'Oh, as for *pity*!' she scoffed.

'Why not? He's a man of intellect and education, shut away in an isolated living with two very young children and a much-loved but exceedingly frail wife—'

'Ah, if you're concerned for his *wife*, might I suggest that you call on her tomorrow? Then you can gratify them both with a full account of the *food* and the *gowns* and whatever else they care to hear!'

Her meanness of spirit staggered him. 'I'll visit them tomorrow', he said, 'and tell them his name was omitted in error. I'll apologize for us both.'

She turned her green eyes on him. 'You would do that? You would betray your wife for the sake of a country cleric? And at such a time as this, when our son's memorial has yet to be completed – when I have put myself through so much for your sake?'

He placed his cup on the window sill and stood for a moment looking down at his wife. 'What you say lacks candour in several respects. If you will excuse me, I have correspondence to attend to.'

*　　*　　*

His dress tunic was buttoned, his belt was buckled, and Norton had been dismissed. Robert stood by the mantelpiece fingering his watch.

His brother had given it to him for good luck on the night before his regiment sailed for Egypt. It was a slim rectangle of plain grey gun-metal, inscribed on the inside with lines from Spencer's favourite poet, Sir Walter Scott:

> 'To horse! to horse! the standard flies,
> The bugles sound the call . . .'

Robert weighed it in his palm.

Dear old Spencer. What would he have made of Violet, if they had ever met?

He could hear his brother's ringing tones as if he were with him in the room. Spencer had never been capable of lowering his voice, and he had never had much time for shades of meaning. 'Capital figure,' he would have said, 'and a dashed pretty face. But hang it all, Robert, the girl has no heart.'

How odd, he thought. Sometimes you can only confront the truth when you're pretending to be someone else.

But was it the truth? Could he really condemn Violet as heartless merely because she chose to exclude an unprepossessing admirer from her guest-list? Or was he simply visiting his own regrets and disappointments – and, yes, damn it all, his own frustrations – upon his wife?

He felt too disgusted and heartsick to untangle all that now. And he wished with passionate bleakness that his brother was still alive.

CHAPTER TWENTY-TWO

The Ralstons' brougham drew up in the carriage drive and two footmen in silver and burgundy leapt from the tail-plate and ran to the doors.

There was a gasp from Mrs Fosdyke as Lady Ralston stepped down from the carriage. Unlike the pale frothing gowns of so many of the ladies, her *tenue de soirée* was of cerulean moiré embroidered with peacocks' eyes, and over it she wore a mantle of sea-green velvet trimmed with brilliants.

Like a tired moth in the wake of a swallowtail, Sir Julian followed his wife up the steps. He wore the simple luxurious black and white attire of the gentleman. 'Anything coloured would be impossible,' whispered Mrs Jordan. 'And as for diamond studs, or – Heaven preserve us – a *gold* dress-watch! Why, only cads and Americans go in for those!'

'Look at the length of that train,' murmured Mrs Fosdyke, her eyes moist with emotion. She hadn't raised her voice above a whisper all evening.

'They say', said Mrs Jordan, 'that Lady Ralston is the scourge of the Skeffington stables. She likes to pass a cambric handkerchief over the horses' necks, and if it's the slightest bit discoloured, the grooms must take them all back in disgrace.'

It was twenty minutes past ten, and still the press of carriages was undiminished. Every window blazed in the darkness. The pleasure grounds were a shimmering tracery of lights: emerald, ruby, topaz and sapphire – as complex and ethereal as the music drifting across the lawns. And in the midst of it all floated white-shouldered ladies in pearly gowns, caught like petals on the arms of sombre gentlemen.

'It's a real fairy castle tonight,' murmured Mrs Fosdyke.

Charity didn't think the Hall looked like a fairy castle, but like some glittering malevolent insect: a many-eyed spider at the heart of a jewelled web.

How naive she had been to believe she could put everything behind her, even for a single night. She wished passionately that she had stayed at home with Will.

Earlier, as she was saying goodbye to him, he had begged her to pat Tully for him, and bring back an Everlasting Strip.

'Oh, Will! Whatever makes you think they'll have toffee up at the Hall?'

'Lord Harlaston *said*. He always wanted an Everlasting Strip when he was a lad, but his grandma wouldn't let him. She was terrible strict an' they never had any sweets.'

An Everlasting Strip! What a strangely workaday treat for a lordly child to have wanted, and for a grown man to remember. She struggled to reconcile it with the enchanted spider-kingdom before her. She pictured him in his great gilded entrance-hall, greeting his guests. Smiling urbanely as he had done at the fête, while discussing with wit and erudition whatever elevated subjects people like him talked about at balls. And his beautiful wife would be by his side in her impeccable *grande toilette,* inclining her golden head and smiling her porcelain smile.

The thought of her made Charity feel hot and graceless, like a small chunky pony. Catch Lady Harlaston wearing a bunch of violets stuck in her hat.

This is the real world for people like him, she told herself. Sometimes they may condescend to take a cup of black tea in a cottager's kitchen, or spin a tale for a village lad, but when they do they're merely acting out a part. Like making a speech at a fête, or doling out parcels at Christmas. Or giving their blessing to their gamekeeper when he gets engaged to a village girl.

If she married Sam, she would spend her life in one of the cottages they had passed on their way up the hill. She would be forever in the shadow of this great stone monster with its golden people gliding about inside. The thought was unbearable.

Down on the lawns she saw a tall, slender, dark-haired man in a scarlet dress uniform proceeding down a rose-lined walk. He took a long narrow glass from a footman's tray and coolly sipped.

'My dear,' said Mrs Jordan, 'you've turned quite pale. Feeling a little seedy? It's the heat, I shouldn't wonder.'

'I'm – all right. Thank you.' Charity tried to smile.

'There's water on the wash-stand. Pour some on your wrists. It'll set you right in a trice.'

'Thank you. Perhaps I will.'

But the water did not help. After a while she got to her feet again. 'You were right, Mrs Jordan. I *am* feeling the heat. I'd better be off home.'

Her mother opened her mouth to protest, but Charity said quickly, 'I'll be fine. I'll ask Sam to walk me back.'

'I suppose it's all right,' muttered Mrs Fosdyke, without shifting her gaze from the window. 'Everyone knows you're as good as engaged already. An' I must say, that young man's the very model of propriety. The very model.'

I can always say I couldn't find Sam, she told herself as she found the track he had shown them after their tea with Mrs Jordan. It led up through the arboretum and round the Cedars of Lebanon before entering Hynton Wood.

The truth was, Sam was the last person she wanted to see. He was present at the back of her mind like a great unresolved cloud of worry. She wanted to go home, away from here, as quick as she could.

But before she went, there was something that needed doing. She had to deal head-on with her foolishness. Punish herself with a last look at the splendour spread out below her.

And most of all she had to catch a glimpse – however distant and fleeting – of the rulers of the kingdom. To drink a deep draught of their magnificence, so that she would know, without a shadow of a doubt, that beside them she was irredeemably vulgar. She needed to see them beautiful and distant and *together*. Then she would think quietly about Sam, and make a decision.

She got her wish.

Pausing in the darkness beneath the Cedars of Lebanon, she saw Lord Harlaston far below on the terrace. He stood out vividly against the golden windows as he bent to give his arm to a tiny, splendid, and very ancient lady in apricot satin. With painful slowness the ill-matched couple crossed the terrace towards the tall silver figure of Lady Harlaston.

The prince in scarlet, the princess in silver. What could be more fitting?

There now, she told herself savagely. Are you satisfied? Now can you go home? Her throat closed. Her head ached with the pressure of unshed tears.

She turned and left.

Ahead of her, the path forked. To the right it led to the short-cut through Hynton Wood. To the left it dipped down to the fields on the other side of the Edge. She took the left-hand fork. It was too soon to return to her own world. Besides, no-one would miss her. Her mother would not be home for hours, and her father was not expecting her yet. Perhaps out here, alone in the moonlight, she would find the clarity she needed.

At the bottom of the field she found a broken gate beneath a hawthorn tree and sat down. Not a whisper of the Ball reached her ears. The familiar country sounds surrounded her. The small secret rustlings of a vole. The distant bark of a vixen.

She took off her hat and let the night air whisper through her hair. Gradually the throbbing in her temples eased. The time for tears passed.

She glanced down at her hat. The violets had wilted. One by one, she pulled them off and dropped them on the grass. Then she unwound the green ribbon from the crown. Holding it up, she opened her fingers and let it float away into the darkness. A section of the brim was frayed and she began to pick at the rough edges. The straw was brittle with varnish and snapped like matchsticks. She broke off larger pieces, working her way around. Soon the hat was a pile of fragments in the grass.

She closed her eyes and tried to think of Sam, and all the *good* things that would happen if she married him. An hour later, she was no nearer a resolution. Slowly she got to her feet and walked back up the Edge. Then she climbed over the stile and entered Hynton Wood.

The moon was bright, and she had no difficulty following the path. If she walked fast, it would take twenty minutes to get through the wood and onto the Moxby road. She would be home before midnight.

But how could she go home, with nothing decided, nothing resolved?

Halfway down, she reached the turning to the Ponds. She took it without hesitation.

She emerged into a moonlit glade surrounded by tall black pines. 'The Ponds' turned out to be three small lakes fringed with water lilies and bulrushes. In the still of the night, the water was as smooth as a looking-glass.

This was where Lord Harlaston had found her brother lying in the nettles. Over by that log-pile which she could just make out on the far side of the clearing.

The grove was silver-blue in the moonlight, and eerily peaceful. She knelt by the nearest pond and dipped her hand in the water. It felt wonderfully clean and cool.

This is *real*, she told herself. This water and these drowned weeds, and that little fish which just brushed against your fingers. The rest is fairy tales.

Whatever you decide to do, it must be real.

You can marry Sam and raise a family, and you'll make a lot of people happy and probably have quite a good life. Or you can ask Mrs Bowles to help you become a stenographer or a schoolteacher, and get right away from Hynton.

But whatever you do, it must be *real*. Not fairy tales.

On the other side of the clearing, the glowing tip of a cigar described an arc.

Still on her knees with her hand in the water, she froze.

He was leaning against the wood-pile with his head tilted back, gazing up at the night sky. Now that she knew he was there, she could see him quite clearly.

He was no more than forty feet away. He had not yet seen her. She could easily stand up and go back – quietly, quietly, the way she had come. He would never know she had been there.

But she wanted him to know.

The words she had said to her mother came back to her: *I'd never do anything I shouldn't.* They glanced off her like leaves drifting down to the forest floor.

She stood up and moved out into the middle of the glade.

When she was ten paces away he came out of his reverie with a start. She heard his quick intake of breath. 'Good heavens! Is that you, Miss Fosdyke?'

'Yes, my lord. I'm sorry I startled you.'

'You did, I confess!' A little shakily he put his cigar to his lips. 'This wood seems to have quite a fascination for your family. May I ask what brought you here?'

She ought to apologize for trespassing. But that would be hypocritical. They both knew he didn't mind. 'I was taking a short-cut home. Mrs Jordan invited us to watch the – your – guests – at the Ball.'

305

'I see. That is, I don't. Who is this ever-present Mrs Jordan?'

'Mrs Jordan is your under-housekeeper, my lord.'

'Ah. And – did you enjoy watching the Ball?'

'My mother did, very much.'

'But you did not?'

' – No.'

'Why is that?'

'I don't know.'

'So you decided to go home.'

'I wanted to see my brother.'

'How is he? I trust he is recovering?'

'Yes. Thank you. Though he was sorry not to come tonight. He was hoping to see your spaniel.'

'Tully?'

'He asked me to pass on his regards if I saw him.'

He gave a quiet laugh. 'To Tully but not to me! The boy shows taste.'

He was trying to put her at ease. She mustered a smile, relieved he couldn't see the effort behind it.

She had so wanted to talk to him again, and the moonlight made it easier than she could have imagined. But in the end he was still just as remote as when he had been down on the terrace with the grand old lady in the apricot satin.

She fiddled with the clasp of her reticule. It bulged with a wedge of seed-cake which Mrs Jordan had given her for Will. The thought of it made her ashamed. She felt like a thief. 'I thought I'd be alone up here. I thought you were down on the terrace with the other lords and ladies.'

'I was. Though you have a rather exalted notion of my guests. There's only one other lord at the Hall tonight, and he went to bed half an hour ago with a boiled egg and anchovy toast.' He drew on his cigar. 'I should have liked to have done the same, but my duties would not permit it. So I came here instead. Which was remiss of me, no doubt.'

'I couldn't say, my lord.'

'Why not? You always tell the truth.'

She shook her head. 'No I don't.'

'You do to me.'

There was no reply to that.

He blew a smoke-ring over the water lilies. Then he said suddenly, 'You're not wearing your hat.'

His change of tack startled her.

'Did you lose it?'

'No. I threw it away.'

'You threw it away? Why?'

She bit her lip. How harsh and uncivilized he must think her.

'Forgive me, Miss Fosdyke,' he said softly, 'I've been firing questions at you like a sergeant-major.'

'I don't mind.'

'And even if you did, you're too well-behaved to say so. Or to ask questions of your own.'

'It isn't my place to ask questions, my lord.'

'But if it were, what would you ask, I wonder?'

'It *isn't* my place.'

'Humour me. What would you ask?'

She frowned. 'I suppose – I suppose I'd ask what *you* are doing here.'

'Straight to the point. You'd make an admirable soldier.'

He was silent for so long that she thought he did not intend to explain his presence to her. Then he said quietly, 'Ghosts are curious creatures, Miss Fosdyke. At first they seem very frail and lonely, as if all they

307

require is the most fleeting attention. But neglect them, and they soon become nightmares.'

He was in a strange mood. Flippant one moment, grave the next. She sensed in him something of the restlessness and pain which had driven him to seek solitude in St Hybald's.

She opened her mouth to speak, then cut herself short.

'Yes? What is it?'

'I – only that the other day, my father showed me Master Linley's memorial plaque. It had just arrived from London. It's very beautiful.'

He paused before speaking. 'How swiftly you grasp the point.'

She wondered if he meant she was impertinent.

I should leave, she thought. If I'm not frightened now I ought to be. I ought to be terrified.

But she knew – she *knew* – he did not want her to go.

'And you, Miss Fosdyke? Are you not afraid?'

'Afraid?' She was appalled that he had guessed her thoughts.

'Afraid of your ghosts.'

'I – don't have any.'

'No,' he said in a low voice, 'of course you don't. And not for a long time to come, I hope.'

She bowed her head. 'I'll be going now.'

'Not yet.'

'It's late.'

'It's not even midnight. You don't have to go yet.'

'I think I must.'

There was silence between them. Then he threw away his cigar and came towards her.

She was suddenly intensely aware of everything

308

around her. The sweet sharp smell of crushed grass. The soft *hoo-hoos* of the young owls gliding between the trees. The gleam of moonlight on his epaulettes.

Because of the heat he had unfastened the top button of his tunic, and when he halted before her she was close enough to see the pale skin at the base of his throat, where the sunburn ended. If she put out her hand she could touch it.

The blood pounded in her ears.

All men are like that with a pretty girl. Specially when they're going off to war.

But he wasn't like that. She knew him. She knew what he felt, because she felt it herself. That was why the danger was so immense.

'Please,' he said quietly, 'stay a while.'

'I can't.'

'You can if I ask it.'

'You shouldn't ask.'

'It isn't that I want—' he frowned. 'What I mean is, you have nothing to fear from me.'

She did not reply.

In the warm darkness she heard him sigh. 'Perhaps you're right,' he said. 'But at least let me see you safely to the edge of the wood.'

'Oh, no. No.'

'But you can't go alone, in the darkness.'

'Yes I can, there's a moon—'

' – which will set in about ten minutes—'

'I'll be home by then.' She hated herself for contradicting everything he said. But she had to leave now, at once, before she started to cry.

He put out his hand to touch her shoulder, but instantly withdrew it. 'I'm sorry. I've upset you. I'm sorry.'

'I'm all right.'

'That's the first untruth you've told me. You are upset.'

She drew a ragged breath. 'Yes. I'm upset. This is wrong. And I'm trespassing and I hate it.'

'You're not trespassing unless I say you are.'

'That's not what I mean, I *am* trespassing! I must go, now, before the moon sets and you'd have to come with me!'

He watched her as she ran from the glade and down the hill towards the village.

CHAPTER TWENTY-THREE

Late July, the Present

'I can't offer you anything to *drink*,' said Leonard
Fielding, motioning Sarah to an overstuffed sofa and
placing himself in what was clearly his favourite armchair. A table at his elbow bore a *Radio Times* and
a half-finished tube of Werther's Originals, neatly
twisted at the end. 'Don't keep the stuff in the house,
I'm afraid, though I know how you writers like to
drink. *Who* did you say was handling your book? It is
a book you're working on?'

'Yes, that's right. For Harlaston College. It'll be
published privately.'

'Privately. I *see*.'

The rector of Hynton's grandson was a stocky man
in his sixties with a large head and truculent eyes.
He wore cavalry twill trousers and a camel-coloured
cardigan which had long ago stretched to accommodate his stomach. His fawn socks were impossible to
ignore, as he wore Scholl sandals rather than the
expected brogues. He caught Sarah looking at them
and raised a combative eyebrow. Catch Leonard Fielding dressing up to be interviewed.

The 'drawing room', as he called it, had cold white walls, ice-blue chintz, and a smell of air-freshener and cat. The few ornaments looked like the remains of a larger collection: a silver skean-dhu; two anaemic watercolours of dreamy cows; silver-framed photographs of school, varsity and the Army. The arrangement of logs in the fireplace had clearly been gathering dust since Christmas.

An estate agent would have described Far View Cottage as a 'character period home'. Sarah thought it resembled a well-furnished, unheated rabbit-hole. She began to regret her choice of short-sleeved shirt and linen trousers, and wished Mrs Fielding would hurry up with the coffee.

Getting dressed that morning, she had been resolutely upbeat. She had been resolutely upbeat for the last four days, ever since she had returned from Lincoln, and stood like a thief listening to Dominic accuse her of cowardice on the answerphone. Of course he couldn't be sure she was listening. For all he knew, he was talking to a machine. And she was not obliged to pick up the phone. The choice was hers. She had simply chosen not to.

Which still left her feeling cowardly, exposed, and bleak.

And when eventually he had rung off, she had resisted the temptation to call Alex, because if Dominic called again he'd find the line engaged, and know she was hiding from him. And she could hardly walk all the way down to the rectory, when that very afternoon she had been severe with Alex about looking after herself.

So instead she had spent a solitary, unsettled evening making half-hearted efforts to watch various videos while rereading what she had written about the Hall.

'So this *book*,' said Leonard Fielding. 'It's for our friends in the colonies, I think you said?'

She told him about the fiftieth anniversary of the college and his mother's connection with the period in question. He accepted her explanation without comment, and seemed to find it natural that Flora Fielding, née Bowles, would be at the forefront of any book about Harlaston.

'And I think *you* mentioned', she said solemnly, entering into his game, 'that your mother wrote her memoirs on her retirement.'

'Yes indeed. Also published privately. Though of course, Mama did not have the resources for a – *local historian*? That *is* what you are?'

'Well, *no*.' Sarah struggled to avoid mimicking his emphatic pattern of speech. 'It's a summer job. Usually I work in television.'

'Tele*vi*sion. I see. We don't go in much for *tee vee* drama. News and cricket. That's our limit.'

She gave a polite smile. 'I produce documentaries.'

'Oh? Anything I might know?'

'I'm not sure. *Tin-Miner. Great Fire Diaries. Memsahib.*'

'You did *Memsahib*, did you? Now that one I *did* rather enjoy.' She saw him mentally transferring her from the category of upstart young professional to that of someone he might conceivably weave into the conversation at the golf club.

'We were in India three years ago,' he said. 'One of those slap-up *package* jobs. India for the *cul-tchah*,' this with relish in a mock-cockney accent, 'Ceylon – *Shree Lunka*, I should say – for the beaches, Honky Shankers for the shopping.'

313

Listening to his grotesque verbal mannerisms, Sarah felt her optimism seeping away. She imagined Dominic's comments on her latest 'lead'.

Oh, Sarah, come on! Is this all you've got to show after seven weeks?

Let's see. What's the grand total to date? Your grandma was a rustic with a loopy brother, who went abroad and became a schoolteacher and had quite a nice line in postcards. Your grandpa was a good-looking, amoral Empire-builder who seduced her, sent her packing to France, and then sloped off to India to prop up the Raj.

That's it, isn't it, Sarah darling? And now you're so desperate that you've gone and jumped down the rabbit-hole with Colonel Blimp. Did I say rabbit-hole? Sarah sweetheart, you're practically through the looking-glass!

'Honeymoon,' said Leonard Fielding, making her jump. 'That's why we went to India. Wasn't it, my love?'

'What's that, my love?' Mrs Fielding appeared with a coffee-tray laden with Royal Doulton.

Her husband leapt to his feet and waited while she poured the coffee. She was a large woman with brown hair set in tight curls like a Fifties housewife. With supreme unconcern for the weather, she wore a yellow sleeveless cotton 'frock' blithely belted over a formidable stomach. 'Oh, yes, *India. Marvellous.* Such *colours.*'

The coffee was somewhere around blood heat, but better than nothing. The sight of Mrs Fielding's happily bared arms sent shivers down Sarah's spine.

She decided it was time to bring up the reason for her visit. 'The period I'm interested in', she began, and

314

Mr and Mrs Fielding looked at her expectantly, 'is pre-First World War. Your mother, Mr Fielding, would have been a young girl at the time? I wondered if her memoirs might shed some light on everyday life in Hynton.'

Mr Fielding sucked his teeth. 'Ooh, I'm not at all sure about that. They're mostly about the Army. Sal*vation* Army, of course.'

'Perhaps there are diaries?'

'Mama never kept them. Far too busy. And, of course, she burnt all her personal papers when she retired. Liked things tidy, you see. *Le superflu est chose* pas *necessaire*, to paraphrase dear old *Vol*taire.' His accent was atrocious. Sarah wondered who would come off worst if he ever came to grips with the old dragon at Dinan Town Hall.

'From what you said on the phone,' she went on patiently, 'I gather that your mother used to visit her parents at the rectory, during the Forties. Did you ever go with her?'

'Oh, *yes*! *Dear* old Nonna and Poppa. Though I can't say I remember too much about them.'

'And did you ever see Lady Harlaston when you were there?'

'Lord, no! The old bat was a recluse by then. Had been for yonks. Often happens when they're stinking rich. Which she was, of course. Most of the money was hers, not his. But you'd know all about that.'

'I've read something about it.'

He narrowed his eyes at the fireplace, searching his memory. 'As I recall, when they sold the estate, just after the First World War, she bought Lyndon Manor. Other side of Tilburne? Moved in, pulled up the drawbridge, practically never seen again.' He paused. 'I

315

do remember her *car*, though. Wonderful old Daimler. Completely black. Size of a swimming-pool. Used to glide about the countryside like a ghost. Never caught a glimpse of her inside, though. Tinted windows. But I remember Nonna saying that she always wore *black*. Always frightfully well turned out. Whole parish was terrified of her.' He gave Sarah a sharp glance. 'This isn't what you're after, is it?'

Politely she disagreed.

Dominic's rich chuckle sounded in her head. *Oh, Sarah! What did you honestly expect? Did you think the rector's grandson would suddenly clap his hand to his forehead and cry: Yes, I remember! Grandad told me all about it – the star-crossed lovers driven apart by the wicked Pearce-Stauntons!*

Oh, shut up, Sarah thought, slamming the door in Dominic's face.

She raised her head and gave Leonard Fielding a defiant smile. 'Your mother married late, I believe?'

'Lord, yes. Met Father at a meeting in 1934. Tied the knot a month later.'

'That's rather romantic.'

Eunice Fielding smiled and smoothed her frock over her knees. 'Oh, you know, the Fieldings all have a streak of romance in them somewhere.'

Leonard Fielding reached over and gave his wife's hand a fervent little shake, and they exchanged mute, tremulous smiles. Then he rubbed his forehead sheepishly. 'Now where was I?'

'You weren't, my love,' said Mrs Fielding, pushing herself to her feet with both hands. 'Why don't I fetch that box of odds and ends you've collected for Miss Dalton, and she can have a quiet rummage through it in the conservatory, where the light's better?'

Mr Fielding had taken some trouble to compile his 'box of odds and ends', and he proudly assured Sarah that it contained 'every surviving vestige of Mama's life – apart from myself, and the papers I made over to the Army.'

The conservatory overlooked a severely clipped garden with a breathtaking view of the Downs. It had wrought-iron furniture with pink gingham cushions and a wealth of Busy Lizzies and parlour palms. Importantly for Sarah, it was several critical degrees warmer than the house.

Mr Fielding carried the box out for her, then went off to do 'commissions in the village'. Mrs Fielding brought out a jug of iced lemonade and suggested opening the doors as it was so stuffy. Sarah quickly assured her that she was fine.

The odds and ends were exactly that.

There was a prayer-book inscribed on the flyleaf in spidery brown ink *To My dearest Flora, from her Papa;* an agenda for a meeting of the Committee on Household Salvage, with Arthur Fielding's name circled in pencil; a handful of programmes from West End musicals of the Forties, and a Sunday-school flyer for a performance of the Nativity in which Leo had played an ox. And, lastly, there were two albums of family photographs.

The first contained a group portrait taken at Hynton rectory in 1902. Sarah recognized the French windows in the background. The rector, standing beside his wife's chair, was a rotund, whiskered cleric with turned-down eyes and a thick clownish mouth. His wife resembled a thin, intelligent stork. At her side stood a small scowling boy in a sailor suit – presumably the missionary son,

Theophilus – and a beetle-browed, distressingly plain girl of about thirteen, in a white pinafore dress and thick black stockings.

A few pages on, another photograph showed Flora aged nineteen: still beetle-browed and unsmiling, but more at ease in a darkly unflattering Salvation Army uniform and bonnet. Then came a wedding photograph, with Flora self-assured and almost attractive in a tailored, wide-shouldered suit. The groom was a fierce-looking man in his late forties with a thin moustache and Leo's gimlet eyes. Then came a naked Leo aged six months on a bearskin rug, disconcertingly like the present-day version, followed by pages of holiday snaps.

Sarah had opened the box at eleven o'clock, and by eleven twenty she had ascertained that the only item of interest was a slim volume bound in navy-blue leather, plainly entitled *My Life by F.M. Fielding*. She settled down to read.

Flora Fielding, née Bowles, had had an axe to grind and had ground it relentlessly. As a young woman with no looks, she had probably needed near-obsessional focus to make headway, but it hardly made for a gripping read.

The first two chapters were an account of her parents' families, heavily slanted to highlight the injustice of mediocre men attaining preferment while talented women were passed over. She dealt with her own childhood sketchily: a dutiful account of her father's parish activities, and a more feeling one of her mother's long fight against spinal tuberculosis. But she seemed uninterested in the people of Hynton, and mentioned none of them by name. For all she cared, the rectory could have been on the moon.

As she approached adolescence, rumours of the suffragist movement began to reach the village, and the pace quickened to a walk. The movement was met with suspicion and contempt by everyone in Hynton, including her parents. '*Surprisingly,*' she wrote, '*the principle of women's suffrage met with greater tolerance from our local aristocracy – although perhaps on reflection one ought not to be so surprised. The aristocracy has traditionally tolerated "eccentricity" more readily than other classes.*

'*I remember one occasion on which this was vividly brought home to me when, as an unprepossessing girl of fifteen, I had the temerity to justify the Movement to our own Lord Harlaston, who had stopped at the rectory for tea, as he occasionally did on his return from his scientific expeditions. "Not two years ago," I argued with the heedless passion of youth, "we fought a war to preserve the right to vote for our South African colonists. If we saw fit to fight for them, isn't it logical to accord English women that very same right, in our own country?"*

'*Of course my parents were horrified at my outburst, but our distinguished guest paid me the compliment of listening to what I had to say, and then agreed that it was neither logical nor just. The principle of women's suffrage he could not argue with, he said, nor did he wish to; but neither could he sanction public disorder as a means of achieving it, hence his opposition to the direction in which the Movement was heading – which, he reminded me gently, was the issue I had originally invited him to debate.*

'*Of course we progressed no further, for Mama concocted an excuse, and I was hustled away.*

However I retained a lasting impression from that exchange. It will be difficult for today's young women, brought up to regard equal opportunities as their Natural Right, to appreciate what such a conversation meant to a young girl in 1904. That a gentleman – a man of intellect and standing in the world – should listen to me as if I were capable of constructing a rational argument, added immeasurably to my self-confidence. It taught me that one may encounter a sympathetic mind where one least expects it – and (I might add) that when one is arguing with a strong intelligence, it is as well to keep one's eye on the dialectical ball.'

Sarah sat back in her chair.

She thought of the portrait in the Long Gallery. 'A man of intellect and standing in the world'. Talking politics with an ugly adolescent girl at a rectory tea.

Whatever else Robert might have been, if Flora Fielding was to be believed – and her account had all the fluency of a vivid memory – he had, on one occasion at least, been kind. 'And kindness', she heard Mrs Favell say, 'is so important.'

She found herself hoping against hope that he had been kind to Charity too. If only for a while.

Getting back to the memoirs, she waded through two World Wars, the early death from leukaemia of Flora's husband – of whom she appeared to have been gruffly fond – and Leo's bout of rheumatic fever, which had ended his career in the Guards. The only section which aroused her interest was a passage describing Flora's support for treating 'lost girls' with greater understanding. *'I felt strongly'*, she wrote, *'that it behoved us as Christians to recognize the existence of different degrees of depravity – and to acknowledge that the capacity for redemption may not be wholly lost.'*

Surely this was the place to have mentioned Charity? In a village the size of Hynton, Flora must have known of the scandal. But to Sarah's enormous disappointment Flora confined herself to generalizations. Her final chapter was a lengthy homily on the changes she had witnessed over the years, and Sarah skimmed the turgid prose with growing disillusion.

'Before the Great War, the prevailing belief was that the Poor are always with us, and the idea of "helping people to help themselves" was still struggling for a foothold. Interestingly, it flourished less among the so-called urban "progressives" than among the more outwardly conservative of our better rural families.

'To take but one example, my own dear mother shrank from progressive ideas, and yet was the first to provide active assistance to one of our village girls.' Sarah sat up and gave the passage her full attention. *'This she did by arranging, through the offices of a friend, a position as a student teacher at a rural lycée in Brittany. At the time, such a course was decidedly unusual, but as Mama explained, she was doing no more than assisting the girl to achieve her own very laudable ambition of seeing something of the Continent – while at the same time allowing us at the rectory to do our small part for the new entente which was then so much on everyone's lips.'*

A distant church bell tolled one o'clock. The Downs darkened with the passing of clouds.

It *had* to be Charity.

There could not have been *two* Hynton girls deported to France before the First World War. Except that, according to Flora Fielding, Charity had not been deported but had gone to France of her own free will, helped by the rector's wife to achieve 'her own very laudable ambition'.

And if that were true, it would do much to explain why Charity had never returned to England after her son was born – not even years later, when the heat of the scandal had presumably died down. Because, quite simply, she had chosen to live in France.

'*I should add*', Flora continued, '*that I was rather put out by the girl's departure, as I was very fond of her, and even cherished a schoolgirl dream of the two of us raising our families in proximious harmony – she happily wed to her sweetheart and ensconced in the gamekeeper's cottage, and I no less happily wed to my father's curate, whom I then affected to admire. My mother, with her countrywoman's good sense, knew better, as usual.*'

Sarah closed the book and stared into the distance.

There had been a *sweetheart*.

Why hadn't she thought of that before? It was so obvious. Of *course* Charity had had a sweetheart! The surprising thing was not that she had had one, but that she wasn't already married, with several children, by the time she'd met Robert. Girls married young in those days, and when Charity became pregnant and went to France in 1908, she would have been in her late twenties. With a good trade as a dressmaker, she must have been a highly attractive marriage proposition. And she could hardly have been plain if she had caught the eye of the lord of the manor.

But *had* she caught his eye?

My God, thought Sarah, going hot and cold.

What if the *gamekeeper* had seduced Charity

Fosdyke, not Robert after all? What if Charity had made up the whole story about her aristocratic seducer, simply to add lustre to a commonplace roll in the hay? In many ways, it made more sense than anything else.

No. It couldn't be. The weight of family legend was too strong. And there was Robert's name on the birth certificate.

'Lunch!' cried Mrs Fielding behind her.

Sarah shot out of her chair.

'Did you find anything useful? You look a little pale. Mulligatawny all right? I hope you like it *hot*!'

Later that evening, Sarah pulled up outside the Old Rectory.

It was raining again. On the radio they were calling it the wettest summer in three hundred years.

The lights were on in Alex's sitting room. The windows were golden squares, warm and peaceful. Stephen would be lying on his stomach on the rug, humming under his breath as he pored over his medical encyclopaedia. Alex would be at the desk, working on his book.

He never talked about his writing. Sarah didn't even know what it was about, except for what Stephen had told her – and much of that was probably wild supposition. But whatever it was, she hoped Alex would finish it, and that it wouldn't turn out to be the sad, delusional waste of time which her brother and Dominic believed it to be.

She wanted to go inside, and tell Alex about Robert's conversation with Flora Bowles, and the possibilities churned up by the gamekeeper sweetheart. He would pour her a whisky and watch her with his cool, brandy-coloured eyes, and ask her what she thought of it all.

How would she answer?

She didn't know.

She eased the Saab into the rectory driveway, turned off the ignition, and got out. Then, quietly, she posted the keys through the letter box, turned up the collar of her jacket, and started up the lane towards the Hall.

CHAPTER TWENTY-FOUR

'*Montague, the Sixteenth Baron,*' wrote Sarah, '*was the first in the family to bring home a wealthy bride. After distinguishing himself at la Corunna, he returned to England with the enormously rich Leonor de Salazar, and devoted the rest of his long life to spending her money. His least successful enterprise was also his personal favourite: the Hynton pineapple plantation – traces of which can still be seen behind the village hall (see map 1).*

'*Leonor bore Montague eight children, then devoted the rest of her life to bee-keeping. According to her obituary in the* Stamford Echo, *she contributed a streak of wilfulness to the Pearce-Staunton character – although many maintained that it had been in evidence long before her arrival.*'

Sarah put the notebook aside and stretched. She was sitting on the Sandalwood Staircase with her files and a mug of coffee. The afternoon sun had burnished the banisters to amber, and brought forth a dusty whiff of sandalwood. Above her head, Father Time brandished his sickle in a bright blue Tuscan sky.

She glanced at her watch. Nearly five o'clock. Almost time to down tools and get back to her own research.

As far as the book was concerned, her self-imposed routine of six hours a day was paying off, and the stack of typescript in the Jade Ante-Room was steadily growing. The really surprising thing was that she had begun to *like* the Pearce-Stauntons. They had not been an outstandingly altruistic race, nor had they produced anyone who had improved the lot of mankind. But they had *lived*. Foolishly, intensely, dangerously – but to the hilt. She wouldn't mind at all if they turned out to have been her ancestors.

There was the Thirteenth Baron, Nathaniel, who had twice lost the entire estate at whist, and only won it back when his opponent went down with measles. And Evelyn, Montague's fifth son, who had set out to be a sheep-farmer in Australia but had boarded the wrong ship and ended up in Peking, just in time to help burn down the Emperor's Summer Palace. And Augustus, husband of the indefatigable 'Grandmama Adela', who had mastered von Clausewitz at the age of ten, Thucydides at twelve, and had spent his life building up the Moxby Hunt with the same devotion which his wife had lavished on the Hall. He had died in 1855 from an attack of apoplexy, brought on by reading of the suicidal cavalry charge at Balaclava.

In another week or so Sarah would catch up with Robert, and the first draft of the book would be finished.

She still wasn't sure what she would say about him. Regarded objectively, the story of her grandmother's seduction, as told her by Alex, her mother, and Mrs Favell, was growing more improbable by the day. Was it really likely that a man of such looks, intellect, wealth and standing should have stooped to notice Charity Fosdyke? And yet, in a way, that was precisely the point. Why would anyone believe so impossible a story, unless it were true?

The important thing, she told herself, is to find out the *facts*. Trace the gamekeeper's descendants and rule him out. Or rule him in, and rule Robert out. But get at the facts.

'Mrs Favell?'

'Who is it? I am afraid I cannot talk now, I have my son with me.'

'It's Sarah Dalton, Mrs Favell. I'm sorry, I'll call back tomorrow—'

'You'll do no such thing, Sarah. I didn't recognize your voice. Charles can wait. He's used to it, aren't you, Charlie? He's taking me to Town. We are going to buy a frame for William's photograph. You are a very *wicked* girl.'

'I'm so glad you like it. Your letter was lovely. It nearly made me cry.'

'Then you are a very *sentimental* girl. You spend far too much time on your own.'

'Mrs Favell, I was wondering – I have one more question. It won't take long.'

'Of course.'

'You're very kind. This may sound strange, but when you visited Hynton in the Thirties, do you remember the gamekeeper at the Hall?'

'The *gamekeeper*.'

'Yes. I know it's odd.'

'No, no. I was trying to remember. May I ask what prompted this?'

'Well, I believe he – or maybe his father, I don't know – may have been my grandmother's – er – sweetheart. Before she went to France.'

'Oh I see. I *see*. You don't think *he* could have—? Do you?'

'It's unlikely, but possible. That's why I need to find out about him. I've gone through what's left of the estate accounts but I've drawn a blank, so I wondered—'

'As a girl I used to play with the daughter of the *retired* gamekeeper. He must have been in his seventies by then. I'm afraid I can't remember the surname.'

'Did you ever meet him? The gamekeeper?'

'I'm afraid not. Of course, he hadn't actually *been* a gamekeeper for many years, not since the Hall was sold. He'd run some sort of garage, I believe, though I don't think it did very well. But everyone always referred to him as the gamekeeper. And I'm afraid I never went to their cottage. I didn't care to. It was not a happy place.'

'Do you remember his wife?'

'Oh, yes. A mousy little thing. Though of course that was hardly surprising. He was not an easy man, I believe. Doreen, the little girl I played with, was the youngest of nine.'

'And you're sure you can't remember his name?'

'It was a short name. One syllable. I think it had something to do with *ducks*.'

'Could you tell me about Doreen?'

'Yes, oh yes. Doreen I do remember. A sweet, bubbly little soul. Of course she was several years younger than me, but that didn't stop us being friends.'

'Did you keep in touch with her?'

'I always felt rather sorry about that. She married an electrician and moved to Norwich, and we lost touch.'

'Do you remember her married name?'

'Now that I *can* tell you. It was Drake. But I'm afraid I can't give you an address.'

'I wonder, you wouldn't know what became of her brothers and sisters, would you? You said she was the youngest of nine.'

'I'm sorry, but I was only friends with Doreen. She was the odd one out, you see. Sort of the black sheep, but in reverse.'

'I understand. Well, thank you very much, Mrs Favell, this has given me something to go on. I'd better not keep you any longer.'

'Did you have your hair cut?'

'I did. I like it.'

'Splendid. What did the others say?'

'Stephen scowled and said it was too short.'

'Ha! Just like a child! They detest change. And Alex?'

'He didn't say anything.'

'Oh, that means it was a success. Though of course I shall want to see it for myself.'

'The next time I'm in London.'

'If you find Doreen, would you give her my regards?'

'Of course.'

'*Webb.*'

'I'm sorry?'

'I remember now. She went from Doreen Webb to Doreen Drake. We used to laugh about it. Ducks and drakes, you see. Webbed feet. There was a pun in it somewhere but we never found it.'

'Mrs Favell, you are quite wonderful.'

'Now I know you've been on your own too long.'

'Goodbye, Mrs Favell. I'll keep in touch.'

'Goodbye, Sarah. See that you do.'

*   *   *

329

'Mrs Drake?'

'Yes? Who's this?'

'My name's Sarah Dalton. I telephoned your son at the shop yesterday.'

'Oh yes. The young lady from the Yellow Pages. Neville told us about you.'

'Well, I'm not actually from the—'

'You know what I mean, dear. Nev said that was how you found him, in the Yellow Pages. But you'll be wanting my husband Ray.'

'No, er, thank you, in fact it's you I want to see. I was given your name by Marion Favell. Her maiden name was Jenkins.'

'Marion Jenkins? I thought she'd passed on years ago!'

'She's very much alive. I spoke to her yesterday. She asked me to send you her regards.'

'Well that's nice to know, that really is! I always thought it was a shame we went our separate ways.'

'Mrs Favell has been helping me with some research I'm doing for a book about Harlaston Hall. I gather you might know something about it.'

'Well I ought to, oughtn't I, dear? I was only born and bred in Hynton.'

'I understand your father used to be the gamekeeper up at the Hall? – Hello? Mrs Drake?'

'What did you say?'

'I was asking about your father.'

' – I don't – what d'you want to know about him for?'

'Only for background.'

'Oh. Well I'm sorry, I can't help. I was the youngest by years. I never really knew him.'

'I understand. Could I come and see you anyway,

330

just for half an hour or so, to have a chat about Hynton?'

'Oh. I don't think so. We're going away next Monday, and I'm up to my eyes, setting the place to rights.'

'Will you be away long?'

'Fortnight. Sorrento. Luxury clifftop hotel. It's the kids' treat for our golden anniversary.'

'That's lovely. You've certainly picked the right time to go.'

'We did, didn't we? Shouldn't gloat, but you can't help it, can you? Only human. Typical British summer.'

'About your family, Mrs Drake—'

'I really can't remember much.'

'Please. Half an hour. For background.'

'The place is in a state.'

'It'd really help a lot.'

'Oh. Oh all right. But I warn you, the place is a sight.'

'I don't mind a bit.'

'Best if you come to tea, day after tomorrow, six o'clock. What did you say your name was?'

'Sarah Dalton. Please call me Sarah.'

'Well, Sarah, mind you don't eat a big lunch. This is Norfolk. We like a proper tea.'

'A proper tea' in Mrs Drake's tiny, immaculate terraced house in central Norwich turned out to be fried sausages, bacon, eggs, baked beans, chips, meat-paste sandwiches, a token plate of tomatoes in vinegar, and several kinds of Mr Kipling's cakes, which Sarah suspected had been bought in her honour, for they were arranged on unmatching plates, and no-one

331

had mastered the knack of passing them round without sending them sliding off their doilies.

Doreen Drake was a round red-faced robin of a woman with a tiny orange mouth and a nice line in placid complaints which she didn't seem to expect to be taken seriously. Her husband and son obeyed her frequent commands with much good-natured rolling of the eyes, and clearly adored her. She treated Sarah with guarded politeness, and seemed to view the coming interview with trepidation.

As with Leonard Fielding the previous week, Sarah made no mention of her grandmother – which turned out to have been a good idea, for the first thing Mrs Drake told her, when finally they were settled in the lounge, and Ray had been sent upstairs for the photo album, was that Charity Fosdyke had jilted Samuel Webb.

'Well she didn't actually jilt him at the altar,' Mrs Drake said, crossing her short arms under her expansive bust and giving it a defensive hitch, 'but she threw him over, which comes to the same thing. Least, that's what my mum always told us when Dad wasn't around.'

'Why when he wasn't around?'

Mrs Drake blinked, as if it was a trick question. 'Well, he'd have taken a strap to her if he'd caught her gabbing about it. He never mentioned it hisself.' She was silent for a moment. 'He used to say digging up the past was all – pardon my French – bollocks, was what he said.' Her cheeks turned a mottled plum, and her glance skittered away from Sarah.

'My mum's exactly the same,' said Sarah. 'When my brother and I were growing up we didn't even know our grandparents' names.'

'Well, there you are then.'

There was an awkward silence. Neville, the son, came and sat beside his mother, who acknowledged him with an edgy turn of the head.

As if on cue, Ray returned with the photo album. Mrs Drake unclenched her hands long enough to turn a couple of pages and pass the album to Sarah. She didn't lean over and point things out, but stared fixedly at the china kittens on the mantelpiece.

The page bore a single photograph with '1916' printed in careful ball-point underneath. It was the only caption.

'They took that the day he went off to Belgium,' Mrs Drake said without taking her eyes off the kittens. 'It's the only one we've got of him. He hated photos.'

Sarah wondered why. Samuel Webb had been a good-looking man, and the uniform had suited his pale, severely regular features. But there was a resentful twist about his mouth, and he had the cold eyes of a man who liked to use his fists. He glared at the camera as if he meant to spit in its eye.

'He had a lot of disappointments,' Mrs Drake said uneasily. 'He used to say he was the unluckiest man alive. Well he was right, wasn't he? In a manner of speaking. Hardly got back from one war when they sent him off on another. That's what he always said. He was bitter about that.'

Sarah nodded slowly. 'And – your mother. How did she meet him?'

Again Mrs Drake blinked. 'Grantham market-day. Met on Saturday, married three weeks later. The year after that other little madam jilted him. He was bitter about that too. Well. He was a bitter man. I s'pose he'd a right to be.'

Sarah waited for her to go on.

'He'd of been rich if he'd ever got the chance to really get his garridge under way. But he never did. For starters he lost face with the parish when she jilted him, and things like that mattered, small place like Hynton. And then before he knew it he had a wife and a bunch of kids, so that was that, wasn't it?' She spoke with the fluency of one telling a tale learned in childhood, and beneath her bosom her hands tightened their grip.

Sarah began to feel guilty. For Mrs Drake, remembering was a painful business. 'When did he – er, pass on?'

'Nineteen forty-five. Just short of his seventy-sixth birthday, and just before the war ended. He always said his timing was off.'

There was silence. Across the coffee table, Ray and Neville exchanged worried glances.

'I'm sorry,' Mrs Drake said abruptly, 'That's all I can tell you.' She blinked hard several times. 'Still. Takes all sorts I s'pose. And it's all done and dusted now.'

'Sarah? It's Alex.'

'Alex.'

'How's it going?'

'Fine. It's going fine.'

'I wondered – I haven't seen you for a couple of weeks.'

'I've been busy. I had to go to Norwich.'

'You could've taken the car. I wasn't using it.'

'Thanks. I didn't want to bother you.'

'It's no bother.'

'I took a cab to the station. No problem.'

' – Are you all right? You sound jumpy.'

'I'm fine. I just haven't been sleeping well.'

'Any reason?'

'If I knew why, I'd be halfway to getting some sleep, wouldn't I? – Sorry, I didn't mean to snap. I'm just – I don't know.'

'What?'

'It's probably this bloody weather getting me down.'

'Mm-hm.'

'You could at least try to sound convinced. And please don't tell me I'm too wrapped up in what I'm doing.'

'I wasn't going to.'

'You were thinking it. I could hear it in your voice.'

'Look, Sarah, I want to bring Stephen up to the Hall.'

'Why? Is anything wrong?'

'No. Except that it's rained every day for the last fortnight and he's bored and he misses you, but he's too proud to say so.'

'So you thought you'd try a bit of emotional blackmail on me.'

'Dead right. I thought we'd come for tea, if that's OK.'

'When?'

'Tomorrow afternoon.'

'Actually, I was planning to work on the book, so it's not really—'

'We'll come about four.'

'I see. I don't suppose there's anything I can do to stop you.'

'No.'

'Right. Well, then. Four o'clock it is. We'll have tea in the conservatory, like proper Edwardians.'

'Good. Stephen will like that. We'll see you then.'

'Sarah?'

'Listen Alex, about tomorrow afternoon, I really don't think—'

'Sarah. This is Dominic.'

' – I thought you were Alex.'

'So it would appear. Is that why you answered the phone so quickly?'

'I answered the phone because it rang.'

'Really? That makes a refreshing change. All I've been getting is some appalling recorded message.'

'That's the bursar.'

'Indeed. Your private screening service?'

'If you like.'

'And very effective she is too. I had no *idea* you'd be so reluctant to speak to me. It's really rather flattering, in a perverse way.'

'What do you want?'

'Be still, I come in peace. – Sarah? Are you there? Ah-ha! Learnt the value of silence, haven't we? Glad I managed to teach you something. Though it was childish of you not to call me back.'

'I wish you'd say your piece and have done with it. I've got things to do.'

'What can you possibly have to do on a Friday evening in Lincolnshire? Unless you and Alex are getting together for a cosy session of Sticking Pins in Dominic.'

'You're not that important.'

'Oh, Sarah, *sweetheart*!'

'Since you ask, I'm making rock buns. Alex is

bringing your son for tea tomorrow, and in case you didn't know, Stephen – that's your son – rather likes rock buns. In fact, they're his favourite.'

'Oh, well *done*, Sarah! Just the right amount of hostility! Understated, under control, but *there*. Not very polished yet, but you're definitely coming on.'

'Get to the point.'

'Very well. Since you refuse to ask, which does enormous credit to your self-control, I am well. And Caroline is well, too. For all I know, her husband is also well, although I shall very shortly cease to care about him, as he will no longer be her husband, but her ex-husband.'

'What makes you think I want to know?'

'Because I am cursed with old-fashioned notions of decency, and I thought you should hear it from me first. I called to tell you that Caroline and I are getting married.'

CHAPTER TWENTY-FIVE

Carefully, Sarah put down the phone and pulled out the plug.

It had occurred to her while Dominic was speaking that here was her chance to make a pointed remark on the eligibility of the wealthy and well-connected Caroline. Now she was glad that she had resisted the temptation, and had simply murmured a neutral acknowledgement, said a firm goodbye over Dominic's objections, and hung up.

It was nine o'clock. Already it was getting dark outside, and raining, as it had been all day.

She went down to the kitchen, made herself an omelette and ate it standing up, then took a small whisky and ginger ale upstairs and watched an American made-for-TV movie about adoption in which she got unreasonably involved. Then she went soberly to bed.

It took hours to get to sleep. She was angry. Angry at Dominic's casual re-entry into her life. Angry at his dishonesty and his insinuations about Alex. And yes, admit it, angry about his engagement to Caroline Harris. But beneath the anger she was vaguely aware of something else: an obscure, nagging anxiety which she couldn't explain.

When eventually she fell asleep, her dreams were full of missed deadlines of heartstopping importance, and endless lines of hostile grey people, and angry voices hissing: *'It's all your fault!'*

At four o'clock she awoke to an abrupt awareness of what had been eluding her. It had nothing to do with Dominic, and everything to do with Robert and Charity.

She lay staring at the canopy above her, willing her heart to stop racing.

Eventually, tired and heavy-limbed, she pulled on jeans and a sweater and padded down to the kitchen. She made tea and took it to the State Dining-Room, where she stood at the window watching the valley slowly emerge from the darkness. At the end of the drive, the great iron gates floated like the masts of a sinking ship in a sea of mist. Hynton was a drowned village, indistinct and ghostly.

She felt like an impostor. As if she had come to Harlaston under false pretences. And, if the suspicion which had crystallized overnight was true, she had.

She couldn't put it off any longer. She went to the Jade Ante-Room to fetch Flora Fielding's memoirs, which a chuffed Leonard Fielding had lent her the previous week. Crossing the landing to the Library, she took down Volume Two of *Edward VII, His Life and Times* and laid it on the floor. Then she sat cross-legged on the parquet and opened Flora's memoirs at the passage about Charity. *'. . . I was very fond of her, and even cherished a schoolgirl dream of the two of us raising our families in proximious harmony . . .'*

'. . . a schoolgirl dream . . .'

The first time she had read it, Sarah had had a vague

sense that something wasn't right, but had been too elated at finding any mention of Charity to give it much thought. Now the discrepancy shouted at her from the page. In 1908 when Charity had gone to France, Flora had been nineteen, and a cadet in the Salvation Army. She hadn't been a schoolgirl for several years. Of course it was conceivable that Flora had used the term loosely, to characterize a foolish fantasy. But it was hard to imagine the woman who had written those memoirs ever using a term loosely in her life. The alternative explanation, which had worked its way to the surface of Sarah's consciousness as she slept, was that Flora hadn't been writing about events in 1908, but about some much earlier time.

Support for her theory was buried in the same passage: Flora's mother remarking that the rectory was doing its *'small part for the new* entente *which was then so much on everyone's lips'*. Sarah reached for *Edward VII, His Life and Times* and flicked through the pages. Beneath an engraving of the King delivering a speech at the Elysée Palace she found what she was looking for. She read the turgid prose with the sinking feeling of someone who sees their unwelcome suspicions confirmed. '. . . *the bitterness of past years was swept away by the brilliance of His Majesty's diplomacy . . . from polite restraint the Parisians swiftly passed to exuberant expressions of affection and esteem . . . The* Entente Cordiale *was established*.' And the *Entente Cordiale*, the drawing-together of the two great sovereign nations, had been on everyone's lips when it was first established: during Edward VII's visit to France in the spring of *1903*.

She had known as soon as she woke up that

morning. Now here it was, confirmed in black and white.

Charity had gone to France in 1903, not 1908. Sarah's father had been born five years *after* his mother left Hynton for the Continent. By which time Robert had been in India for three years.

The conclusion was inescapable. Robert was not her grandfather.

She remained sitting on the floor while the sun came up and burned off the fog, and the birds awoke in Hynton Wood. Finally, she went downstairs and made more tea, which she drank in the Long Gallery, staring at the portrait of the man she had begun to accept, for better or worse, as her grandfather. The black un-English eyes regarded her coolly. A handsome, thoughtful, worldly face, giving nothing away.

There was no doubt about the dates. But still she was not convinced.

She waited until half past eight, then rang Mrs Drake. Apologized for the early call, thanked her for the lovely tea, and could she ask one more question? In what year had Samuel Webb got married?

July 28th 1902 of course, Mrs Drake wasn't hardly like to forget a thing like that, was she, her own mum and dad's wedding anniversary? And yes, they got married the year after he was jilted by that other little madam, that went abroad.

Finally, Sarah called her mother.

'Sarah? What's wrong?'

'Nothing, Mum. I'm fine.'

'You don't sound fine. Something's happened. It's too early. It's only ten to nine.'

'Look, sorry about this, but I'm doing some routine

341

checking, and – um, Dad *was* born in 1908, wasn't he?'

There was a long silence at the other end of the phone. Sarah shut her eyes and waited for the outburst.

It didn't come. Her mother gave a deep sigh, and said tiredly: 'Oh, *Sarah*. What on earth are you on about now?'

'I know it sounds ridiculous, but bear with me? I've got to check everything. It's just routine.' Just routine. Like a detective in a thriller, hoodwinking a suspect.

'Well consider it *checked*! He was born on the sixth of August 1908, as you well know! I've only got his birth certificate, haven't I? What d'you want, a bloody certified copy? And you don't need to be French to read the essentials, even I can do that! Sixth of August nineteen hundred and *eight*. Mother: Charity Elisabeth Fosdyke. Father: Robert High-and-Mighty bloody Pearce-Staunton. Now suppose you tell me what on earth's going on?'

'Sorry, Mum. Like I said, I just—'

'I wish to goodness you'd do what I said at the beginning and give the whole thing up as a bad job! I don't know what Alex was thinking of! You're obviously going round the twist out there on your own. I've half a mind to send Nick this afternoon and fetch you home!'

'Nick's in Perpignan, Mum. You know that. I got a postcard from them last weekend.'

'Well, then.' She sounded mollified, as if the fact that Sarah could remember her brother's whereabouts was proof of at least a vestige of sanity. 'But consider yourself warned, my girl. Any more of this nonsense and you're coming home!'

'I will. And Mum – thanks.'

'Are you sure you're all right? You sound all shaky. You can't be eating properly.'

''Course I am. In fact, I'm having Alex and Stephen round to tea. I'm even doing some baking. You'd be proud of me.'

'Oh, yes. From a cake-mix, if I know my daughter.' She was right of course, and when Sarah told her so she did her best not to sound reassured.

'*In memoriam, Robert Percival D'Authon Pearce-Staunton, Nineteenth Baron Harlaston . . . I Corinthians 13, 1–3.*'

A fugitive shaft of sunlight slanted through the east window of St Hybald's. The alabaster tablet glittered like frost.

Sarah sat in the front pew with her notebook before her. A fortnight earlier, she had borrowed Stephen's school Bible and copied down the text from Corinthians. '*I may speak in tongues of men or of angels, but if I have no love, I am a sounding gong or a clanging cymbal. I may have the gift of prophecy and the knowledge of every hidden truth; I may have faith enough to move mountains; but if I have no love, I am nothing. I may give all I possess to the needy, I may give my body to be burnt, but if I have no love, I gain nothing by it.*' What had Lady Harlaston intended to convey by that reference on her husband's memorial? An ironic comment on her marriage? Or merely a conventional wifely tribute?

Sarah would never know.

What she did know was that Charity Fosdyke had gone to France of her own accord in 1903, and had not been pregnant at the time. Nor was there a shred of evidence to suggest that her departure had been surrounded by scandal. She had gone for reasons of her own. Perhaps it was as Flora Fielding had said, a 'laudable ambition to see the Continent'. Or perhaps Samuel Webb's fury at being jilted had driven her away. Who could say? Whatever the reason, Charity had stayed in France, formed a liaison with an unknown man, and had a child – five years *after* she left Hynton.

It was unlikely in the extreme that this unknown man had been Robert. Sarah knew from the annals of the Royal Society that he had returned from his last plant-hunting expedition to South America in March 1905; and according to Aubrey's account, he had left for India soon afterwards, and served there until 1915. To have sired Julian D'Authon, he would have had to return from India, trace Charity to an obscure school in provincial France, seduce her, then go back to India – all a good five years *after* he had last set eyes on her, if indeed he ever had.

In fact, were it not for the vague oral tradition in the Dalton and Hardy families, there was no evidence linking Robert and Charity at all, except for the appearance of his name on the birth certificate. As to that, it was far more probable that poor Charity had simply given the midwife a false name. It wouldn't have been the first time a lonely young woman had lied about the identity of her baby's father. Maybe Charity *had* once been in love with Robert. He was rich and good-looking; lots of village maidens must have felt the same. And maybe he *had* seduced her when she was living in Hynton, and years later she had still harboured tender feelings for him. Or maybe, and this was far more probable, he had simply never known of her existence. Then, five years later, when she was alone in France – perhaps abandoned by her real-life lover, and with the dream of a new life in another country rapidly tarnishing – she had tried to cheer herself up with this pathetic fantasy. And had kept the fantasy alive while her son was growing up. And Julian himself, lacking a real father, had mistaken it for fact, and in time had passed it on to his own family. Just as William Fosdyke had passed it on to his daughter, who in her tight-lipped way had perpetuated the story by telling Alex. Family legends had taken root in thinner soil than that.

But if all that were true, then who had been Sarah's grandfather?

She sat in the pew staring into space. Fitful sunshine flooded the church and was abruptly dimmed, as the first drops of rain pattered onto the roof.

'So if I've got this right,' Alex said that afternoon as they wandered about the terraces after tea, 'you've got a little nearer your grandmother, which is pretty encouraging, but you no longer have any idea who your grandfather was. Correct?'

'Correct,' said Sarah.

'Christ,' he said succinctly.

She had waited till after tea to tell him. As they'd solemnly worked their way through rock buns, iced fingers, Jammy Dodgers and orange juice, the conversation had been confined to lichens, fossils, and the bat sanctuary. Alex did not ask if Sarah had spoken to Dominic, nor did she mention the news of his engagement. Dominic wasn't uppermost in her mind. Besides, she assumed that Alex already knew – though it was clear from Stephen's unclouded countenance that he did not.

They left the terraces and wandered along the Italian Walk. Rose trees dripped gracefully onto mossy flags. In an arbour at the end, a bust of Boadicea contemplated their approach.

Stephen had run on ahead to compare the patches of lichen on Boadicea's magnificent bosom with those he had noted down a month ago. Four rock buns, three iced fingers, and countless Jammy Dodgers had done nothing to slow him down. He kept racing up the slope to the summer-house and back, like a puppy squeezing double the distance out of a walk.

'So do you think', said Alex, 'it might have been this gamekeeper, Samuel Webb?'

She shook her head. 'At one time I thought so, but then the penny dropped about the dates. I suppose he *could* have gone across to France and found her, but it's pretty unlikely. He didn't have that kind of money. No, I'm sure it was someone she met in France.' She shivered, and buried her chin in the neck of her sweater.

Alex watched Stephen climb a mulberry tree, and treated Sarah to one of his expectant silences.

She broke off an overblown yellow rose and started pulling off the petals. 'To tell the truth, I didn't want it to be Samuel Webb. I didn't want it to be anyone but Robert.'

He glanced at her. 'I thought you didn't approve of him.'

'I don't. Oh, I don't know. He wasn't all bad. He could be kind.'

'That's basing a lot on Flora's recollection of something which happened over seventy years before.'

'So? You're basing a whole book on a piece of bog oak over seventy *thousand* years old. Who's kidding whom?'

'It's a novel,' he said briefly.

She threw away the remains of the rose. 'And this is fact. And yes, I do know the difference.'

They walked a little further. Then she said, 'Look, I'm sure you think I'm making too much of this. But I've told you before, it isn't some kind of New Age identity thing with me. I know who I am, whatever the hell that means, and compared to a lot of people I'm bloody lucky. I had parents who loved me, and that's more than a lot of people ever get. It's more than poor little Stephen has, isn't it? But I just – I just want to know the truth.'

He stood watching her with his hands in his pockets.

'This is going to sound sentimental and illogical,' she went on, taking a shaky breath, 'but in some way I feel I owe it to her – and to him too, for that matter – to find out the truth.'

He didn't ask if she meant Robert or her father, and, if he had, she wasn't sure what her answer would have been. 'Don't worry about me, Alex. I can handle it. Honestly.' She held out her hand. 'See? Steady as a rock bun.'

They reached Boadicea and turned back. Alex said, 'I called Dominic yesterday.'

She glanced at him. 'That's a bit out of character for you.'

His cheeks darkened. 'I made him tell me why he's so keen to speak to you.'

'I know why. He called me too.'

He turned sharply to face her. 'When?'

'Last night. Probably as soon as he'd finished

talking to you. He wouldn't want his little brother stealing his thunder, would he?' She paused. 'I take it Stephen doesn't know he's getting a new stepmother?'

'Not yet.'

'What about Clare?'

He shook his head. 'She's in Germany. Dominic couldn't reach her. I suppose once she knows, she'll come back and tell Stephen herself.'

'I wouldn't bet on it. She'll probably ask you to do it.'

'Mm,' he said without relish.

They watched Stephen tumble out of the mulberry tree, grin broadly to reassure them he wasn't hurt, and head off at a gallop towards the Japanese Garden.

'Knowing Stephen,' Alex said, 'he'll pretend to be more worried about the effect on his mother. But what about you? You don't seem too bothered.'

She shrugged. 'All I could think of when Dominic called was how bloody pompous he sounded. In fact for the first time I wondered what I'd seen in him. He's such a prick.'

He laughed.

They were back at the terraces. Halfway up the slope, Stephen beckoned to them. He was standing on one leg on the narrow stone bridge which marked the entrance to the Japanese Garden. When they reached him, he glanced from Sarah to Alex. 'Were you talking about me?'

'Yes,' said Alex. 'I was telling Sarah how good you are at looking after your mother.'

So as not to look pleased, Stephen sucked in his lips till they disappeared. Then he said to Sarah, 'D'you want a tour of the Japanese Garden? Mr Hinde told me about it and I looked it up.'

'Yes please,' she said.

That night, Sarah dreamed she was in Robert's study, searching for her father.

She was standing by the big leather-topped desk, which was just as it appeared in the portrait in the Long Gallery. Robert stood on the other side of the desk beside the great bowl of orchids, in the same graceful pose as in the portrait, but turned away from her. All she could see was the back of his sleek dark head.

She desperately wanted him to turn and face her, and his silent refusal filled her with grief.

Then she became aware of a woman sitting in an armchair beside the desk. She couldn't see her face, but had a vague sense that she was young.

Where's my father? she demanded of Robert's long elegant back. He never moved. He didn't even turn his head.

Silently she pounded the desk, but her fists were soft and useless as putty. *What have you done with him? I haven't got time for this, I have to find him!*

Without turning round, Robert spoke. He sounded puzzled, and faintly impatient. *Why? Why must you find him?*

I can't lose him twice!

Robert's shoulders lifted in an elegant shrug. *He's probably looking after his mother. He takes good care of her. He worries about her.*

But what about you? she cried. *Why don't you worry about her? Why don't you take care of her?*

He did not reply.

The young woman in the armchair slowly faded to nothing.

Where have you put them? Sarah cried, and the part of her brain which knew she was dreaming heard her mewing like a puppy in the waking world.

You know, Sarah, Robert told her calmly, still without turning round, *this isn't my fault. I'm not the one you should blame. But you've known that all along. Haven't you?*

That's not true! she cried. *Turn round and tell me to my face! Why can't you turn round? I can't, I can't, I can't, lose you twice!*

She woke with a start to the steady falling of the rain. It was five o'clock in the morning. Grey light was seeping round the edges of the curtains.

Sleep was impossible. The dream had left her shaken and confused.

She got up, pulled on jeans, sweater and socks, and took the duvet downstairs to the Jade Ante-Room. She made tea, padded back to the Ante-Room, and curled up under the duvet.

The rain intensified. Beyond the tall bay windows the curtain of grey almost obliterated the Lion Steps. The Hall was cut off, adrift on a sea of rain.

Her hands shook as she held the mug. Her stomach was a tight hard knot.

She thought back to the previous day, when Stephen had shown them round the Japanese Garden.

'It's nothing like a tea garden,' he had explained severely, 'it's a *Kare-Sansui*. A sort of dried-up water garden. The last Lady Harlaston had it built. Mr Hinde said his dad told him it was her favourite place. You see how they dug this channel winding all the way up the slope, and made it look like a river-bed, with a bridge and banks with little trees and things, all the way up to the summer-house? That's where the spring's supposed to be. Only there *isn't* a spring. Or a stream. The whole thing's built to make you *think* there's water but there isn't any. D'you get it? It's a dried-up water garden.' The paradox delighted him.

In the Jade Ante-Room, Sarah's tea had grown an oily film. She put the mug on the floor. She felt sick. Her head throbbed from crying in her sleep.

'I wanted it to be Robert,' she had told Alex fiercely, as they contemplated Lady Harlaston's arid horticultural lie. 'I know it's ridiculously sentimental but I wanted him and Charity to have been in love, if only for a while. Otherwise it's all so bleak. Sometimes I think everything's so bleak!'

She had felt such a fool. Pressing her fingers to her lips to stop herself crying, and forcing a smile for poor scared little Stephen, who thought it was something he had said about Lady Harlaston's garden, while Alex rubbed her back with one hand and said, I know, I know, over and over again.

And now, curled up under the duvet, she began to cry again, which was ridiculous, and nothing but the effect of the dream on an empty stomach and her own bloody fault; what did she expect if she kept skipping meals?

Alex and Helen. Helen and Dominic. Dominic and Clare. Dominic and Sarah. Damage and more damage, on and on like a paper-chain. Was that all there was?

Why couldn't there just for once have been something that didn't end in damage and bitterness and regret?

Why couldn't Robert and Charity have been together?

She was crying more wrenchingly than she could remember since the day her father died. Deep noisy hiccupping sobs. And like the time in the car when she had split up with Dominic, she was outside herself, and the animal noises beat at her ears with alarming violence.

CHAPTER TWENTY-SIX

Sunday 2 September 1900

Break of day brought little relief from the heat of the night.

In nightgown, shawl, and bare feet, Charity went downstairs into a kitchen submerged in an exhausted copper glow. Her face felt stiff, her eyes gritty with fatigue. There was a rhythmic throbbing in her temples.

She longed for a cup of tea, but couldn't risk waking her mother and facing the inevitable questions about why she was up so early on a Sunday.

What could she say? *'Last night I had an extraordinary conversation in Hynton Wood, and now nothing feels right any more'?*

She had lain awake all night with dark thoughts crowding in on her. She told herself that this desolation – this bleakness – was her own fault for behaving in a wicked, unwomanly way. But she knew it wasn't true. It wasn't the wickedness that kept her awake. It was the impossibility.

On the kitchen table lay an old straw hat and a length of pink ribbon. She had unearthed them from her trunk as an excuse, in case her mother came down. Trimming a hat had the advantage of truthfulness, at least. She must have something to wear for morning service.

Morning service. The thought of seeing him in church made her mouth go dry. She would plead a sick headache and stay at home.

Her glance strayed to the *Sybarite's Reward* on the wall. She remembered how he had studied it. At the time she had wondered what was going through his mind.

Every time she thought of him her stomach turned over. He had stood close to her in the darkness. So close that she had felt his breath on her hair. If her mother knew – if Mrs Bowles, if anyone knew – they would be appalled.

So why wasn't she?

Was she a fool not to believe the worst of him? She didn't know. She didn't *know*. All night she had veered from one extreme to the other. She kept hearing what her mother would say: that she had acted foolishly, brazenly, wickedly. But she knew – she *knew* – that there had been nothing wrong in it. He had simply wanted to talk to her, because he was lonely and unhappy, and because for some extraordinary reason they understood each other.

But the worst was remembering how *she* had behaved, and wondering what he must think of her. Thinking about that made her go hot and cold. Her cheeks burned. Shamelessly seeking him out when he wanted to be alone. Marching up like a hussy and keeping him there in stilted conversation.

For the first time she understood her mother's burning need for respectability. She longed for a chance to behave in his presence with the very extremity of decorum, so that he would see how respectable she really was.

She put her face in her hands. Oh *God*. What must he *think*?

The sound of footsteps on the stairs. She just had time to pick up the hat before her mother entered the kitchen.

Mrs Fosdyke stood blinking in the doorway, her face puffy with sleep. 'I overslept. I never oversleep.'

Charity applied herself to the hat. 'What time did you get back?'

She sat down heavily at the table. 'Must've been gone one. One in the morning! Shame you left early. You missed the dancing.'

Charity put the hat down and went to the dresser for the oilcloth table cover. 'I was tired.'

'You're pale. Shadows under your eyes. Didn't you sleep?'

She shook her head.

'Is anything wrong?'

'No.'

'Is it because it's Sam's last day?'

' – Maybe. I don't know.'

'You won't like me saying this, but you'd feel easier about that if you were engaged.'

Charity unfolded the cover and spread it on the table. She looked down at it, her hands on the back of the chair. 'Mother,' she said softly, 'what did happen to Cousin Ruth?'

Mrs Fosdyke went very still. 'Why – do you ask?'

'I don't know. Because.'

'But why now?'

'I don't know.'

Mrs Fosdyke stared at the oilcloth, her gaze lost in the swirling black and purple patterns. 'We used to say Nanny Rot got her in Jericho Wood. D'you remember Nanny Rot?'

'The old widow woman who lived by herself.'

'You children were terrified of her. "Don't you go near those woods," we'd say, "or Nanny Rot'll get you."'

Quietly, Charity sat down. 'You were the same age as Cousin Ruth, weren't you?'

Mrs Fosdyke paused before answering. 'Like as two peas in a pod, we were. Her family lived in Crow Water Fen, just like us. An' they were poor, too.' She shook her head. 'You don't know how poor! They lived in a turf hut with one room. Sedge on the floor to soak up the wet. Hole in the roof to let out the smoke.'

'Were you friends?'

'I 'spose. She was a good girl. Good little worker. Got a job on a farm when she was eleven. Kitchen girl. Oh, it was *hard* work. Humping coals, blacking grates. But we loved it. They fed you well on those big farms, an' you always knew exactly what you had to do.' She paused, remembering. 'After four years they put her up to housemaid, just like me. She loved that too.'

'What happened then?'

Slowly Mrs Fosdyke spread her hands on the table, placing each finger with deliberate care, as if her balance depended on it. 'One Sunday she meets this boy coming out of church. He's this great strapping fellow, but when she looks at him he goes as red as a rosehip.'

' – And?'

Her mother flinched. Charity felt cruel. But she had to know.

'Come the time for the harvest-home supper. The horkey, they called it in those parts. An' they did it the old way, the whole village an' the farms together. Then all of a sudden it's *after* the horkey, an' he says enough's enough, I'm walking you home.' She looked down at her hands. 'They strayed too far into the wood. An' Nanny Rot got her. You can work out the rest.'

'Was she found out?'

''Course she was! Hard to hide after the fourth month.'

Charity swallowed. In all her speculations about Cousin Ruth's crime, she had never imagined a child.

'The Bible's *wrong,*' said Mrs Fosdyke. 'There is no forgiveness.'

'You mean she lost her place?'

'Lost everything. Farmer's wife had her up in front of 'em all with a sign round her neck. Bible words, about unclean, an' wickedness. Then sent her packing. We never saw her again. Never will, neither. Not in this life.'

'But couldn't she go home to her family?'

'Oh, she could never do that! Farmer's wife wrote to the parson's wife, who told the whole village.'

'But they'd have understood. It can't have been the first time something like that had happened—'

'You don't understand!' Her eyes were fierce. 'It weren't what *they* thought, but what *she* thought! She was a good girl. She'd have died of the disgrace. It was bad enough for me, an' I was just the cousin.'

Charity sat back in her chair. So that was what made her mother so fierce about respectability. Always on the watch in case her daughter showed signs of her ill-fated cousin's waywardness.

Well you've shown it now, haven't you? she thought.

'Now then,' said her mother, the steel returning to her voice. 'I've done what you wanted. I've told you about Cousin Ruth. Now it's your turn. Why were you so keen to know about Cousin Ruth?'

'I told you, I don't know.'

'That's not good enough.'

'I'm sorry. It's all the answer you're going to get.'

They traded stares.

'Then tell me this, my girl. Last night when you were walking home, did something happen with Sam?'

'Nothing happened with Sam.'

'Are you sure?'

'Of course I'm sure! I'll swear it on the Bible if you want.'

'Charity—'

'Leave me be, Mother.'

'But Charity—'

'I said leave me be!'

What must she *think* of me? thought Robert as he climbed the stairs to the nursery and looked about him with the deceptive clarity that comes from too much champagne and staying awake all night.

Out on the west lawn, an army of journeymen was dismantling the remains of the Ball: taking down the pavilions and the strings of lights and bearing the potted orange trees back to the conservatory. They worked in silence. It was six o'clock in the morning, and the house was full of sleeping guests who must not be disturbed.

The conversation in the wood had acquired the quality of a dream. What had possessed him to behave in such a way? What must she think? What *could* she think – save that her landlord had attempted a rather ill-conceived seduction which she had foiled at the last minute by running away. *Ill-conceived?* To that poor girl it must seem infinitely worse: a base, contemptible abuse of power perpetrated against a young woman made pathetically vulnerable by age, class, experience – whatever measure one cared to use. How could she think otherwise?

If only he could talk to her. Explain, make her understand. But what would he say? How could he make her understand when he didn't understand himself?

With his hands in his pockets, he wandered from room to room.

To his surprise, the nursery had hardly changed since he was a boy. Poor little Linley had scarcely left a mark. In the night nursery he found the same square of grey hardcord on which he and Spencer had taken their baths. In the day nursery the old low table was still covered with scuffed brown linoleum. In the schoolroom he found the same handwritten lists of Sovereigns and Capital Cities tacked to the picture-rails, and the same patch of blistered paint which he had always fancied resembled the Sphinx.

But against the wall in the day nursery were two deal toy-chests he hadn't seen before. The lid of one was propped open to reveal a jumble of board-games. It looked as if Gibbs had been called away in the middle of sorting them out, and had never returned.

He stood looking down at the toys. Someone ought to pack them up and send them away. They wouldn't be wanted now.

Then he noticed a small cedarwood box which

looked familiar. Hadn't it once contained a rather splendid set of glass marbles? Yes, it was the same box. One long-ago Christmas, Aunt Margot had given it to them as a joint present, and thereafter it had caused many a nursery feud.

Taking the box to the table, he pulled up a chair and tipped the marbles onto the table. How much smaller and less luminous they were than he remembered.

Idly, he began an old game. One marble equals five years. Set out fourteen marbles in a line: that's three score years and ten, the biblical span. Now roll away the marbles you've already used up, and count how many are left.

Two rows of marbles, with seven marbles in each. Thirty-five years gone, thirty-five years left. Always supposing that somewhere on the veldt there wasn't a Mauser bullet with his name on it.

Is that what this is about? he wondered. You feel your life slipping away, and you want another chance at happiness? My God, if that's the case, you're even more of a coward than I thought.

But that was not the worst of it. The worst was that he had offended her. He knew from the catch in her voice, and the way she had run from him.

Ah, *God*.

And now there would be no chance to see her before he left Harlaston. No chance to apologize, to explain – to convince her that he wasn't as contemptible as she must think. Tomorrow he would take the train to London, and two days later he would board the steamer for Durban.

Suddenly he realized it was impossible to leave this unresolved. He had to see her again.

He got to his feet and pocketed three of the marbles.

You're still drunk, he told himself, trying to make light of it. Give up this ridiculous notion. Go downstairs, have a bath and a glass of seltzer water. And then if you hurry, you'll just have time to catch poor old Bowles before he leaves for church, and apologize for Violet's appalling discourtesy in crossing him off her guest-list.

He would see to all that. He would. But first there was something he must do. He crossed to Gibbs's little writing desk and found a sheet of notepaper, an envelope, and pen and ink.

He wondered how best to persuade her to see him again. How to get the note to her in the first place.

In the end he brushed all that aside and simply wrote: '*I must speak to you alone. Be at the same place at noon today. Harlaston.*'

'What you must understand', he told Ederic Bowles an hour later, leaning forward on the sofa with his elbows on his knees, 'is that Lady Harlaston was so overcome – so mortified at having unintentionally injured a dear old friend – that she was quite unable to accompany me this morning.'

A flicker at the corner of his vision told him that Gwendolen Bowles repressed an involuntary protest.

The rector and his wife had been at breakfast when he was announced, and had entered the drawing room in an anxious flurry: Bowles supporting his wife on one arm, with his napkin forgotten in his collar and a drop of egg-yolk on his chin. He did not look as though he had slept well, and his too-ready protestations of ignorance as to the reason for Robert's visit betrayed his bewilderment at being excluded from the Ball.

'I fear', Robert went on, 'that since my return, Lady Harlaston has believed it her duty – mistakenly, I need hardly add – to put herself under great strain for my sake, while endeavouring to conceal the depths of her grief about our son.' God help me, he thought, but what else can I say? 'You, my dear fellow, to our infinite regret, have been the unintended casualty of too much taken on too soon, by too sensitive a nature.'

Another recoil from Gwen – which, mercifully, old Bowles didn't catch. It was doubtful if he caught anything at all. His eyes were brimming with tears.

'Needless to say,' Robert added with belated prudence, 'I must ask you never to broach this with Lady Harlaston herself. To do so would, as you will no doubt appreciate, only cause her the keenest distress.'

'Oh my dear Lord Harlaston,' spluttered Bowles, 'of *course* not! Why, I should never dream – oh dear *no*! The poor dear lady – oh, of *course*!' Grasping Robert's hand in both of his, he muttered something unintelligible, and fled the house.

The poor old chap had swallowed it whole, which only made Robert feel worse.

He wondered if he would have the courage – the black-hearted gall – to deceive Gwendolen Bowles into passing on the note. Before leaving the Hall, he had gone to his study and chosen a small volume of Italian travel writing, and slipped the envelope inside. He had a vague idea that he might find some way of asking Gwendolen Bowles to pass the book to her 'little reader' under the pretext of a loan.

But as he was riding across the park, he was struck by his lack of invention. To say that he was not good at subterfuge would be a kindness he did not deserve. He was simply inept.

And he was only too well aware of the risk he would be running, for both of them.

If you bungle this, he told himself, if Gwendolen Bowles uncovers the note and you get that poor girl into trouble (he flinched at the unintended double meaning), you will never forgive yourself.

But then, you will never forgive yourself if you don't find a way to see her again and apologize.

Suddenly he realized that since the rector's departure he had been sitting in silence. 'Gwen,' he said gently, 'this affair of the Ball. I am so sorry.'

She gave him a tremulous smile. 'I know you are. And – thank you.'

'For what?'

'For what you just did for Ederic. It was a *great* kindness.'

'Please. I told a lie. You know that as well as I.'

'But it was such a *fine* lie. How can I condemn you for it?'

His cheeks darkened with shame. What had he been thinking of? To abuse a friendship which had lasted since childhood? The book must remain in his pocket. He must find another way.

Riding slowly back along the Tilburne road, he spotted William Fosdyke trying out his new crutches on the verge. He was appalled by the fierce rush of hope that surged through him.

He is a *child*, he told himself savagely. You cannot make use of a *child*.

'Good morning, Will,' he called out, 'you're abroad early.' He thought he sounded horribly jocular and false.

The boy shaded his eyes with his hand, and shyly smiled. 'So are you, my lord.'

'I thought I'd give my horse a farewell ride.'

'May I ask what he's called, my lord?'

'His name is Viscount.'

On cue, Viscount put down his head and allowed his nose to be stroked.

'Will you be taking him to Africa, my lord?'

'Oh, no. He wouldn't care for the sea journey.'

'I don't s'pose he'd like the big guns, neither.'

'I don't suppose he would.'

'May I ask something else, my lord?'

'Of course.'

'In Africa, will the Dutchmen shoot at you?'

'Without a doubt.'

'And will you shoot back?'

'I'm afraid I shall. That's what it comes down to in a war.'

The flaxen head nodded sagely.

Robert gathered his reins and put Viscount forward.

He had ridden some distance along the road when he turned the horse's head and cantered back to the boy. Quickly, before he could change his mind, he took the volume from his breast pocket and extracted the note. 'Give this to your sister. Show it to no-one except her and tell no-one about it. That's very important. Do you understand?'

'Of course, my lord.' The blue eyes met his without a shadow of surprise or complicity. They made him feel a hundred years old.

On impulse he reached into his pocket and brought out the three glass marbles. He leaned down and put them into the boy's palm. 'Here. Something to remember me by.'

The boy gave a low murmur of delight. 'Why, my lord! They're *spells*!'

'Spells?' Robert was intrigued. 'I thought they were marbles.'

'Oh, no sir! They only look like marbles.'

'But – how can you tell they're spells?'

'Because you can cast 'em, sir. An' they're mortal hard to break. An' because they're what your lions hold between their paws.'

'My lions?'

'Up at the Hall.'

'Ah, yes. And – tell me, Will. Those spells in your hand. Are they good or bad?'

Gravely the boy looked up at him. 'Depends how you use them, sir.'

Robert nodded. 'Well, then. Take care how you do.'

The boy smiled. 'You may be sure of that.'

'Goodbye, William Fosdyke.'

'Goodbye, my lord. I wish you good luck in the war an' a safe journey home when it's all done.'

Robert looked down into the handsome, earnest little face, and felt a sudden absurd pricking behind his eyes. 'Thank you. Thank you,' he said.

'*I must speak to you alone. Be at the same place at noon today. Harlaston.*'

Charity knelt at the foot of her bed with the note spread in front of her on the counterpane.

When Will had hobbled into her room and given her the envelope, black spots had darted before her eyes. It hadn't been a lie when she told her mother that she had a sick headache and must stay behind from church.

The note was an overwhelming presence in the

room: alien, yet intensely, unbelievably personal. She pictured him writing it, seated at his great gilded desk in his marble study.

The words leapt out at her, black and crisp and elegant. His handwriting. His name. The thick ivory paper even carried a faint whiff of cigar smoke.

With her finger she traced the forthright black letters. It felt shockingly intimate. Like touching him.

My God, she thought. My God. What do I do now?

Midday in Pond Hollow.

A warm wind soughs through the pines and rustles the dusty teasels by the path. A summer snowstorm of thistledown drifts across the clearing. The air is heavy with the scent of resin.

He was standing on the far side of the hollow, looking the other way.

With the clarity of a dream she observed the fit of his tunic across his back. The narrowness of his waist. And like the time in St Hybald's, the sharpening of his shoulder-blades filled her with a sense of protectiveness and desire.

She took a deep breath. It was like inhaling the air from a furnace. Picking up her skirts, she walked towards him.

Before leaving the end house, she had changed from her Sunday best into her everyday sprigged blouse and navy skirt, with the plain leather belt, the old straw hat, and her much-darned, workaday woollen gloves. She knew it was irrational, but the change of clothes was essential to her sense of propriety. No-one could accuse her of dressing up for him.

No-one had.

Her mother, returning from morning service gasping

in the heat, had wondered at her going out at all in the noonday sun. But she had accepted her daughter's excuse with surprising ease: that she needed to be on her own, to make a decision about Sam. Such ready trust made Charity feel like a criminal.

The ponds were a milky turquoise in the flat noon light. The lilies were hot and waxen, drained of colour. The only movement was a stirring of wind in the bulrushes, and the bright cobalt dart of a dragon-fly.

She knew that coming to this place was the height of folly – that she was doing what no respectable woman would ever do. But precisely *because* she must prove her respectability, she had no choice.

I will make him see me as I truly am, she resolved with a kind of savagery. He must understand that last night was a brainstorm. That I am not, and never could be, fast.

He felt her watching him, and turned. His face was drawn. 'I knew you would come,' he said.

She stopped three paces away from him. 'You left me no choice, sir. Your note was not a request but a command.'

That made him flinch. 'Had I merely asked, you wouldn't have come.'

'It was wrong of you to make me.'

' – Perhaps. But I had to explain my conduct of last night. Not only explain. Apologize.'

'There's no need.'

'There is. Listen to me. This is important.' He searched for words. 'Last night you must have gained the impression that my intentions were not— that is to say, that I wanted not merely to talk to you, but—' he broke off, frowning, and in a rush of pity she perceived his dilemma: he could not bring himself to offend her by speaking too frankly. It moved her to see so articulate a man struggling for words. 'What I'm trying to say', he went on, 'is that anyone observing my conduct last night would have believed the worst.'

She felt her face growing hot.

'I assure you, Miss Fosdyke, that any such impression was utterly false. You must understand. I never meant to offend you.'

She felt trapped and breathless, and angry – though whether with herself or with him, she couldn't tell. Why did I come here? she asked herself. I risk everything, and for what? To be reminded once again of what I can never have?

She wondered if it was the same for him. Did he truly believe that he had come here simply to apologize? Or did he also perceive how they were trapped in a downward spiral, both clutching at any chance of another meeting, no matter how brief or painful or disastrous it must be. How every time they saw each other it went a little deeper, hurt a little more. Like a splinter working its way into the flesh.

'Why don't you speak?' he said.

Her throat worked. She didn't think she could speak without breaking down.

'You're right,' he said at last. 'It was wrong of me to make you come here. Forgive me.'

To her horror, she felt the tears beginning to spill down her cheeks.

She heard his intake of breath. The rustle of grass as he came towards her. When he spoke, he was very close. 'Don't. Charity.'

Her name hung in the air between them.

'God, I'm sorry,' he murmured. 'I wanted to make it better! Instead I've only made it worse.'

She couldn't look him in the face. Through a mist of tears she saw his ungloved hands open and close at his sides. He wanted to put his arms around her. She wanted it too.

Instead, he reached out and very gently put one hand on her upper arm. Not as a restraint, but a caress. Tentative, involuntary.

It made everything ten times worse. The warmth of his fingers through the cotton blouse. The way his thumb lightly stroked her inner arm. Making her dizzy. Making her want to go to him and lean her head against his breast, and feel his arms about her.

She wished savagely that she was not still wearing her woollen gloves – and that, if only for a moment, she might reach up and put her hand on his. And feel his skin against hers.

Oh, she should have pulled away the *instant* he touched her! The instant. Now every second was making it harder. She was sick with tears.

'Forgive me,' he said again.

She couldn't speak.

Shakily she took his hand in hers – in her gloved hand – and put it from her arm. For a moment their fingers linked and held. Then she withdrew her hand from his grasp and picked up her skirts, and turned and walked away.

She left him standing in the sunlit clearing, surrounded by water lilies and celandine and brilliant dragonflies.

The end of evensong in St Hybald's.

The party from the Hall had filed out to the carriages,

and the farming families were gossiping in the church-yard. The Fosdykes, the Goldsbrows, the Ruddocks and the Hares were shuffling out of their pews.

Charity told her mother she would be out in a moment, and not to wait for her, as Sam would walk her home. She bent her head, pretending absorption in her prayer-book.

She had managed very well on entering the church, and she meant to be as successful on leaving it. By dropping her prayer-book twice and keeping her eyes stubbornly on the floor, she had avoided seeing or being seen by the party from the Hall. If he had chanced to glance in her direction as he and Lady Harlaston left with their guests, he would have seen her as she wanted him to see her. Decent and respect-able. And newly engaged to Keeper Webb.

Sam would be waiting for her in the churchyard. 'Don't be long,' he had hissed when she indicated that she would stay behind. 'I've only got this afternoon, I want to show you off.'

It was the closest he had ever got to a compliment. In the service yard that afternoon he had been curt, still vexed at her equivocation of the night before, and embarrassed at her blurting out in front of the grooms that, yes, she would be his wife.

But later, when he had come by the end house to walk her to church, he had looked almost happy, accepting with diffident pleasure Mrs Fosdyke's tearful smiles and Mr Fosdyke's abashed handshakes. Out in the churchyard he would be telling Dr Bowles, and anyone else who cared to listen, of their betrothal – and when she did emerge, she would be greeted with one of his rare smiles. It was always easier for him to behave like a lover in the company of others.

You did the *right* thing by accepting him. Now everything can go back to normal. You did the right thing.

She heard the last carriage rattle down the lane. It was safe to leave the church. She rose and went out into the evening sun.

Dr Bowles was standing with Sam in the shade of the lych-gate, talking to an elegant couple in a high-sided black and yellow dogcart.

Oh no, she thought. *No.*

Her parents had gone. Will was hanging over the gate looking miserable, as he had been since learning of her betrothal. Sam stood, hat in hand, squinting up at Lord Harlaston – who sat beside his wife in the dogcart, holding the reins.

As Sam turned to look for her, Charity slipped behind a table-tomb. She saw him give an impatient frown, then turn back to the couple in the dogcart.

'Lord Harlaston, Lady Harlaston!' Dr Bowles cried. 'A *thousand* pardons for detaining you in this inclement heat, but I could not let you depart without sharing our simple rustic joy! We have a *summer betrothal*, sealed this very afternoon! Is it not delightful? Our very own Keeper Webb, and artisan Fosdyke's daughter – whom I fancy my dear wife introduced to you the other day, and who is none other than our own little reader at the rectory!'

From behind the table-tomb, Charity watched the handsome sunburned face become very still. 'Why, what splendid news,' he said smoothly. 'Sam, I am sure Lady Harlaston joins me in wishing you every happiness.'

He and Sam and Dr Bowles talked on, while the grey gelding nodded sedately at the flies, and Lady

Harlaston softly pressed her husband's arm, and murmured about rejoining their guests.

This can't last much longer, thought Charity dully. Soon it'll be over. Soon they'll go back to the Hall. All you have to do is wait till they've gone.

Forgive me.

It had cost him a great deal to say that. His voice had shaken with emotion. And she had said nothing in reply.

She watched Lady Harlaston sitting beside her husband in her beautiful snowy dust-coat, her great white hat resplendent with bird of paradise feathers.

Compared to such a woman, Charity Fosdyke had nothing. Neither looks nor poise nor breeding. All she had was her good name. She couldn't bear it if he thought she didn't even have that. Far better if he thought her a respectable woman whom he had offended, and who could not forgive him.

Suddenly he turned his head and scanned the churchyard. He was looking for her.

Forgive me.

She pictured him lying on some desolate African hillside with a bullet in his forehead. Never knowing that there had been nothing to forgive.

She couldn't bear it.

She stepped out from behind the table-tomb just as he flicked the reins and the dogcart moved off.

She picked up her skirts and ran down the path.

She was too late.

The dogcart had disappeared in a haze of dust.

CHAPTER TWENTY-SEVEN

'*Tues. 4th September,*' Charity wrote in large clear letters, so that her mother could read them. '*Gone to Tilburne to send goodbye telegram to Sam. Back late. C.*'

She didn't like writing it, or leaving it propped against the teapot on the dresser. A written lie seemed worse than a spoken one. But her mother could not have taken the truth.

Her first thought had been to go to Tilburne and send him a telegram, saying simply that she wasn't offended and there was nothing to forgive.

Then it occurred to her that she would be recognized in the telegraph office at the railway station.

The alternative was to take the train to Grantham, where nobody knew her.

Or go to London and see him herself.

She couldn't. She couldn't march up to his house and rap on the door. Cousin Ruth might have done that, but not her.

Then she imagined how she would feel if she did not go. If she let the days slip by and did nothing to make it right between them.

Make it right? No-one could do that. But perhaps she could make it better.

Sometimes she told herself that she had got it all wrong, was making something out of nothing. Then there were other times when she would sit on the floor by her window with her hot cheek pressed against the glass and *know* that this mattered, to both of them.

She dressed before dawn, pinning her savings inside her reticule. Then she walked out to the Tilburne road to wait for Mr Burridge's wagon.

Two hours later, she climbed down just before the wagon reached Market Square. The square would be full of people who might know her. Her guile astonished her. Maybe this was the family taint working its way out.

In the railway station she walked up to the booth and asked for a ticket to London.

'I take it you've pre-booked?' asked the clerk, knowing very well that she hadn't. He was a corpulent little man with moist aggrieved eyes and a clipped grey beard that sat bizarrely atop his heavy jowls.

'No I haven't. I didn't know you had to.'

He looked affronted. 'Lot cheaper if you pre-book. All sorts of discounts if you think ahead.'

She thought of the five shillings and eightpence in her purse: the remainder of her savings after the button boots, the green hat-ribbon, and a reckless second-hand copy of *Stenographic Shorthand and Epistolary Form*. She couldn't afford more than three shillings for the fare if she was to have enough left over for getting about in London – whatever that might cost – and something to eat. 'I didn't know about the discounts,' she said, humouring him.

He snorted. 'I can see you haven't been on a train before.'

She forbore from mentioning that she had, once, when she was twelve, on a school outing to Spalding to see the bulbs.

'I could do you a third-class excursion ticket for four and six.'

Four shillings and sixpence?

That left exactly one and tuppence for everything else. She'd have to do without food, for a start.

'Well?' said the clerk testily, as if an imaginary queue was building up behind her.

'I'll take it,' she heard herself say. 'Four shillings and sixpence.'

He gave her a disappointed look and opened his ledger. 'Next train to Little Bytham's the eight oh five. Arrives Little Bytham eight thirty-six. Then it's the fast train via Peterborough at eight fifty-seven, arriving King's Cross at eleven thirty-eight.'

'When does it get to London?'

He stared at her over the top of his spectacles. 'Like I *said*. Eleven thirty-*eight*.'

'Oh. Thank you.'

With a long-suffering flourish he seized a handbill of flimsy mauve paper and wrote on the back, speaking slowly, as if to a child. 'Now, then. The return. Four ten from King's Cross – that's King's Cross *London* – gets you to Little Bytham at six twenty-eight. Six forty-one from Little Bytham, arrives Tilburne at seven twelve. Back before dark. All right for you?'

Home by half past nine if you walk fast, she thought faintly. She gave him a brisk smile. 'That will be perfect.'

*   *   *

375

The fast train to London tore through countryside she could only guess at. The blinds were down to keep out the soot, and inside it was stifling – and startlingly different from the slow train to Little Bytham. The seats were upholstered in dark green plush, and there were overhead racks of varnished teak, with gaseliers of amber glass.

The seven other seats in the carriage were amply filled by seasoned passengers. The men looked like commercial travellers, with old-fashioned frock-coats, striped trousers and heavy brass watch-chains. The two older ladies wore patriotic khaki dust-coats trimmed with red. The third, a heavy-faced woman in lilac, had paper roses lavishly piled on her hat. All were equipped with travelling-bags, walking-sticks, umbrellas, picnic baskets, and little velveteen cushions for their backs. No-one spoke, which Charity found disconcerting.

After the first half-hour, the ladies began dispensing to their menfolk an impressive selection of flasks, paper-wrapped sandwiches, cake and hard-boiled eggs. Still no-one said a word – except to decline indignantly the ticket-collector's suggestion of 'something from the refreshment carriage'. This presented no temptation to Charity, since a Great Northern luncheon basket cost two and six, and a tea-basket sixpence.

In the face of so much stoutly corseted respectability, her journey struck her as increasingly insane. After all, what did she have to go on? By apologizing to her, he had only behaved as a gentleman should towards a woman – any woman, be she a duchess or a fishwife. It was she in her ignorance who had mistaken it for something more.

For the first time she wondered how he would react

to a village girl pitching up on his doorstep to tell him he was forgiven.

He would be astonished, embarrassed, irritated – or perhaps simply amused. But she doubted if he would betray much emotion. He was too well-bred and too kind for that.

Waiting for the train in Tilburne, she had formed a vague idea of sending some sort of message to his house. At the platform bookstall she had paid an extortionate penny a piece for an envelope and a sheet of notepaper. They were inside her reticule, folded in three so as not to get creased. Fortunately, she had brought her own pencil, or no doubt that would have eaten up another tuppence.

But now the absurdity of writing to him struck her anew. And how *could* she write to him, when she hadn't the faintest idea where he lived, other than that it was in 'St James's Square'. Her mouth went dry. She was hurtling towards the largest city in the world, and she didn't even know his address.

Suddenly she remembered the slip of paper Sam had given her on which he had written his address 'for letters.' She had been touched that he wanted her to write to him, though in the next breath he had said that he wouldn't have time for replies.

Aware of the scrutiny of seven pairs of eyes, she rummaged in her reticule and brought out the slip of paper. It bore a regimental address in the Orange River Colony.

At the sight of Sam's careful capitals, she felt a wave of shame. He deserved better. What did it matter that he had been brusque on his last day? He was going to war, wasn't he?

She had asked him if he was worried about going

back to the fighting, but he had met that with suspicion. 'You'd like it if I was scared, wouldn't you? Poor sort of man I'd be if I took fright at a lot of Dutchmen and darkies!'

As they had stood together in the porch, he had kissed her for the first time, quick and hard on the lips. She had felt the weight of his hands on her shoulders and smelt the peppery smell of his moustache. Then he was gone, striding down the garden path without a backward glance.

My God, she thought, crumpling the slip of paper in her hand, what on earth am I doing?

Nothing could have prepared her for King's Cross station.

It was like St Wolfram's in Grantham only ten times bigger, and instead of stained-glass windows it was covered with enamelled signs shrieking from every surface: Wills' Gold Flake! Oakey's Knife Polish! W.H. Smith & Sons! Lost Property!

The whole concourse teemed with grey-faced people: a torrent of humanity of all shapes, ages, classes and descriptions, striding along at astonishing speed. Every few minutes another train arrived in a cloud of steam and soot, and a fresh river of people poured through the platform gates. The high cathedral arches echoed to the shrill whistles of the guards, the slamming of doors, and the pounding of feet. And beyond the station portals came a deafening roar: the clamour of thousands of iron-shod wheels and tens of thousands of iron-shod hooves on the paving-stones of London.

She approached an outside porter and they held a shouted conversation above the roar of traffic. Could he tell her the name of the nearest public museum? The idea of meeting in a museum had been a great comfort when it occurred to her. They would be safer there, on neutral ground, with less risk of being recognized.

'You'll want the *British* Museum, miss!' shouted the porter. 'Oldest, biggest, and best in the world!' Correctly judging that her resources wouldn't stretch to a hansom fare, he pointed to a line of omnibuses drawn by the scrawniest horses Charity had ever seen. 'That's the one you want! Swiss Cottage via Holborn, sixpence any distance!'

The omnibus looked complicated as well as expensive, and Swiss Cottage sounded like another country. She decided against it.

Her next conversation was more productive. She caught the attention of one of the less disreputable-looking lads who thronged the station entrance in the hope of carrying bags or running errands. Despite the boy's swagger, she felt better able to deal with him than with an omnibus. Even Tilburne had its share of station loungers.

He was several years older than Will, but frighteningly thin, with a sandy moustache above chipped yellow teeth, and feral grey eyes that flicked over her with good-humoured insolence.

'How much to take me to the British Museum,' she shouted, 'and run a message to St James's Square?'

'Shilling the lot, lidy!' he shouted. His words came so fast and in such an impenetrable accent that she had to make him repeat everything he said – but then, so did he with her.

'I'll give you sixpence!' she shouted.

'Do us a fivah! Ightpence or nuffink!'

'What? Oh all right! Eightpence for the lot!'

'Done! Money up front!'

'What? Oh, no, my lad, I'm not a complete fool! Half now, and half when it's done.'

He grinned. 'Oh hor! *roight*! *Hof* we goes then!'

She handed over four pennies, and was about to ask how far it was to the museum when he started off at a brisk trot. She was obliged to follow or be lost for ever.

For the next quarter of an hour, talking was a waste of breath. The heat, the din, and the dust were indescribable, the stench of horse-dung so strong it was almost visible. They shouldered their way down a huge street choked with hansom cabs, horse-trams, omnibuses, and legions of private broughams and clarences. Many of the horses looked as if they were on their last legs.

The pavements were thronged with garishly dressed women hanging on the arms of men in boaters, with mothers holding pallid children, with soldiers in khaki. Hawkers sold bunches of skinned rabbits on strings; tailors walked up and down with cloth caps stacked on their heads like pancakes; urchins swept crossings for a penny a go. And above the roar of the carriages loomed the silent assault of the printed word: posters, placards, lurid enamelled signs.

They came to a street of tall stately houses, silent as a churchyard. The boy – 'call me 'Arry, miss' – told her the 'nobs' who lived there had 'shut up shop' and gone away for the summer.

The tall white columns reminded Charity of Harlaston. Perhaps the house in St James's Square looked like this. Again she felt the impossibility of what she was doing. This was his world. The world of town houses and soireés, and dinners at the club. For him, Harlaston was only a summer interlude between Seasons.

They turned off the main road into a maze of narrow streets. Here the crowds were thinner, the carriages slower. The swells with their fancy women had given way to grim, grey-faced men in dark suits, whom Charity supposed to be attorneys. Then suddenly they were out in a broad open space dissected by glittering black railings tipped with gold. Behind the railings rose a serene, enormous temple of many columns. It was almost as large as the Hall, though not nearly so ornate.

This ought to be grand enough even for him, she thought, as she stood blinking on the pavement.

The ladies' cloakroom of the museum was deserted, except for a sour old woman on a stool who exacted a ha'penny for letting Charity in. The walls were gleaming expanses of blue and white tiles. The wash-basins rested on fluted columns of white porcelain, and had taps of polished brass.

After the din of the street, the silence throbbed in her ears like a heartbeat. She could still feel the pavement vibrating beneath her feet to the thunder of the carriages.

Ignoring the attendant's stare, she took off her hat and gloves and tidied her hair. When she wetted a corner of her handkerchief and cleaned her face, it came away speckled with black.

Her hands began to shake. She held them under the cool water and took a deep breath. In the looking-glass above the wash-basin a strange girl stared back at her, her expression as severe and inward-looking as a Londoner's.

Silently she addressed the stranger in the looking-glass. There is nothing wrong in what you are doing.

There is no impropriety, if you behave properly. You simply came to clear up a misunderstanding, so that he will know you took no offence, and you will know that he knows. Then you can go your separate ways and be at peace.

She went out into the echoing marble entrance-hall. The staircase alone was as wide as the end house, and rose to uncharted heights above her head. Harlaston Hall must be like this inside. So much the better, she told herself. He will feel at home here.

She did not like to wait in the entrance, so she crossed to a marble hall filled with enormous foreign-looking heads in speckled granite. Gazing about her, she collided with an attendant: a severe old gentleman in a top hat and dark blue frock-coat, who met her apology with a narrow stare, as if he suspected her of plotting to rob the museum of its treasures.

She passed into another hall, then another, and finally into a smaller, less intimidating chamber peopled by half a dozen statues. Shafts of dusty sun-light illuminated the attendant at the far end, and a lady and gentleman murmuring over a catalogue.

She composed herself to wait, trying not to think of Harry 'asking his way around' with her note in his yellow fist.

She had pencilled it on the balustrade in the museum colonnade, while Harry tried to read it over her shoulder. His knowing air when she told him whom it was for made her realize afresh the lunacy of what she was doing.

She didn't even know how to address a letter to a lord. How then could she convey in a few scant lines the reason for her coming? How could she explain, make good the cowardice of Sunday – without confusion, deception, or, worse still, anything which he might misconstrue as impropriety?

In the end she gave up, and simply wrote: '*I shall be at the British Museum for an hour and a half. C.F.*'. She addressed it to 'Lord Harlaston, St James's Square.' He could make of that what he would.

At least there had been one glimmer of light in the darkness. Harry had confidently shrugged off the problem of the incomplete address. He had a tongue in his head, didn't he? He could ask round the square, someone'd know the house, him being a lord. He had been quite indignant at her lack of faith.

But that had been forty-five minutes ago. It was now a quarter past one. The relief she had felt on gaining the safety of the museum was wearing off. There was nowhere to sit down, and she had eaten nothing since the night before.

And the statues were no help at all. Their faces were severely beautiful, but their ineffectual marble drapery only drew attention to their finely muscled limbs and smooth bare chests. She found such pensive nakedness deeply disturbing.

Hours passed, or so it felt.

Soon she would ask the attendant in the next room to tell her the time. She had asked the one in this room twice already. Then at half past two, Harry or no Harry, she would go out into the street and find her own way back to the railway station.

She thought about Harry with her note, and her stomach turned over.

Despite his blithe assurances, he had not been able to find the house after all. Or else he hadn't got as far as St James's Square, but had chanced on some more lucrative employment and had simply tossed the note in the gutter and gone on his way. Or he *had* found the square *and* the house but Lord Harlaston hadn't been at home, and Harry hadn't cared to wait. Or – and this was by far the most probable – Lord Harlaston *had* been at home, and had simply read the note and tossed it in the waste-paper basket with a puzzled or perhaps a faintly irritated shrug. How tiresome. Another muddle-headed village girl who'd got up some ridiculous notion, and had trailed all this way on the strength of precisely nothing.

She came to a halt in front of a marble horse which in a distracted way had become her favourite. Whoever had sculpted it had known about horses. The cheek was flat and muscular, the forelock swept to one side to keep it out of the eyes, and it was chewing on its bit, as horses do.

She stood before it lost in thought. She pictured herself trailing back through the crowded streets. She pictured the note rolling around in a gutter, undelivered and unread.

The hansom cab rattled through the side-streets on its way to the museum. Robert hadn't waited to have his own carriage brought round from the mews, but now he cursed the slowness of the spindle-shanked mare between the shafts.

The note had said that she would be at the museum for an hour and a half. Yes, but when had she written it? And where in the museum would she be waiting, assuming she had not already gone?

He had been on the point of leaving for the club when the urchin had arrived with the note, and been paid off by an astonished and affronted Norton. Robert had stood in the drawing room with the note in his hand, struggling to take it in. Staring at the forth-right copperplate which baldly stated her whereabouts but said nothing about her purpose.

Why had she come? It was extraordinary. For a village girl who had probably never been further than Grantham in her life to embark on such a journey – it was not merely extraordinary. It was magnificent.

No.

He gave himself a mental shake.

This has gone on long enough. You are deluding yourself. For the past three weeks you have behaved like a romantic puppy. You have persuaded yourself that in a stonemason's daughter you have found more than a handsome face and a pretty figure. You have not. It's a delusion. The truth is simpler and more contemptible than that. The truth is, you have allowed your wife's excessive delicacy and your own con-founded reserve to keep you from feminine company for too many years. And instead of facing up to it like a man, you have persuaded yourself that this feeling is something finer and deeper than it really is.

Now the least you can do – the very least – is to behave like a gentleman. You will be beneath contempt if you don't put her on the first train back to Little Bytham.

And there can be *no question* of seeing her yourself. You have shown by your past conduct that you are incapable of behaving towards her with propriety. It's imperative that, when you find her, you withdraw at once – without letting her catch sight of you. Pay the cabby to take her to the station and see her safely onto her train, but for heaven's sake don't do it yourself. If you do, you will be sure to mishandle it, as you mishandled it so spectacularly with Violet.

Violet.

Every time he thought of that last appalling exchange with his wife he winced. Why, why, *why*, had Violet chosen that night of all nights, his last at the Hall?

He had returned from evensong on Sunday prickling with self-disgust to face an interminable dinner with the Mayhews, the Brabazons, and the Cornwallis-Dennistouns. And when finally the last of them had retired, his only thought had been to find oblivion in a bottle of cognac. But then Violet had dismissed Paige and done the unthinkable, gliding towards him and asking, with a peculiar, resigned intensity, if he could bear to carry her lamp up to her room.

Why had she chosen that particular night to fix him with those incomparable eyes, from which she had been quite unable to banish her distaste?

He knew the answer perfectly well.

She had left it to the last possible moment to do what she believed to be her duty, because it had taken all that time – nearly three weeks – to summon the resolve to commit so repugnant an act. To overcome her revulsion and embark upon what was required to conceive another heir.

The problem was, when she had made her elliptical, unmistakable request, he had been conscious only of a vast dismay – a dismay he had been unable to conceal from her.

For the space of a heartbeat her face had mirrored his own astonishment. But she had been the first to recover. With a contemptuous twist of her long neck she had swept from the room, leaving him hot-faced at the window.

The hansom clattered to a halt outside the museum.

He gave the cab-driver a sovereign and told him to wait, and ran up the stairs.

There was no sign of her in the entrance-hall. How long had she been waiting? Had she already gone? If she had, how would he ever find her in the crowded streets? How would she find her way back to the station?

He checked the rooms on the ground floor which he thought would interest her most. The King's Library, the Elgin Gallery, the Egyptian Sculpture Room. She wasn't in any of them. He went down into the basement, then checked the upper floors. Prints and Drawings, the Townley Collection, the Waddesdon Bequest. She was nowhere. She must have left.

Finally he went back to the ground floor and started again, methodically checking every room. He should have done this at the outset. While he had been upstairs, she had probably already gone.

He was standing in the doorway to the Mausoleum Room when he saw her.

She was contemplating the chariot horse from Halicarnassus. She had not seen him.

Now was the time for him to leave. To hurry back to the entrance-hall and down to the waiting cab. Tell the driver where to find the girl in the green dress, perhaps leave her a brief message to reassure her about taking the hansom, then hail another cab for himself, or walk, or run, if it came to that. But be gone by the time she reached the hansom.

If he did not leave now, if he allowed her to catch sight of him, there would be no going back.

She stood before the great stone horse, absorbed and unaware. She looked small and upright and brave. And easily hurt.

As if seeing her for the first time, he took in the slow sweep of her lashes as she traced the line of the horse's neck. The clarity of her profile. The warmth and tenderness of her mouth.

All his careful reasoning collapsed about him.

He was left with a line of Greek from some half-remembered snatch of verse. *As the oak tree is shaken by the wind on the mountain, so my heart is shaken by love.*

That is the essence of her, he thought. The warmth and the tenderness. The bravery and the truth.

He went towards her.

CHAPTER TWENTY-EIGHT

He walked swiftly towards her, his boots echoing on the marble floor. He was not smiling. He looked as young and unlike a lord as on the day when he'd carried Will into the end house kitchen.

'Have you any idea', he said in a low voice, 'just how enormous this confounded place is?'

She shook her head. Her heart was beating so fast it was making her dizzy. 'The porter at the station said it was big.'

'Big!' He took her hands in his and began to smile. 'Oh, yes, it's big! I can personally vouch for that, I've been over most of it myself in the last twenty minutes!'

'I'm sorry. I didn't think of that.'

He shook his head and laughed, and she knew with a painful twist of joy that he was glad she had come.

'Do you know', he said, 'it was only by chance that I was at home when your note arrived? The house is practically uninhabitable – something's gone wrong with the drains in the square – and last night I nearly gave up and removed to my club.' She guessed he was talking to overcome her nervousness, and perhaps his own as well.

'Have you seen enough antiquities?' he asked. 'I

have a cab waiting. I thought we might go to the Russell.'

'What is the Russell?'

'It's an hotel. It's very close, just around the—' he sensed her recoil and stopped. 'For tea,' he said gently. 'Only for tea.'

'Oh. Thank you. But I don't think I really—'

'Ah, but you see, I do. Really. You're beginning to resemble one of these marbles. It's high time you sat down and had something to eat.' Then, with a graceful gesture that was to stay in her memory for years, he placed her hand on his arm and they left the museum.

'The Russell' turned out to be an imposing red-brick edifice like an extremely elaborate iced cake. It was smaller than the museum and much less crowded than King's Cross, so it should have been easier to deal with than either.

It was too early for fashionable people to take tea, so they had the enormous salon to themselves, except for two sleekly elegant couples who, like them, kept to the tables among the potted palms nearest the walls.

They probably shouldn't be together either, Charity thought, her euphoria vanishing as swiftly as it had come.

She contemplated the pink and gold carpet and the little round table draped in dazzling linen. All this beauty and elegance, not quite concealing what lay beneath.

She glanced at him across the table. She couldn't deceive herself. Khaki might be a great leveller, but, despite his uniform, anyone seeing them together could not fail to be struck by the difference between them.

It was there in the over-careful way in which she laid

390

aside her gloves to pour the tea, and in the very gloves themselves: plain black wool instead of narrow-fingered kid. It was there in the easy grace with which he disposed of his own gloves and hat and cane, and gave instructions to the waiter, and took his tea from her hand as he made her describe her journey, and ate a slice of Dundee cake which no doubt he didn't really want. All to put her at her ease, and ensure that she ate something too.

At least after all her afternoons with Mrs Bowles, she knew how to pour tea like a lady. And she noticed that when milk was available, he forgot his preference for taking it black. But in a strange way that only made her feel more of an impostor.

The waiter had brought a silver tray covered with an immaculate lace cloth on which were disposed a small silver kettle over a spirit-lamp, a silver teapot and strainer, and all the other appurtenances of afternoon tea. He had also brought a revolving stand bearing three porcelain plates arrayed with hot breads, little cakes, and tiny crustless sandwiches.

The least item on the stand would have drawn a famished moan from Will. She wished she could enjoy it, but her throat had closed.

So far, the day had gone wildly better than she had imagined, but she felt like a criminal.

This is wrong, she thought, struggling to answer his questions. It's no good feeling pleased with yourself just because you know the right way to pour tea. You're here on false pretences. Everyone can see it. They're all thinking the worst.

From the look on his face, he had guessed what was troubling her. He drew out his watch. 'As your train's at four, we have just under two hours. If you'd care to, we could go to the park and feed the ducks.'

She folded her napkin and placed it on the table. 'Thank you, but I don't think I—' she broke off, wondering how to go on without appearing ungrateful.

'What don't you think?'

'It's just that – I'd prefer not to go to the park.'

He was silent for a moment. 'If you're concerned about whom we might meet, please don't be. This time of year Town's practically empty.'

She looked down at her hands. She had not expected to feel this vulgar or this cheap.

He leaned forward and said softly, 'Charity. Look at me. No, *look* at me. That's better. Now tell me why you came to London.'

Close up, she saw that his eyes were not black, but a very dark, warm brown. He was looking at her as he had done in St Hybald's. As if he needed to know the truth.

'I was going to put it in the note,' she said, 'but I couldn't think how to say it. And I only had one sheet of paper.'

He waited for her to go on.

'After we talked on the night of the Ball, I was horribly afraid you'd think me fast.' He opened his mouth to protest but she shook her head. 'Please let me say this. I had to show you that I'm not like that.'

'I never thought you were.'

'I had to make you understand. That's why I hid in the churchyard.'

'You hid?'

She coloured. 'Behind a tombstone. I know it sounds ridiculous. I saw you looking for me, but I was a coward. And then it was too late and you were gone.' She paused. 'I told myself I'd got it all wrong – that it wasn't important. But then I thought, what if I'm mistaken? What if it *does* matter, and he's killed out there in Africa, or ends up in some hospital for months and months, without ever knowing? I couldn't bear that. So I came.'

'You are', he said gravely, 'the most extraordinary young woman.'

They rejoined the hansom cab and he told the driver to take them to Regent's Park.

The streets became wider and less chaotic, the pavements fringed with plane trees whose soot-blackened leaves rustled like newspaper. Gentlemen in immaculate overcoats strolled beside cool parasolled ladies in promenade gowns. Nurses waddled after clean little boys in sailor suits.

It was an enormous relief not to be out on the pavement in the teeth of that well-bred parade. To sit back against the cracked leather seat while the mare lifted her scrawny neck and the great buildings and elegant pedestrians slid harmlessly by.

At first he pointed out the landmarks, but he soon gave that up and began talking about the Hall instead. He told her how his grandfather had built it to spite the old Duke of Kyme, and how he and his brother had grown up there with their amazing old grandmother, who had believed in the 'Spartan' way of bringing up children, which seemed to have meant daily cold baths, riding in all weathers, and no nursery fires between March and November. But there had been compensations, for she let them keep silkworms and monkeys in the conservatory, and read anything they found in the library. Tutors who objected were summarily dismissed, and in the end they were left with Dr Bowles and old Edic the nurse, whose grey alpaca dress exactly matched the colour of her moustache.

He talked amusingly and made her smile, which she knew was his way of overcoming her misgivings at being alone with him in a hansom cab.

About herself she was reluctant to speak. In the end she told him about being a scholar at the Higher Grade School, and the time Will had freed Mr Pechey's rabbits, which he seemed to find genuinely amusing, and finally about the typewriter. He wanted to know where they could be purchased, and how one learned to use them, and she began to see where he was heading.

'Would you let me buy you one?' he said at last. 'I should like to.'

'No. No.'

'Why not? A typewriter's rather innocuous, don't you think?'

'It's not the thing itself. It's how I come by it.'

He was silent for a moment. 'We could make it a loan. You could repay me when you've found a position as a stenographer—'

'No.'

' – and that way you wouldn't have to marry Sam.'

It shocked her to hear him speak the name. She had assumed that, like her, he would avoid all mention of Sam. But seeing his taut face, she realized he had only been biding his time. It revealed a ruthlessness she hadn't previously suspected.

'I don't *have* to marry Sam,' she said at last. 'I want to.'

'I don't believe you.'

She turned her head away. 'I can't talk about him to you. Promise you won't mention him again.'

'No.'

The hansom clipped along past glossy black railings.

After a while she turned to see if he was angry. He was gazing out of the window with the same closed expression he had worn at the Hynton fête. If he decided to withhold something, as he was doing now, he would be a hard man to reach.

They turned a corner and came upon a newspaper boy shouting headlines. 'Wynborne Murdahs, Two Arrested! Dutchess leaves 'arf a million ta Childer's 'Ome! 'Evvy Failyahs in Americky, Scores Ruined!' The war in South Africa was conspicuously absent.

Charity asked: 'What will happen when you go back to Africa?'

Startled, he turned to her. 'Why do you ask that?'

'I – I want to know.'

He seemed taken aback.

'I'm sorry,' she said. 'If you don't want to tell me—'

'It isn't that. It's just – I'm not – I don't talk of it much.'

That struck her as extraordinary. Didn't his wife ever ask him? What did they talk about? 'I wanted to know', she said, 'if you'll be doing what you were doing before.'

'You mean, will I be burning farms and turning out women and children?' He shook his head. 'I told the chaps in Whitehall that I won't.'

'Can you do that in the Army?'

He stroked his moustache. 'You can try.'

Presumably you could, if you were a lord. 'What will you do instead?'

His lip curled. 'I'm to command a rather dreary little railway garrison.' He paused. 'Being given a railway garrison is like being put out in deep cover in cricket. It's fearfully dull, but someone has to do it.'

'And – if you change your mind about the farms, you won't have to command the garrison.'

'Although no-one has said it as plainly as that.' He seemed surprised to find her still interested. 'Three weeks ago, I made myself rather unpopular by telling some important gentlemen certain things which they didn't care to hear. Yesterday I made matters a good deal worse by doing it again, only more so.'

'What happened?'

He shrugged. 'They asked me to retract my reports. I declined. That was when I was given to understand that, if I persisted, I should serve out the war on the railways.'

'But your reports – don't they still exist?'

'Oh, no doubt some junior staff officer has already been told to lose them in some convenient paper mountain.'

'That's not fair.'

He smiled. 'That's the Army. Though I admit it's somewhat hard on those Dutch families out on the veldt.'

He spoke lightly, but she remembered the way he had looked in St Hybald's. The tension in his shoulders. His haunted eyes.

She tried to picture a railway station in Africa. 'This garrison – will it be near the fighting?'

'From time to time. Though it's not the sort of fighting that finds its way into the newspapers.'

She studied his face. Then she said softly, 'Are you afraid?'

'Afraid?'

'Of what might happen.'

' – You mean, am I afraid of being killed?'

She nodded.

He turned the silver-headed cane in his fingers. At last he said, 'I'm not afraid of death. But of dying – dying slowly, or being mutilated, or blinded. Oh, yes. I'm afraid of that.'

She put her hand on his arm.

He had taken off his hat, and the breeze from the open window stirred his hair, which was soft and black except for a gleam of chestnut where the light caught it. He was looking down at her hand on his arm, and in his face she fancied she saw the thoughts passing: all that he had told her of himself, and what he thought of Sam, and his feelings about the war. She saw the boy he had been and the man he was now, and the man he would become if the war let him live. She was shaken by the depth of her feeling for him. It wasn't his beauty or his otherness which moved her so much as his likeness to herself. Meeting his eyes was like looking into her own self.

She pictured what her life would be without him. Even if she married, she would always be alone, because she wouldn't be with him. And she felt a kind of anger towards him for evoking feelings he could never satisfy.

He asked her why she looked so sad.

'Do I?'

'You know you do.'

She shook her head.

He put his arm around her and drew her to him so that her head rested against his shoulder.

After a while, the hansom drew to a halt.

He said, 'Here we are. Come along, let's go and feed the ducks.'

They walked down a gravel path to a beautiful curving lake, and he bought a bag of crusts from an old woman. They found a bench by the water in the shade of a willow tree and took off their gloves and fed the ducks. He had been right about there not being many people about. To Charity's relief they had this section of the lake to themselves.

Eventually, a large black swan glided up and scared away the ducks. Charity powdered the last crust in her fingers and scattered it on the water, so the swan wouldn't get it.

He said abruptly, 'Forgive me for what I'm going to say, but you cannot marry Sam.' When she remained silent, he added with more force, 'Charity, he is not for you.'

Slowly she dusted off her fingers. 'Please can we not talk about this.'

'That's not possible.'

'I don't see why.'

'Because I say so.'

She stood at the water's edge and crossed her arms about her waist. 'I must marry someone. Sam's a good man.'

'You don't love him.' When she made no reply, he said, 'I'm right. You can't deny it. You're too honest. You don't lie.'

'Yes I do lie,' she retorted, 'I lie every day! I lie to Mrs Bowles and the parson. I lie to my parents and my brother. I lie to Sam—'

'But not to me.'

' – No. Not to you.'

'Listen to me. He wouldn't make you happy.'

'Why not? Because he's a gamekeeper? Because he says "hisself" instead of "himself"?'

'Because he doesn't think as you do.'

'How do you know?'

'Because I grew up with him! Because I know you.'

There was such certainty in his voice. 'What do you know?'

'I know there isn't a woman in ten thousand who would have done what you did today. I know you have a capacity for getting to the truth which is a rare gift. I know that with Sam you wouldn't have a chance.'

The way he said it made her feel cold inside. 'He's a good man,' she whispered. 'He'll make a good husband.'

'This isn't you talking. You don't realize what you're saying.'

'Yes I *do* realize! I do. That's why I won't talk about him. And it's the same for you. You don't talk about your w— about Lady Harlaston.'

There. She had spoken the name.

'That', he said at last, 'is different.'

She sat on the bench and picked up her gloves, and twisted them in her hands. 'I see. Yes, of course. It's different.'

'It *is* different. But not in the way you think I meant it. It's different for this reason alone. *You* still have a choice. I do not.'

A great sadness welled up in her throat. 'Why are we doing this? Talking won't make it better. All we do is spoil the time we have left.'

He came and sat beside her.

'Today', she went on shakily, 'is something separate. Sam has nothing to do with it. Neither has your wife. And when it's over – when I'm on the train and you're back in St James's Square – it'll be over for good. It'll be as if it never happened.'

'No,' he said quietly, 'it can never be that.' He took her gloves and laid them on the bench, then took her hands in his. He sat looking down at them. Then, lightly, his fingers moved over hers, learning the feel of her skin and the pulse on her wrist, and the fine soft places between her fingers.

A distant clock-tower chimed half past three.

He met her eyes. Then his gaze dropped to her mouth, and she knew that he wanted to kiss her – but would not, because they were too exposed.

He said, 'We must start for the station if you're to catch your train.'

A little dizzily, they walked back to the waiting cab.

After driving in silence for some time, she said, 'When we get near the station, I'd prefer it if you dropped me outside and then drove on.'

He looked horrified. 'I can't do that.'

'I'd prefer it,' she repeated.

'I'm sorry, it's out of the question. I can't leave you alone outside King's Cross station.' After a strained silence he added, 'Do you have any idea what is in fact "outside the station"? I'll tell you. There are two other railway stations – the goods station and St Pancras, both of them huge – as well as a gasworks, an ale depot, and the largest, most disreputable cab-rank in Town. Oh, and they're taking the paving-stones up along the Euston Road, so the whole area is crawling with navvies.'

'But—'

'If I left you outside, I should worry for weeks that you hadn't reached your train safely, or that you had ended up in the wrong sort of carriage with the wrong

400

sort of people. And I should have no way of finding out. I cannot believe you would be so unfeeling as to sentence me to such anxiety, and I'm not going to give you the chance.'

'That's not fair.'

'I agree, but there's nothing you can do about it. Driver! Stop here for a moment.'

They were in a quiet winding street which she recognized as being near the museum.

Telling her to wait in the cab, he stepped down and disappeared into a dingy little shop with grimy windows and a peeling yellow door which rattled dolefully shut behind him. She couldn't see the shop's sign, but guessed it to be a jeweller's shop or perhaps a better sort of pawnbroker's.

She guessed he was buying her a brooch or a bracelet. Something discreetly beautiful and no doubt horribly expensive that would make her feel wretched and unutterably cheap. She would have to explain why she could not possibly accept it, and if he insisted, she must make sure to lose it on the way home.

Watching him spend his money on her had been the one awful thing about the afternoon. It would have been different if she had been with Sam. With Sam it would have been unnatural if he *hadn't* paid for everything. But she wasn't with Sam. And the sums were so enormous: a ceaseless flow of ridiculous amounts of money.

'Now this,' he said, getting back into the cab and tapping on the roof with his cane, 'you must accept. It cost nothing, and it's so far beyond reproach that I could give it to Gwendolen Bowles without a qualm.'

He placed in her unwilling hands a small oblong

parcel the size of a prayer-book. It was wrapped in beautiful glossy green paper dotted with tiny silver lilies, and tied up with green satin ribbon in a complicated double bow.

'I told you,' she said harshly, 'I can't take anything from you.'

'It's only a book, Charity. A writer's account of his travels in France. You told me you like reading about France, so I thought you might enjoy it. And you needn't worry, I haven't written anything on the flyleaf.' When she remained stubbornly silent he sighed. 'If old Bowles gave it to you you'd accept it, wouldn't you? Well, then.'

She stared at the problem in her lap. 'I'm sorry. I can't take it.'

He bent closer to her. 'You've done so much for me by coming here. Let me do something for you. It's so little! You'll be cruel if you don't accept it.'

'You've used that argument before.'

'Well, it worked, didn't it?' She heard the smile in his voice. 'Now please. You can hardly throw it from the train, as no doubt you'd throw anything else I tried to give you. Destroying books is a crime.'

She suppressed a smile. 'No it isn't.'

'Yes it is. Please. Take it. Read it. Learn a little French.'

After an inner struggle she gave in to her curiosity. 'Do you know any French?'

He inclined his head in a sort of nod, and immediately she realized her stupidity. Of course he knew French. He probably spoke it like a Frenchman.

'I've never heard it spoken,' she said, to excuse the question. 'Would you say something in French?'

He thought for a moment. Then his face became

grave and he spoke what sounded like poetry: a wistful soft-flowing stream of rounded sound.

'That's beautiful. What does it mean?'

But he declined to tell her. When she asked again, he looked into her face and leaned down and kissed her gently on the lips.

After a moment she reached up and put her arm about his neck. The kiss deepened. She felt the softness of his hair against the bare skin of her wrist. The strength of his hand on her waist. The unbelievable warmth of his mouth.

Minutes later, the hansom drew up outside the station. She clung to his arm as they moved down into the concourse – dazed by the clamour and the glare and the suddenness.

There was little chance to speak as they were swept towards the platforms by the jostling torrent. They had a brief argument about the first-class ticket he wanted to buy her – an argument she won through sheer stubborn refusal to brook opposition; then another, shorter dispute over an elegant little refreshment basket which he sent a lad to fetch from a platform trolley – because, he said, she had scarcely eaten at the hotel, and it was a long way back to Hynton. This he won easily, for by the time he had found an empty 'Ladies Only' third-class carriage and had settled her in the window seat, she was too sick at heart to put up much resistance.

Moments before, the whole afternoon had stretched before them. Now suddenly they were down to seven minutes.

To have *so* little time. And such harsh things still to say before he left. She sat beside him with the book in her lap, wondering how to begin. At last she said, not looking at him, 'When the war is over, and you come back—'

'Charity, don't—'

' – when you and Sam come back,' she went on doggedly, 'and when we meet again, I'll be married to him. It'll be as if this never happened.'

She sensed his rejection of everything she said.

'As long as this is the end,' she insisted, 'we haven't done anything wrong.'

'Whom are you trying to persuade? Yourself or me?'

'I can't even write to you,' she said unsteadily. 'Sam collects all your letters.'

'I know. I thought of that too.'

'And if anything came for me from South Africa the whole parish would talk.'

Footsteps in the corridor. They stiffened. A sharp-faced young woman hovered in the carriage door, but he gave her such a hostile stare that she flushed and hurried away.

He turned back to Charity. 'You know how I feel about you and Sam so I won't repeat myself, except to beg you to *think* before you do anything irrevocable. And promise me, if you come to your senses and decide not to marry him – if you need help to get away, anything at all, you must promise—'

'I can't do that.'

'Why not? It doesn't change what you said. There need be no contact between us—'

'That's not the point.'

'*Why* must you be so stubborn? Why can't you simply promise, because I ask you to?'

'If I gave you a promise I'd have to keep it. And I never would.'

'My God, you can be so absolute at times!'

'I have to be. It's all I have.'

He put his elbows on his knees and kneaded his fist in his hand. 'I understand how you feel. I really do. But can *you* not understand that your attitude only shows how hugely you've underestimated my regard for you?'

The first whistle blew.

He stared out at the platform and saw none of it. 'I saw your expression when we stopped at the bookseller's. I've been trying to work out what goes through your mind when you look like that. Do you imagine that for me this is just a passing fancy? That I've done it before? Do you think that I simply liked the look of you when I first saw you on the Tilburne road, and told myself, yes, why not, I have three weeks to while away, that ought to keep me amused? Is that what you think?'

She shook her head.

'Don't ever think like that again. Don't ever think that what you've meant to me – what you *mean* to me – can be cheapened in such a way.'

'There's the last whistle,' she said. 'You'll have to go.'

He took up his hat and cane. 'What I'm telling you is that there isn't a woman alive I respect more than you. I wish you'd believe me.'

'You shouldn't say that. Not to me.'

'Oh, I know. I know. But it's the truth. And I want you to remember it.'

She couldn't bear to see the bleakness in his face.

A stout middle-aged woman in a Watteau hat entered the carriage. She carried an umbrella, a tea-basket, a capacious tapestried handbag, and two bulky brown paper parcels, and she was not about to be

405

intimidated into leaving. But she noted his uniform and their taut faces, and with an air of kindly tolerance turned her back and became elaborately engrossed in settling her belongings into the furthest corner.

The train gave a lurch. The guards moved along the platform slamming the doors.

He took her hand and pressed it hard, and looked into her face. She knew he wanted to kiss her again, but would not, because of the lady in the corner. 'Goodbye, Charity,' he said quietly. 'I hope – you'll be happy.'

'And you. And—' her voice broke. 'Come back safely.'

The kindly lady ostentatiously blew her nose.

He left the carriage.

As the train moved off, Charity watched him walk away down the platform. He did not look back. For as long as the station remained in view, she watched his tall figure walking away into the crowd.

Opposite the platform, in a filthy passage between the booking-hall and the Lost Property office, a soldier was spewing up his lunch.

A sandwich-board man shuffled past and glared at him. 'Bloody drunk! Bloody disgrace to 'er Majesty's uniform!'

Shakily, Sam Webb straightened up and wiped his mouth on the back of his hand. He leaned against the wall and shut his eyes. In vain he tried not to picture what he had just witnessed on the concourse. A tall khaki-clad figure and a girl in green, walking arm in arm towards the Peterborough train.

CHAPTER TWENTY-NINE

Early August, the Present

'*Crow Water Fen*', read Sarah, sitting in the sun on the south terrace, '*was once the loneliest, rottenest fen in England. The "fen tigers" who inhabited it were a law unto themselves, and tolerated no interference in their bleakly chaotic lives. As recently as 1858, when the authorities decided that the parish of Jericho should have its own police officer, the locals showed their disapproval by murdering him. Unsurprisingly, a replacement could not be found until the early years of this century.*'

Sarah put down the book which Alex had lent her, *A History of the Fens of Southern Lincolnshire*, and sat back in her chair. Even allowing for dramatic hyperbole, the region in which Charity's parents had been raised must have been a harsh one.

She turned to her notes of the Fosdyke births and deaths. They had been surprisingly hard to track down, since she didn't even know the first names of Charity's parents. And Fosdyke, as the Lincoln Archives were at pains to point out, was one of the more common Lincolnshire surnames. But then she had found a reference to '*Jack Fosdyke, stonemason*' in one of the Hall's account-books, and a search of the parish records in Lincoln had produced the rest.

Charity's mother, Alice Fowler, had come into the world in the hamlet of Jericho in 1861. She had borne her husband five children, although only Charity and William had lived past infancy, and she had died in Jericho in 1902. Her husband had swiftly married again and moved to the coast, where he had lived until his death in 1921. His second marriage had produced a daughter: a half-sister for Charity and William. The half-sister had died in 1983, but according to Doreen Drake, the half-sister's daughter had been a 'tee-vee personality' in the Sixties. The name Anita Hopkins meant nothing to Sarah, but it might to her friends at the BBC. Now it was just a matter of waiting for them to get back to her.

She found the wait unnerving in the extreme. Anita Hopkins might be the breakthrough she had been hoping for, or just another dead end.

'*At the beginning of the twentieth century,*' she read, '*the "fen tiger" had not changed in a thousand years. He was stubborn, superstitious, and still as fiercely independent as his Jutish forbears. He wore a red necktie against marsh demons, lived on starlings and water-rats when times were bad, and was ravaged by bouts of malaria, which he called the "shakes". He kept the disease at bay with "paigle tea", a potent distillation of potatoes and poppy-seeds which he laced with laudanum when he could get it. There is little doubt that this lethal concoction contributed greatly to the high incidence of lunacy in the fen.*'

God almighty, thought Sarah, what a legacy. Lawlessness, insanity and drugs.

Beside her lay the clear plastic wallet which contained her grandmother's postcard. It had landed on the doormat three days before, along with a note from Mrs Favell explaining that '*on reflection I believe this belongs to you rather than me. Besides, it is only fair trade for William's photograph.*'

Sarah studied her grandmother's sloping hand-writing. It was still the most revealing thing she possessed about Charity. A confident and amusing woman, independent and given to speaking her mind, who had enjoyed painting and apparently life in general, and who seemed to have loved her son.

What on earth did such a woman have in common with the dark, disease-ridden life of Crow Water Fen? Or was it precisely *because* of her ancestry that she had been able to shape her life as she had? For how else would a twenty-three year-old dressmaker at the dawn of the century have had the courage to emigrate to France and raise an illegitimate son, if she *hadn't* had the independence and tenacity of a fen tiger?

The fact is, Sarah reminded herself, you don't know. All you know is that she went to France in 1903, had her son five years later, and never came back. You don't know what she did in France. You don't even know what she looked like.

Once again she found her place in the book and began to read. '*Crow Water's most famous inhabitant was St Gudwal, who founded an abbey in the fen in 738. Gudwal was a man of noble blood and education who, in the words of an early chronicler, "had determined to become a hermit, and sought a place in the wild wilderness, far from the abodes of men." Gudwal found such a place in Crow Water, and "dwelt there without heed for his earthly life, but for his soul's salvation."* '

Again, Sarah put down the book. It was no good. Her concentration was shot to pieces, as it had been for the past week. Ever since she had broken down in front of Alex in the Japanese Garden.

And what made it worse was that she still could not give up on Robert, even though it was now clear that he could not have been her grandfather.

She turned to the map at the back of the book and scanned the featureless waste of Crow Water Fen for the place where his forbears had originated. She knew from the Lincoln Archives that until the Pearce-Stauntons bought the Harlaston estate in the early sixteenth century, theirs had been a far less grandiose seat, about fifteen miles to the north-east of Hynton. She found Merriot Hall and marked it with a cross. To her surprise, she saw that it was roughly equidistant between the birthplaces of Charity's father and mother. One could draw a circle with a six-mile radius and encompass all three.

Which meant that Robert and Charity had come of similar stock.

And which of course was neither here nor there, because Robert had not been her grandfather.

Rationally, she knew that he was nothing to her now, and yet she still ached to discover what his life had become. Everything she knew about him made her want to learn more. Here was a man who had grown up with no expectation of inheriting a title, whose life had been abruptly overturned by the death of a much-loved brother. A man who had come into an estate on the brink of bankruptcy, and had turned it around. For a decade he had done what was expected of him: he had made a 'brilliant' marriage, and had then devoted his wife's money and his own abilities to the estate. Then, suddenly, in 1903, it had all fallen apart. He had left his wife to wander in the far places of the world, and had then disappeared into the great Imperial maw of India.

A man of noble blood and education who had determined to become a hermit.

If she was honest, she knew why she couldn't give him up. She couldn't get rid of the lingering hope that family folklore would turn out to have some truth in it after all. That he and Charity *had* meant something to each other, if only for a time.

But even that seemed increasingly unlikely. And time was running out. The book would be ready for the Board of Governors in a matter of days, and in three weeks the college would re-open, and she must return to London and get a job.

The idea of leaving Harlaston brought her up short.

She looked around her. After weeks of rain the weather had finally turned, and it was hot on the terrace. A faint breeze carried the fragrance of the rose garden, and across the lawn, the sleeping lion frowned gently in his dreams. At the top of the steps two cast-iron wolves guarded the Upper Terraces, each attended by a pug-faced cherub. The wolf on the right carried his cherub on his back like a Labrador. The one on the left straddled his cherub wolfishly: neck stiffly arched, lips peeled back from fearsome canines. Not much could be seen of the cherub except for his flailing limbs.

Like the rest of Harlaston, it was hopelessly over-blown. And like the rest of Harlaston, she would miss it.

As she would miss Stephen, and Alex.

As if on cue, Stephen appeared on the slope above the Japanese Garden. Usually he took it at a gallop, or simply lay down and rolled all the way to the bottom. Today he planted his feet as carefully as an adult. His face was expressionless. He looked like his father when he had lost a case.

Five days before, Clare had called Alex from Germany and asked him to break the news about Dominic's engagement. Alex had rung Sarah the following evening and told her about it.

According to Alex, Stephen had listened in wary silence, then gone to his room and spent the rest of the day poring over his medical encyclopedia. 'When he came down,' Alex said, 'all he asked was why they have to get married. He keeps asking. He seems to think that if he understands the reason, it'll stop hurting.'

Sarah said, 'I suppose you can hardly tell him about Caroline's money, or her father's position in the City.' She knew that sounded waspish but she didn't care. She didn't want to have this conversation in the first place.

'No,' Alex replied thoughtfully, 'I can hardly tell him that.'

There was a silence. He seemed to sense her reluctance to get involved, although, being Alex, he made no comment. She pictured him lying on the sofa, with his long legs crossed at the ankles and a tumbler of Bruichladdich balanced on his chest. 'Well,' he said. 'Now you know that he knows. Though I don't think he'll want to talk about it.'

Stephen asked what she was reading.

She showed him the cover and told him about the

murdered policeman and the paigle tea. He listened politely, but his attention was elsewhere. 'What about you?' she said. 'I haven't seen you for a week.'

He shrugged. Then he smiled to show he wasn't being rude.

She could think of nothing to say to make him feel better. Until Alex told him about Dominic's engagement, he must have cherished the usual fantasies about the return of the ex-father. The rebuilding of the broken family after the swift clearing-up of what had just been a huge mistake. Now he must face the fact that it was never going to happen.

She said, 'Would you do me a favour?'

He looked at her warily.

'Go and check the post-box in the hall? I'm expecting some letters.'

Gratefully he sped off, and returned a few minutes later with a book-sized padded envelope. 'It's from the BBC,' he said, trying not to look impressed. 'I think it's a video.'

Sarah's fingers shook as she tore open the envelope. Briefly she told Stephen about Jack Fosdyke's second family, and the tee-vee personality.

With growing excitement she read aloud what her friend Sally had to say about Anita Hopkins – skipping the media gossip, Sally's complicated love-life, and the treatment (in precise anatomical detail) which Sally felt should be meted out to Dominic.

According to Sally, Anita Hopkins was still very much alive and still acting, although her finest hour had been in the early Seventies, when she had starred in a popular sitcom. '*Sort of* My Wife Next Door *meets* Please, Sir,' wrote Sally, '*and absolutely cringe-making – bucket-loads of innuendo – but quite popular in its day. Though anyone into retro-chic should take a look at what the seventies were really like – from which you'll gather I made the ultimate sacrifice and did just that (video enclosed), and for which you owe me lunch when you break out from under the greenwood tree. Which must be soon, surely? We miss you!'*

'What's innuendo?' asked Stephen.

Sarah told him, and he filed it away for future use.

He said, 'This actress lady. Are you going to see her?'

'Like a shot, if she'll see me.'

'Do you think she'll know what Charity looked like?'

'Well, as her mother was Charity's half-sister, I'd say there's a pretty good chance. She's bound to know something.'

'My headmaster says it doesn't matter what people look like. I think that's rubbish.'

'So do I.'

'Can I come with you when you see her?' He said it apprehensively, as if he expected to be turned down.

She wished she could say yes. But interviewing Anita Hopkins would mean talking about remarriage and stepchildren, the last things he needed to hear about. She said gently, 'I don't think that's a good idea.'

'Oh, *please.* I'm *bored.* And Alex has been in a bad mood for *days.*'

'Alex?' She was astonished. 'Alex doesn't have bad moods.'

'He does now.'

'Why?'

He gave an exaggerated shrug.

She put that aside to think about later. 'Listen, Stephen. Anita Hopkins is divorced and never had any kids. Some women who've never had kids don't like them much.'

He gave her his unblinking stare. '*You've* never had kids and *you* like them.'

'Well, I like you. It's not the same thing.'

He put his chin on his hands.

'I'll tell you all about it as soon as I get back. OK?'

He heaved a sigh. ''kay. But you'll have to tell me everything.'

'Everything. I promise.'

They sat for a while in silence. Sarah reread Sally's letter and wondered if this was the breakthrough she had been looking for, and Stephen leafed desultorily through *A History of the Fens of Southern Lincolnshire*. After a while she sensed that his attention had wandered.

He was gazing up at the Pearce-Staunton coat of arms in the Library window. She told him what the guidebook said, that although 'the untutored' would call it a 'coat of arms', it was in fact an 'achievement' – whatever the hell that meant – and he liked that, because he liked learning the proper names for things. After a while he began silently mouthing to himself, and she realized he was trying to decipher the motto: backwards, back to front, and in Latin.

'*Ani-mum – lu-crum – sequi – tur*. What does it mean?'

'Profit follows courage. I looked it up.'

'Does that mean: if you're brave, you'll get rich?'

'I think so, yes.'

He looked crestfallen. He had probably been hoping for something noble and inspiring. Such cold ambition was clearly the last straw.

What, she thought savagely, were Clare and

Dominic *thinking* of, leaving it to Alex to break the news? Did they honestly believe that their bright, observant ten-year-old didn't realize they couldn't be bothered to tell him to his face?

She said, 'Did you read the bit in the book about the riots in the Middle Ages?'

He shook his head.

'Here we are. "*In the reign of King John, the prior of St Gudwal's Abbey was forced to watch his lands ravaged by half-naked savages from the fens – whom he called*," ' she paused for effect, ' " *the very* scum *and* offscouring *of the land*." '

His lower lip thrust out. With the toe of his boot he scuffed a clump of thyme between the flags. 'The very *scum* and *off-scouring* of the land.' Another kick at the thyme. 'The very *scum* and *off*-scouring.' He was still chanting it as he wandered off to inspect the lions for lichen.

I probably shouldn't have told him that, she thought. He'll probably use it when he next sees his father. Or when he meets Caroline for the first time. Heigh-ho.

Her gaze shifted to Sally's letter on the table. She wanted to go inside and call Alex and tell him all about it, and find out if Stephen was right and he really was in a bad mood – whatever that meant when you were Alex Hardy.

Apart from the one brief conversation about Stephen, she hadn't spoken to him since he had stood beside her in the Japanese Garden, stroking her back and talking to her as if she were a horse that needed calming down.

Afterwards she had been awkward and ashamed, and had avoided him. She was avoiding him now.

But she would miss him when she went back to London. She missed him already.

Which is proof in itself, she told herself briskly, that it's high time you went back to your own life before you drop off the map altogether.

CHAPTER THIRTY

'I wondered how you found me,' Anita Hopkins said, pushing down the plunger of the cafetière and raising an expertly pencilled eyebrow. 'So they remember me at the Beeb, do they?' She barked a mirthless laugh. 'What did you do, look me up in the archives?'

'I've got a friend who—'

'I'm in them, you know. Auntie's archives. Puts me in my place, doesn't it?'

Sarah smiled, but offered no comment. The last thing she wanted was a discussion of *Teacher, Teacher*. After ploughing through Sally's video, she'd had her fill of *doubles entendres*.

Anita Hopkins had been briskly professional on the telephone, and readily agreed to an interview when she learned that a book was involved. She had indulged in no more than the usual pretence of a packed working schedule. Sorry she couldn't see Sarah before Friday, the week was booked solid.

Sarah had used the interval for more background work on *La* Hopkins. Sitcoms, game shows, character parts in Sunday serials, as well as provincial panto-mimes and musicals. All in all, a moderately successful career. Although Anita Hopkins was no longer a household name, she was probably still well-known in the seaside resorts.

She's a trooper, thought Sarah as she sipped her excellent coffee. I ought to admire her.

She could not.

She wasn't sure what she had been expecting, but it wasn't this brittle over-groomed fifty-something with the bitter eyes and the resentful mouth. She was hugely relieved that she had stood firm about not bringing Stephen. To Anita Hopkins, youth was something to be loathed and denigrated whenever the chance arose. Already Sarah had lost count of the waspish little jabs at the awfulness of one's friends' children, and the clothes sense of the young.

And Holt Place, a substantial Queen Anne house just outside Bourne, didn't help either. It put Sarah in mind of a film set assembled by someone with no eye for character. Soulless brass carriage-lamps and potted bay trees on the outside, an expensive *House & Garden* monotony within.

Ms Hopkins rose from the sofa and sashayed across the room to close the door. She was expensively dressed in a crêpe de Chine blouse and well-cut navy slacks, with slightly too much gold jewellery, and high-heeled pumps that lowered the tone by a couple of notches. Her dark sharp-boned good looks reminded Sarah of someone extremely familiar whom she couldn't quite place.

Once again the actress arranged herself on the sofa, and as if from long habit her gaze came to rest on the portrait above the mantelpiece. It was a competent depiction of a thirty-something Anita Hopkins, gracious in a shift of burnt-orange silk on a white leather sofa. The painter had added a white fur rug and a glass side-table on which he had placed a single lily in a tall vase. Perhaps he had been going through his Hockney phase.

Sarah took the tape recorder from her bag and asked if she could use it.

'I'd think it amateurish if you didn't, dear. Now, what do you want to talk about?' A discreet glance at her Rolex, which Sarah was meant to catch. Don't hang about, will you, dear? I haven't got all day.

They had dealt with the preliminaries over coffee. Anita Hopkins had asked if Sarah was married and Sarah had replied that she was not. Anita Hopkins had searched Sarah's face for signs of regret, found none, and given an irritable shrug, as if Sarah's unmarried status was meant as a subtle criticism of herself. Curiously, the common ground between them – the successful careers in television, the absence of husbands and children – had seemed to breed mistrust rather than empathy. Perhaps *La* Hopkins thought they were in competition.

'As I mentioned on the phone,' Sarah began, 'I'd like to talk about your mother's family, though I appreciate that must seem a bit unusual.'

'Why?' The baldness of the question was almost offensive.

Oh God, thought Sarah wearily, I'm going to need kid gloves with this one. 'Well, presumably most of your interviewers are interested in your work, not your family.'

Thumpingly unsubtle, but it went down surprisingly well. Ms Hopkins clearly didn't believe a word of it, but at least Sarah had paid the necessary dues.

Given the way things were going, Sarah thought it best to leave Charity till later, so they spent twenty minutes on Ms Hopkins's early years in show business. Eventually Sarah said, 'About your family. I'm particularly interested in your grandfather's *first* marriage, especially the children, William and Charity. Do you know anything about them?'

Anita Hopkins's lips twisted in a knowing smile. 'I was wondering when you'd get around to them.'

Sarah's heart jerked. 'I take it you know something?'

'Oh, yes,' she said drily. 'You can take it that I do.'

Sarah waited.

Anita Hopkins reached for a silver cigarette-box, and Sarah watched in fascination as she went through the ritual played out in a thousand black and white films: the tapping of the cigarette, the tilting back of the head, the slit-eyed inhalation. Any minute now, Sarah thought, and she'll pluck a speck of tobacco from the tip of her tongue.

She knew the actress was playing with her, but she didn't mind. For all Sarah cared, Anita Hopkins could stage a solo performance of *Hamlet*, as long as she told her something worthwhile about Charity afterwards.

The actress gazed at her portrait. 'William and Charity,' she said at last. 'God-awful names, weren't they?'

Resisting the urge to wave away the smoke, Sarah said, 'Did your mother talk about them?'

'Did she ever! And Gran too. I practically grew up with William and Charity. At least, that's what it felt like.'

'Why d'you think your mother went on about them so much?'

She shrugged. Then she said, 'Maybe it was the slur on our "good name", if you take my meaning.'

'Um. I don't think I do.'

Anita Hopkins stubbed out her cigarette and reached for another. 'Pretty obvious. The boy was the village idiot and the girl was the local scarlet woman. Very Mary Webb, if you know what I mean.' There, said the sharp unsmiling eyes, you didn't think I knew any Eng. Lit., did you?

Sarah's heart was thudding against her ribs. 'You say she was the local scarlet woman—'

Anita Hopkins threw her a look of frank mistrust. 'You must know *something* if you're writing a book.'

'I do. But I want to hear your version. If that's OK.'

'She had an affair with the local squire, didn't she? Heaving boobs and screwing on the billiard-table. Now come on, you know that much, surely?'

'I'd heard something.'

She gave Sarah a knowing look. 'I'll just bet you have.'

Sarah asked pleasantly, 'Did your mother ever meet them?'

'God, no. Why would she? Even Grandad wasn't allowed to keep in touch. *Persona non* bloody *grata* in our household. Though in case you're wondering, all this took place just a tad before my time.'

'Yes of course, I appreciate that.'

Anita Hopkins gazed at her portrait and blew a thin stream of smoke towards the ceiling. 'Funny, isn't it. Some people spend their whole lives in the limelight, and others just grub around in the dark.' Her gaze pulled away from the portrait and fastened on Sarah.

'In what way was Charity in the limelight? If that's what you mean.'

Another shrug. 'Notoriety, I suppose you'd call it.' Again she inhaled deeply. 'I don't know. When I was a kid I used to look at that face and think, what makes you so bloody special?'

It was a moment before Sarah grasped the sense of what she had said. 'Do you mean you've got a picture of her?'

Anita Hopkins flicked her an amused glance. 'Would it matter if I did?'

Sarah attempted a casual shrug. 'Photos bring a story alive.'

'Well if you're hoping for a doe-eyed heroine for your book, forget it. She wasn't much to look at.'

'You mean she was plain?'

'Oh I suppose some men might have found her quite attractive, in an ordinary sort of way. Quite a nice little figure on her. But nothing to write home about. Nothing to justify all that hoo-ha.'

My God, thought Sarah, astonished and repelled, she's *jealous*. To Anita Hopkins it didn't matter if you'd been dead for sixty years. If you were a woman you were a rival. She said carefully, 'And the hoo-ha. What do you know about that?'

Another cigarette was stubbed out. A fresh one took its place. Sarah began to feel nauseous.

'What *don't* I know? Like I said, in my family they couldn't leave it alone. Mum and Gran were always picking away at it. I'm not sure why. Maybe it was the "disgrace to the family". Or maybe,' she added with surprising insight, 'it was because she'd actually *done* things, and they hadn't. Still,' she added, as if to reassure herself, 'when you think about it, she didn't do so bloody well for herself, did she? More like *Upstairs, Downstairs* than King Cophetua. If you're old enough to remember *Upstairs, Downstairs*.'

Sarah gave a polite smile. 'Just about. You said she'd done things. D'you mean the affair with the squire?'

'And the rest. Getting out of the village and going

abroad. Though much good it did her in the end.'
Another thin smile. 'Quite a kerfuffle when they were
found out. Huge disgrace. Huge. Never darken my
door, that sort of thing. Her mum – my grandad's first
wife – went mad because of it. Sent her scuttling back
to the fens. Split up the family. Like I said, all very
Mary Webb.'

'What happened next?'

'Village idiot gets adopted by local vicar, and grandad marries a buxom wench with all her marbles – my
gran – and starts a boarding-house.'

'And the scarlet woman?'

'Far as I know, she follows her mum to the back-
woods. Mum pegs, scarlet woman slopes off to the
Continent, goes on plying her trade – if you take my
meaning. Ends up living the life of Riley. Never comes
back. *Et voilà.*' She spread her bony hands. 'That's all
I know.'

Sarah said carefully, 'I think you mentioned a photograph.'

Anita Hopkins gave a brittle smile. 'I think I did,
didn't I?'

'Did you ever see it?'

''Course I did. The last time was when my mum was
turning out the spare room.' She paused for effect.
'Just before she chucked it.'

There was a silence.

Sarah pressed her lips together in a smile. 'Well,' she
said. 'That's quite a story.'

'I used to think so. In fact a couple of years ago, I
thought it might make a series. Bashed out a treatment,
hawked it round a bit. No takers. Too ordinary, they
said. Been done before.'

God, thought Sarah, she's absolute poison.

Suddenly she remembered where she had seen that face before: in an illustration in a book of fairy tales which had been her favourite as a child. Anita Hopkins was, to the life, the Bad Fairy at Sleeping Beauty's christening. In contrast to the usual depictions, the illustrator had made the Bad Fairy gauntly attractive, which had enormously impressed the eight-year-old Sarah. It wasn't the Bad Fairy's fault if she was bad, she had argued; it was just that everyone was nasty to her. Nonsense, her mother had retorted, the Bad Fairy started off just like everyone else, but was forever on the lookout for slights, and hated it when her friends were happy, so what did she expect? Her mother had left Sarah in no doubt that the Bad Fairy had been the author of her own misfortune.

Anita Hopkins was beginning to look impatient. Sarah said quickly, 'You said Charity led the life of Riley when she moved to the Continent. Do you know any details?'

Another knowing smile, as if the real reason for Sarah's visit had finally surfaced. 'Oh there was always money. Don't ask me how she came by it, though you can guess, can't you, I don't have to draw a picture. There was money all right. The village idiot's kid went to some posh private school, then university, no expense spared – and you don't do *that* by weeding the church marigolds.'

'I'd heard most of the money was lost after the war. When they sold the vineyard.'

A shrug. 'All I know is, we never saw a penny of it. Mum never said two words to any of that lot in sixty years.'

Well then, what did she expect? thought Sarah. Out loud, she asked, 'Do you know when all this took place? The squire and the scarlet woman?'

'As it happens, I do. It was always part of the recital. The squire and the scarlet woman were doing their bit on the billiard-table in the year before Queen Vic popped her clogs. Last decadent breath of a dying Empire, that sort of thing. The scarlet woman and the mad mum left straight after.'

Queen Victoria had died in January 1901. So if Anita Hopkins was right, it meant the affair had begun in 1900, with Charity and her mother leaving for the fens some time in 1901 – which would tie in with Charity's mother dying in Jericho in 1902. 'What about the squire?' Sarah asked. 'What happened to him?'

'Oh he didn't get away scot-free, either. Much good the whole thing did *him*. Apart from the obvious. He became an explorer. Ended up in Delhi or somewhere, doing his bit for the Empire.'

'When did he leave England?'

'1903,' Anita Hopkins said with surprising promptness. 'Gran never forgot that because it was the same year she and Grandad got married. *1903!* Bloody *centuries* ago! Don't put that in your book or I'll never live it down.'

'What about the squire's wife, Lady Harlaston?'

Another thin smile. 'She must have thought she had it all, at one time. Money. Looks. Title. Handsome husband. Much good it did her. First the handsome hubby leaves, then he dies, the estate's sold, and instead of living it up on the Riviera, she goes and buys another mouldy old pile practically round the corner. Ends up a recluse.' She shook her head. 'Forty-seven years on her own. Imagine. You'd think she'd have been glad to see the back of Lincolnshire, wouldn't you? But it's like she couldn't keep away. Or maybe she just couldn't live it down, him leaving like that. Almost makes you feel sorry for the poor old cow.' But it wasn't pity that was making her reflect. It was scorn. Catch Anita Hopkins making the same mistake.

Her relentless cynicism was dragging Sarah down. And yet everything she said could very well be true. Certainly, the Hopkins version tallied exactly with the few facts Sarah knew. But did that mean that the affair between Robert and Charity was also true?

She put the thought aside to deal with later.

Ms Hopkins reached for another cigarette. 'Funny thing about old Lady H.,' she said. 'Well, maybe funny isn't the right word. When she died, she left an absolute packet. Whole parish got its hopes up. But do you know what she did? She went and left the whole bloody lot to some old cousin. Forget any nice little nest eggs for the loyal retainers. *Big* disappointment all round, I can tell you.'

Sarah thought about that. 'The cousin – would that have been Aubrey Vincett-Searle?'

'God, how should I know? They all sound the same. It'll be in the will, won't it? Can't you look it up?'

In the act of reaching for the recorder, Sarah froze.

'What's the matter?' snapped Anita Hopkins. 'You look like you've seen a ghost.'

The *will*.

Sarah you fool. You bloody *fool*. You've gone and missed the most glaring lead of all. Robert must have left a *will*.

Anita Hopkins looked pointedly at her watch.

For the first time since the interview began, she and Sarah were in perfect accord. Suddenly Sarah wanted to leave as much as Anita Hopkins wanted her gone.

CHAPTER THIRTY-ONE

'I still can't believe I missed it,' said Sarah, sitting at the kitchen table while Alex and Stephen made supper. 'It was so obvious. And it never occurred to me.'

Stephen, drying lettuce leaves with a tea towel, asked, 'Can I come with you to London and see Lord Harlaston's will?'

'Of course you can,' she said. She turned to Alex. 'And that's another thing. It *would* be on a Friday that the penny finally drops. Now I've got to wait till Monday to find out what he said.'

Alex stood at the ancient gas cooker, making kedgeree. Without turning round, he asked, 'What he said about what?'

She threw him a glance. 'About anything.'

'That's not what you mean. You mean, what he said about your grandmother.'

Sarah turned her wineglass in her fingers.

'You don't give up, do you?' Alex said. 'In the teeth of all the evidence, you're still hoping they got together. It doesn't matter that he was the Nineteenth Baron and she was a stonemason's daughter and they probably never got within fifty yards of each other.'

At the other end of the table Stephen met her eyes and glanced quickly away.

'It's not against all the evidence,' she said, the heat rising to her face. 'Anita Hopkins told me—'

'And even if it were true, what makes you think it would be mentioned in the will?'

'Maybe it isn't. At least, not in the one in the public registry. But he might've left a secret will. They weren't unheard-of in those days. You should know, you're the lawyer.'

'But in that case, how the hell would you find it?'

He had been in this mood since she arrived, hardly listening to her account of the Bad Fairy of Holt Place, and brusquely declining the Sauvignon Blanc she had bought in Bourne to take away the aftertaste of the interview. Instead he had poured himself a huge whisky, then promptly ignored it.

He wore his usual checked shirt, faded cords and hiking boots, and presented a bizarre contrast to the rectory kitchen, which had all the unrelenting chirpiness of an Italian sandwich-shop: a riot of dancing vegetables on the walls, with frilly yellow curtains, and cabinets of apple-green Formica.

Oblivious of his surroundings, he leaned against the fridge with his arms crossed, and contemplated the kedgeree.

He's lost weight, she thought with a shock. Always rangy, he now looked positively gaunt. She reached for the wine bottle and refilled her glass. It shook her to see him like this without knowing why.

Stephen had finished drying the lettuce and was cutting each leaf into strips which he laid one by one in a blue glass salad bowl. Beside the chopping-board, three tomatoes, half a cucumber, and a yellow pepper awaited execution. He was either too absorbed in his task or too intrigued by the notion of a secret will to notice what was wrong.

'You're missing the point,' said Alex. 'The point is, Robert was not your grandfather. Robert is irrelevant to you.'

Sarah blinked. 'I still want to know what happened to him.'

'You know what happened to him. He—'

'I mean if he was happy. What he did with his life.'

'Why?'

'What d'you mean, why?'

'*Why* do you want to know about him? *Why* is he so important?' His eyes were bright and angry. He was cross-examining her like a witness in court. She had a sudden flash of what he must have been like as a litigator.

Stephen tipped the last of the tomatoes into the salad bowl and said in an execrable Welsh accent – his new skill – 'Shall I do some chicory as well?'

Alex ignored him.

'All I want', Sarah said slowly, 'is to take a look at the will. I don't see what's so—'

'But can't you see that the man's will is neither here nor there? It's irrelevant.'

'Stop saying that! It isn't irrelevant! Not to me.'

'It's simply an excuse to go on hiding out down here, instead of moving back to London and getting on with your life.'

'What have you got against him?'

Stephen watched them, with the knife in his hand. 'Alex . . .' he mumbled. 'The chicory . . .'

Alex said quietly, 'You're in love with him, aren't you?'

'I'm *what*?'

'You're in love with Robert. It's not as far-fetched as it sounds. You identify with Charity, and you want him to have been in love with her, because he – or rather, the man you tell yourself he was – is the exact opposite of my brother.'

'*Dominic*? How does he come into this?'

'I've just told you.'

'Alex,' said Stephen, beginning to look alarmed, 'what about the chicory—'

Alex turned on him. 'Not now!'

Silence echoed round the kitchen. For Alex to snap was like another man yelling obscenities.

Stephen blinked several times. Then he got off his chair, walked over to the fridge, and took the bottle of vinaigrette dressing from the door. Carefully he shut the fridge and went back to his chair. Then he poured dressing into the salad server. He managed to hold bottle and spoon nearly steady throughout.

Sarah took forks from the dresser and laid three places at the table. She tore off three pieces of kitchen paper from the roll, folded them in half, and put one beside each fork.

Alex took the pan off the cooker and told Stephen that if he wasn't fed up with chopping vegetables, yes please, he could do some chicory as well. Having accomplished that act of apology and reassurance, he waited patiently for his nephew to finish making the salad, then divided the kedgeree between three plates, and they sat down to eat.

At least, Sarah and Stephen ate. Alex had a mouthful, put down his fork, and contemplated his whisky with distaste.

'Don't you want any more?' Sarah asked.

'Evidently not.'

Stephen's fork froze on its way to his mouth. His eyes went from Alex to Sarah and back again.

Sarah went to the sink and poured tumblers of water for herself and Stephen. Absurdly, she felt on the verge of tears.

'I'm sorry,' Alex said, to both of them. To Stephen he added, 'Do you want some of mine? I'm not hungry.'

Sarah watched Stephen scrape half Alex's kedgeree onto his plate. 'Alex,' she said firmly, 'You're going to have to tell me what's wrong. I'm no good at guessing. Especially not with you.'

'Nothing's wrong.'

'Oh come on. This isn't like you.'

'I said nothing's wrong.'

She helped herself to salad.

'I'm sorry,' he said again.

'For what.'

'For behaving like a child. I suppose one often does where one's family's concerned.'

Sarah said, 'Could *one* stop distancing *one*self with abstractions and explain what *one* actually means?'

The first smile of the evening. A bit twisted, but a smile nevertheless. He said to Stephen, 'Your father rang this afternoon. He and Caroline are coming down to see you at the weekend. They'll be staying at the Bald-Faced Stag in Stainton Hamer.' He glanced at Sarah. 'They're taking Stephen out tomorrow, and on Sunday Dominic's booked lunch for everyone at the hotel. That includes you. I've no idea why, and he wouldn't say. But there's absolutely no need for you to come and I can't imagine you'd want to.'

'Hmm,' mused Sarah. 'Sunday lunch with Dominic

432

and Caroline. High Noon at the Bald-Faced Stag.' She sat back and began to laugh.

When the light began to fade, Alex walked Sarah home. Stephen had gone on ahead, whistling through his teeth to demonstrate his complete unconcern about the weekend arrangements.

It was a warm blustery evening and the sky was an ominous pinkish-grey. There would be rain in the night and possibly thunder.

When they turned into the drive the wind lost itself among the rhododendrons, rattling the leaves like a bad-tempered child.

'I just couldn't help seeing the funny side of it,' Sarah said. 'It's so theatrical. So like Dominic.'

In the kitchen when she had started to laugh, Alex had been astonished. It made him look unlawyerly and young. Now he walked gravely beside her with his hands in his pockets. She wished he would say something.

When the silence had gone on long enough, she said, 'And there's something else. He couldn't have picked a worse weekend if he'd tried. My mother's coming tomorrow for the day. She says it's just to bring my car, which has *finally* been repaired, but really she's coming to check up on me. She thinks it's unnatural to be alone for so long.'

'It is.'

She glanced at him but his face was impassive. 'One thing's for certain,' she said. 'We'd better make bloody sure she doesn't bump into Dominic. She never liked him, and since we split up she's blamed him for everything. The job, the pneumonia, the lot.'

Alex made no comment, but clearly he thought her mother had a point.

'Alex,' she said suddenly, 'lighten up. It's your brother coming down for the weekend, not a death in the family. OK, I wish he wasn't coming, and I'm sure you do too, and I can't imagine Stephen's looking forward to it either. It's intrusive and inconvenient and bloody annoying. But that's as far as it goes.'

And if you really want the truth, she added silently, with a sideways glance at his stony profile – and there's no way of telling, because when you're like this you might as well be on Jupiter – I'm far less worried about Stephen than I am about you. What were you *thinking* of, letting Dominic manoeuvre you into this? Sunday lunch at the Bald-Faced Stag? What's got into you?

As if he guessed her thoughts, he said, 'I agree with all that. I suppose I just dislike having to defend what I don't have a claim to. Though in this case I don't have a choice.'

'I haven't a clue what you mean.'

He made no attempt to enlighten her, and they walked on without speaking. Stephen flitted in and out of the rhododendrons like a lost soul from a Victorian ghost story. Of the three of them, he had the most reason to be upset by Dominic's invasion, but was putting on a convincing show of indifference.

Suddenly Alex said: 'I wish you wouldn't come on Sunday.'

She stared at him. 'Why?'

'I don't think you realize the damage he did to you when you split up.'

'Well I think I do—'

'I mean long-term. I mean—' he broke off, frowning.

'Dominic undermines people. Women. He takes away their confidence.'

She wondered if he was thinking of his wife.

They reached the bridge and watched the mallards skimming in to land on the darkening lake. The evening star glimmered above Hynton Edge.

Sarah asked, 'Why *did* you leave the City?'

He threw her a glance. 'What on earth makes you ask that now?'

'I don't know. Maybe it's what you just said. It put me in mind of – um – Helen. And I wondered why you left.'

He hesitated, then said, 'It was pretty trite, really. I'd turned forty. Realized I wasn't sure if I still liked my job. Or why I was doing it. If anyone had asked, I'd probably have trotted out the usual arguments. The status. The intellectual challenge.' He paused. 'It's not like your job. You create nothing when you practise law.'

'You seem to create a good deal of money.'

He shrugged. 'Well. One day I decided I didn't want to do it any more. I told you it was trite.' He contemplated Stephen in the distance. 'Perhaps it would have been different if we'd had children.'

They turned and continued up the drive. Against the luminous blue of the twilit sky the Hall was a goblin's kingdom of fantastic complexity.

The gathering dusk made Sarah bold. 'How did Helen fit into your quitting the City?'

'She didn't,' Alex replied. 'Although we took longer to realize it than we should've done. Especially me.'

'Why do you always blame yourself? I mean, I know she wasn't well, but she didn't *have* to have affairs.'

'They didn't matter any more.'

She wondered if he really believed that.

'We just needed to be apart,' he said after a while.

'Did she see it like that too?'

He shook his head.

'You mean, she didn't want a divorce.'

'Not to begin with. I think she still needed the security of a marriage. She'd had a bad time the year before. In and out of hospital. Then the Dominic thing.' He rubbed a hand over his face. 'He really screwed her up. And I wasn't much help. But in the end I realized we couldn't live together any more. So I made her agree to a divorce.'

'Do you *know* that everyone thinks it's the other way around? That *she* left *you*, and you were so shattered that you dropped out and buried yourself in Hynton?'

He looked surprised. 'Is that what they think?'

'Yes,' she said, exasperated, 'that's what they think.' When he remained silent, she asked, 'Don't you mind?'

He thought about it. 'No. I suppose people need to make sense of events. And if the events don't fit the pattern they want, they rearrange them till they do. No, I don't mind.'

'And you're not angry? Not even a little?'

'With whom? With Helen? No, of course not.'

Sarah waited for him to go on.

'I'm not angry with Dominic either, if that's what you're getting at. Though I was at the time. She was still so fragile when he came along. And it meant nothing to him. Just one of his stupid little games. But I'm not angry now. Dominic just does these things. Well, you know that better than me. It's his nature.'

She had never found that a convincing argument. Dominic was a human being, not an animal. He had a choice about what he did. It surprised her that a man as intelligent and perceptive as Alex could persuade himself that what he'd just told her was the truth.

They entered the carriage drive. Perseus and Andromeda glowed faintly in the gathering darkness.

Sarah said, 'You mentioned that people rearrange the truth to make sense of it. Is that what you think I've been doing this summer?'

He watched Stephen scramble onto the back of one of the stone lions and sit swinging his legs and tunelessly humming. 'I could understand', he said slowly, 'the need for something completely engrossing when you came to Harlaston. You'd been ill. Dominic had knocked you sideways. And there was some sort of backlog about your father that you'd never had a chance to deal with. But then I thought you got better. I thought you put Dominic behind you – '

She opened her mouth to say yes, she had indeed put Dominic behind her, but he didn't give her the chance.

' – but just when I thought you'd dealt with all that, you seemed to go even deeper into this thing about your grandparents. To become more absorbed, not less.'

'It's important to me.' She knew how lame that sounded.

'Why?'

'I don't know why. You can't always explain *why* you feel things. Maybe it's because of my father. Maybe it's because I think it's important that someone should find out the truth. I'm not like you, I can't stand by and let people make up their own version if it's plainly wrong.' She stirred the gravel with the toe of her boot. 'I just think they deserve better. Charity *and* Robert. I refuse to let that appalling woman turn them into some kind of soft-porn melodrama just because she feels like it. I want to get at the truth—'

'You can't. It's impossible.'

She raised her head.

'You can't ever know the past. No-one can. Whatever you find out, you'll never know if it's even close to the truth.'

'Oh well, in that case, why does anyone bother with history?'

'What I'm talking about', he said, suddenly brutal, 'is the kind of truth you're looking for. About your grandmother and that man you want so much to have been in love with her. How can you think you'll ever discover what really happened? The only people who knew that particular truth were that one woman and that one man, and they've both been dead for decades.'

'So according to you, I might as well pack my bags and go.'

'Exactly.'

Abruptly, Stephen stopped humming.

'That', Alex went on quietly, 'is exactly what you should do. Pack your bags tomorrow and go back to London.'

Sarah stared at him in disbelief. 'Why?'

'Because your job here is finished. You've written the book. You've done what you were paid to do.'

'Do you *want* me to go?'

'What the hell sort of question is that? Stephen, get down from there. We're going home.'

'Oh, *I* see. This isn't about Robert and Charity at all, is it? This is just another exercise in Alex the totally uninvolved recluse – I *don't* think – trying to get poor defenceless little Sarah out of the way of his morally delinquent brother!'

'Sarah, come off it—'

With shaking fingers she fumbled for her keys in the pocket of her jeans. 'No, *you* come off it! Stop taking responsibility! I'm not Helen, and I'm over the pneumonia, and I'm well and truly over Dominic, and I really, really wish you'd take all that on board.' She paused for breath. 'If I want to leave tomorrow, I will leave tomorrow. If I want to stay till I find out the truth about Charity – or that part of the fucking truth which I *can* find out at this distance – I will do so. And if I want to go to the showdown at the Bald-Faced Stag, I will do that too. The point is, if what I do gets me hurt or disappointed or disillusioned, it will be down to *me*, and no-one else. Especially not you.'

CHAPTER THIRTY-TWO

Letter to The Lady Maltby, 36 Eaton Square
12 December 1900
near Patrysdraai, Orange River Colony, South Africa

Dear Stella,

What a delightful surprise it was to receive your letter, knowing as I do what it must have cost you to renege on a promise never to darken the saddle-bags of your disgraced nephew with further correspondence.

I hope this arrives in time for the Society's luncheon. If not, I plead the rains and a persistent if unheroic dialogue between Mausers and Lee-Metfords which disrupts the postal service here.

You tell me it's my duty to provide 'everyday details' of the campaign for the Society, so I shall of course obey. In return, I beg you to send me news of home. Everything. Particularly of your recent visit to Harlaston. Anything about the village and its inhabitants, however trivial, will be welcome. I confess to a bad case of homesickness.

And so to the 'everyday details' – and like a good Englishman, I shall begin with the weather. It's late in the afternoon but still scorchingly hot, for the rains passed a week ago. I'm writing this lying on the banks of the Vals river, where we made camp an hour ago. Already the dust is littered with tobacco-papers, bully-beef cans and butchers' leftovers. The smells I leave to your imagination. The river-banks are strikingly English in appearance, with swallows and poplars and weeping willows. Were it not for the weaver-birds, I might be at Harlaston, tossing pebbles into the Lyde.

My subaltern, Lieutenant Marchand, is watching the horizon through his field-glasses. He's a delightful young fellow, with something of the water-spaniel about the eyes, particularly when he tries to be severe with the men – while hiding his blushes at their language. It's like watching a puppy in charge of a pack of wolfhounds. They treat him gently, for they are fond of him, but they call him Marjorie behind his back.

I should perhaps explain that I am no longer at my little garrison at Heuweltop. After four weeks of acting the shopkeeper, I was ordered back to my company, and now rejoice in the command of a small supply column. Thus from being a shopkeeper I have become a tinker – albeit with two fifteen-pounders and a stout company of Lincolns to protect my wares.

Like Dante's lost souls we drift across the veldt, bestowing ammunition and compressed vegetables on one lonely little outpost after another. Since the principal activity of these outposts is to 'clear' the surrounding farmlands, one might say that it's become my task to support the man who lays waste the countryside, whereas before, I was that man himself. The Army has shown an unexpected talent for irony, has it not?

I wish I could convey to you the extraordinary

flatness *of this part of the Colony! It reminds me of that phrase on our wonderful, useless FID maps: 'Vacant spaces indicate that data are wanting, rather than that the ground is flat.' Here one may hazard a pretty fair guess that the ground will indeed be flat. Unfortunately, this means there's no cover to speak of. Stella, if there is a Mauser bullet out there with my name on it, I hope to Heaven it does the job cleanly. Lying low in this country would be an infernally tricky business.*

We are all in a state of continuous siege. Sometimes my company makes up the rearguard for one of the larger columns, and that can be interesting, for if the enemy presses at the rear, the main column's advance quickly leaves us stranded. The principal difficulty, however, lies in the very nature of the enemy. We are fighting an invisible army which knows the country to the last anthill, and fires smokeless cartridges from trenches we cannot see. By the time our big guns have come up, Brother Boer has simply ridden off into the grass. How he must laugh to see our columns trailing after him, for all the world like oxen in earnest pursuit of gazelles! It's little wonder that your newspaper clippings caused such hilarity in the Mess the other night when I read them aloud. 'Now that hostilities are over, only a few desperadoes remain in the field . . . With the conclusion of the war in South Africa . . .' *When those words were written, five Boer commandos were invading the Colony, we had lost a garrison at Dewetsdorp, and the railway had been blown to pieces in a dozen places.*

But I digress, and for the space which remains I shall mend my ways. Christmas will have passed by the time this reaches you, so I hardly know in what tense to

442

write, but I was reassured to learn that Violet will be with you at Wynburne; and of course I shall understand if her letters are less frequent. I should be dismayed if she felt obliged to sit up till all hours, penning notes to me. Which brings me to the hints buried so adroitly in your letter (and those of Margot and Lily, my love to them both). I shall answer them as plainly as I can.

I was not, as you suggest, vexed to learn that the three of you have become Violet's confidantes – though it is a daunting triumvirate to have ranged against one. I cannot help observing, however, that I found the extent of her confidences to you surprising.

Plainly I can't confide in you as Violet has done, but I will be as blunt as I may without betraying her confidence in me. You are correct in that we didn't part on the best of terms, and if there was misunderstanding, I must bear the lion's share of blame. As you have gathered, Violet has been torturing herself with a conviction that the world, her family, and her husband require her to produce another heir. I only became aware of this on the eve of my departure, and was unable to reassure her as I should have done. Anything you can do to dispel this notion would place me in your debt.

Soon it will be dark, for in Africa there are no lengthy sunsets. I am not eager to welcome snipers by lighting a lamp, and shall therefore plead cowardice and sign off. Write soon, particularly with news of Harlaston and the village. I mean it about the homesickness.

As always, your affectionate nephew
Robert

Letter to The Rev. E.L. Bowles, DD, the Rectory, Hynton
12 December 1900
ORC, South Africa

My Dear Bowles,

I trust you and the family are well. You will be surprised to receive a letter from me and I must ask you to forgive its brevity. I am writing in the remaining minutes of daylight and as there are rumours of a scrap tomorrow I don't care to put this aside unfinished. I require assistance and only you can provide it.

You will be aware that latterly I have taken an interest in the Fosdyke boy, who sustained an injury in my wood as the result of a negligently placed snare. I have just learned through the Hynton 'bush telegraph' (i.e. Sam Webb) that the boy's wound is ulcerating, and the mother has also become unwell through the strain of constant nursing. No doubt our excellent Dr Young could remedy both ills swiftly enough, but I understand the family hasn't called him in, presumably because they can't afford his fee.

So here is the matter: I want Young to treat the boy and his mother forthwith, at my expense. And here is the difficulty: these people are infernally proud, particularly the mother and I believe also the daughter; thus the thing must be achieved sub rosa. *My attorney Gerard Vane (Vane, Lanyon & Co. in Holborn) will establish a small charitable trust with a thousand guineas for the purpose of meeting the medical expenses of such of my tenants as the Trustees (myself, Vane and you, if you will consent to act) consider deserving – &c., &c. I need hardly add that the trust*

444

*must be bona fide; in any event it is high time that I
put something of the sort in place.*

*I have no time to write to Vane as well, and would
ask that you send him this letter by way of instructions. He will see to the details as a matter of urgency.
More importantly, I should be grateful if you would
take it upon yourself to ensure that the trust's first
beneficiary is the Fosdyke family, and that Young is
called in without delay. I know I may rely on you to
handle this affair with discretion. If you would send
me a line now and then to say how the boy and his
family go on I'd be immensely in your debt.*

*Once again, forgive the brevity of this note and be
assured of my gratitude and good wishes.*

Harlaston

12 December 1900, Hynton

Mrs Fosdyke entered her daughter's room and sat
down heavily on the bed.

The room was freezing. Her breath steamed. She
didn't mind. It eased her to come here when Charity
was doing her reading at the rectory. Sometimes she
would move from bed to washstand to window-seat,
touching the neatly folded clothes, the carefully placed
comb and brush and hat-ribbons. Sometimes there
would be a piece of writing left on the trunk: a
shopping-list or a note of some errand for Mrs Bowles.
Mrs Fosdyke liked to examine such things, for she was
proud of her daughter's facility with letters.

It amazed her that Charity never saw the wonder of
being able to write so fluently, without having to think
about each separate letter – just as she took in her

stride the visits to the rectory. The very thought made Mrs Fosdyke grind her teeth in fear.

But Charity was not like her. Charity was brave. You had to be brave to go alone to the telegraph office in Tilburne and 'send a wire' to your intended in London. '*A wire*'. What familiarity! What ease!

An angry cry from the other room. Something was thrown against a wall.

She sighed and rubbed the back of her neck. Once again, Will's leg had kept him up all night. He said it felt like a nest of vipers, crawling and trailing poison. All day he had been wretched with exhaustion, fretting for something to distract him from the pain. A story. A recipe from *The Young Housewife's Daily Assistant*. This afternoon he had got it into his head that nothing would do except a kerchief sprinkled with Charity's lavender water.

Charity wouldn't mind. She'd do anything for her brother.

But it was with some unease that Mrs Fosdyke lifted the lid of her daughter's trunk. She felt like a thief.

She found the unknown parcel by chance, tucked beneath a neat pile of underclothes. Afterwards, the intimacy of that juxtaposition was what haunted Mrs Fosdyke most of all.

As if handling something alive, she unearthed the parcel and set it on the bed, and stood looking at it for a long time. The wrapping-paper was pale-green sprinkled with silver flowers, and tied with green satin ribbon of unbelievable delicacy. The parcel had been opened and rewrapped and retied so many times that the paper was white along the edges, the ribbon beginning to fur.

Mrs Fosdyke reached down and gently tugged one

end of the ribbon. The bow unravelled with a soft satiny slithering. The paper unfolded of its own accord.

14 December 1900, Kaalspruit Farm

Sam pretended to take a last look at the horses. Twenty feet away, Lieutenants Marchand and Payne sat beneath a clump of thorn trees, wide-eyed with exhaustion and shock. Lieutenant Marchand was still babbling. Wondering how it could have happened, what had become of the rest of the column, whether anyone else had got away.

What's the bloody point, thought Sam. You take your chances like the next poor bugger, and if you end up alive and he doesn't, why waste your breath?

Four yards upstream, Robert was taking a wash in the beck. He had stripped to the waist and was crouching on a flat rock at the water's edge, using his mess tin to sluice his head and chest.

Sam couldn't take his eyes off him. He was no longer a servant watching his master, or a soldier his captain, but a jealous man studying his rival.

He had never looked at another man's body with such attention. The breadth of the shoulders. The black hairs on the forearms. The flex of muscle beneath the smooth, pale skin.

If only Sam could have sneered at him as a weakling. But he wasn't weak. He was quick and strong, and he knew how to fight. When they were lads, Sam had never been able to take him down. It wouldn't be any different now.

Suddenly he was overwhelmed with bitterness. His chest was a fluttering hollow. His belly clenched.

That man, enjoying his wash in the afternoon sunshine. *That* man, who had reached down and snatched what was Sam's, and made it filthy.

He still didn't know how he had got back from King's Cross that day. It was a blur. From when he had turned on the concourse and seen them: her hand on his arm as she looked up and spoke with that grave, precise way she had of shaping her words; him leaning down to listen, not smiling exactly, but with a kind of inner tension as if he *wanted* to smile. From then on, everything was just a blur until he got back to the house, where Norton met him at the door and asked if he'd made it to 'Lost Property', – which set him off all over again, retching into the gutter.

She had played it cool enough with 'her Sam', hadn't she, the lying little bitch. *Trollop. Whore.* Filthy lying little *cunt*. She had lied from the start. Ah, *God*, how she'd lied.

Like the time when they'd gone looking for her soft-as-shit brother and found *him* instead, smoking his fancy cigar, and she had *pretended* to be surprised. That was where they did it, wasn't it? In that old railway cart. Bet they'd had a proper laugh next time they met.

And then when he'd asked her to marry him and she'd been all coy and wanted time to think. To think? Women don't *think* except with what's between their legs. What she'd wanted was time to go tripping off to her lover and have another bloody good laugh.

He pictured them together. His mouth on hers, his body straining against her. She would be so white. So white. And her hands would be deep in his black hair, and the sweat would be running down their sides . . .

When I *think* what she owes me. And this is how she pays me back. Spreading her legs for the first toff who'll toss her a sixpence.

'I say, Webb!' called Lieutenant Payne. 'Stop keeping the horses awake or we'll finish your coffee!'

Sam went over to the fire and held his cold hands over the flames. 'Don't want any, sir.'

'Take it,' said Lieutenant Marchand, holding out a steaming mess-tin. The colour had returned to his cheeks, and he no longer looked like a frightened rabbit.

'Are you all right, Webb?' Robert asked sharply. He was buttoning his shirt and his hair was damp. Droplets of water clung to the base of his throat.

'Yes, sir. 'Course, sir.'

'There's no "of course" about it, you know.'

'Yes, sir.' And I hope you rot in hell for all eternity. *Sir*.

Robert regarded him thoughtfully, and slowly nodded. 'All right, then. Get yourself some sleep. That goes for everyone. We'll move off before dawn to spare the horses. In the meantime, three-hour watches. Mr Payne, organize lots.'

Sam drew the final watch. He took his haversack to the shade of a thorn bush and lay down.

You think you're so bloody clever, he thought, watching Robert fetch his saddle for a pillow. But I know. *I know*. And I can tell anyone, whenever I like.

In the three months since London, that knowledge had been a deep source of comfort. No-one else knew. Her mother and father, the parson and his wife, everyone at the Hall. The whole bloody village. Only

449

Sam Webb had the power to change their lives for ever.

He liked to picture how he would tell them. How their expression would change as they struggled to take it in. Disbelief, bewilderment, bitterness, horror, rage.

Only with Lady H. would he do it in a letter, so she wouldn't know who he was. She wouldn't forgive the man who had ruined her wonderful life.

The best would be when he told Charity herself. He pictured her on her knees before him like the girl in the lithograph in the end house kitchen. Her hair all dark down her back, her face chalky-white and streaming with tears. Begging him to forgive her and take her back. *Begging* him. He turned onto his front and ground his loins into the dust.

He wouldn't give her an answer straight off. What, after all she'd put him through? It was his *duty* to make her see the full horror of her crime, and how better than to make her sweat for a couple of months? Only then would he agree, reluctantly, to take her back.

Which was strange, because most men would have sent her packing. But he'd known from the beginning that he would marry her just the same. It was a matter of justice. Why should she escape as easy as that? When they were married he would take her away from Hynton for ever, and that way he'd have his revenge on both of them. She'd have to do what he wanted for the rest of her life.

He pictured all the things he would make her do.

The sun hit him smartly in the eyes and he jerked awake, convinced he'd been hit by a shell. He lay gasping like a fish. Dazed, heart pounding.

Twenty feet above his head, Lieutenant Marchand

crouched on the edge of the gully and swept the veldt with his field-glasses. A couple of yards away, Lieutenant Payne slept like a schoolboy with his mouth open. Robert lay on his side, fast asleep.

How can they sleep? Sam wondered, his heart hammering. The sun was orange above him. Orange like shell-bursts. He couldn't close his eyes for fear they'd come at him again.

It had started four days ago, when they were ordered to escort a big support convoy south to the mountains. The column commander had taken it into his head to split up 'B' Company, and had ordered most of them, including the guns, to march in the body of the convoy. What was left – a couple of platoons, including Sam's own, and a handful of mounted officers – were sent to join the smattering of Mounted Infantry in the rearguard.

Robert had kicked up a proper stink: everyone heard the argument in the colonel's tent. 'But the guns are no *use* stuck in the middle of the column, *sir*! This enemy doesn't give you time to get into position! You've got to take the guns to *them*, or you might as well not *have* the bloody things!' In the end the colonel had accused him of wanting to save his own skin by hanging onto his guns. At that, he had gone quiet for a moment, and then said wearily, 'Well all *right*, then,' as if the whole thing was suddenly too much trouble.

As it turned out, he had been right about the guns.

The first three days were quiet enough, though as the land became more hilly, the convoy slowed to a snail's pace. It was perfect Boer country. Everyone could see that except the colonel. Robert rode with Lieutenant Marchand's platoon in the rear and kept his eyes glued to his field-glasses, and Sam marched behind, and watched him watching the veldt.

They reached a long low hill and began to climb, but by the time the rearguard had crested it, the convoy was far ahead, a dusty brown caterpillar inching across the veldt. That was when the Boers landed their first shell.

In disbelief Sam watched the caterpillar bulge and fan outwards, the tiny khaki figures scuttling between puffs of yellow smoke to the low mutter of rifle fire and the rat-a-tat-tat of the Boers' big guns. Then someone was yelling commands and he was running down towards the convoy, and then the scrub on either side of the road sprang to life and he forgot everything in his first taste of a Mauser fusillade – a drumming roaring hammering storm of bullets, whining and spitting and sparking off rocks, and sucking the breath from his lungs.

Men dropped like shot rooks. Lieutenant Jordache came galloping straight for him, pitched over his pony's head, and lay still with a foot-long piece of shrapnel jutting from his back.

In a daze Sam grabbed the reins and clawed his way onto the pony's back, yanking its head round and digging in his heels and galloping back up the slope and away from the convoy.

Some time later, he pulled the pony to a walk. The rattle of gunfire had fallen away behind him. He slid to the ground and stood with his hands on his knees, retching into the road.

That was how they found him, Robert and Lieutenant Marchand and a plump red-haired officer of Mounted Infantry who he later learned was Lieutenant Payne. They too had tried to reach the convoy and been driven back. Everyone else was either dead or captured, babbled a wild-eyed Lieutenant Marchand, cut off behind a wall of shells, Christ, it was appalling, where the hell were the bloody *guns*?

By then it had been getting dark, but there was enough of a moon to ride by, so Robert decided they would keep going. Go east cross-country, then veer north and head back to Reitz to sound the alarm.

They rode all night, and the red glow in the sky faded behind them. Just after dawn they came to the burnt-out ruins of a farmhouse beneath a low hill. A wagon-track skirted the base of the hill. There was the usual blackened barn and tangled garden, and a dam and a pasture, surrounded by a barbed-wire fence. And there were clear traces of a large, very recent Boer encampment. Sam guessed maybe five ox-wagons and about fifty mounted men: a full Boer commando.

Once he was satisfied the place was deserted, Robert called a halt, though out of caution they made camp in a gully about a quarter of a mile south of the farmhouse. They tethered the horses among thorn bushes at the deepest end of the gully and Sam made a small fire for coffee.

Robert went and sat alone by the water, and Sam could tell he was thinking of his men. Old Spencer would have gone red about the eyes and said, 'Dashed bad luck, eh? Though I'm hanged if I know what I could've done to prevent it.' Which would have been the truth. Robert wasn't like that. He was too ready to take the blame. Even when it wasn't his fault.

That was Sam's last coherent thought before he slept. Then someone was shaking his shoulder and saying it was time to move off.

It was only beginning to get light when they led the

horses out of the gully. The night-crickets were still sawing away and the air was cool and smelt of cinnamon.

In half-darkness they rode through the pasture to the wagon-road which showed pale in the gloom. Then they rounded the hill and left the farm behind. Five hundred yards ahead, a man's voice shouted a challenge in Dutch.

Sam's heart jerked.

'*Christ*,' muttered Robert. 'They must have left a bloody picket!' He raised his head and shouted back: '*Frints! Frints!*' He sounded Dutch enough to Sam, but the indistinct figure in the distance became very still.

'Keep riding towards them,' Robert said quietly. 'Slowly. We can't see them, but they can see us against the sky, so any sudden moves and they'll open fire. If they do, turn and ride back to the farmhouse. It's a good position, we can deal with them there . . .'

A bullet whined past Sam's shoulder, and behind him someone grunted. Another bullet thudded into the dust by his pony's hock. Then another. The air crackled and tore apart.

Sam's pony didn't need urging. With a squeal it wheeled and galloped back the way it had come, streaking past the others as it headed for the farmhouse. Sam grabbed its mane in both hands and hung on, his rifle bumping against his hip. Pounding hooves and men yelling in English and Dutch, and the dull vicious *crick-crack* of Mauser fire.

It was still too dark to see much. All he could make out over his shoulder were shadows looming out of more shadows. Then as they rounded the hill and the dark bulk of the farmhouse hove into view, he saw Marchand's pony bolt up the slope and put its foreleg in a hole and pitch over with a horrible drawn-out squeal. Marchand struggled out from under it and started limping towards the ruins, staggering and firing his revolver uselessly over his shoulder. He'll never make it, thought Sam as he galloped past.

He reached the farmhouse and slid down behind a ruined wall. Bullets whined and spat around him, and his hands shook as he struggled to reload his rifle.

Dimly in the distance he saw Marchand struggling towards him across the hillside. Robert was still five hundred yards behind Marchand, lashing Mahomet's neck with his reins. Sam couldn't see Payne or the Boers. Blindly he fired into the hillside where he thought they might be.

On the crest of the hill above Marchand, a pair of Boers appeared and started heading down towards him. Robert yanked Mahomet's head round and spurred the pony up the slope. He reached Marchand just before the Boers, leaned down and pulled the boy up behind him. Sam fired to drive the Boers back, and dropped one with a lucky shot.

A few minutes later, Robert reached the shelter of the wall. Marchand slithered to the ground in a heap, teeth bared, clutching his right thigh. 'Ah, God! God! Sorry sir! Think I've bought it! Tell the old dad I died game!'

'Don't be ridiculous,' snapped Robert, 'you're not going to die!' He whipped out his handkerchief and tied it round Marchand's thigh with such firmness that the boy yelped.

'Where's Payne?' Robert said over his shoulder.

'Don't know, sir,' Sam replied without breaking fire.

Marchand raised himself on his elbow. 'By the dam, sir. I saw him take the fence but I don't think he made it. Pony got stuck on the wire.'

'Bloody hell,' muttered Robert. 'Sam, how many did you see? I counted five but I think you dropped one.'

'Four left, I think, but they're hanging back.'

'Fine. Cover me.'

'What?' Marchand pulled himself up against the wall. 'You can't go *back*, sir! They'll pick you out against the sky!'

'What about Payne?' said Robert. 'We can't just leave him on the wire!'

At that moment they saw four dark shapes moving across the hillside towards them. The Boers had slowed to a trot, knowing their quarry had already reached the ruins.

'Bugger,' muttered Sam. '*Bugger*. Bastards are keeping off the road so they won't show up.' He took aim and fired several rounds, all wide of the mark.

At the corner of his eye he saw Robert pull his revolver from its holster and swiftly drop the cartridge into his palm, gauging by its weight how many rounds were left before snapping it back in place. He often did that when he didn't have time to count, and Sam used to think it a handy trick. Now he hated himself for ever admiring the man.

The *bastard*. The bloody *bastard*. Tears ran down his cheeks. Angrily he brushed them away.

Robert remounted and yanked Mahomet's head round and spurred him towards the dam.

The light was improving rapidly, and Sam could see clearly now. He stopped firing and scanned the hillside. Down by the dam he could see Payne struggling beneath the frantic pony on the barbed wire fence. He could see the four Boers converging on Robert. He could see Robert galloping towards Payne.

Sam took careful aim and shot Robert in the back.

CHAPTER THIRTY-THREE

15 January 1901
Letter from Mrs Gwendolen Bowles to Mrs Myles
Gifford
Ridgewell Terrace, Chelsea

My Dearest Loelia,

*What unhappy days are these, when daily we
dread the newspapers' reports of Her Majesty's ebbing
vitality! I wish I could begin more cheerfully, but I do
not feel cheerful. It is a freezing cold morning, we have
heard nothing from Lord Harlaston since the beginning of December, and on top of everything we have
had a most distressing occurrence, for one of our
parishioners has lost her reason!*

*It came to my attention only yesterday. I was resting
in my drawing-room when, 'out of the blue', Rose
announced Mrs Fosdyke, the mother of my protégée.*

*Oh, Loelia, the alteration in my poor fen tigress!
Where was that fanatically orderly materfamilias I
have heretofore described? Who is this broken old
crone, her gown so sadly spotted, her hat-ribands so
sorely in need of a pressing? The lips work constantly
to the accompaniment of a perpetual grinding of the*

jaws – and the hands! They pluck, they rub, as if working out some imaginary stain. Verily, if I have sketched a rural Lady Macbeth attacking in vain her moral blot, I do not exaggerate one whit.

For your sake, I shall condense a most lengthy and distressing interview to a few brief lines. In short, the poor woman had been brooding for weeks and working herself into a perfect mania over a suspicion that her daughter is guilty of – an attachment – with an unknown gentleman of quality. I can scarcely pen the words, they are so inexpressibly repugnant! My Charity, accused of such baseness – and by her own mother!

You may imagine what I experienced as the poor deluded woman's tale unfolded in that halting Lincolnshire brogue. And all of it founded upon so pitifully little! Upon the girl's hesitation at her sweetheart's proposal of marriage, and on her impetuous journey to Tilburne to wire him a last farewell (ah, the sweet folly of young love!)

If the above were all, I should have dismissed it as the sorry fantasy of a deranged imagination. Indeed, I am still disposed so to dismiss it. Yet there remains one further, more disquieting item of 'evidence'. A volume: a small, opulent thing which the poor woman found in her daughter's trunk, and which I confess causes me unease. For how could a nineteen-year-old country girl have come by a mint-new copy of Mr Henry James's A Little Tour in France, lavishly illustrated with photogravures, and beautifully bound in green kid tooled in gold? Why, such a volume must have cost three guineas if it cost a penny. Small wonder, then, that the poor fen tigress was so broken by its discovery. Such a volume would seem, would it *not, to indicate some sort of communication with one of far superior rank?*

Of course, I revealed none of this to the fen tigress, but merely dismissed her, having stated my intention of retaining the volume and interviewing the girl myself, to ascertain the truth.

That interview takes place this afternoon when she comes to read to me. I do not look forward to it at all. Indeed, I long to put the whole affair out of my mind. But even as I sit here, the volume lies beside me. Mute, accusing, exquisite. Unspeakably repugnant.

I must lay down my pen if this is to catch the morning post. Oh Loelia, spare a thought for your poor sister – for when you read these lines I shall have confronted my protégée and learned the truth!

Your loving, deeply uneasy
Gwendolen

He is riding Mahomet up the lane to St Hybald's.

Something is wrong with the pony's neck. It is soaking wet and twisted to one side.

His hands are wet. He wipes them down his thighs. He doesn't want the blood to frighten her.

'You mustn't mind my horse,' he calls out as he rides through the wall of the church. 'He's dead, you see. When that happens their legs go stiff, and they swell up in the middle. Don't be alarmed.'

Mahomet's legs get longer and longer as they walk up the nave towards her. By the time they reach the pulpit, his head is near the rafters. He wonders how he is going to get down onto the flags.

She is kneeling in her green dress, arranging marbles around the foot of the pulpit.

The marbles trouble him. 'But you have put them all

on the wrong side,' he tells her from somewhere near the ceiling. 'That can't be right, can it? I can't have used them up already. I'm still only halfway through.'

She doesn't turn round. He wonders if it is because she can't hear him, or if he has angered her. He longs for her to turn and look at him, but she doesn't move.

'I'm sorry,' he tells her. 'Charity. I'm sorry.'

Rain patters on the flags. It streams down her back like a torrent of dark hair.

A small child stands behind her, contemplating the marbles.

Robert reaches down and takes the child's hand in his. As he straightens in the saddle, the child's fingers lengthen endlessly.

'Oh but you're not real,' Robert says in disappointment.

'I know,' the child says in a cool adult voice. 'But I'm more real than you.'

The child disappears. Once again Robert is alone with Charity in the church. Still she refuses to turn to him.

He stands behind her, watching her long dark hair streaming down her back. Flowing, flowing like rain.

As he watches it, a great sense of peace steals through him. It no longer matters that the marbles are all on the wrong side. As long as she allows him to remain, he will be at peace.

He reaches out and sinks his hand into the streaming current of her hair. Silently, sinuously, it flows around his fingers, but when he tries to grasp it he cannot. Like mercury, it slips away.

The sound of rain fills his head. Cool, obliterating rain.

Robert awoke.

His eyelids were heavy. Too heavy to lift. He gave up trying. It was an enormous effort simply to breathe, so he concentrated on that. Then it occurred to him that it was unusual for him to have difficulty breathing, and perhaps he had been wounded. Yes. That must be it.

He began to carry out a slow inspection. His lips were cracked, his tongue swollen and enormous. When he tried to shift his limbs, his skin rustled like paper against the sheets. His skull was splintered glass, piercing his brain in a hundred places. When he moved his head the splinters dug deeper. Blinding white lights flared behind his eyes.

The pain in his side was worse than anything he had ever known. It was a presence inside him: a white, malign, burning thing, crouching, waiting to engulf him. His swollen throat struggled to release a moan. The presence flared. His body ceased to exist. He disappeared into the pain.

Much later, he opens his eyes.

He is lying in a dim, canvas-coloured twilight. The wind in the poplars sounds like rain pattering on window panes. But it can't be rain, for he smells hot spicy dust, and through the gaps in the tent-flaps the African sun is fierce. He glimpses other tents, neatly aligned and bordered by whitewashed stones.

The white burning presence is with him in the tent. He feels it watching him, waiting to engulf him again. If he lies completely still, perhaps it won't be able to take him away. He bites down on it, catches it between his teeth. As long as he holds it there, caught fast, it can't escape and engulf him again. He can't cry out

462

because that would release the pain. His jaws ache, but he is determined not to let go.

He wonders if anyone will come. If anyone will notice the burning white presence.

The tent-flap opens. The light dazzles, sending fresh darts shooting behind his eyes. A woman in a white cap and scarlet pelisse leans over him. She is amazingly neat and clean, and she smells of soap. Gently she touches the back of her cool hand to his cheek. She smooths the sheet across his naked chest and takes his wrist in her fingers.

He is immensely comforted. She knows about the presence. She has come to be with him, to keep it away.

Later, he opens his eyes again. The woman is still there. He wants to thank her for staying, but can't find the words. 'So neat,' he murmurs at last. His lips are pasteboard, and his tongue is too big for his mouth. What he utters is something between a croak and a groan.

With a puzzled frown she bends closer.

He tries again. 'So *neat.*'

Her slow-dawning smile is the last thing he sees before he drifts away.

When he awoke again, the glow behind the canvas had deepened to a rich late-afternoon gold. The presence had gone. In its place was a hot throbbing ache the length of his side.

Charity sat beside the bed.

'I knew you'd come,' he told her. 'I saw you in the church but you wouldn't turn round.'

She sat with her hands in her lap, smiling at him with her warm brown eyes.

463

'I'm sorry,' he murmurs. 'I'll make it up to you. I love you.'

'You're awake,' she said, and resolved into Marchand. 'How do you feel?'

He shut his eyes, clinging to the last swift-fading traces of the dream. Retaining nothing but his disappointment.

When he opened his eyes again, Marchand was still sitting in the canvas fishing-chair beside the bed. His face was a patchwork of blisters and pink new skin. He wore blue Army shirtsleeves and a pair of filthy flannel trousers several sizes too big, held up by frayed red braces. He looked like a pantomime clown. He sat with his right leg stretched before him. The trouser-leg had been slit to accommodate heavy bandaging about the thigh. A pair of crutches was propped against the foot of the bed.

'I feel', Robert said, 'like a squeezed lemon. Forgive me if I close my eyes.' For several minutes he concentrated on breathing. Then he asked, 'Did I say anything while I was unconscious?'

'Nothing we could understand. I think at one point you were talking to your wife.'

He opened his eyes. Marchand was blushing beneath his blisters. Robert said, 'Where are we, what's the date, and where's Sam?'

'It's Boxing Day. We're in a field hospital in Frankfort. They picked us up a week ago. Sam's fine.'

'Was he hurt?'

'Only sunstroke and dehydration. I saw him this morning in the Tommies' quarters.'

'Good. Good. What about you? You look frightful.'

'Thank you, sir. So do you.'

Robert arranged his lips in what he hoped resembled a smile.

Marchand said, 'Actually I'm not doing at all badly. My leg got into a bit of a state, but thanks to Major Creagh – he's the chief surgeon here – I've almost decided to keep it. The major's awfully decent. You'll meet him now you're on the mend.'

'Someone was crying out for rather a long time. You or me?'

'Um. Me, as it happens. Sorry. I came down with some sort of beastly fever thing. It gave me the most frightful head.'

Robert opened his eyes. Beneath the sunburn the boy's face was skeletal, the eyes sunk in sepia shadows.

Marchand frowned. 'Sorry. Sorry.'

For a while they were silent. Robert tried to concentrate on the clean cool feel of the sheets and the chatter of birds beyond the tent-flaps. But the dream had left him with a deep melancholy he couldn't dispel.

Marchand said abruptly, 'It's most awfully good to see you on the mend, sir. We didn't think you'd pull through.'

Robert did not reply.

'You lost gallons of blood out there. Then the water ran out and we thought you couldn't possibly make it. I kept thinking how beastly unfair after what you'd done for me—'

'That'll do, Marchand.'

'No,' Marchand said with surprising firmness. 'It won't do. You saved my life. If you hadn't picked me up on that hillside when my pony went down, I'd have been done for. I'll never forget it.'

'*Now* will you go away and leave me in peace?'

Marchand smiled and left.

16 January 1901
Letter to Mrs Myles Gifford
Ridgewell Terrace, Chelsea

My Dearest Loelia,

Terrible, terrible, terrible. *Such* unspeakable *occurrences – and all happening at once!*

I had just finished my letter to you and sent Rose to the post, when Ederic entered the drawing-room with the most appalling *news. There has been an incident in South Africa. Details are scarce: we know only that Lord Harlaston lies gravely wounded. Indeed – and I can hardly bring myself to write the words – it is uncertain if he will live. You may imagine my feelings. But there is still* more. *Young Samuel Webb was with him in the incident and is also indisposed (although not seriously), and it is he who has unwittingly provoked the revelation which I can scarcely bear to relate.*

It came about as follows. In the midst of my distress over Lord Harlaston, I knew at once that it was my duty to inform my protégée of her sweetheart's narrow escape, to prevent her hearing it in some garbled and doubtless more alarming form. And of course I at once postponed my plan of questioning the girl over the mysterious green volume; that would have to await another, less fraught, occasion.

The afternoon came, the girl arrived, and once Rose had brought the tea tray and departed, I told the girl of the incident in which her sweetheart had been injured: calmly and succinctly, which as you know is always my preference. I made it clear that although Lord Harlaston's life hangs in the balance, young Webb is in no danger whatsoever. What was my

astonishment and alarm when I observed the girl turn
frighteningly pale! If I had announced her sweetheart's
death upon the battlefield the effect could not have
been greater. O Perfidy! O Falsity! No, no, I cannot
write it yet!

Perhaps what I did next was wrong. Certainly it was
harsh and uncharitable, and impulsive. But Loelia, I
was so perplexed by the girl's reaction! And I confess it
revived in me certain fantastic suspicions which her
poor deluded mother had sown the day before. In
short, I brought out the volume and confronted her
with it, even as she was reeling from what I had just
told her.

Mrs Bowles put down her pen and lay back against
the cushions. Her eyes came to rest upon the armchair
where Charity had sat the previous afternoon.

She had sat very straight, with her hands together in
her lap. After hearing of the incident in South Africa
she had rapidly regained her composure. Too rapidly
for Mrs Bowles, who would have found tears or
palpitations more reassuring. And when Mrs Bowles
brought out the volume and laid it on the table
between them, the rigid composure had scarcely
altered. Only the girl's colour had changed: the raspberry lips draining of blood. And she had sat so still.
Such terrifying stillness.

'Well?' Mrs Bowles had said, to break the silence.
'What have you to say?'

At last Charity replied. 'Nothing. I have nothing to
say.'

'That cannot be. You must tell me – it is your *duty*
to tell me – how you came by this volume.'

'I'm sorry, Mrs Bowles. I can't do that.'

'You must! If not because I ask it – though that

should be enough – but because the worry is making your poor mother ill!'

Charity looked down at her hands. 'I was given it,' she said in a low voice.

'By whom?'

'I can't tell you.'

'How so, you *can't* tell me? Insolent girl!'

'I'm very sorry, Mrs Bowles. I don't mean to be insolent. But I can't.'

'Not even to save your mother's sanity? Can't you see this is robbing her of her reason?'

At that the girl's face contracted, and Mrs Bowles felt a twist of remorse. But she had to know. Not for the sake of the mother, but for herself. 'Charity,' she said sternly. 'If you don't tell me the truth, you will drive your mother insane. I don't think you could live with such a crime on your conscience. Now tell me. Who gave you the book?'

Again the girl looked down at her lap. Then she raised her head and a flush crept into her cheeks. 'This is not about my mother,' she said softly.

Mrs Bowles felt her face growing red. 'What do you mean?'

Charity regarded her steadily for a long time. 'Very well,' she said at last. 'I will tell you. Not because of my mother, but because I want to tell you. Lord Harlaston gave me the book.'

Absolute silence reigned in the drawing room.

Mrs Bowles breathed shallowly, as if the least movement might precipitate the explosion she could feel building inside her. 'Dear God in heaven. You are as deranged as your mother.'

The girl flinched. 'I'm not mad. Though I understand why you must think I am.'

'You *are* mad! Mad, wicked, deluded, deceitful! Wicked, deceitful, *wicked* girl! To utter such lies – such *falsehoods*!'

'It isn't a falsehood!' the girl burst out. Then she reined herself in. 'I wouldn't lie about such a thing. Especially not to you. I hold you in too great esteem for that.'

'So now you would flatter me, you wicked, deceitful girl!' To her horror, Mrs Bowles found that she was close to tears.

The girl's hands clenched in her lap. 'The important thing', she said with quiet ferocity, 'is that you understand it wasn't his fault. You must believe that.'

'Not his *fault*?'

'He was so unhappy. With his little boy dying, and all the things they made him do in the war. He couldn't help it. And there was never any – impropriety – between us. You must believe that. He never—' her voice broke. 'He wasn't to blame.'

Alone in her drawing room, Mrs Bowles took up her pen and stared at it, and put it down again. The girl's face had held such passionate conviction. Such passionate truth.

But it could not be. *It could not be.* Perhaps if she kept repeating that to herself, she would come to believe it.

Once again she took up her pen, and forced herself to write out a brief summary of the interview.

At this point, she continued, *I put an end to the deplorable speech with great firmness. Indeed, I lost my temper. You may imagine my anger at such* inconceivable *presumption!* An attachment to Lord Harlaston? *Can you credit the gall? To dare to assert that a man of such quality and intellect would seek solace not from the Church or from his lifelong friends (among whom I believe I have the honour to number myself) or even from his own wife – but from some chit of a village girl! Why, it flies in the very face of Reason!*

For make no mistake, never for one instant did I believe Lord Harlaston guilty of the slightest impropriety. Why, a man of such calibre is incapable of misconduct towards any member of our Sex, be she a lowly rustic or the most exalted of peeresses. The moral constitution is simply too finely wrought. What I do believe, as I informed the girl in a few apt and cutting phrases, is that she believes it, no doubt on the basis of a single act of impetuous charity on his part: namely, the gift of the volume. I have since come to understand that such a gift would be perfectly consistent with his generous nature. One may readily imagine the sequence of events: the poor deluded creature's quest for a final glimpse of her fancied 'Beloved'; the 'Beloved's' understandable horror, then dawning pity as he perceives the extent of her mania; his impulsive seizure upon some random volume from a side-table, in the hopes that it might send her away consoled. Little would he suspect that such a gesture must only fan the flames of her pathological affliction.

Yes, Loelia, that is the only tenable explanation. The poor girl has simply 'dreamed up' the whole tale out of 'thin air'. Such passionate imaginings are regrettably not unknown among our village girls, whose inherently coarse natures inevitably incline them towards indelicacy.

'Yes,' she whispered to herself, staring ahead with haunted eyes. 'That is the only tenable explanation.'

Of course, she continued, *I had no choice but to*

dismiss her at once from my employ. The falsehood was too black, and I have my children to protect. On that point I know I did rightly, and have no regrets.

When I informed her of her dismissal, she once again subsided into that perfect, almost ladylike composure, regarding me steadily – not with impertinence, but with a certain wondering surprise, as if beholding me for the first time. Then, with that unaffected candour for which I once held her in such affection, she thanked me for my past kindnesses and took her leave.

Under other circumstances I should have been gratified to observe that my lessons in comportment have borne such remarkable fruit, but now I find it agonizing, and worse: I feel guilty. Yes, guilty – for I feel that by educating her I have sown the seeds of unwomanly ambition in a heretofore simple nature.

Oh, Loelia, what am I to do? How am I to find peace? Can you find it in your heart to visit me and bring the girls, that they may distract their meddlesome aunt with their pretty ways?

Write soon, for I am very wretched.
Your loving, greatly distressed
Gwendolen

CHAPTER THIRTY-FOUR

Letter to Mrs Lilian Vincett-Searle
28 January 1901
No. 17 Stationary Field Hospital
Frankfort, Orange River Colony, South Africa

Dear Lily,

With your usual flair for making an impression, you have set our little tent-hospital agog with the extravagance of your wire. I had no idea that getting shot would prove such an effective short cut to re-habilitation within the family.

I understand that Aubrey wishes to know 'every detail' of how it felt when the bullet struck, and everything which happened afterwards. That's a 'tall order', as the Colonials would say. I'll do my best.

Being shot, Aubrey, feels like being hit extremely hard with a cricket-bat. There is no pain when it happens, though it arrives with commendable speed a few minutes later. As to exactly what occurred, my own recollection is hazy and incomplete – so in the account which follows, I shall rely upon Sam Webb's description of events. Sam was the only one who saw it all, for, by the time I was shot, Marchand had fainted from his wounds.

I remember putting my pony at the barbed-wire fence, in the hopes of rescuing Lieutenant Payne. I never reached him, and we discovered afterwards that he had passed beyond my help. At the time, however, I was so intent on getting to him that I didn't notice one of the Boers peeling off from the others and riding round to my rear, to cut me off. It was he who shot me in the back. After that, things are a little hazy. Somehow I turned my horse's head and made my way back to the others as fast as I could. Or rather, my gallant little pony made his way back, with me lolling inelegantly over his neck. I'm told that when we reached safety, I slid unheroically to the ground in a dead faint, while my poor brave pony fell lifeless beside me. As for the Dutchman who shot me, I never even saw him, for Sam Webb shot him immediately afterwards. And I'm afraid, Aubrey, that I cannot comply with your other request, and send you the bullet from my side as a souvenir – for (mercifully for me) Sam dug it out and cast it aside while I was still insensible. You must excuse Sam for this: he was, understandably, more intent on rendering me some much-needed first aid, than on preserving the evidence for posterity. And I must say, he did it with great skill: no doubt his long experience of tending dogs and horses came in useful when dressing my wound!

The rest is briefly told. Sam, who had seen off the remaining attackers single-handed, dug a grave for Lieutenant Payne, and I stammered out a few words. Then with the remaining horse we struck north for Reitz. This was not a journey I remember with *pleasure, for we had but one water-bottle and a few opium tablets between us.*

Fortunately, after a few days we were picked up by a 'body-snatching' detail, which tipped us all into a Scotch cart and took us to the little town of Frankfort – although I must take all this on trust, for by then I had progressed from being a 'sitting-up case' to an emphatically 'lying-down' one, and remember nothing of the rescue.

I awoke in this splendid little hospital, which lies beside a lazy brown river and comprises nineteen large bell-tents, an operating marquee, a mortuary tent, and a burying-ground. And we are in luxury, for there are iron bedsteads, straw mattresses, and sheets! Further details must await a subsequent letter, however, as I still tire ridiculously easily, and must now move on to other matters.

The news of the Queen's death reached us yesterday. It's strange, but one feels it more than one would have anticipated – perhaps because the old lady was always with us, and it's scarcely conceivable that it should be otherwise. Do you feel the same, Lily? I should be interested to hear your views, and to see the newspaper editorials, if you have time to collect a few.

You will be glad to learn that my men are now all accounted for. Twenty-three ended up here, and in recent weeks Marchand and I have spent much time with them. Six have died, victims of the shelling with injuries too horrific to describe. I was with them in their last moments, and took down their final words to their wives and sweethearts. They preferred me to do it, as they feared to embarrass the Sisters with the love passages. I can only say that any woman would have been proud to have taken down the words they entrusted to me.

The strangest case by far is that of Hynton's own Sam Webb. Day after day he sits alone, gnawing his fingernails and snarling at those who approach him. Most remarkably, he cannot bear to be praised for his conduct during the incident, though, as you know, he saved my life by dropping the Boer who shot me. I had to speak to him sharply about this, pointing out that it's carrying modesty too far, and that I've written to the colonel recommending him for decoration. At this he became so angry that I wondered if his reason had been impaired. Fortunately, however, the physicians say it's only nervous strain, and he'll recover within a month. I hope so. I find his affliction baffling, as well as profoundly affecting. We played together as boys, and I owe him my life.

I must end soon, for Sister Doherty is looking fierce. Tomorrow I start for an officers' convalescent home in Pretoria. They tell me that if I'm obedient, I should be back in harness in about a month. (Not so Lieutenant Marchand, whose wound still plagues him, and who has been packed off to Durban to await a passage home.)

You asked what you might send out, and I'll give you an honest answer. Send me books, news, and cigars! As regards books, you know my tastes, though please avoid anything about the sea. We only have two books here: List, Ye Landsmen! and The Adventures of the Iron Pirate, and I've read both several times (they are terrible), and had my fill of sea-faring.

By far the most important request, however, is for news, especially local news from Harlaston. If you or Aubrey or anyone can provide details of how things go on there – at the Hall and in the village – particularly the village – I should be eternally grateful, for I miss the old place terribly. Before Christmas I petitioned Stella and even the rector for news, but have heard nothing from either. It's probably only an accident of the post, but I confess I am becoming uneasy. Has something happened? Is there sickness in the village? Whatever it is, you must tell me, or I'll imagine the worst.

Aubrey, as I have done my best to satisfy your desire for 'details', so you must satisfy mine. Go down to Hynton and reassure me that all is well. Find out how the repairs at St Hybald's are progressing, how the stonemason's boy is faring (as I recall, you can already lay claim to some slight acquaintance with him), and ascertain how his family and the others in the village go on. Write soon and leave nothing out.

My love to you both,
Your nephew and cousin
Robert

PS. Aubrey, an important point. While in Hynton, take the utmost care not to mention Sam Webb's peculiar mental affliction to anyone, and particularly not to the Fosdyke family. As I believe you know, the daughter – whom you will no doubt come across – is engaged to be married to Sam, and it would be unconscionable to alarm her. In fact it would be best if you didn't mention the incident or our injuries at all. You may appreciate bloody details, but I'm quite sure that it would only distress her, as it would the rest of Hynton's female population.

*   *   *

Robert sat alone on the river-bank and watched the sun go down.

Above the veldt the sky was aglow with lines of pure colour: lemon, orange, scarlet, mauve. A breeze rustled in the eucalyptus trees around him. In the uppermost branches, a colony of weaver-birds clamoured incessantly. Swallows wheeled and swooped over the water.

Some of them would have flown south from the English winter. He wondered if any had passed over Harlaston.

My God, man, he thought wearily, listen to yourself. Why can't you stop? What good does it do?

He had thought that being thousands of miles away would make it easier. It didn't. He never knew when something would remind him of her. That afternoon he had been playing chess with Major Creagh when a little nurse had hurried past and brushed her temple with her wrist, and instantly he was in Regent's Park, watching her brush back her hair as she frowned at the black swan and tried to shoo it away.

He didn't want to think about her. Thinking about her hurt. But he couldn't help it. It was as if something had got inside his mind and was rifling through his memories, throwing things to the surface whether he wanted them or not.

A spasm of pain shot through his side. He straightened his back.

The worst thing about being wounded wasn't the pain. It was having so much time to think. To realize what his life had been before, and to face the fact that when the war ended and he returned to England, he must resume it exactly as it had been. All those perfect, meaningless dinners and luncheons and teas.

And *why* would no-one tell him the news from Hynton? Neither Bowles nor Stella nor even poor Sam would tell him anything. Was he imagining it, or were they all conspiring to keep something back? But what could be so terrible that he must be kept in the dark?

There was no-one in England he could ask. No-one to whom he could send a wire saying simply: *Go to Hynton and make sure that she's all right.*

Behind him they were lighting the fires for supper. Blue acacia smoke drifted across to him, sharp and aromatic on the evening air.

He watched the sky drain of colour and resolve into darkness; the stars come out between the bone-white branches of the trees.

He couldn't imagine spending another thirty-five years like this.

19 March 1901
Letter to Mrs Myles Gifford,
Ridgewell Terrace, Chelsea

My Dearest Loelia,

I had so hoped to be welcoming you all to the rectory within the week! And yet I quite understand; with head-colds one can never be too careful. You are indeed wise to suggest that we await more clement weather.

In the meantime, you asked for news, and I shall oblige – though I am afraid that in Hynton these days 'news' only means the wretched saga of the Fosdyke family.

It will not surprise you to learn that the full details of my ghastly interview with the Fosdyke girl were

*known to all of Hynton within the hour. No doubt
Rose was to blame, for, as you are aware, she always
listens at the door after she has brought the tea. On
this occasion, however, I am afraid I was too sick at
heart to scold her for eavesdropping.*

*Hynton's judgement on the girl was swift and
absolute. The village swallowed the tale whole,
and believed the very worst. While I persist in telling
myself that any sort of liaison between that girl and
Lord Harlaston is wholly impossible, our good rustics
simply muttered 'No smoke without fire', and left it at
that. And, of course, the fact that she was summarily
dismissed from my employ has only supported their
verdict.*

*As you will appreciate, Fosdyke mère and père
have taken their daughter's disgrace extremely hard –
particularly the mother, whose mental decline worsens
by the day. By degrees, she has conceived an absolute
horror of encountering her fellow-villagers. At first she
would only venture from her cottage after dark; then
not at all; now she has been housebound for weeks.*

*You may imagine the effect on the rest of the family.
The father and daughter maintain a dignified front
which under other circumstances would be admirable,
but the boy is far too young for concealment, and has
been driven to the brink of delinquency. Why, only last
week he instigated a most regrettable bout of bull-
baiting, in which two young lads (Ned Webb and
Jim Bacon) were rather badly injured. It subsequently
emerged that our flaxen-haired seraph was a champion
bull-baiter in his previous parish! To prevent a recur-
rence, I have taken it upon myself to intervene, and
have retained him as a sort of 'boy of all work' here at
the rectory – a plan of which Fosdyke père thoroughly*

approves, for he himself has accepted a post near Oserby, and has clearly been wondering what to do with his son.

But what, you will ask, is to become of the unhappy mother in all these relocations? Is she also to remove to Oserby when her husband takes up his new position? No, Loelia, it is far more remarkable and reprehensible than that! A week ago, she declared her intention of removing herself and her daughter to her old parish in the fens – there to live out her days in miserable seclusion. In short, she intends to abandon her husband and son!

Ederic has been tireless in adverting to the wickedness of her intent, but she remains impervious – and supported in her resolve by her daughter, who has sold a much-prized typing-machine to render the removal possible. It is set for the twentieth of March (i.e., tomorrow). Discreet enquiry has established that mother and daughter have taken a tiny, isolated cottage in windswept farmland about three miles from a hamlet aptly named Jericho. No doubt the father will send them some pittance when he is able, but it cannot be sufficient, for the girl intends to take an ill-paid post as a 'supplementary' at a very low sort of dame school, and to work for her teacher's certificate in her 'spare time'.

'But why', you ask, 'has Gwendolen made any enquiry about the wicked pair? She should rejoice, for tomorrow they depart, and leave Hynton unsullied!'

Oh but Loelia, I have come to believe that in this affair I have acted very badly. I did not behave as a Christian ought, and have suffered accordingly.

Make no mistake. I do not for one instant regret dismissing the girl from my employ. What I do regret,

*and bitterly, is how I dismissed her – and my sub-
sequent withdrawal of all guidance and assistance.*

*She is wicked and an outcast – that we know. But
for that very reason should I not have extended the
hands of Pity, Forgiveness, and Charity? Should I not
have guided her towards Repentance, while proffering
such material aid as lies within my power to provide?
Instead, I – who had such lofty plans for her improvement – have only cast her back into the Slough of
Despond.*

*Ederic tells me sternly to put the whole affair out of
my mind, and no doubt he is right. But I confess that I
do not find such advice of great assistance. I remain
perturbed and unhappy, and, yes, remorseful over my
harsh treatment of the girl. I long to render her some
assistance, but I cannot think how.*

*I entreat you, dearest sister, help me in this trial.
Write to me soon with your frank opinion, and advise
me as to how I might make amends.*

Your sorrowing, remorseful
Gwendolen

20 March 1901, Hynton

Charity sat on the naked mattress rereading the letters
she had spent the last hour writing. Downstairs her
father was helping Mr Burridge take their trunks
outside. Her mother was already inside the carrier's
wagon, safe from prying eyes behind the black canvas
sides.

Will was nowhere about. After pressing his farewell
present into his sister's hand he had run off to the
churchyard, too overcome to stay and see them off.

His little bottle of rose water lay on top of her reticule.

Her letter to Sam was brief. It didn't take long to break off an engagement, and she hadn't gone into details. By now he would know the reason why. Someone from the village – his brother probably – would have written and told him all about it. She didn't think Sam would believe the *very* worst that people were saying of her, but he would understand why she couldn't be his wife.

Her letter to Robert was longer.

My dearest Robert, it began. She had never called him by his name before, and writing it had felt wonderful.

You'll wonder why I'm writing to you, when we agreed we wouldn't. Why am I? I don't know, exactly. I suppose it's to warn you. My mother found the book you gave me and took it to Mrs Bowles, and there was an awful scene, and I told her about you and me. She didn't believe me. She said I'd made it all up. (At least, that's what she said, although I think she does believe me really, in her heart.) I don't think you need worry that your wife will find out. Lady Harlaston never comes here, and so is unlikely to hear anything. And even if she did, she wouldn't believe it, would she?

But if I'm honest, warning you isn't really why I'm writing. It's because it makes me feel better. I'm lonely, and I miss you.

But I'll stop being maudlin, and give you some good news. Will's leg is entirely better now, thanks to your wonderful Trust, and he has taken his revenge on the boys who attacked him. You'd approve of how he did it, and I'd like to tell you about it, but I don't suppose I'll get the chance.

I'm afraid that's all the good news I can think of.

It's strange, but everyone in the village believes the worst about you and me, and no-one believes the truth. They point, they snigger, they call me your 'fancy woman'. But they won't believe the truth. Except perhaps for my poor mother, although it's harder and harder to know what she believes. Sometimes I don't think she knows herself.

She put down her pencil.

'But Mother I'm not *like* Cousin Ruth!' she had cried on that first awful afternoon after the scene with Mrs Bowles. 'I didn't do anything wrong!'

'I know. I believe you.'

'Then why are you crying?'

'You can't help it, my poppet. It isn't your fault. It's in the blood.'

'But I didn't do anything wrong!'

'I know. I believe you.'

That was when Charity had first wondered if her mother was losing her reason.

You're probably wondering why I told Mrs Bowles. I've wondered that myself. I could say it was because I was tired of lying, but that wouldn't be the whole truth. The truth is, I wanted her to know. Can you understand that? It's odd, isn't it? I knew it would bring my whole world crashing down about me, but I wanted someone to know. I think that's why I didn't hide your book very well, either. Because deep down, I wanted someone to find it. (Oh, I wish I still had it, but Mrs Bowles wouldn't give it back, she said it would only 'fan the flames of my pathological affliction'. I think she was cruel to keep it, and I told her so.)

But the worst, the very worst, is that no-one will tell me how you are. I know you're out of danger, but that's all I know, and I keep thinking about what you told me in London – about being blinded or mutilated. Oh God, Robert, you're all right, aren't you? You're not in pain? I could bear anything if I knew you weren't in pain.

That was as far as she had got.

Down in the road, Mr Burridge's horse snorted and stamped, impatient to be off. Soon her father would come to the foot of the stairs and call her name.

She hadn't put anything in the letter about leaving Hynton and moving to Jericho. If she told him he would be worried, and try to find her.

But, of course, as soon as he read the letter he would do that anyway. It was his nature. It was also the one thing which would incriminate him in the eyes of the world.

She picked up her pencil and signed her name. Then she folded the letter carefully into three, and tore it up. She placed the fragments in her reticule along with Will's rose water, and got up and went downstairs to her father.

CHAPTER THIRTY-FIVE

Early August, the Present

On Sunday morning at half-past twelve Sarah turned the car towards Stainton Hamer. Dominic had booked the table for twelve fifteen, as he and Caroline had to be away by two. Alex and Sarah wouldn't mind making it an early lunch, would they? He had a stack of work in Chambers, they had people coming to dinner, and a horribly early flight to Venice the following day.

Sarah wouldn't have minded not making it at all. Her hands were shaking, and she had to take deep breaths to still the butterflies in her stomach. Which was ridiculous, because Dominic couldn't hurt her any more.

Except that this was no longer about Dominic. It was about having a row with Alex on Friday night and not making up properly afterwards.

It had rained all night and was still raining now. After weeks of driving Alex's car, her newly returned Golf felt light and skittish on the wet roads. She felt tired and slightly hung-over. Her mother had brought her car from Coventry the previous day and stayed the night, and they'd sat up till after two with a bottle of wine. Both were surprised at how well they got on, and Mrs Dalton had only just caught the noon train back to Coventry.

Sarah took a short cut down a side-road and got stuck behind a tractor held up by a gaggle of mountain-bikers in purple cagoules. By the time she reached the hotel's griffin-topped gates, she was forty minutes late.

In the parking area she pulled into a space next to Alex's car, and sat watching the rain take over the windscreen.

The front seat of Alex's Saab contained the usual clutter of rucksacks, maps, and Stephen's medical encyclopedia. Dangling from the rear-view mirror was a fat furry bat with green fluorescent eyes which Stephen had given Alex for his birthday. That was Alex all over. If Stephen had given him a pair of fluffy dice he'd have hung them up just the same, because, deep down, he didn't care what people thought of him. Just as he didn't care why Dominic had manoeuvred him into having lunch at the Bald-Faced Stag – though he must have been aware that it would serve no purpose but Dominic's own.

The trouble was, *Sarah* cared. Because even if Alex shrugged off his brother's motives, he could still be hurt. And Dominic was a black belt at hurting people.

A week ago, she would simply have rung Alex and told him what she thought. But the row in the carriage-drive had created a distance between them.

He had called her very late the previous night.

'Sarah.'

'Alex.'

'I know it's late. Um. How's your mother?'

'She's fine. She's upstairs taking a bubble bath under the Bohemian chandelier.'

'What does she think of the Hall?'

'Actually, she likes it. Much to her surprise. And mine.'

'Good. That's good.'

This was unlike Alex. Normally he said what he wanted and rang off. He hated long phone calls.

'Look,' he said. 'I'm sorry about last night. I was out of line. It's up to you to decide when to go back to London.'

'It doesn't matter.'

There was a silence. 'It's just that I don't —'

'Yes?'

He sighed. 'Nothing. I'll see you tomorrow.'

'High Noon at the Bald-Faced Stag. Wouldn't miss it for the world.'

He said goodbye and rang off, and she was left feeling bleak and unsatisfied, wishing she had the self-confidence to call him back.

The Bald-Faced Stag was a sprawling Jacobean manor with coldly staring mullioned windows. Imposing on the outside, it mysteriously dwindled within to a handful of stark interiors full of steel, glass, and strident Modernist prints. Sarah had trouble finding her way. There was no reception, and everyone was so artfully dressed-down that it was impossible to tell which were staff and which were guests.

The washroom, when she found it, was clinical brushed steel with a single branch of ocotillo in a tall glass tube. An enormous flask of scent provided a solitary note of deep purple. Sarah unstoppered it and sniffed, and decided against it. Caroline wouldn't notice, but Dominic's knowledge of womens' perfumes was extensive. *Poison* would be bound to elicit a comment.

She glanced at herself in the mirror and was not reassured. Earlier, she had stumbled downstairs in her T-shirt to find her mother cooking an enormous breakfast and fretting about railway timetables. After toying with bacon, tomatoes, and scrambled egg, she had dashed upstairs, showered and washed her hair, and pulled on whatever was clean and went vaguely together. Black jeans and loafers, an oversize black silk shirt; a stack of malachite bangles from a market in Zimbabwe, and a pair of dangly copper earrings that turned her ear lobes green if she wore them for more than two hours.

Now, in the unforgiving halogen splendour of the hotel washroom, she realized that the ensemble didn't come off. She looked neither elegant, idiosyncratic, nor subversively chic: merely scrappy and out of date, like a not very successful presenter on children's television. But at least Alex wouldn't get the idea she had dressed up for his brother.

When she reached the dining room the others were tackling their starters at a large round table by the French windows. Dominic was talking energetically, while drizzling olive oil over his *crostini*. He looked as he always did: solid, expensively well-groomed, his black eyes roving and watchful. Beside him, Stephen was messily dismembering an artichoke, while trying to follow his father's jokes, and checking if Alex was laughing. Caroline sat on Dominic's right, baring her teeth and waving her hands so that her gold bracelets clashed. She looked much the same as Sarah remembered: confident Julie Andrews features and a good but over-generous figure, which women found reassuring,

and most men strangely erotic. She was unimagin-
atively well-dressed in a beige silk blouse and trousers
and expensive suede jacket. Even on location she
always dressed like a merchant banker, and it never
bothered her that she looked wildly out of place.
Maybe she thought everyone else was underdressed.

Alex sat on Caroline's right. He seemed to have
skipped the starters and was leaning back in his chair
studying the wine-list, slowly nodding at whatever
Dominic was saying. Sarah noticed that Dominic,
Caroline and Stephen kept flicking him little glances,
as if monitoring his reaction. She had seen people do
that before. Perhaps it was because he was quiet and
listened to them, so they ended up wanting to know
what he was thinking.

A place awaited her between Alex and Stephen,
opposite Dominic. That would be Dominic's doing.
Right in the line of fire. The butterflies started beating
a tattoo in her stomach.

'Sorry I'm late,' she said briskly, striding up
and clashing cheeks with Caroline. 'The traffic was
murder coming from the station and I got stuck behind a tractor.' The earrings were a mistake: they
swung wildly back and forth and increased her self-
consciousness tenfold. Slow down, she told herself.
There's no need to put on a show.

From the corner of her eye she saw Alex looking down at her and Stephen watching him, and
Dominic watching all three. She turned to Alex
and gave him a brilliant smile. Uncertainly, he returned
the smile.

Dominic gave her a rapid once-over. '*Marvellous* to
see you, darling! And what a wonderfully *disturbing*
haircut. Alex you sly bastard, why didn't you warn

me? And whatever were you doing at the station? Last-minute attack of nerves? Oh I remember, Alex said something about Shirley coming down. God almighty,' he gave a rich chuckle. 'I'd love to have been a fly on the wall when you two got going over a bottle of wine!' Clearly he thought they'd talked of nothing but him. 'So what did your mama think of our dear old Harlaston?'

A waiter hovered into view and Sarah ordered a vodka martini and whatever Stephen was having. 'She loved it,' she said. 'Over the top, but great—'

'Good Lord,' Dominic murmured, 'don't they *have* socialism in Coventry any more?'

' – and we wondered what Dad had made of it,' Sarah went on, unperturbed. 'It's a shame we never got around to asking him.'

She caught his slight surprised recoil. He raised his glass. 'Oh, well *done*, Sarah darling. You *are* coming on. Jolly good for you.'

Alex reached for a bottle of Perrier and filled Sarah's glass, and smiled at her with his eyes.

She raised her eyebrows and smiled back.

'Are you two friends again?' Stephen asked her.

'Shut up, Stephen,' said Alex.

Sarah laughed.

Dominic made a point of not noticing.

Caroline told Alex how much she'd adore it if he took her round the Hall. 'I hear it's absolutely amazing. Oodles of false doors and weird angles, like a hall of mirrors. Oh do say I can come!'

'Caro, darling,' said Dominic, 'with your co-ordination it'd be a disaster. You'd never make it round in one piece and nor would the Hall. Poor old Sarah would have to follow you round like a prison warder, to make sure you didn't break anything. Wouldn't you, Sarah my love?'

Caroline flicked Sarah the sort of look usually reserved for importunate sellers of charity flags, and resumed her attack on Alex.

Sarah's drink arrived, and the first long swallow hit her stomach with a welcoming burn. The butterflies fluttered weakly and gave up.

She found herself looking at Dominic's hands and wondering why she used to find them erotic. If he didn't watch out, in a few years his stockiness would become serious. And there was a petulant twist to his mouth which reminded her of Leonard Fielding, the rector's grandson. In fact, he might end *up* like Leonard Fielding if he didn't take silk and wasn't made a judge. The idea of a disappointed Dominic was a heartening one.

Caroline was still badgering Alex for a tour of the Hall. Sarah wondered if he found her attractive.

Stephen plucked up his courage and shyly told Caroline: 'There's an open day in two weeks. If you like, you could come to that.'

'*Lovely!*' said Caroline with the kind of warmth which Sarah had once mistaken as genuine.

'Stephen, what a *marvellous* idea,' said Dominic. 'Why don't we all come? We could stage a reading of Robert's will in t'auld Library. Wouldn't that be fun? '*And the name of Sarah's grandfather is . . .*' Or shall we try to winkle it out of the old chap directly, in a séance? What do you think, Sarah?'

How the hell does he know so much about it? thought Sarah. She shook out her napkin with a snap and said smoothly, 'Not much point in a séance,

Dominic. With you around the ghosts would never get a word in.'

He raised his glass in a silent toast.

She felt Alex watching her and shot him a warning glance. *Don't even think about jumping to the rescue. I can handle this.* His face lightened and he lifted his hand a fraction off the table. *As if I'd dare.*

Caroline put her chin on her hand and asked Alex to tell her *all* about his book. Sarah gave him a wry smile and turned to Stephen, who was looking guilty. 'You rat,' she said quietly. 'You told him about Robert, didn't you?'

'Sorry. Actually I didn't, I told Caroline, but only because she made me. She's quite—'

'Yes, I know.'

'Even Daddy does what she says.'

'Crikey!' Sarah laughed. 'That makes up for letting the cat out of the bag!'

He looked relieved.

'So,' she said, 'what did we order for the main course?'

'A fish called turbot in a sauce.'

'Good. And what are we working up to?'

'Frozen chocolate souffl – I think they mean ice-cream – *or* peaches in cider. I'd go for the peaches, but—'

'But?'

He lowered his voice. 'The prior of St Gudwal's had a supper of peaches after his estate was ravaged by the scum and off-scouring of the land, and the next day he died of the bloody flux.'

Alex cast him an amused glance. 'You can't get the bloody flux round here. If you want the peaches, go for them.'

'What bloody flux?' said Caroline loudly. 'What *are* you talking about?'

Dominic roared with laughter. Stephen beamed.

Bottle followed bottle as the meal wore on. Dominic and Caroline drank most of it. Alex drank sparingly (for him), and Sarah had one glass and then switched to Perrier. With Dominic around, she would need her wits about her. Especially when, as now, he was cross-examining her about her research, and dropping in little references to the 'Hynton literary community' while flicking sideways glances at his brother. She began to have a nasty suspicion about the reason for his visit, and hoped she was wrong.

Suddenly she was overtaken by a wave of sadness. This was *Dominic* she was regarding as Public Enemy Number One. She had lived with him, laughed with him, slept with him. They had shared each other's doubts and insecurities. He knew how she felt about her father, and she knew how he felt towards his brother. And now it was as if all that had never happened.

Caroline was still gamely trying to elicit the plot of Alex's novel, and still being gently deflected. She kept darting little puzzled glances at Dominic, as if his brother wasn't at all what she had been led to expect.

Sarah wondered what Caroline *had* been led to expect, and what she saw when she beheld her future brother-in-law. 'Good-looking, isn't he?' her mother had remarked with startling candour the night before. Mrs Dalton had 'dropped in' on Alex on her way to the Hall, specifically to make an inspection. 'I'd never really looked at him before, but then he's like that, isn't he? The kind of man you hardly notice at first, then suddenly you take a good long look, and you think, oh *yes*.'

He was explaining something to Caroline, using one hand to emphasize a point. Sarah had always liked his hands. They reminded her of the effigy in St Hybald's: the same long narrow fingers and veins across the back.

In the beginning, she had tried and failed to detect some resemblance to Dominic. The eyes in particular were utterly different. Clear and brandy-coloured, with light brown lashes that were unremarkable until close range, when they became breathtaking.

Suddenly her stomach disappeared.

With great care she set down her knife and fork and looked down at her plate. No. No. It couldn't be.

She remembered the day in London when she had loftily told Clare that there was no *possibility* of anything happening between herself and Alex. The thought of that now made her go hot and cold. She felt as if she'd been happily paddling about in the shallows and had suddenly gone over the edge into bottomless black water.

Alex had probably already guessed how it was with her, and in typical Alex fashion was trying to let her down gently. That would explain his behaviour on Friday night. The silences. The brusqueness. Telling her to pack her bags and go back to London. He'd seen it coming and was warning her off, to prevent her being hurt. He didn't want to get involved with her. He didn't want to get involved with anyone. He wanted to live quietly at the Old Rectory and finish his book, far from the *Sturm und Drang* that had wrecked his marriage.

She sat turning her glass in her hands, wishing she

hadn't come. Everyone must have guessed by now. Dominic. Caroline. Probably even Stephen. It was so bloody obvious, to everyone but herself. Stupid, pathetic little Sarah. Dumped by one brother and now hopelessly hung up on the other.

She glanced up and found Alex watching her. He smiled. Then as he met her eyes, the smile slowly left his face. She glanced quickly away so that he wouldn't see her eyes fill.

Across the table, Dominic had been studiously ignoring them. Now he turned to her and winked. He hadn't missed a thing.

Well he wouldn't, would he, she thought bitterly. This is why he came to Lincolnshire. Clare tipped him off, and he decided to see for himself how the land lies between his ex-girlfriend and younger brother.

The waiter arrived and they ordered coffee, and peaches for Stephen. When he had gone, Dominic turned to his son and waited for a gap in the conversation so that everyone would hear, then casually asked if he would like to come and live with him and Caroline in the new house in Holland Park.

Caroline toyed with her coffee spoon with the self-important air of someone at a meeting whose colleague has just embarked on a delicate manoeuvre. Her expression was so smug and knowing that Sarah wanted to hit her.

'It's another month till school starts,' Dominic said. 'Why not give Uncle Alex a bit of peace to give his book a good seeing-to. Or whatever.' He didn't glance at Alex or Sarah, but Sarah knew he had them in his sights.

Stephen blinked several times. His eyes went from his father to Alex, then to Sarah, then back to Alex.

His face was a curious blend of dismay and resignation, as if he had known all along that some grown-up plot would eventually conspire to send him away from the rectory.

Alex fished in his jacket pocket and brought out his keys. He handed them to his nephew. 'Wait in the car. I'll be out in a minute.'

'Can't I—'

'No,' Alex said gently, 'you can't.'

'Why?'

'Because I want to find out what Dominic's talking about and it'll be grown-up talk. Go on, it won't take long.'

Sarah watched Stephen slide off his chair and weave a path between the tables. He looked small and straight-backed and unnaturally composed.

'Not rushing after him, Sarah darling?' said Dominic. 'Not in the mood for maternal – sorry, *quasi*-maternal support?'

'Dominic,' she said, 'don't be such a prick.'

'*Sarah!*' gasped Caroline.

A middle-aged couple at the next table applied themselves to their puddings.

'Can we please deal with this like adults?' Caroline went on. 'After all, Dominic *is* the boy's father.'

'Oh for Christ's sake, Caroline,' snapped Sarah, 'this has nothing to do with Stephen! It's just Dominic playing games.'

'Well really, if you're going to be like that—'

'Mrs Harris,' said Alex, addressing Caroline in a soft voice that made her nose turn pink, 'I think you'd better keep out of this.'

'Simmer down, old son,' murmured Dominic. 'People are beginning to stare.'

Alex leaned back and put his hands in his trouser pockets and smiled. 'Which isn't my problem, since I'm not the one who wants to become a judge. Now let's get the facts straight, shall we?'

'Don't be ridiculous. We're not in court.'

'Clare has sole custody. That's right, isn't it?'

Dominic gave a long-suffering sigh. 'Of course.'

'And Clare is in Germany. Correct?'

'Correct.'

'And she knows nothing of this.'

'As *yet*, but—'

'Is that correct?'

Dominic humoured him with a smile of great ill temper.

'Correct.'

'Well then, you have three options. First, you agree to do nothing till you've spoken to Clare. Second, you drop the whole idea. Third, we thrash it out here. And everyone stares.'

'*Alex,*' murmured Dominic. 'There's no question of *thrashing* anything out. It's remarkably straightforward. We simply decide who gets to play mummies and daddies for the next month or so.'

'Listen,' Alex said briskly. 'If you want to find out if I'm sleeping with Sarah, ask. Don't use Stephen to weasel it out.'

Caroline stared at Alex in fascinated horror. The couple at the adjacent table had given up all pretence at conversation.

Dominic arranged his mouth in a tolerant smile. 'Don't you think you're overreacting?'

'To the sight of you kicking your son around for a bit of fun? No, I don't. Now are you going to drop the whole idea or are you going to phone Clare?' He got to his feet and stood looking down at his brother. His eyes were bright and angry. Sarah thought he looked marvellous.

Dominic gave a heavy sigh. Then he spread his hands. 'Very *well*. If it makes you feel better, I'll talk to Clare this evening.'

'Good.' Alex flicked Sarah a glance which could have meant anything, and left. There was a general breathing-out at the surrounding tables.

With ostentatious steadiness Dominic reached for the coffee-pot and refilled his cup. He shook his head in weary dismay, enjoying himself enormously. 'Caro darling, you mustn't mind poor old Alex. It's just boring old sibling rivalry rearing its ugly head – as it always does when he feels threatened. And the sad fact is, he always does feel threatened when I'm around. Ridiculous, I know. But there it is.'

'And the only problem with *that* remark', Sarah told Caroline, dropping her napkin on the table and picking up her keys, 'is that Dominic's got it the wrong way round. For "poor old Alex" read "poor old Dominic", and you're pretty much there.' She turned to Dominic. 'If I were you I'd stop trying to keep up with your brother. You'll never make it. Thanks for the lunch.'

Dominic returned her glance without a flicker.

She turned to Caroline. 'He's had rather a lot to drink, hasn't he? If I were you, I'd do the driving.'

'Thanks for nothing,' Caroline snapped. 'As if I'd let him near my Lancia in his condition. Dominic. Keys. Now.'

To Sarah's astonishment, he didn't snap back. With a show of humouring Caroline, he simply put the keys on the table. He was clearly furious. God almighty, Sarah thought, I hope he thinks it's worth it.

She reached her car just in time to see Alex pulling out of the gates. She watched him drive away, feeling shaky and slightly sick.

Suddenly she realized that he was right about leaving Harlaston. What was the point in hanging on for a few more weeks? She *had* been using Robert and Charity as an excuse. The fact was, it was time to stop procrastinating and go back to London. Find a job and bloody well get *on* with her life.

When she got back to the Hall there was a message on the answerphone from her friend Sally at the BBC. 'That will you called about on Friday? My assistants managed to pull some strings – well, quite a lot, actually, and it should be waiting for you on Monday afternoon. And another thing. That job at Synergy. They're really really keen and they want to see you ASAP if you're still interested. I've got the details and I'm around for most of the week. Give me a call.'

Sarah rang Sally and they talked about Synergy, and finding somewhere to stay until the tenant moved out of her flat. Then she rang Alex and got the engaged signal. A few minutes later she rang again and got the answerphone. He was screening, as he often did when he was writing.

She thought about going down to the rectory and telling him in person that he was right and she'd be leaving the following day. But she knew he wouldn't try to stop her, and she didn't think she could take that face to face. In the end she hung up without leaving a message.

Then she went upstairs and started to pack.

CHAPTER THIRTY-SIX

31 October 1902
near Jericho, Lincolnshire

A gust of wind soughed in the poplars. Charity put a fresh block of peat on the fire and wondered if the starlings would come tonight.

Summer was the time for owls, and the first frost of winter brought the greylags, but the starlings always came in the autumn. She would see them at dawn as she walked to Jericho: a great wavering shadow darkening the fields. Then at dusk they would sweep up to roost in the poplars, engulfing the cottage in a raucous clamour.

Her mother *hated* them. Their coming always marked a downturn in her spirits. For starlings brought autumn, and autumn stripped the land of cover, and without cover there was nowhere to hide.

It must be long past midnight, Charity thought numbly. That must be why the starlings haven't come.

She knew she should rise and make a start, but couldn't summon the energy to stir from her chair. She had pulled it close to the fire, but still couldn't get warm.

Her mother's body lay on the cot in the corner. Death had caught her unprepared. She looked tiny and ill at ease, like a faintly perplexed wax doll.

Charity straightened her back to ease her stiff shoulders, and the sheaf of papers crackled in her lap. Sam's letters. She looked at them in distant puzzlement. Why had she kept them all this time? What had moved her to bring them out tonight? She could not remember. All she remembered was sitting by her mother's body as the cottage darkened and the wind got up.

She had received the first letter six weeks after she broke off their engagement. She had picked it up at the Jericho post-house and opened it on her way home, and the unfamiliar words had leapt from the page. Whore. Bitch. Other names with meanings she could only guess at, but all neatly shaped without blot or hesitation, as if he'd practised the spelling. She had leaned over the edge of the dyke and retched till her stomach ached.

Eighteen months on, she felt nothing but distant pity. Poor Sam. Letting loose a torrent of filth to conceal his pain.

Slowly she rolled up the letters and used them to poke the fire. The paper crackled and flared like last year's leaves.

She thought about her mother on the morning they left Hynton. Her strange, distant, terrifying resignation. As if the blow she had been dreading all her life had finally fallen.

'It's not your fault,' Mrs Fosdyke had murmured as they watched the village disappear behind them.

'Of course it's my fault! It's all my fault! *I* brought you to this, *I* tore the family apart, *I* made you ill—'

'No, no, my poppet,' she said in that horrible, calm, unfamiliar voice. 'It's my fault an' nobody else's. It always was.'

If only I'd listened when she talked like that, thought Charity. If only I'd tried to understand.

But for the first few months in the cottage, things had seemed to be getting better. Her mother was almost her old self again, especially after they reserved the plot in the churchyard at All Saints. She had started sewing, and looking forward to the weekly letter from Will. She missed him terribly, but wouldn't let him visit. It was as if she and Charity had contracted some shameful disease and he mustn't risk infection.

But when the days shortened and the starlings came, her mind would darken again. She would spend hours counting her burial money and discussing arrangements for her funeral. Or she would scrub the cottage from end to end to rid it of stone-dust. 'I can *smell* it,' she whispered to Charity one night. 'It smells of dead things left in holes to rot. An' I can *see* it, all over everything like a coating of frost. An' sometimes I lie awake an' I can *feel* it. Settling on my face like a shroud.'

The fire was dying down again. She ought to build it up, heat water and make a start. She had never done a laying-out before, and didn't know how long it would take.

She glanced at the workbox at her feet. She vaguely remembered dragging it out from under the bed, intending to sort through her mother's things. Now she leaned down, picked it up and put it on her lap.

It felt wrong to lift the lid without permission. There was the best collar of Nottingham lace, and a picture of Jesus healing the blind man which Will had crayoned when he was little. There was *The Young Housewife's Daily Assistant*, and Lady Harlaston's magazine, neatly wrapped in brown paper and un-examined since they left Hynton. And there was a bracelet of dried peas threaded on cotton, which Charity had made when she was eight.

Lastly she found a small parcel wrapped in nainsook that she had never seen before. She peeled away the covering to reveal an old-fashioned embroidered sampler: a block of Bible text exquisitely worked in tiny red and black cross-stitch.

'You can't never have children,' her mother had told her slyly the day before.

Charity had been out in the vegetable patch cutting a cabbage for their supper when her mother had drifted up like a thin grey ghost, startling her into snicking her finger on the paring-knife.

Mrs Fosdyke had clutched her daughter's arm and muttered in her ear, 'You can't never have *children*. You know that, don't you?'

'Why not?' Charity said shortly, sucking her finger. There were days when she was sick and tired of her mother's nonsense.

'*She* said so,' muttered Mrs Fosdyke. 'Parson's wife up village. She made me work it in stitching so I'd remember. She knew.'

'What did she know?'

'Come inside an' I'll tell.'

That had been yesterday.

Now Charity sat blinking at the black and red text on her lap. '*A bastard shall not enter into the congregation of the Lord; even to his tenth generation shall he not enter into the congregation of the Lord.*'

16 February 1903

The great blue heron regarded Charity with a narrow eye from the other side of Wadlands Dyke.

She leaned into the wind as she struggled up the lane, one hand on her hat, the other clasping her books to her breast. As she neared the crossroads, the heron spread its wings and lifted off, and rowed away across the sky.

On either side of the lane the bare fields unrolled their flatness to the horizon, transected by dykes which gleamed dull silver in the low winter sun.

She was fiercely cold. Her short cape whipped about her as if tugged by an angry child, and despite her gloves she couldn't feel her fingers. The wind had a bitter edge which promised snow by nightfall.

She was taking the long way home, as she had every day for the four months since her mother's death. She hated returning to the empty cottage. She hated the thought that, while she was inside, her mother lay unprotected in the frozen churchyard.

When my time comes, she told herself, they'll never bury me in the ground. They'll burn me like a pagan on a great hot blazing fire.

But she hadn't hesitated about staying alone in the cottage, and had forbidden Will to join her. What would he do out here? He was better off with the parson and his wife. It had been painful for both of them when they met at the funeral.

This country suited her. The bleakness. The loneliness. She wanted to see no-one, and she wanted no-one to see her.

Each morning she walked the four miles to Jericho and taught the three R's to a row of gaping infants,

504

and each afternoon she walked back, prolonging the journey for as long as the cold would allow.

Only in her dreams did life and feeling sometimes break through. Like last night, when she had dreamed of the Hall. A vivid, miraculous, heartbreaking dream. She had been standing on the emerald lawn looking up at the great house, and its enchanted turrets had floated above her and pierced the stars. Someone had freed all the stone lions from the roof. They came leaping down with great elastic bounds, lashing their marble tails like huge joyful cats as they raced across the park. Watching them break free, she had been exhilarated. But when she awoke her cheeks were wet with tears.

She never dreamed of Robert. There was no need. Sometimes she'd be digging in the vegetable patch, or chalking letters on the children's slates, when she'd be visited by a flash of memory as vivid as any dream. The way he narrowed his eyes when he smoked his cigars; his brown hand stroking the spaniel's ears.

The war had ended the previous spring, and he would have returned to England. She pictured him safe and well at the Hall: walking with Tully on Hynton Edge, or leaning down on his tall chestnut horse to talk to Will. They had not exchanged letters, nor had she returned to Hynton in the hope of seeing him. She was proud of that. Her mother would be at peace.

But there were other times – like today, when the dream had left her raw and restless with longing and the sky was limitless around her – when she felt that everything might have turned out differently. At such times it seemed that all things were possible for those who had courage, and the true secret of life was that it was much, much simpler than people thought.

She wondered if Robert ever felt the same. She wondered if there wasn't some way for them to be together.

She hated feeling like this. It ploughed up the calm surface of her existence and threw unanswerable questions to the surface. The brutal truth was, she had no idea if Robert thought as she did, or what he would feel if he ever learned what her mother had revealed the day before she died.

She reached the cottage and stopped in the vegetable patch to cut a bunch of kale for supper. Then, with the kale balanced precariously on her books, she elbowed open the latch and went in, and found Robert standing by the hearth.

He watched her enter the cottage with her arms full of books and some kind of greenery piled on top.

Her face was thinner than he remembered. Whatever she had been through over the past two years had refined her features and burned away the last traces of girlishness.

There had been times when he had almost hoped that his feelings would have changed. Now he needed all his self-control not to take her in his arms.

She deposited the books and the greenery on the table and looked at him, her eyes blank with shock.

'I startled you,' he said, 'I'm sorry. The door was unlocked.'

She fumbled at the neck of her cape and took it off, and laid it over the back of a chair. She was wearing a high-collared mourning-dress of plain black. Black suited her. It made her look taller, and brought out the straight-backed dignity he had always admired.

'I came as soon as I found out where you were.'

For a long moment she searched his face. Then she said in a low voice, 'We agreed not to see each other.'

'I had to know you're all right.'

She took off her hat and gloves and smoothed her hair. Her hands shook. 'I'm all right.'

Which was manifestly absurd, given the state of this appalling little hovel. Patchy clay walls streaming with damp. A floor of black earth scattered with reeds. So cold that his breath steamed.

He said, 'Shall I light a fire? It's freezing in here.' Without waiting for an answer he knelt before the tiny grate and took a block of peat from the basket.

She seemed perplexed to see him on his knees. 'Let me do that.'

'I can manage.'

'But it isn't—'

'If I can get this going, you could make some tea.'

'I – I don't have any milk.'

'That doesn't matter.'

'You prefer it with milk.'

Their eyes met and his heart leapt, for he thought she would smile. Then she said, 'How did you find me?'

'I asked Will.'

'Oh, you shouldn't have done that.'

'I know.'

'You shouldn't have come.'

'That', he said with force, 'is easy for you to say, but quite impossible for me to carry out.' He paused with a block of peat in his hand. 'I'd heard nothing about you for over two years. No-one would tell me anything. My God, the number of times I nearly wrote to you!'

She put the kettle on the hob, then sat down on one of the rickety chairs, smoothing her skirt over her knees. Her fingers were red, her wrists raw-boned and boyish.

He pulled up a chair beside her. 'No-one told me you'd moved away. You can't imagine the shock when I found another family in the end house. It was as if you'd never existed.'

'Didn't Sam tell you?'

'Sam? I haven't seen him. After we got out of hospital he went back to his platoon and I was seconded to another regiment. When the war ended he went home and I was ordered to Natal. But surely he told you all this?'

'I haven't seen him either. I thought you'd been back in England for over a year.'

'My ship docked five days ago.' He watched her take that in. Then he said gently, 'I need to know how it's been for you. Will told me about your – scene – with Gwendolen Bowles. I need to understand why you told her. And how it's been for you since then.'

She shook her head. 'Why I told her? How can I tell you that? I don't understand myself.'

'Please. Try.'

She studied the first licking tongues of fire. 'Did you ever play hide-and-seek as a child? Do you remember how it felt when everyone else had been found and you were the last one left? You're alone and scared, and in the end you just want to stand up and say, here I am, and get it over with.'

'So you got it over with.'

She gave a slight smile. 'I did indeed.'

'What happened then?'

'I don't want to talk about it.'

'Why not?'

'It'll only make you angry.'

'You're stubborn!'

Again she gave a slight smile. 'I have to be.'

The fire crackled and spat. A faint warmth stole through the cottage. Rain rattled the windows and dripped into a tin pail by the bed.

The entire cottage was smaller than his own gun-room, and a good deal lower: on entering, he had cracked his head dizzyingly on a cross-beam. The only furniture was a cot-bed (neatly covered with a patchwork coverlet), the two chairs by the fire, an old tin trunk, and the table with the books and the pile of greenery. Compared to this, a Boer farmhouse was a veritable palace.

He could contain himself no longer. 'My God, Charity, this *place*! *Why* didn't you ask me for help?'

Two spots of colour appeared on her cheeks.

He reached for her hand. Her fingers were cold and worryingly thin.

'Why did you come?' she asked.

'I missed you. You can't imagine how much.'

'Yes I can.'

'I came to take you away from here.'

She took her hand from his and got to her feet. 'And where would you take me? Where they'd call me those names again?'

'That's not what I—'

' – where I'd be your "fancy piece"?'

'You know that's not what I mean.'

'Then what do you mean?' Once again she searched his face, and he had a strange feeling that she was seeking something which she knew she wouldn't find. Then her features contracted and she turned away. She crossed her arms about her waist, and he saw with pity and unease the sharpness of her shoulder-blades. He was on the point of going to her and taking her in his arms when the kettle whistled.

Without turning round, she said, 'I'll make the tea. Then I'll tell you something about myself.'

CHAPTER THIRTY-SEVEN

'My God, Charity, this *place*!'

He was right, of course. And seeing him here, so effortlessly elegant in his tweed riding-jacket and breeches and top-boots, only made it worse.

Why, she thought, must he be so graceful in everything he does? Sitting there cradling the chipped enamel mug as though he always takes his tea this way.

Even the things he had cast upon the table – the mackintosh, cap, gloves, and riding-crop – seemed to possess an incongruous glamour.

I'll tell him everything, she thought. Once he knows, it'll be easier for both of us. For then it really will be impossible, and I can put aside these ridiculous notions once and for all.

She poured her own tea and sat down. 'I need to tell you something. It's important. It makes a difference.' Beside her, she sensed him become very still.

'My mother died last year,' she began.

'Will told me. I'm sorry.'

She nodded. 'It was sudden. I was outside and I heard a chair go over. She was only thirty-nine.'

'You miss her.'

'More than I expected. She was—' she paused. 'She was a difficult woman. But sometimes I'd catch a glimpse of who she might have been if things hadn't gone wrong.' Again she paused. This was harder than she thought. She would have to fix her eyes on the fire and not look at him until she reached the end. 'From when I was little, she used to warn me about her Cousin Ruth. "You behave, now," she'd say, "or you'll end up like Cousin Ruth." Cousin Ruth, who went to the bad.'

'*The Sybarite's Reward.*'

'You remember that? For years she wouldn't tell me *what* Cousin Ruth had done. Not until three years ago, the year I met you.'

He waited for her to go on.

'When Cousin Ruth was seventeen, she had a child out of wedlock, and disappeared. She was our Family Secret. My mother lived in terror – real terror – of anyone finding out. She was so ashamed. Then the day before she died, she told me the truth. There *was* no Cousin Ruth. My mother was Cousin Ruth. She was so horrified when she realized she was going to have a child that she couldn't even tell my father. She let him go away to look for work without telling him, and when he came back she was gone. He only found out about me when I was two. Of course he married her, but by then the damage was done. She'd lied to everyone. She lied to the midwife when I was born so it wouldn't show on the birth certificate, and she told everyone she was a widow. My father had to pretend he was her second husband. And because of the lies she thought she was a criminal. She lived in terror of the police coming to arrest her. And I never suspected.' She glanced down at her lap. 'So you see, on top of everything else, I'm a bastard.'

The fire crackled and spat. Rain beat at the windows.

She stole a glance at him. He was watching the fire, his face unreadable. At last she said: 'Why don't you say something?'

He shook his head.

'I told you it would make a difference,' she said. 'Or maybe I'm already so far beyond the pale that this can't make it any worse.'

'Don't say that.'

She studied his face. 'Do you know what "ruth" means? I do. I looked it up. It means compassion and remorse. For my mother it only meant remorse. She lived her whole life in remorse. She was blasted by it. And for *what*? For one sin, committed when she was little more than a child! For something which happens up and down the country, and to which so many people turn a blind eye. I've thought about that a lot since she died.'

He turned the mug in his fingers. 'What are you trying to say?'

'Sometimes I think life wasn't meant to be this complicated, and it's only us who make it so. Was *anything* worth the lifetime of fear she went through? What would it have mattered if they'd *never* married?'

What would it matter, Robert, if *we* never married?

He was trying his best to follow her, but she could see that he did not, and suddenly she realized that the impossible notions she had dreamed up in her loneliness were simply that: impossible notions. He would never leave Harlaston to be with her. He could not. It had never occurred to him to try. Harlaston had possessed him since he was a boy, and was too powerful to escape. Desolation opened up before her. Until that moment she hadn't realized how much she had relied on this hope to sustain her.

He placed the mug on the floor and leaned forward and took her cold hands in his own. 'You're very tired', he said softly, 'and hungry and cold. You must come away from this place. I can't leave you here.'

'And what would you do?' she said wearily. 'Set me up in some pretty house at a discreet distance from the Hall, so that I may become what all of Hynton already believes me to be?'

'That's not what I meant.'

'I know. But it's how it would be.'

He did not reply.

'Think, Robert, how should we go on? With you slipping out from the Hall every now and then to visit me?'

'Don't talk like that.'

'If you'd wanted that sort of arrangement you'd have done it long ago. But I don't think you ever have.'

'I spoke without thinking. I'm sorry. There's a simpler way. I'll open an account for you. It'll be entirely at your disposal. We need never meet. We need never even correspond if you don't want to. My attorney shall handle it all.'

'You know that's impossible.'

'You needn't even tell me where you are. But at least I'll know that you've a roof over your head which doesn't leak.'

'I can't take money from you.'

'Why not?'

'Because I can't.'

He went to the window and looked out at the rain. 'Why must you be so perverse?'

'I'm not. Try to understand. To everyone in Hynton I'm already a lost woman, but *I* know they're wrong. If I took your money I would be.'

He shook his head.

'It's all I've got left, Robert.'

So why, she thought, would it be any different if he left Harlaston and we went away together, to some far place where nobody knows us? I'd still be taking his money – so why would it be any better? Perhaps the answer was that, if they went away together, the difference between them would no longer be so immense. She would be giving up her reputation, but he would be giving up the Hall, and in a strange way that might make it possible.

But why think of that now? It was never going to happen.

'So what is it you want?' he asked without turning round. 'You want me to leave you here in this horrible place and go back to my great, warm, ridiculously opulent house, where the lowest kitchen-girl is better treated than the woman I love, and that is to be the end, for the rest of our lives? No. It's unthinkable. I won't do it.'

'I won't be in this "horrible place" much longer. Soon I'll have my certificate. Then I can find a better position.' She tried to smile. 'Somewhere with a roof that doesn't leak.'

'Oh, how much better *that* makes me feel!'

'I had a letter from Mrs Bowles. I think she's sorry for how she behaved. She wants to help me find a position.' She wished he would turn and look at her. It would be terrible to waste their time together in anger.

'So you'd accept help from Gwendolen Bowles but

not from me. I don't understand. Why can't you accept my help? Don't you trust me?'

'You *do* understand. You don't want to, but you do.'

He was shaking his head. 'I can't do this. I need you.'

Charity stood up and went into his arms. She put her forehead on his breast and felt him tremble against her. They stood together for a long time.

He said: 'When I was in South Africa, I thought my feelings would have changed. I told myself that these things don't last.'

Her arms tightened about his waist.

He said: '*Why* didn't you write to me when all this happened?'

'You'd have tried to protect me.'

'And that would have been wrong?'

She raised her head and put her palm against his cheek, and he leaned against it. 'Promise you won't come back again.'

'I can't do that.'

She had a sudden vision of the days and months to come. Waiting and hoping and dreading that he would come again. The slow slide into what they both wanted and feared. And she realized that she must leave Jericho, and go as far away as she could. She said, 'We have to get this over with quickly, or I won't be able to bear it.'

He put his hands on her shoulders and held her at arm's length. 'You really mean this.'

She made no reply.

He released her and turned away, and put his hands on the sill. Then he went to the table and stood looking down at his belongings, as though wondering how they had got there. Then he picked up his long riding-mackintosh, came over to her and put it around her shoulders. It was heavy, and smelled of cigars and horses. 'This stays with you whether you like it or not. When spring comes you can sell it. It'll take you wherever you want to go.'

'It's raining. You'll be soaked.'

He picked up his crop and cap and gloves from the table. The bleakness in his face was unbearable. 'Goodbye Charity.'

A few minutes later, as she stood at the window with his mackintosh around her, she heard hoofbeats disappearing into the darkness. 'Goodbye, Robert,' she said.

What, thought Robert, dressing for dinner, did you honestly expect? Nothing is changed. It's exactly as it was in London. Except that having seen her in that dreadful place, you'll always remember her there.

Always. What does that mean? For the rest of your life? Twenty, thirty years? Dear God, I hope not.

Norton had brought in his clothes from the dressing room and was laying them out on the bed.

Robert had never given much thought to what he wore, but suddenly he was acutely conscious of the opulence of everything before him. All in the best possible taste, of course, and all sickeningly extravagant.

In the great tombstone fireplace a fire was burning brightly. Norton, that paragon among valets, always made sure it was well-stoked when his lordship came in from his bath. Especially on a freezing February evening when his lordship had arrived home soaking wet, having unaccountably mislaid his mackintosh.

It had a lining of woollen cloth, Robert recalled, which should at least provide some warmth. And he hoped to God that when she found the tie-pin slipped beneath the lapel she wouldn't try to return it. It wasn't a large pearl. She could hardly raise a serious objection. He wished savagely that it had been a diamond: a huge, vulgar, American millionaire's three-carat affair.

Norton was waiting by the door as if he expected some kind of response, and Robert realized he'd been asked a question. 'What is it?' he snapped.

Norton discreetly cleared his throat to register affront. 'Your lordship enquired whether there is an engagement this evening.'

'Did I. Well? I take it there is. There usually is. Are we dining in or out?'

'Out, my lord. Mr and Mrs Poynter at Lyndon Manor.'

Robert closed his eyes. 'When do we leave?'

'I believe, my lord, the carriage is ordered for eight o'clock.'

Robert took his watch from the chest of drawers and sprang the catch. Twenty past seven. 'Very well. I shall be in my study. Not to be disturbed. Is that understood?'

Again Norton cleared his throat, this time with an air of pained apology. 'Perfectly, my lord. However – '

'However *what*.'

'I understand that her ladyship greatly desires your lordship's presence in the Blue Drawing-Room.'

'Really?' Robert bit back a sarcastic comment. Since his return from South Africa, Violet had not been remarkable for desiring his presence. 'Well no doubt it can wait for thirty minutes.'

'My apologies, my lord, but I do not believe that to be the case. Her ladyship was most particular.'

Violet was waiting when he entered the Blue Drawing-Room.

With the exception of her own apartments, it was the only room in the house which she had adapted to suit her own taste. The furnishings were ice-blue damask, with spider-legged gilt chairs and a white marble fireplace of implacable simplicity. The only ornaments were eight untinted engravings of formal French gardens, and an enormous alabaster vase which was invariably filled with white amaryllis. The waxen petals reminded Robert of funerals.

His wife was seated on a sofa at the far end of the room. She looked magnificent. In fact, he noted dispassionately, she had never looked lovelier. Her aquamarine gown glittered with thousands of tiny crystal beads which lent a pearly glow to her marble shoulders.

He said, 'Maud Poynter must have snared an ambassador this evening. You look positively regal.'

She acknowledged the compliment with a slight inclination of her golden head.

He took the other end of the couch and leaned back, crossing his legs. 'I understand you desire my presence "most particularly".'

She fixed him with her incomparable green eyes and smiled. 'I merely wished to enquire about your afternoon, and whether you managed to entertain your mistress. Or should one put that the other way around?'

He studied her. If she was expecting him to turn pale with shock she would be disappointed. 'What gives you the idea that I have a mistress?'

She adjusted a fold of her gown. 'Some time ago I received a rather unsettling little note. It was of a very low kind, so I thought nothing of it. But then – ' Delicately, she let that remain.

'I see. And what do you want of me?'

'Why, an explanation. At the very least.'

'Then you'll be disappointed. You see, I've never had a mistress. Though God knows,' he added evenly, 'I've had cause, if any man has.'

A faint flush visited her porcelain cheek. 'What an extraordinary thing to say! How *can* you be so coarse!'

Robert laughed. He reached for the bell-pull.

'Why do you ring? I particularly wish us not to be disturbed.'

'We shan't be. At least, not by a glass of champagne. Would you care to join me?'

'Don't be ridiculous.'

'Thank you, Paige, a bottle and just one glass.'

They waited in silence while the champagne was duly brought and poured, and the doors were once again closed.

Robert thought: we are like two great cats circling each other. Why can't we say what we mean? He felt desperately tired. At last he understood what people mean when they speak of being sick at heart.

'Mrs *Bowles* and I', began Violet, emphasizing the name to show her disdain, 'believe it would be best if the creature were sent out of the county. A position has been found in a mining town somewhere in the north. Shall you object?'

'Of course I object. As will the lady in question, without a doubt. She is not afraid of making her opinions known.'

'Indeed. I have heard that can be an advantage in the practice of her profession.'

'And that', said Robert with a sharpness which brought the colour to his wife's cheek, 'is the sort of remark I'd expect from one of the practitioners of the profession to which you refer. You will withdraw it at once.'

'I will do nothing of the kind. How dare you speak to me like that!'

He tilted back his head and gazed at the ceiling. From now on, this was what his life would be. Sniping and silences and small spurts of violence. The aridity of the whole exercise appalled him. 'I merely want you to understand that you must leave her alone. And that you'll regret it if you do not.'

'Are you threatening me?'

'Yes. That's exactly what I'm doing.'

Their eyes met. She was the first to look away. He knew he had frightened her, but he had no choice. Charity had no-one to protect her but himself. 'Tell me,' he said, 'when did you receive this anonymous intelligence?'

'Last October.'

He was aghast. 'But – Violet. That was five months ago. Why didn't you mention it before?'

'I wished to be sure. And to be frank, I could not believe it. I could not *bring* myself to believe the – the creature's identity.'

'Why?'

She coloured at the baldness of his question.

'I see. It's the nature of the choice which offends you, rather than the fact that I made a choice at all.'

She regarded him with loathing, and he knew he was right.

He sighed. 'Violet, Violet. I haven't made you happy, have I?'

She flushed, as if he had addressed her in the most indelicate terms.

He went on: 'I used to feel so sorry for you—'

'*Sorry* for me?'

' – for your desperate need for approval. But you've gone far beyond being frightened of doing the wrong thing, haven't you? You do everything superbly. You don't need a husband any more.'

'How dare you speak to your own wife in such a fashion! If these are the manners you acquired in South Africa, perhaps you had better return there.'

'That's precisely what I was thinking.'

She threw him an impatient glance.

He got up and refilled his glass, and stood looking down at her. 'A few months ago, a friend of mine asked me to join him on an expedition to Ecuador. It sounded rather ill-conceived, so I turned him down. Now I think I'll find out if he still has a place for me.'

'That's absurd.'

'It is rather sudden, and for that I apologize.'

'What do you mean?'

'He leaves on the twenty-third.'

'Of this month?'

'Yes.'

'But that's next Thursday. You forget, on Saturday we go down to Wynburne for a fortnight.'

He was amused. 'I believe you're more exercised by the thought of missing an engagement than by the prospect of losing a husband.'

She raised an incredulous eyebrow. 'Is that what this is about?'

He considered her. 'Yes, Violet. I rather think it is.'

'You really are contemptible.'

'I should have thought you'd be glad,' he said tiredly. 'Without me you can remain as you've always been: beautiful, unapproachable, and unapproached. You'll lose nothing by this. In fact, you'll gain. Everyone we know will stand by you. You're so clearly the wronged party.'

Her bosom rose and fell. 'I warn you. If you go to her, I'll ruin you both. I'll ruin you *utterly*. And I'll never, *never* give you a divorce!'

'I never thought you would. But please understand, I'm not leaving you for her.'

She gave him a disbelieving stare.

'How could you imagine I'd put a woman I care for through the horror of contested proceedings? Or do you think I intend to dishonour her by the sort of arrangement you so readily believe already exists?'

'Ah, so you *have* thought of it!'

'Well of course I have! I've thought of little else for the past two years!'

She leaned back, appalled at his violence. 'I don't believe a word of this,' she stammered. 'But even if it were true, what is it you intend to do?'

He rubbed his temple. 'That's a matter of profound indifference to me. I only know that I shan't stay here.' As soon as he said it, he knew he would never stay at Harlaston again. It had become impossible for him. Hynton Wood, the village, the end house. The memories were too strong. He had a sudden vision of Charity's face: her warm brown eyes searching his. 'I shall travel,' he said. 'Perhaps I'll try to atone for my sins. That ought to keep me occupied for a good many years.'

She tossed her head in scorn. 'You have consumed

the better part of a bottle of champagne. You are perfectly disgusting. I cannot imagine what the Poynters will say.'

Robert laughed. 'How very like you to bring me back to what really matters: our dinner engagement! And you're quite right to remind me. Time is indeed pressing. I have, let's see – ' he drew out his watch – 'eleven minutes to pack a valise before they bring the carriage.'

'Whatever do you mean?'

'You'll be passing by the railway station on your way to Lyndon Manor. I should just manage to catch the last train for London.'

Realization finally dawned. 'You really mean to leave me.'

'Yes, my dear, I really do.'

'That's impossible.'

'It'll be impossible tonight, unless I make haste.'

'But whatever shall I tell the Poynters?'

Robert raised his glass to her and drained it in a silent toast. 'Anything you like.'

CHAPTER THIRTY-EIGHT

Late August, the Present

On Monday morning Sarah started for London.

The previous evening she had finally left a message on Alex's answerphone telling him she would be leaving Harlaston the next day. He had not called back. Maybe he was busy tracking down Clare and sorting out who would take charge of Stephen. Maybe he thought there was no point in contacting her. After all, she was only following his advice.

She took her time loading the car, and kept the front door open in case the phone rang. Then she had a last mug of coffee in the Long Gallery and said goodbye to Robert.

At ten o'clock she called her friend Sally and told her there had been a change of plan. She would move the bulk of her belongings to Sally's flat, but keep back her files and a holdall as she needed to spend one last night at the Hall. There were some loose ends she hadn't had time to tie up. 'Loose ends,' said Sally, wisely refraining from comment. 'Right. Whatever you say.'

Having bought herself a reprieve, Sarah called the rectory. Stephen answered. He sounded breathless, as if he had run for the phone. No, Alex wasn't around. He had gone off in the car while it was still dark, and left a note saying he wouldn't be back till later. Swallowing her disappointment, Sarah told him she was going to London to read Robert's will, and did he want to come? A pause. He *would*, but Alex had promised to take him to the old leper hospice at Market Upton, which he'd been wanting to see for *ages*, so he'd said yes. Fine, said Sarah. Tell Alex she'd be back in the evening after all, and enjoy the leper hospice.

It was a beautiful morning: crisp and clear, with the elegiac feel of early autumn. As she left the carriage-drive, Harlaston rose behind her in the rear-view mirror. Magnificent and remote, and already slipping back into the past. She wiped her eyes with her fingers and switched on the radio full blast.

She made good time and arrived at Sally's flat in Bloomsbury shortly after two. A neighbour let her in, helped carry her bags upstairs, and handed her a note from Sally, with a Fee Sheet from the Probate Search Room. Then she took the tube to the records office on High Holborn.

She hadn't been there since it had re-located from splendid old Somerset House to a modern office block, but the impact of the main record room was still overwhelming. The tall, thick burgundy ledgers filling the bookshelves. Hundreds of thousands of finished lives, neatly noted down in double columns.

She handed in the Fee Sheet which Sally's researchers had completed on Friday afternoon. The clerk told her it would take five minutes or so to locate the will. She knew she was incredibly lucky to be able to see it so soon. Usually it took at least a week to retrieve an original from storage. Sally's researchers had performed miracles through their network of unofficial contacts.

But, now she was here, she didn't want to go through with it at all. Seeing the will would be so stark. So final.

Reluctantly, she went to one of the bookcases and scanned the spines of the more recent ledgers. It would be horrible to find him in one of these great clinical books, but she knew she had to do this, to start making it a reality.

The volume entitled '*WILLS & ADMONS 1917 L-P*' was thicker than most, but it took her no more than a minute to find his name. '*Pearce-Staunton, Robert Percival D'Authon, Nineteenth Baron, on active service in France on 27th November 1917. Probate: London, to Violet Florence, widow.*' There followed a bald statement of his total effects in pounds, shillings, and pence. It was not a large fortune – but then, Sarah reminded herself, most of the money had been Violet's. And under the marriage settlements of the time, Violet's fortune would not have been Robert's to dispose of on his death.

Slowly she closed the ledger and put it back on the shelf. She stared out of the window, into a deserted side-street. A bicycle chained to a railing. A cellophane sandwich carton, discarded in the gutter.

Five minutes later, she was sitting at a table in the middle of the room with the original will before her. She untied the green ribbon that bound it up. Once released, the springing cream-coloured pages would not lie flat.

Robert's vivid black signature sprawled across the bottom of the last page. Bold, clean strokes, with an idiosyncratic energy all their own. Underneath he had written the date: 7 September 1908.

It was a very brief will: clear in its language and simple in effect. To his wife, Violet Florence Pearce-Staunton (née Redfearn), he had left such of his personal property at the Hall as she wished to keep, but nothing else. The estate itself was to be sold, and the proceeds divided in three equal parts. One third went to the St Francis Hospital-School for Orphans, Frankfort, Orange Free State, South Africa; one third to his son, Julian Spencer D'Authon; and one third to Charity Elisabeth Fosdyke. Should Charity predecease him, her third was also to go to their son. The final paragraph ended with a brief stipulation that his remains were to be cremated, and his ashes buried with Charity's on her death.

It was the classic division prescribed by medieval tradition: one third to the widow, one third to the issue, and one third for 'the soul's part', for its salvation. Robert, who had read History at Oxford, would have known about that. The only departure from tradition was that in this case the 'widow' was not Lady Harlaston, but Charity Fosdyke.

Across the table from Sarah, a middle-aged man pulled back a chair and threw down a tattered cardboard folder stuffed with papers. He had a doughy disapproving face, and scowled at her when she looked up. Amateurs, his expression seemed to say, should stay away from the search room if they couldn't handle it without crying.

You are *perverse*, she told herself savagely as she started the drive back to Hynton. You spend the whole summer hoping you'll find something like this, and when you do, you feel like the world's come to an end.

She felt terrible. She wanted to put back her head and howl. It was like the withdrawal symptoms she underwent when a feature she'd been steeped in for months was at last nearing completion. It was like the end of a love affair.

It wasn't *enough* to prove that Robert was her grandfather. It wasn't *enough* to know that he had loved Charity – that he had loved her so much that he'd wanted to be buried with her, and had said so in a public document for everyone to see.

'But *why* is it so important for you to find out?' her mother had asked when they'd been drinking wine in the conservatory. 'Surely it doesn't matter *how* your dad came into the world? So *what* if it was a backstairs fling! So *what* if it was the affair to end all affairs. The important thing is that he was loved, and he grew up happy. And he did, you know, he really did. What are you trying to do, love, reinstate him? Wipe away the stain of illegitimacy?'

That had brought Sarah up short. In the beginning, she *had* wanted to reinstate her father. But she had ended by wanting to reinstate Robert, too.

And now she had done it. She had proved that he wasn't the casual philanderer of family legend. She had got closer to him than she had thought possible. Just close enough to realize how far away she would always be.

She thought of the pensive, unsmiling face in the portrait. It wasn't the face of a man who could 'make his own contentment', as Mrs Favell had put it. It was the face of a man with too great a capacity for being haunted by his ghosts. Perhaps that was why he had needed someone like Charity: the warm, resilient woman of the postcard.

She wondered when he had left India and caught up with Charity in France; how long they had stayed together before he went back to India; whether they had been happy. She would never know. All she did know was that he had loved Charity Fosdyke, and had given their son as much of his name as he could, without letting scandal sour his life. She knew that the Bad Fairy of Holt Place had got it wrong.

Suddenly she felt enormously tired. All she wanted was to get back to Harlaston and switch off the phone and have a drink. Probably several.

As she left London behind, the traffic thinned, and she made good time. Her decision to take the A1 instead of the motorway looked like the right one. But just outside Peterborough she ran into a roadblock. An articulated lorry lay on its side surrounded by police cars, an ambulance, and a set of temporary traffic lights.

To cheer herself up she turned on the radio, and a newsflash announced the death of a much-loved film star who had flown his twin-seater into a mountain. She turned off the radio. The day had begun in brilliant clarity but was swiftly clouding over. A dank early twilight was already descending.

Waiting for the lights to change, she became aware that the car in front of hers was a hearse. Through the window she made out a mound of what her mother called floral tributes. The most distinctive was a three-foot wreath of yellow rosebuds packed together to spell a name. She could make out an 'E' and a 'D', followed by either an 'I' or maybe a 'W'. Edith? Edward? Edwina?

She had progressed to 'Meredith' when something floated to the surface of her memory. Something was wrong. It didn't take her long to work out what.

Robert's will had stipulated that he should be buried with Charity. But according to all the guidebooks, he was down in the Pearce-Staunton mausoleum with his wife.

Had that been deliberate, or simply an oversight?

Another thought struck her. She rummaged in her bag for her notebook and turned to the text of the biblical reference inscribed on Robert's memorial tablet. Stephen's school Bible had translated it as: '*If I have no love I am nothing*.' But if her hunch was correct, a different translation gave it a completely different meaning. And if *that* was right, then the conclusion was inescapable. Violet had coldly and deliberately ignored her husband's last wish.

And that, thought Sarah, would be horrible.

For the past six weeks, St Hybald's had had a new sexton. In the first flush of his reforming zeal he had placed ruby-coloured night-lights on either side of the altar, and set them to come on promptly at half past seven.

They had been on for some time when Sarah reached the church. Outside, the sky glowed with the deep blue of an August twilight.

She didn't feel like turning on the overhead lights. Instead, with the aid of a candle from the repository on the wall, she found what she was looking for in a cardboard box under the table: a maroon clothbound copy of the Authorized Version. She took the Bible and the candle up the nave and sat in the front pew nearest the pulpit. She quickly found the text she was looking for. She had been right. The passage in the Authorized Version *was* different from Stephen's modern version. It was exactly as she remembered it from school.

The night was fine and still. Around her the dust of the old church settled sorrowfully on her discovery.

Oh, *Violet*. How *could* you?

Behind her in the porch, the door creaked. A man's footsteps echoed on the flags.

Alex came up the nave towards her. He stopped a few paces away. 'I thought you'd gone,' he said. It was too dark to see his expression, but he sounded startled.

She said, 'Didn't Stephen give you my message?'

He shook his head.

'I didn't have time to sort out my files, so I decided to come back and do it tomorrow. And I haven't had the heart to tell him I'm leaving, so I'll have to do that too.'

He sat in the pew across the nave from her, leaned back and shut his eyes. 'Did you find the will?'

'Yes.'

'And?'

Briefly she told him.

He turned his head to her. 'So now you know.'

'As much as I ever will.'

'Is it enough?'

She looked down at the Bible in her lap. 'No. You knew it wouldn't be, didn't you?'

'I wondered.'

'Well. You were right.'

He closed his eyes again, and she studied his profile in the candlelight. He looked tired. He had probably spent much of the day on the phone. She said,

'Dominic doesn't really want Stephen to live with him, does he?'

'I doubt it,' he said, without opening his eyes. 'Though he's not admitting it. As a boy he liked to drop pebbles into ponds and watch the ripples. Some things never change.'

'How wide are the ripples this time?'

'Pretty wide, as it happens. When I talked to Clare, she said she hasn't exactly told Dominic to go to hell.'

'*What?* I thought she hates Stephen spending time with him!'

'So did I. But she's caught up in the pace of things in Frankfurt, and enjoying being the centre of attention over here. Lots of agonized little chats with Dominic on the phone.'

And, with you too, thought Sarah sourly. I'll bet she just loves those.

'And, of course,' he went on, 'she's thoroughly enjoying winding up Caroline, who's the only one who's come clean and said she definitely *doesn't* want an instant family, not even for a month.'

'What are you going to do?'

He shrugged. 'Wait for them to come to their senses. Clare will when she realizes what this is doing to Stephen. Dominic will when he realizes that Caroline means what she says – and, more to the point, that her father means it too. Dominic won't risk losing her for a bit of mischief.' He rubbed a hand over his face, and Sarah wondered how she could ever have thought he wasn't good-looking.

He turned his head and caught her watching him. 'What brought you in here?'

'Oh.' She ran a thumbnail along the spine of the Bible. 'Something occurred to me on the way home. It wasn't particularly cheerful, so I thought I'd find out straight away if it's true.'

He gave her his enquiring silence, so she repeated what the will had said about Robert's ashes. 'It was a short will for its time, so I thought if he'd bothered to put it in at all, it must have been important to him. And that's the horrible thing. It didn't happen the way he wanted.'

'What do you mean?'

'Violet wouldn't let it. He's buried with her – with Violet – in the mausoleum. She said in *her* will that they should be together, and they are, it says so in the guidebook. I remembered it while I was driving home. And I bet she made bloody sure that her cousin Aubrey obeyed her to the letter. Who knows, maybe that's why she left him all her money.' She drew a shaky breath. 'So Robert's down there in that "horrid stinky old crypt", as Stephen calls it, with a wife he didn't love, and Charity's out in the open air among the trees.'

Alex opened his mouth to speak but she didn't give him the chance. '*Don't* tell me it's just ashes and it doesn't matter. I *know* that. But it *does* matter. Because it mattered to him. And that's not the worst of it. What makes it *so* much more horrible is the reference on his tablet up there on the wall, the one Violet put up when he was killed. All this time I've been reading it wrong. I thought it meant: "*Without love I am nothing.*" I thought it was just a standard thing for a wife to say. I was wrong. That's only how it reads in the modern translation. Just now I looked it up in the Authorized Version.' She opened the Bible and read: "'*Though I speak with the tongues of men and of angels,* and have not charity, *I am become as sounding*

534

*brass, or a tinkling cymbal. And though I have the gift
of prophecy, and understand all mysteries, and all
knowledge; and though I have all faith, so that I could
remove mountains,* and have not charity, I am nothing.
*And though I bestow all my goods to feed the poor,
and though I give my body to be burned,* and have not
charity, it profiteth me nothing." Do you see? It was
Violet who had that tablet made. *"If I have not
charity, I am nothing."* She had that horrible vindictive
little pun cut in his own bloody memorial stone. She'd
kept them apart, and she wanted everyone to know it.
Christ, how she must have hated him! It's the most
desolate, lonely thing I've ever heard. Why do people
do these things to each other? Why do they do it to
themselves?'

They sat in silence. Then Alex said, 'I'm sorry. This
wasn't the best way to spend your summer.'

She gave him a strained smile. 'There you go again,
blaming yourself. I told you not to do that.'

'Oh yes, so you did.'

Another silence. He seemed about to say something,
and for one wild moment she thought he was going to
ask her not to leave tomorrow: please, Sarah, don't go,
I need you. But in the end he just got to his feet and
said, 'Come on. Let's get out of here. You need a drink
and so do I.'

Suddenly she wanted to cry, or put her arms around
him and bury her head in his chest, and hear his heart
beat. She stood up and the Bible slid off her lap onto
the floor. 'I can't,' she said shakily. 'I've got to sort out
my files.'

'D'you want any help?'

She shook her head.

'Right. Well, then – '

'Alex – '

Quickly he turned.

'I have to tell Stephen – I mean, that I'm leaving. Could you send him over tomorrow?' She pressed her lips together and tried to smile. 'And I'll have to tell him about the will, or he'll never forgive me.'

He looked puzzled. 'Doesn't he already know?'

'Well, no, I haven't spoken to him since this morning.'

'This *morning*?' He went very still.

'I called to leave a message for you. We'd sort of agreed that he'd come to London with me, but he said he'd already arranged to go to the leper hospice.'

'He changed his mind,' he said blankly. 'He left a note. He said he was taking the bus to Grantham.'

'Wh-at?'

'He was meeting you there and you were going by train to London to avoid the traffic.'

Their eyes met.

'Jesus Christ,' they said.

CHAPTER THIRTY-NINE

Forty minutes later, Alex had rung the police, Grantham railway station, six of Stephen's schoolfriends' mothers, the vicar, and the bat sanctuary. He had failed to get hold of Clare, and left messages all over Frankfurt. After several attempts he'd reached Dominic – who was only too ready to vent his spleen on his brother.

'It's not your fault,' said Sarah as they sat bleakly in the sitting room.

'Of course it is,' snapped Alex. 'A child in your care goes missing, it's your bloody fault.' He picked up his keys from the desk. 'I'll go and check the lanes.'

'I'll stay by the phone.'

'There's no point, Sarah. The answerphone's on. Go home. I'll call you if anything happens.'

Sarah went.

Letting herself into the Hall, she half expected to find Stephen on the Sandalwood Staircase. It would be just like him to pick Harlaston as a bolt-hole.

She started checking the downstairs rooms, leaving a trail of blazing lights behind her. The Hall had never seemed so empty or so vast.

She told herself to concentrate on what she was

doing, but images seeped relentlessly into her mind. Stephen tottering down an alleyway, menaced by crack addicts and pimps. Stephen's small stocky body lying in a crumpled heap among used needles and condoms. People all over the country shaking their heads at his school photograph smiling from the front pages of the papers: '. . . *hope is now fading for ten-year-old Stephen Hardy who was last seen leaving his uncle's house in the village of Hynton on Monday morning . . .'* '*Police have found a body believed to be that of . . .*'

'Oh *God. Please* let him be all right.' She was wringing her hands like an actress in a silent film. It's true, she thought distractedly. People really do that.

After two hours she had searched the whole of the ground floor, all the outhouses, and the Science Complex. Not a trace of him anywhere.

She went upstairs to the bursar's office to call Alex, and found Stephen asleep in an armchair.

'You left the window open in the conservatory,' he said defensively.

Shakily she slumped into a chair. 'Where the *hell* have you been?'

He blinked. 'I was going to see Daddy. I got as far as Grantham but I didn't have enough money for the train so I came back again.'

'When? When did you come back?'

'Ages ago. I wandered round town for a bit, but I didn't have enough for a film either, so I got the bus back but Alex wasn't in and I'd forgotten my key so I came here but you weren't in either so I thought I'd better just wait.'

'*Jesus*, Stephen! Alex wasn't in because he was looking for you!'

He swallowed.

'Why the *hell* did you do it? I thought you had more sense than to run away from home!'

'I didn't run away from home!' he said indignantly. 'I'm not stupid, I haven't got enough money to live by myself! I was going to see my father and sort things out.'

She studied him. 'You really are impossible. We've been frantic.'

He looked hopeful. 'Was Alex frantic too?'

'What do you think? He's out there now combing the lanes. And to make matters worse, Dominic gave him a bollocking on the phone.'

His face fell. 'But it wasn't Alex's fault.'

'Try telling that to your father.'

'Oh *Jeez*.'

'Exactly.'

Suddenly he was on the verge of tears. 'Why's everything the wrong way *round*! I wish Alex was my father.'

There was an awkward silence. Sarah said, 'I know you do. But he loves you just the same. So do I, come to that.'

After a while he stopped crying and wiped his nose with his fingers. 'You know,' he mumbled, 'you had the most rotten taste picking Dominic the first time.'

She gave a weak smile. 'I know. God, don't I know!'

'I mean, yesterday at lunch! It's like plonking down a Ladybird History next to a Penguin Classic.'

Sarah laughed and cuffed him on the back of the

head. 'Come on, you precocious little monster! Let's phone the Penguin Classic and put him out of his misery.'

Alex answered on the first ring, and she said simply: 'He's with me and he's fine.'

'Jesus. *Jesus.*'

'D'you want to talk to him?'

'No. Just bring him home.'

Alex was standing in the open doorway when they arrived. Behind him on the hall table was a tumbler half full of whisky. The fact that he had obviously forgotten about it impressed Stephen enormously.

Alex stood looking down at his nephew. 'Never, *ever*—'

'I won't,' Stephen said quickly. 'I promise. Honestly, for ever and ever. And I'm really, *really* sorry I got you into trouble.'

'What are you talking about?'

'With Dominic. Sarah said he gave you a bollock-ing.'

Alex glanced at Sarah, and started to laugh.

Later, Sarah poured herself a glass of wine and sat on the steps on the rectory porch. It was a warm night. A damp smoky tang rose from the wet leaves on the garden path.

Stephen was in bed. Alex was in the sitting room talking to the last of the schoolfriends' mothers on the phone.

She thought back to the night three months before when she had stormed down and announced that she couldn't possibly do this job and would be leaving in the morning. Alex had sat opposite her and listened in that casual way he had of eliciting confidences.

He hadn't tried to change her mind then, nor had he this time. He wanted her to go.

The door opened and yellow light streamed onto the flags. Alex came out and sat beside her on the step, nursing a whisky.

'Sorted?' she asked.

'Getting there. Clare's flying back and Dominic's giving up his Saturday on the links and driving down for the day.'

'What, both of them, down here?'

'Both of them down here.'

'Crikey. A summit meeting at the Old Rectory. They're going to love that.'

'Tough. It's time they thought about their son for long enough to work out what to do with him.' He turned and smiled at her with his eyes, and she felt a sudden uncomplicated rush of love for him.

'Knowing those two,' she said, 'the summit could get nasty. Especially with Caroline in attendance, which I assume she will be.'

'God knows.'

'I don't think Stephen should be around, do you? If you like,' she added cautiously, 'I could stay on for a few days and he could come to me.'

He fingered his glass. 'Thanks, but that's already sorted out. I've asked the bat sanctuary to keep him occupied. They jumped at it.'

'Oh. Well, good. He'll like that.'

'That's what I thought.'

She attempted a smile which didn't come off. 'You know, it's funny. I hated Harlaston to begin with, but now I can't bear to leave it.'

Alex looked at the sky. 'This will sound trite, but I think you'll feel better once you're back in London.

You need to put some distance between yourself and this place. All this business with Stephen and Dominic. It hasn't been the best way of helping you get over him.'

She opened her mouth to reply, but he went on quickly, 'I know you don't believe me, Sarah, but it's true. You need – ' he frowned ' – perspective.'

'Perspective. Right.'

He turned his head and their eyes met.

Now was her chance to tell him quite simply that Dominic was irrelevant. She didn't want to go because she didn't want to leave *him*, Alex. Because she loved him. But she couldn't say it. She couldn't risk seeing the dismay in his eyes as he wondered how to tell her. *Sarah, I'm sorry. I like you, but I don't love you. I thought you knew.* She just couldn't risk it.

'It's OK, Alex,' she said softly. 'I'll go quietly.'

For a while they drank in silence. Then he said, 'Are you all right for somewhere to stay? I've got a place in Highbury which I only use now and then. It's just a studio, but you can have it for as long as you like.'

'Thanks. But I'll be staying with a friend till the lease is up on my place.'

'Oh, right. It's good you've got that sorted out.'

She stood up. 'I'll be around tomorrow until about four. Could you send Stephen over?'

'Sure.'

'Well. Goodnight.'

'Goodnight, Sarah.'

By the time she got back to the Hall it was nearly midnight. She had eaten nothing all day, but was long past hunger. It felt as if weeks had elapsed since she went to London and read Robert's will. She sat on the Sandalwood Staircase for a while, then went upstairs

542

to bed. She couldn't sleep. She ended up having another drink and standing dry-eyed before Robert's portrait, wishing Alex would call and knowing he wouldn't, and cursing herself for not having the guts to call him instead.

The next morning she awoke with a thumping headache in the armchair in her study. Stiffly she unfolded her cramped limbs. Her face in the overmantel mirror had the creased look of a dog who's slept with his muzzle pressed against the side of his basket.

By tea-time she had put everything in the car except for a couple of files, and had wandered through the rooms saying goodbye. She had left the files till last, as Stephen was still going through them. Alex had told him at breakfast that she was leaving, and he had arrived soon afterwards, trailing after her like a small forlorn sheepdog. Eventually she hit on the idea of giving him her papers and telling him to read them critically in the light of Robert's will. Anything to make her feel less like a deserter.

It's for the best, she kept telling herself as she wandered about the grounds. I can see both of them whenever I like. I can come down for weekends.

She made two mugs of tea, tucked a packet of chocolate biscuits under her arm, and climbed the Sandalwood Staircase to where Stephen was poring over her files. He looked up warily at her approach. He had been crying, but would be mortified if she noticed.

They sat side by side on the stairs in self-conscious silence. Stephen worked his way through the biscuits and Sarah leaned back and contemplated the ceiling. Fat plaster putti swung from painted garlands, and

Father Time brandished his floor-plan and his wicked-looking scythe.

Beside her on the stair lay the photograph of her father. It was the last thing she'd removed when she cleared out her study. She picked it up and looked at the back. *St Francis Hospital-School, Frankfort, South Africa, 1903–53; Founder: RPDP-S.* Beneath it was a shield bearing an oak tree in leaf, supported by two dreamy-looking griffins, and entwined with a Latin motto on a fluttering scroll. '*Dum vivimus, vivamus.*'

She turned it over and looked at the picture, and her father smiled back at her with Robert's dark almond-shaped eyes. Her father, attending the fiftieth anniversary of the school *his* father had founded.

The cynical motto of the Pearce-Stauntons drifted into her mind: *Courage brings profit.* How different from the motto which Robert had adopted when he founded his little school, and which perhaps he had also adopted for himself. *Dum vivimus, vivamus. While we live, let us live.* The Pearce-Staunton achievement. Not such a bad legacy after all.

She shut her eyes and breathed in a dusty whiff of sandalwood.

I wish, she told Robert silently, I wish I *knew* how long you had with Charity. And whether you were happy. Even if it was only for a little while.

'If Lord Harlaston left two-thirds of his fortune to your father and Charity,' said Stephen through a mouthful of biscuit, 'why aren't you stinking rich?'

She opened her eyes. 'Death duties, blight, and my father's rotten choice of investments. Plus, most of the money was Violet's in the first place.'

'Yes but *he* had the estate.'

'But remember, he'd have spent quite a bit of his

own money when he founded the hospital in South Africa, and then when he bought the vineyard for Charity. And after he died and the estate was sold, it didn't fetch all that much. Especially not after death duties. Big places didn't in those days, they were a liability. And then—' She broke off, smiling and shaking her head.

'What?'

'Well, my dad wasn't exactly brilliant with money. It used to drive Mum wild. Just after the war – the Second World War – the vineyard went down with some kind of blight, and, instead of hanging onto it, he sold it for a pittance. And most of *that* he spent on our education. What was left, he lost on the stock market. So there you are,' she finished. 'That's why I'm not stinking rich.'

But Stephen's attention was already elsewhere. He was reading Sarah's notes at the end of the file. 'It says here that Lord Harlaston died in 1917. But it doesn't say how.'

She was silent for a moment. 'It was in the First World War. He'd gone to fight in France in 1915.'

'How old was he?'

'In 1915? He'd have been fifty.'

'Wasn't that a bit old to be a soldier?'

'I expect if you were a lord you could bend the rules. And by then they needed all the officers they could get.'

'But why would he *want* to bend the rules?'

'Well, in those days people thought it was their duty to fight for their country.'

He looked bemused. 'What happened then?'

She gazed up at the ceiling, and Father Time gazed impassively back. 'There was an enormous battle called Cambrai. It went on for days. The citation doesn't say very much about what happened.'

'What's a citation?'

'It's what they write about you when they give you a medal.'

'Oh.'

'All it says is that he was leading a patrol and there was a mix-up with the communications, so they walked straight into a German machine-gun post which they'd been told had been destroyed. He managed to get most of his men out safely, and disabled one of the guns, but then the other one turned round and started firing. He must have died pretty well instantly.'

Beside her, Stephen was silent.

After a while she glanced at his profile. He was scowling down at the file on his knees, his dark lashes casting spiked shadows on his cheeks.

I shouldn't have told him that, she thought. He isn't old enough to take it.

Still scowling, he looked up and said, 'You know, I think you're wrong about the ashes.'

She blinked. 'What?'

He heaved the file higher on his lap and flipped to a place he'd been marking with his finger. 'This photocopy from the 1935 book? It's a photo of Lord Harlaston's memorial.'

'Yes I know. So?'

'*So*. The Bible reference – the one you said Lady Harlaston put in about Charity? It isn't there.'

'*What?*' She took the file from him.

He was right.

'The only *logical* conclusion', he said, sounding

incredibly like his father, 'is that someone added the reference *after* 1935. And it couldn't have been Lady Harlaston because by then she was a recluse, and I bet she was past caring about things like that.' He beamed at her. He seemed to have forgotten all about being miserable.

'All right,' said Sarah slowly. 'But I don't see where you're going with this.'

He picked up a copy of the Authorized Version which had been lying beside him, and said triumphantly, 'The *brother* did it.'

'The brother.'

'William Fosdyke. My great-grandad.'

'You're saying that William Fosdyke put the reference on Robert's memorial about twenty years *after* it was made.'

He nodded.

'Why?'

'Because it doesn't mean what you *think* it means.'

She took the Bible from him and read the verses to herself. The second time around, understanding dawned. 'Without Charity I am nothing,' she murmured.

'*Exactly*,' said Stephen. 'Without Charity he's nothing, because he isn't *there*. He isn't *in* the mausoleum, he's outside, in the churchyard, by the ash tree, with *her*. The way they were meant to be.'

He was right. He had to be. And thinking about it, it would have been easy for William Fosdyke. He had trained as a stonemason and was always doing odd jobs around St Hybald's. No-one would have thought it unusual to see him pottering about in the mausoleum or the churchyard. So, sometime in 1938, he had simply removed Robert's ashes from the mausoleum, and placed them with Charity's, in her grave, by the south porch. Then, with a touch of bravado, he had added the reference to Robert's tablet.

A further thought struck her. 'Where's the bit in my notes where I copied down what's on Charity's headstone?'

'Ephesians chapter two, verse fourteen,' Stephen said promptly. 'I was just looking it up when you brought the biscuits.'

Crikey, thought Sarah. Another lawyer in the making.

She found Ephesians and read the verse to herself. She caught her breath. 'You're right,' she said, passing the book to Stephen. 'We could check the mausoleum to make sure but I don't think there's much point. Your great-grandad knew his Bible, all right.'

Stephen read aloud, and with growing understanding, what William Fosdyke had added to his sister's headstone: '*For he is our peace, who hath made both one, and hath broken down the middle wall of partition between us.*'

CHAPTER FORTY

18 May 1905, Dinan, Brittany

'*Dear Will,*' wrote Charity as she sat in the schoolroom taking detention. '*Last night, spring made a final bid for attention by flinging one of its more spectacular tantrums – which was downright churlish, in view of the Historical Society's picnic to the priory at St-Magloire. Another outing rained off, just like the last two we've attempted!*'

Frowning, she laid down her pen.

How peevish I sound. Like a disgruntled old spinster who got out on the wrong side of bed this morning.

But of course, she *had* got out on the wrong side of bed. Or rather, as she came sleepily downstairs at six o'clock, she had inadvertently trod on Amélie's paw and sent her shooting out into the garden, where she had sat lashing her tail under a gooseberry bush, refusing to come inside.

And I *am* a disgruntled old spinster, Charity thought, trying to make light of it.

'*Please don't think from the above*', she continued, '*that I didn't enjoy the outing! Luckily St-Magloire isn't more than a mile from town, so at the first*

raindrop we beat a dignified retreat to Maître L
Bihan's drawing-room, where Philomène (his house
keeper) rustled up hot poiré *and some of he*
wonderful langues de chat. As you may imagine, th
poiré *put everyone in much better spirits than the poo*
old priory would have done, and the party was ver
gay. It was six o'clock by the time I got back t
my house, by which time the storm was howling i
earnest, and Amélie was half-way up the parlou
curtains with fright. What a storm it was! One of ou
honest-to-goodness Breton tempests which makes one
so glad to be inside, and which no doubt Madame la
Comtesse would describe to her chère *Madame Bowles*
as being "the very mirror of her own tempestuous
soul" – that is, when the soul is safely ensconced in the
luxury of her own appartements!'

No, no, that's not right either, now I sound snide.
What's wrong with me? I *like* the countess.

She put down her pen and reread the letter from the
beginning. It struck her as falsely cheerful and annoyingly arch. 'The party was very gay'! What would Will
make of that? He would be worried, and would guess,
correctly, that she was going through one of her low
patches.

It was the first warm day of the year, and the storm
had left a clear sky of rain-washed blue. Through
the schoolroom window the wet rooftops of Dinan
gleamed like pewter in the sunshine. The rue de Jerzual
sloped steeply down towards the quayside, its cobbles
glistening. From her desk she could see a seagull
perched on the weathercock of St-Sauveur, and the
blue and white pennants fluttering gaily on the clock-
tower. Across the street, the mignonettes in M.
Pennec's window-boxes were brilliant with raindrops.

It was the sunshine which had put her in a temper. The onset of summer always brought on one of her dissatisfied periods, when nothing felt right and the smallest mishap reduced her to tears. Her pupils were well aware of her moods and had learned to be on their best behaviour when the weather turned fine, for then Mademoiselle Charité could be liberal with detentions.

To their cost, the three eleven-year-olds who sat at their desks sucking their pencils had forgotten about that, and each had earned an extra English composition for passing notes in class.

Gwenolée Damplesmes wrote steadily, her large freckled face bent close over her *cahier*, her hair a copper-wire halo in the sunlight. Of the three, she would finish first. Her English would be correct and uninspired, with an occasional flash of genuine feeling which she would probably cross out.

Augustine Vigeac would finish second, for she was practising the old trick of making her writing large to fill up the lines. Charity would let that pass, for she disliked the girl's sly ways, and had to stop herself from showing it.

The youngest, Madeleine Le Bihan, was scowling at the rooftops, her sallow elfin face tight with concentration. The story had taken over as it always did, and Charity knew that when the clock struck five she'd have to chase the child from the schoolroom. The title Charity had selected for the composition – 'helping Mother prepare dinner' – had been chosen for its romance-free content, but watching the flicker of emotions across the girl's face, she guessed that Madeleine had already widowed the mother and invited a mysterious gentleman to dine. She had just asked Charity how to spell 'swoon'.

Down in the street, M. Maurice was asking Mme Rinan how her brother-in-law was faring after his *syncope*. For a time they argued mildly about the merits of *tisane de romarin* and *tisane de genêt à balais*, then drifted imperceptibly to the proper cleaning of lampshades.

Charity became aware that Madeleine was gazing at her with speculative eyes.

Madeleine asked, '*Pourquoi n'êtes-vous pas mariée, Mademoiselle Charité?*'

Gwenolée and Augustine bent their heads and applied themselves to their *cahiers*.

'*Tais-toi, Madeleine,*' said Charity evenly, '*et finis ton travail.*'

'*Pardon, Mademoiselle, mais c'est pour mon histoire.*'

Charity returned her gaze firmly, and the child was chastened. But moments later she said cunningly, '*La belle veuve anglaise dans mon histoire, elle aussi est assez jeune encore, et le père de sa petite pupille, qui est veuf, est tombé amoureux fou d'elle . . .*'

Augustine gave a sly grin, and Gwenolée gaped at Madeleine's audacity.

'*Ça suffit, Madeleine!*' said Charity. What could one do with such a child? If she gave her another detention for impertinence she'd probably be delighted.

'*Elle va se remarier bientôt,*' muttered Madeleine contentedly. '*Le bel étranger va lui demander sa main juste après le café.*'

Charity glanced down at the half-written letter to Will. Perhaps she oughtn't to have mentioned the Historical Society picnic. Once or twice in his letters, Will had asked after Madeleine's father, Maître Le

Bihan, whom Charity had rashly described when she joined the Society the previous year. She had become sensitive to such casual-seeming enquiries, even from her own brother.

Glancing out of the window, she saw Mère Barbans toiling up the hill. Although the day was warm, the old lady had bundled herself up in half a dozen wrappers against the evils of the *courants d'air*. It was half past four, so she would be on her way to select her daily *tartelette aux myrtilles* from M. Gallouédec's in the place des Merciers.

Charity watched the old woman's slow progress. She thought: if things had been different, I'd be married by now. If Father had found a position at Stainton Hamer instead of Hynton, I'd be living in a cottage somewhere, with a husband, and children running about under my feet. Or maybe I would still have come to France, but I wouldn't be like this. For one thing, I'd have married Maître Le Bihan. I *ought* to marry Maître Le Bihan. He's a good man, and his little girl needs a mother. And I'm *twenty-four*. What's the good of a cat and a budgerigar at twenty-four? And a mackintosh folded at the bottom of my trunk which I still can't bring myself to part with.

She took up her pen and a fresh sheet of paper and drew an angry cat hissing beneath a gooseberry bush.

I wish, she thought savagely, it was forty years from now, and I was old and fat like Mère Barbans, with everything behind me and nothing to think about except my daily pastry and whether the neighbours will find out about my secret *coups de rouge* in the evenings.

If I was old, I'd have forgotten him years ago. I wouldn't still search through Will's letters for scraps of news about him. I wouldn't have long bitter arguments in my head with Lady Harlaston.

'*Vous êtes triste, Mademoiselle,*' said Madeleine. Her dark eyes were troubled.

'*Mais non, ma petite. Quelle idée!*'

'*Alors, en* ce *cas,*' persisted Madeleine with the logic of childhood, '*vous êtes heureuse.*'

Charity forced a smile.

Gwenolée and Augustine were ruling neat lines beneath their essays with undisguised relief. Charity dismissed them and told Madeleine to hurry up, as it was a nice day and she ought to be outside in the fresh air.

Madeleine cast her a frankly disbelieving glance. Unlike the other two, she regarded the outdoors as no more than an uncomfortable interlude between books.

When Gwenolée and Augustine had clattered down the stairs and the front door had slammed shut behind them, Madeleine plucked up her courage once again and asked, '*Mais* pourquoi *êtes-vous triste, Mademoiselle, quand il fait si beau aujourd'hui?*'

'*Mais* vraiment, *Madeleine, pour la dernière fois, tais-toi!*'

Three weeks earlier: 28 April 1905, Ravenna, Italy

Tom Nilsson, lounging among the plaster centurions, waited as he had waited all afternoon for his employer to descend from the upper gallery of the Accademia. Tom regarded the dying gladiator with a jaded eye, and thanked God he had been born an American.

Not that he didn't have a lot of time for Europe. In the past two years he had seen a great many splendidly done paintings and thousand-year-old churches. But always after a fortnight's trailing about he began to be overwhelmed by the weight of all that history.

Fortunately, their European 'holidays' rarely lasted more than a month, as his employer was a restless man. He never stayed in one city for more than a week, and his travel plans would have kept a small department at Thomas Cook's fully occupied. As it was, he made a fine old pile of work for one private secretary.

But Tom didn't mind. It suited him down to the ground. He had taken the position in order to see the world, and seeing it he was. And if he was more bemused than ever by Europeans, he was also more determined than ever to figure them out.

For Tom knew he wasn't destined to be a private secretary for long: no sir, he was destined to be a journalist. But he was shrewd enough to know that a realtor's son from Eureka, Idaho needed experience before tackling the Pulitzer Prize. So he had worked his way to London and hung around that Royal Society of theirs, attending whatever lectures they'd let him into and generally making himself agreeable, and eventually his diligence had been rewarded with a job.

He liked it just fine. And he liked his employer, for he was a wealthy man and a cultivated one, and Tom had a great deal of respect for both qualities.

At first, though, it had taken him a while to adjust to the man. Oh, he was generous all right, and easygoing, and almost American in his directness. Which made it all the more unnerving when he lapsed into what Tom had taken to calling a 'brown study'.

And that sense of humour! It was true what they said: the British liked their humour black. Why, Lord

Harlaston seemed to enjoy himself most when things were at their worst. Like the time in Ecuador when their guides ran off and left them stranded eight thousand feet up in a cloud-forest, with no food, no mules, and no idea of how to get out; just two canisters of beautifully labelled botanical specimens. Lord Harlaston had lit one of his cigars and offered one to Tom, and as they stumbled about in the forest in what they hoped was the right direction, he had talked so amusingly that Tom actually laughed. But at the same time Tom had got the uncomfortable feeling that his employer didn't give a damn about the outcome of their 'little jaunt' – although out of courtesy he'd probably do his best to ensure that at least his private secretary survived.

That was Lord Harlaston for you: at his best when things were worst, and in the darkest of moods when things were looking pretty bright to everyone else. That was when Tom had to tread most carefully: when his employer was in one of his brown studies. Most often he got like that when something had reminded him of his estate back in England. Once, Tom had dared to suggest that, as he missed it so much, maybe they should pay it a visit. That was the only time his employer had ever snapped at him, and Tom wouldn't be making the same mistake again.

Lord Harlaston was in a brown study now. He had been all afternoon. The elderly museum attendant had just waddled upstairs to check on him, and had come down shaking his jowls. The English *signore*, apparently, was still sitting just where they'd left him two hours before, in front of that statue – with his hands on his cane, so deep in thought that he might be a statue himself.

Tom yawned and stretched. He didn't mind. He could think of worse places in which to wait. The Accademia was housed in what had once been an old monastery, and the cloisters were built around a small quiet courtyard, with a fountain encircled by lemon trees. It was good to sit here and smoke a cigarette, away from all the clutter of the churches.

That was what made him sorry for Europeans. Over here things got so *cluttered*. Take this town, for instance. Ravenna. Nice enough little place. Friendly people, plenty of sunshine, pretty good food. And some fine solid buildings in nice plain brick. But there was just too damned *much* of everything. Centuries of the stuff, all piled up together. No space for a man to catch his breath.

Funnily enough, the only place he'd felt at ease was in the tiny thick walled church among the mosaics. They'd had an eye for colour, those Byzantines. Bright, unassuming primary colours: seaweed green, snow-white, blood-red, sky-blue. And good clear designs, simple and joyful. Dolphins and turtles in a wavy green sea; a deep blue sky scattered with golden stars; Jesus in a meadow, with a flock of sturdy sheep picking their way towards Him. What more could a man want?

Ah well. To each his own. If you were an American that sort of thing *spoke* to you. If you were a British lord, it apparently did not. Yesterday he had watched in surprise as his employer turned sharply away from the mosaics with every sign of irritation.

Still, who was he to complain? If Lord Harlaston didn't have the eye to enjoy something as straight-forward and happy as those mosaics, and instead preferred to sit for hours gazing at some marble knight, he was welcome to do so. Meanwhile, Tom would take his ease among the plaster centurions and enjoy the scent of the lemon trees in the sunlit courtyard.

The knight lay upon a bier, his helmeted head resting on a pillow of plain white marble. To Robert it looked as if his companions had only just carried him from the battlefield. The air still seemed to carry the bitterness of smoke, to ring with the cries of men and horses.

The knight's limbs had the doll-like awkwardness of a body rearranged by others. The hands were laid one upon the other on the hilt of his great sword. Someone had unbuckled his spurs and laid them by his ankles, where the straps had curled from the heat of his still-warm body. In death, the head had fallen slightly to one side, and the visor had been raised to reveal the face: the intense, exhausted, luminous face, which had held Robert's gaze since early afternoon.

The lips were slightly parted to reveal a glimpse of clenched teeth. The nostrils were flared: his final breath had been an intake. The flesh of the cheeks had just begun to settle. Above the great hooded eyes, whose lashes were still spiked with sweat, the brows were drawn together in a frown. Life had been painfully extinguished, after a struggle lost only seconds before. Moments ago, this was a man. He had shouted and fought alongside his companions – his companions who still cannot grasp that he is dead. Their disbelief is palpable: one feels it in the air. Surely, *surely* he isn't really gone? Surely the lashes will tremble, the parted lips will speak.

How extraordinary, thought Robert. I must have seen tens, perhaps hundreds of men die suddenly. Real, living, breathing men, whose names I knew, blown to pieces in combat. Yet it takes a four-hundred-year-old effigy to bring home the finality of death.

This man before me, whom Baedeker quaintly describes as '*a man of arts and counsel, beloved by all*', was killed at the age of twenty-six. The same age as Spencer when he died. At twenty-six he would have thought himself immortal. He must have thought there would always be time to fulfil his plans; and time for all the vague, half-formed intentions which haven't even matured into plans.

And suddenly there was no more time.

The end could come to *me* as suddenly as it did to him. It could come tomorrow. It could come to-day.

He was intrigued to find that he minded.

Why?

Could it be that, despite what he had been telling himself for the past two years, he still harboured some secret, unadmitted hope? That somehow, at some future time, everything would come right?

His reason told him it was impossible.

But *why* was it impossible? In the face of this vast finality before him, everything became wonderfully simple.

It really was extraordinarily simple. So much simpler than he had always thought.

His mind flashed back to the little cottage in the fens. Her face: pale, intense. Searching his own. Was *that* what she'd been trying to convey? Was that what he had signally failed to grasp? 'Sometimes I think life wasn't meant to be this complicated, and we're the ones that make it so . . . what would it have mattered if they'd *never* married?'

What a fool I've been, he thought, as the enormity of his mistake began to reveal itself.

For the past two years he might as well have been dead for all the good he'd done anyone, including himself. It would have amounted to the same thing if he'd simply handed the money to young Nilsson and said: here is so much for Peru and for South Africa, and so on, and so on; now get on with it, and leave me to sit quietly in this corner and grow cobwebs.

Was it really too late?

His hands tightened on the silver head of his cane. His pulse quickened.

Rationally, there could hardly be any doubt. Time would not have stood still for a woman like her. And she had been in France for over eighteen months. That much at least Will had thought fit to tell him, though the boy had become more reticent about his sister as he grew older.

She would be married by now. She must be. She was twenty-four. And if she were, then of course that was the end of it.

Strangely, however, that thought did nothing to lower his spirits.

Tom had tired of the courtyard and was smoking on the lawn in front of the Academia. A few yards away, a small boy in a sailor suit and an enormous straw hat played on the grass under the eye of his nurse.

According to the guidebook, the building next to the Accademia was the Basilica of Santa Maria in Porto: a fine, straightforward sixteenth-century affair on which the eighteenth century had slapped a horribly pompous façade of blue-grey marble. Even Tom could tell it was a mistake. Fat women tangled up in billowing drapes gestured wildly from over-decorated alcoves. Patience, Prudence, Charity, Hope. A hotchpotch of virtues, ugly enough to turn a man to sin.

The afternoon sun was hot, and the inside of the church looked invitingly cool. He was considering stepping inside when he saw his employer walking towards him across the grass.

Immediately Tom sensed a profound alteration. A clarity. A lightening.

'I'm afraid, my dear fellow,' said Lord Harlaston, 'I'm going to be eccentric again. We shall have to forego the Giottos of Padua. Will you mind?' He smiled at Tom's ill-concealed relief. 'We must go to Paris at once. Tomorrow if we can. I wonder if you'd make the arrangements.'

'Of course, my lord,' Tom said brightly, for he adored Paris. 'The usual hotel?'

'To begin with. But if all goes well we shan't need to stay for more than a few days.'

'Oh. And then – may I ask?'

'And then I'm not sure. It rather depends upon what we find out in Paris.' He lit a cigar and narrowed his eyes against the smoke as he watched the small boy tumbling about on the lawn. 'Somewhere in the Côtes-du-Nord, I believe.'

'But you're not sure where?' Tom couldn't keep the surprise out of his voice.

Lord Harlaston's lip curled. 'Not yet. I believe I shall have to hire someone to find out. Perhaps we can ask your fellow Americans to help.'

'My lord?'

'Pinkerton's. Isn't that their name? I gather they're rather good.'

Pinkerton's? Tom blinked. What was the man talking about?

Lord Harlaston's smile broadened into a grin. 'Don't worry, Tom, I haven't gone off my head just yet.'

Not so sure about *that*, thought Tom. If this is what sitting in front of a lump of marble does for a man, then Heaven preserve me from an interest in sculpture.

'I shall leave you to make the arrangements,' his employer said briskly. 'We'll dine at the hotel at, say, nine o'clock. And Tom – I mean it about Pinkerton's. You might send their Paris office a wire and arrange an appointment for as soon as we arrive.'

At this point Tom hazarded an enquiry about what his employer intended to do until dinner. Normally Tom took care not to be inquisitive, but he was becoming seriously concerned for his employer's health. He had heard that the onset of fever could bring on a radical change in spirits, and he felt it his duty to maintain a watch. Besides, he *liked* the man. And there was a brightness to Lord Harlaston's eyes that could only be described as feverish.

The question seemed to amuse Lord Harlaston. 'Have no fear, Tom. I can still be trusted to venture out on my own, and even to find my way safely back to the hotel. But since you ask, I thought I might just take another look at San Vitale.'

'San Vitale, my lord?'

'Those mosaics – which you thought so fine, and I couldn't stand.'

After that, Tom Nilsson had no option but to step aside and watch him go: a tall, unmistakably English figure in a white linen suit and a panama hat, walking purposefully up the via di Roma. And Tom realized with a flicker of regret that pretty soon it would be time to start looking out for another position.

Charity tidied her desk and started wiping English adverbs off the blackboard. Outside, a carriage rattled up the rue de Jerzual.

Now that Augustine and Gwenolée had gone, peace had descended upon the schoolroom. The muslin curtains swelled gently in the breeze, and dust-motes floated in shafts of sunlight. The clock gave out its measured, slightly disapproving tick.

Madeleine had finished her composition and was standing at the window looking down into the street. She was never in a hurry to leave, for she was an only child and her home was a quiet one. '*Voilà un* très *beau cheval brun,*' said Madeleine. '*Bel équipage, très bien conduit. Et bah! Ce méchant Goulven Lebesque s'est engagé de tenir le cheval pour le beau monsieur, quand tout le monde sait qu'il ne mérite pas cet honneur-là!*'

'Madeleine,' said Charity without turning from the blackboard, 'you know it isn't done to pass comment on passers-by.'

Madeleine snorted with laughter. She found it inexpressibly funny when Mademoiselle Charité spoke to her in English outside lessons. '*Mais c'est comme dans mon* histoire,' she replied. '*Ce monsieur-là ressemble à l'étranger mystérieux qui est arrivé pour dîner avec la belle veuve.*'

'Madeleine—'

' – *ce monsieur-là, lui aussi est très grand, comme l'étranger dans mon histoire, et* très *bel homme. C'est vrai que je ne peux pas exactement voir son visage d'ici, mais il* doit *être beau, habillé comme il est, et avec son air de grand seigneur.*'

'And that's quite enough,' said Charity, joining Madeleine by the window. 'If you don't come away from there *now* I am going to prise you away – *there's* a new English word for you, *prise* – and *throw* you down the stairs head over heels!' She grasped Madeleine by the shoulders and shook her till she squealed in delight.

Down in the street, the little Lebesque boy was clutching the bridle of a glossy bay carriage-horse which stood patiently between the shafts of a fine-looking trap. The gentleman who had so intrigued Madeleine had his back to them, and was reaching into the pocket of his long tan dustcoat. Charity saw a flash of white cuff as he stretched out his hand towards the boy, his long narrow fingers tendering a coin.

Her own hands tightened on Madeleine's shoulders.

The gentleman seemed to be asking questions, for Goulven was shrugging and shaking his barley-coloured head, miming 'I don't know' with all his might. Then at last comprehension dawned and the boy broke into a gap-toothed smile, and nodded and pointed up at the schoolhouse.

Then the gentleman took off his hat, and the wind lifted his dark brown hair as he turned and looked up at the window.

CHAPTER FORTY-ONE

Early December, the Present

'Alex.'

' – Sarah? Is that you?'

'Yes it's me. How are you?'

' – I'm fine. It's good to hear from you.'

'Good. Look, Alex, can we meet up, d'you think?
For lunch or something? I mean, do you want to?'

'Of course I do. In fact I'll be up at the flat for the
next couple of days. I was just leaving. But I suppose
that's too soon.'

'How about tomorrow?'

'Can you fit it in?'

'Oh, yes.'

'I thought you'd be too busy. I hear you're working
on something big. A series.'

'I am. But I'm a bit less driven than I used to be.'

'Is that good or bad?'

'Oh, good. Definitely good.'

The traffic was terrible, the cab-driver complained
non-stop about Christmas gridlocks, and she was
late by the time she reached the restaurant. She had

particularly wanted to be early, so she could have a drink by herself, to calm her nerves before he arrived. She hadn't seen or spoken to him in over three months.

She had been on the point of calling him dozens of times, but always reasoned that if he'd wanted to see her he'd have called her himself, and he hadn't – which could only mean that he didn't want to see her. And yet when she'd asked him to lunch he'd jumped at it, so what the hell did *that* mean?

Deciding what to wear had taken forever. She wanted to look good, but not so sharp or glitzy that he'd think she'd changed, and be put off. In the end, she chose narrow stone-coloured jeans and loafers and a wonderfully subtle gilet in eau de nil silk jersey that was neither clinging nor loose, and had cost a week's salary in Harvey Nichols the day before.

She had also agonized over the choice of restaurant, and eventually settled on Stephanie's, as it was in a not too fashionable street off the Fulham Road, and therefore free from raucous office parties. It was also good without being flashy; she didn't think he would appreciate anything too recherché after three years' seclusion in Hynton.

As it turned out, she needn't have worried about overwhelming him with urban chic. When she arrived at the restaurant he was already seated at the table, looking sleek as a greyhound and startlingly unfamiliar in a pale grey suit which had Armani written all over it.

'Jesus,' she said shakily, 'you look like a film star. What happened to the checked shirt and cords?'

He stood up, startled. 'What? Oh. These are just old work clothes. I've been to see my publisher.' He stooped to pick up his napkin which had fallen to the floor, and sat down again, and moved his knife and fork a fraction to the right, and she realized with a shock that he was as nervous as she was. Then he said abruptly, 'You look marvellous,' which rattled them both.

She busied herself with her napkin to stop her hands from shaking, but it was no good. His eyelashes were still breathtaking. His shirt was pale grey, with a tie of darker grey, but instead of making him look colourless, all the greys only brought out the light in his eyes and the fine sharp planes of his face. She imagined standing very close to him and putting the flat of her hands against his chest, and feeling the thin soft cotton of his shirt and the warm blood coursing underneath.

She drew a deep breath and exhaled slowly. 'So,' she said brightly, 'when *is* the book coming out? My spies tell me it's pretty good.'

'Oh, Christ, you haven't seen it, have you?'

'What's the point of having friends in publishing if you can't sneak a preview now and then? Don't look so crestfallen. You'll have to get used to people reading it. It's good. I enjoyed it.'

She meant it. His novel had surprised her. It was more optimistic in tone than she'd expected, less elliptical, and at times genuinely funny. If her friend at Gates Willoughby was anything to go by, the sales would be more than respectable for a first novel. Pippa said it was the sort of book which was intelligent enough for people to like being seen with on the tube, but with enough of a plot to let them enjoy it as well.

'Is that why you called me?' Alex asked without looking at her. 'To talk about my book?'

'Not exactly.'

'So why did you? I mean, why now?'

She did not reply. What could she say? That two

nights ago, she had dreamed that she was sitting in Robert's study talking with her father, and he had told her she'd be crazy not to call Alex and give it another try.

Her father had looked the way he did before he became ill. He'd sat at Robert's big leather-topped desk, steepling his long fingers and studying her with affectionate irony, as he used to do when he was about to cut through her convoluted reasoning and get to the truth.

'So let's get this straight,' he had said, smiling at her with Robert's direct black gaze. 'You love this man, and you think there's a chance that he loves you, but neither of you has *done* anything about it. And now you've left him alone for – what, over twelve weeks? Oh, *Sarah*!'

Dum vivimus, vivamus.

While we live, let us live.

Alex took the hint from her silence and didn't press her for an answer. The waiter came and they ordered drinks, and talked of other things until the wine arrived. She told him about her new job at Synergy. The teething period was over, she was delegating more, and getting a kick out of putting the new series together. He said that the book on Harlaston was coming out in February in time for the run-up to the College's anniversary, that advance orders had been encouraging, enrolments were up, and the Board of Governors was delighted with what she had done. Lastly, he told her that Stephen was back in London with Clare.

'I know,' Sarah said. 'In fact, a couple of weeks ago I took him to the Science Museum.'

He was surprised. 'Clare didn't tell me. How did you pull that off?'

'Clare and I have sort of declared a truce. For Stephen's sake.'

'Ah.'

'I think she finally accepts that my taking him off her hands from time to time can actually be quite convenient.'

'Yes. Well, it would be.'

She rearranged her napkin on her lap and tried not to stare at his hand on the table. Suddenly she asked, 'Do you miss him?'

'Oh, yes.'

She took a sip of wine. 'Do you miss me?'

He gave her a long steady look which brought the heat to her face. 'Yes. Very much.'

'Good,' she said at last.

The waiter came back and Alex warded him off with a sharp glance.

Sarah said, 'You know, at any time over the last three months, it would have been open to *you* to call *me*.'

'I know.'

'So why didn't you?'

He did not reply.

'Because', she said, 'you think I've already been through enough with your brother. That's it, isn't it?'

He turned his glass in his fingers and frowned.

'*Dammit*, Alex, I told you before—'

'I know. Stop being overprotective, you can look after yourself, it's insulting to think you can't. I know, I know, I know.'

'Well, then.'

'I'm sorry. Old habits. Sorry.' After a while he said, 'I know you think I'm overprotective, but maybe you've forgotten the state you were in when you first arrived at the Hall.'

'Alex—'

'You looked as if you'd just been let out of Belsen. You didn't want to talk to anyone, you didn't want to see anyone. You were falling apart at the seams. And it was my brother who did that to you.'

'With a little help from a bout of pneumonia and an employer who didn't want me back.'

He ignored that. 'The point is, between Dominic and me, we'd already managed to screw up Helen pretty comprehensively, and I was damned if I was going to watch the same thing happen to you.'

'Why can't you get it into your head? *I'm not Helen!*'

'I know. I know that now.'

Their food arrived and they stared at it.

Alex pushed his plate aside and took an envelope from his jacket pocket and gave it to her across the table. 'This came for you about a week ago. The bursar asked me to pass it on. I thought it might be important.'

It was a blue airmail envelope which had obviously done some travelling. The handwriting was Continental and old-fashioned, and the return address on the back was unfamiliar. *Mme Gwenolée Lebesque, 7 rue Gambetta, Dinan, 22100 C. d'Armor., Bretagne, France.*

Suddenly she knew what it was. 'My God,' she said. 'The teacher from Charity's school.'

Alex leaned back in his chair. 'Is that who it's from. I couldn't work it out.'

Her heart began to race. She tore open the envelope and began to read.

'*Elle était d'un vrai chic, je me souviens,*' wrote Madame Lebesque, recalling the summer in 1924 when, as a child of ten, she had helped her mother entertain a pretty English lady and her son at their house in Dinan.

Mme Lebesque's mother had been a teacher at the same school in which she herself had taught for thirty years. And long ago, when her mother was still a child, 'Mademoiselle Charité' had been her English teacher, and they had retained an affection for each other, and sometimes Mademoiselle Charité would visit Dinan and do a little teaching, *pour se distraire*.

'*We had tea beneath the almond tree,*' wrote Mme Lebesque in her clear, precise French. '*I was very much in awe, for the lady was so chic, and it was the age of the great couturier Vionnet, whose clear colours suited her extremely. Her hair was cut in a bob, straight and shining, and I liked it extremely. And I remember that her shoes were beautiful: simple, but very fine.*

'*We had tea and she and my mother talked, while I became shy of the young man. From what you say, Mademoiselle, I suppose he must have been your father. At that time he was a boy of about sixteen, but to me he was quite the young gentleman. Tall, lean, dark, rather handsome, and so mysterious, because he was English! He was kind to me, and one could see that he and his mother understood each other well.*

'*I am afraid I do not remember much more, for I was only a child. There was some mention of the lady's property just outside Pau – a vineyard, I believe – and at one point I summoned the courage to admire a locket she wore: a fine gold locket on a ribbon at her breast. She opened it and showed me a photograph of her husband who had been killed in the Great War. I remarked how sad that was, for he had been very*

*handsome, and Mademoiselle Charité said, yes, it was
very sad, but that she'd had twelve wonderful years
with him—*'

'*Twelve* years!' exclaimed Sarah. She stared at Alex
in astonishment. 'It says here they had *twelve* years
together! But how could that be? He was in India.'

'Um, no,' said Alex, 'actually he wasn't.'

'What?'

'He never went to India.'

'He never— but he did, Aubrey said so. Anyway,
how do you know?'

'I checked.'

She stared at him. 'How? I tried the private archives
but they never wrote back.'

'I know. I got through to an old biddy at one of
them who's been sitting on your letter. She got
quite shirty with me. Seemed to think I ought to know
the answer already. It turns out that anyone who
knows anything about these things knows that the
Lincolnshires weren't an "Indian" regiment, but
an "African" one. She was categorical about it. His
battalion never went to India. And, according to her,
Robert definitely didn't serve in the decade before the
First World War. She didn't even need to check her
records, she remembers his name because he got the
MC after Cambrai. She was going to write and tell you
but she never got around to it.'

Sarah stared at him in disbelief. 'And you did this?
For me?'

His cheeks darkened. 'It was only a couple of phone
calls.'

'But why do it at all?'

'It seemed to matter to you. I thought if you didn't
find out it'd bother you.'

'It did.'

He gave a slight smile. 'Well, then.'

'But – what about Aubrey? He said Robert spent ten years in India. D'you think he just made it up?'

'It looks that way. I suppose India was a lot more acceptable to Violet than the thought of her husband living with another woman in the south of France.'

'Twelve years,' murmured Sarah, shaking her head. 'From his last expedition in South America to when he was killed.' She went back to the letter. '. . . *she'd had twelve wonderful years with him, which she said she had never expected to have. I did not understand what she meant by that, but did not think it proper to ask.*

'*After they had gone, my mother and I agreed that Mademoiselle Charité seemed content, and was fortunate in having such a son to comfort her. But for myself I sensed a certain distance in her: as if nothing could really touch her now. And I thought it a pity she never remarried.*

'*I am afraid, Mademoiselle, that I never saw your grandmother again. My mother did, for they remained friends, and once Mademoiselle Charité brought her brother with her to Dinan when he was on holiday from England. But by then I was a young woman and had other concerns.*

'*I remember nothing more which might interest you, except that in 1937 my mother received a letter from the son saying that Mademoiselle Charité had died. It was influenza, and it took her quickly. She was only fifty-six. For myself, I think maybe she did not fight it very hard . . .*'

Sarah folded the letter, and passed it to Alex. She felt tears pricking her eyes, and blinked them back.

Alex refilled their glasses and they sat in silence

while he read the letter and Sarah stared out of the window. Then he looked at her, and took a manila envelope from his pocket and put it on the table between them.

'What's that?' asked Sarah. 'Not *another* letter?'

To her surprise, his face was grave. 'No. It's something you should have had a long time ago. It comes with a confession and an apology.'

'That sounds serious.'

'When you know what it is, you'll probably never speak to me again.'

She couldn't tell if he meant it or not. 'In that case I'll take the confession first. What exactly are you confessing to?'

'Arrant stupidity and criminal negligence.'

She gave an uncertain laugh. 'Well you'd better get it over with, you're starting to worry me.'

With his forefinger he traced a diamond on the envelope. 'When your father became ill, he gave some family things to *my* father for safe keeping. He wanted you and Nick to have them, but he knew how your mother felt about his family, and didn't want to hurt her feelings by leaving them for her to deal with.' He added gently, 'I think by then he was getting a little over-anxious, as people do when they're very ill.'

She swallowed. 'I know. After he died, your father sent everything to Nick and we went through it together. But that was years ago. It's just old cricket photos from his schooldays and things like that. I went through it again earlier this year, to make sure. There's nothing in it.'

Alex winced. 'That's where the confession and the apology come in. I have no *idea* why my father did what he did, but, somehow, something got separated from the rest. I only came across it the day before yesterday, inside one of the photo albums. I was going to call you and see if we could meet up so I could give it to you, but then you called me.' He drew another diamond on the envelope. 'It was in a different album from the one with the picture of William. That's why I missed it. I should have checked there before, I can't imagine why I didn't. But I didn't. That's where the arrant stupidity comes in.'

'Don't forget the criminal negligence,' said Sarah, her heart pounding. 'Are you trying to tell me that *all this time* you've had a photograph of Robert and Charity and you didn't even know it?'

He pushed the envelope across the table towards her. 'I can only think that because it was so special, my father slipped it into the album for safe keeping and then forgot about it. I'm sorry.'

'*Sorry?* Alex!' She didn't know whether to laugh or cry or hit him over the head with the wine bottle.

'I know. If you'd had it from the beginning you'd never have had any doubts about Robert and Charity and your father. I'm so sorry.'

'All this time,' she murmured. Then a suspicion crossed her mind. 'Tell me you haven't known about this all along. Tell me you haven't been letting me find out for myself as some sort of exercise in self-discovery.'

To her relief he looked appalled at her suggestion. 'Absolutely not. I swear to you, I've only just found it. Jesus, Sarah, who d'you think I am, Machiavelli?'

She picked up the envelope and stared at it. Then slowly she drew out the contents.

It was a photograph in soft sepia tones, about eight inches by five, mounted on pasteboard. She looked at it for a long time.

At last Alex said quietly, 'You're not going to cry, are you?'

She shook her head. The slow tears spilled down her cheeks. Charity was staring directly into the camera, her dark elegant eyebrows arched in amusement. She had clearly defined features which only missed true beauty by a hair's breadth, but were wonderfully alive, and she looked as if she had just said something funny and was making a valiant attempt to keep her composure. A small dark-haired boy sat on her lap. He had twisted round to share the joke, and was looking up at her with a wide delighted grin. Robert sat beside Charity with one arm along the back of her chair and his hand resting on her shoulder. He wore a white linen suit, and he looked very handsome and relaxed. And he wasn't smiling, he was *laughing*.

Sarah drew a ragged breath and caught her lower lip in her teeth. 'They look so happy. They look so *happy*.'

After a while Alex reached over and put his hand on hers. 'Sarah,' he said quietly, stroking the back of her hand with his thumb, 'I'm going to pay the bill and get us a cab.'

She wiped her eyes with her other hand and sniffed. Then she nodded.

He looked at her steadily. 'Will you come home with me?'

'Yes,' she said. 'Of course I will.'

THE END